An Apology for Autumn

David Turrill

An Apology for Autumn

The Toby Press

First Edition 2004
The Toby Press LLC

P.O. Box 8531, New Milford, CT 06776-8531, USA
& P.O. Box 2455, London W1A 5WY, England
www.tobypress.com

ISBN 1 59264 090 7, *hardcover*

A CIP catalogue record for this title is available from the British Library

Typeset in Garamond by Jerusalem Typesetting

Printed and bound in the United States by Thomson-Shore Inc., Michigan

"Sometimes one finds in fossil stones the imprint of a leaf, long since disintegrated, whose outlines remind us how detailed, vibrant, and alive are the things of this earth that perish."
— Diane Ackerman, *Why Leaves Turn Color in the Fall*

"Fair youth, beneath the trees, thou canst not leave
Thy song, nor ever can those trees be bare;"
— John Keats, *Ode on a Grecian Urn*

Chapter one

I f you spend any time observing the human race, you begin to believe that the only way heaven could have *any* occupants at all is through sloppy bookkeeping. We're such a miserable lot, incapable of any real charity—or even the right kind of faith. We've taken faith and mixed it up so badly with religion that the Prodigal wouldn't have a prayer today. I know *I've* always sided with the good son who resented his father's forgiveness of his other wayward brat. Hell, if you accept *that* idea, then what happens to justice? If there's no justice, what point is there to ethical behavior?

Herkimer's primary peeve was the whole judgment thing. He didn't give a fig for justice, something I'd always considered pretty important. He kept harping on 'mercy' as if it weren't aggravating to believe that a repentant serial killer could slip into paradise at the last minute. I don't think I'm pharisaical so much as I'm envious that, if last minute redemption really is the case, *I* didn't have more fun taking advantage of the system. Judgment, Herkimer told us, is for those who have given up on God, or those who're arrogant enough to think they know Him better than anyone else. We're meant, he told me, to wonder about it all. The most comfortable people are always the most judgmental, and if there's one emotion we should *never* feel in regard to the Almighty, it's comfort.

Herk believed, as I said, in mercy. He used to talk about something he called his 'apology for autumn'. "People are like deciduous trees," he'd say. "We're green for most of our lives. Some of us flash brilliantly, and all of us change, just before we die and fall. It's our nature. Should the leaves blame each other for which falls first, or which has the spot closest to the sun? Should the leaves hate the tree that lets them go? Should God damn the leaves? It's just the way it works." His point? Without autumn, there is no spring.

How could a man like that, like Herkimer Gudsen, believe that he would die by crucifixion? I scoffed of course. No one except for a few guilt-crazed Catholics in South America and the Philippines had been crucified for centuries—and they had *arranged* their own agony. Legally sanctioned crucifixion had exited the world with paganism. Lethal injection had made our century civilized about murder. How could he be crucified?

As was my usual error in listening to my brother, I took him literally—and he was almost never literal. I don't mean to indicate that he was evasive or deceptive. In his own circuitous way, he was the most honest man I knew.

He never intended us to think that he'd be hung up somewhere for public entertainment. He only meant that his death would come slowly, by degrees, and would involve what he referred to as 'piercing'.

I knew, of course, that he was right. He was always right. The piercing had been going on most of his life. In one way or another, it was bound to get the better of him. He once confided to me that although his 'execution' was expansive rather than narrow, progressive rather than static, and instructive rather than punitive—it *was* a crucifixion. It was true. Even though the piercings occurred gradually over several decades and were often not sensational, or even conspicuous, they were no less authentically and lethally *relevant* to the fulfillment of Herkimer's calling than the sufferings of any other Christian martyr. It just takes some men of God a little longer to get nailed, that's all.

According to our mother, Virginia Gudsen, (known to all, except her oldest son, as Ginny), the piercings started early in Herk's life. She has a reel of 16-millimeter film tucked away somewhere, which I've seen, several times. Herkimer, then eight months old, was the star, as usual. I wasn't yet conceived in Ginny's mind, let alone her body. In the film, baby Herkimer was in a little chair of some kind, designed for infants, with springs on it, and he was constantly bouncing up and down, as *I* would later, in a very different sense. Herk was perpetually in motion.

The tiny chair had been placed on our front lawn and his bare feet had trampled the grass in front of him. You could see that the weather was warm—the baby was dressed only in cloth diapers and a tiny tee shirt, the kind that snapped at the shoulder. His right hand was heavily bandaged, and he held it away from his body as if to protect it from the frivolous activity of his other limbs. He bounced and bounced, but his eyes, squinting against the summer sun, were steady and sure. I think he knew, even then, who he was.

Though Ginny could vouch for the world being in color then, I always think of that part of my brother's past, the time before me, as being black and white. It was 1945. Our uncle, my mother's only sibling, was there in his army uniform, having avoided becoming added refuse on the trash heap that had once been Europe. I knew, as I watched the film with Ginny, that Judy Garland had stepped from bland Kansas into Technicolor Munchkinland six years earlier. But even then, color lied. Baum's little people were really blue. Winkies were yellow. Only the Emerald Ozians were depicted in their true colors. Perhaps that's why green is the color of envy. Maybe that's why most of us see each other in black and white.

As we watched, my mother and I, I could see that the person who held the camera loved that baby, doted on him in fact. Dad wouldn't leave the family until I came along in '49. Herk's pudgy arms and legs flailed around to no purpose, the bandaged hand held aloof—but it was all purposeful to the recorder of the moment. The baby was surrounded by the two family dogs and curious neighbor children rather than sheep and magi, but it was no less a nativity to the shooter. I've often wondered how many deep and thorny theological questions would have definitive answers, had Mary and Joseph owned a camera. Still, the life it recorded would have been in black and white, as so many see it now.

The first time I saw this film was years ago, just before my brother almost died. I asked our mother, at the time, why Herkimer's hand was bandaged. She told me that he'd driven a needle through the soft flesh between his thumb and forefinger while crawling on the shag carpeting of her sewing room. The needle had become entangled in the carpet during one of Ginny's many tailoring marathons, a hobby that would, of necessity, become an occupation. The baby had been shuffling across the room on his hands and knees, since he'd not yet learned to walk. His forward momentum, as was so often the case in his life, had forced the piercing.

Characteristically, Ginny Gudsen's voice shook as she spoke of the incident concerning her oldest boy. (I was the second son, a position I would have held even had I been born first). Her face was aging even then, and was weary in the harrowing recollection. The smooth forehead had been furrowed by the rough plow of anxiety; the searching blue eyes had dulled and retreated back into the deepening caves below her brow. I think they only wanted to be left alone and not see. Fear, not age, had turned her ebony hair to gray. Her voice, once steadied by the ebullient courage of youth, was timid and halting as she spoke of it.

Perhaps it was because her eyes had withdrawn so far away from the world that they could see the past so clearly. She moved her head, as if to turn away from the old sewing machine that was no longer there. She lifted her foot from a ghostly pedal. She looked down at the yellowing linoleum of the kitchen, but she saw the shag carpet and she saw her baby, literally pinned to the floor. The needle was still embedded in the carpet as well as Herkimer's little hand.

"He tried to pull free," our mother said to me, "but he just made it worse. Oh Jimmy, the blood! There was so *much* blood!" She always called me Jimmy—never James or Jim. It was, I think, due more to status than age.

Her eyes glinted briefly, representative of a general euphoria she frequently seemed to experience in her memories of Herkimer.

"Even though he was less than a year old," she told me, "the pain or the blood didn't seem to bother your brother so much as...as being...*interrupted.*"

How many times had she related stories like this one about Herkimer? She had none like them to tell about me. I should have been jealous and, as a child, I was—bitterly so. But as I matured, I was forced to give it up. I gradually learned that she didn't love him any more or less than me. There *was* favoritism, yes, but it was deserved. It was *necessary*, for God's sake. That's why Herk was different—for God's sake.

"I felt terribly responsible," she said. "I'd dropped the needle somehow. I should have been more careful. A good mother wouldn't have let it happen." The tears came again and even though I probably could have stopped them with a few words of comfort, I didn't. My brother was *supposed* to be pierced, but she would always feel responsible. So would I. I once abetted God by providing the weapon too.

I was probably nine or ten. Herk was stumbling into gawky puberty. Randy O'Connor, the Irish kid next door who was two years my senior, talked me into it. He was behind most of the pranks in our neighborhood. He smashed pumpkins and waxed car windows at Halloween. He stole Christmas lights. His shenanigans were not restricted to holidays either. He put garter snakes in cars and wrote swear words in fresh cement. He never got caught for two reasons: One; he could run faster than a hungry cheetah, (he would run the hundred meters in college), and two; he always picked a younger kid, (such as myself), to be the fall guy. He was full of more mischief than anyone I knew, but he was also an altar boy at St. Mark's Parish, a brilliant student, and always polite around adults, who were easily duped into urging their children to emulate him. This casuistry served him well.

Randy had, that summer of 1959, discovered an innovative and inexpensive form of weaponry with which to terrorize the other kids of our neighborhood—the water bomb. He'd stolen a bag of a hundred or more balloons that his mother was planning to use for his sister's birthday party and he quickly initiated me into the specialized art of water warfare. Like a West Point general instructing a plebe, he showed me how to stretch the lips of the balloons over the outdoor faucet and control the flow of water so that the missiles were filled to lethal distension without rupturing. Then, his green eyes wide with perfidy above the innocence of his freckled cheeks, Randy would tie them off, a procedure he referred to as 'arming'. This delicate operation required the hands of a surgeon, (which occupation Randy eventually embraced).

We would stash them in various armories behind trees or the backyard shed, so that after a sortie, when flight was required, we would not be left without a cache to cover our retreat. (Randy explained to me the intricacies of guerrilla warfare, but I thought then, and for a long time after, that he meant we were simian soldiers). Our victims were frequently younger than we were and would usually run off crying to their mothers after a single strike. An exception was the newspaper boy. He was big, a lineman on the high school football team. We counted coup (a term I'd proudly added to our martial vocabulary after reading a book about Crazy Horse) on him as he passed on his bike below the maple tree where Randy and I were concealed. He was doused, and so were most of the newspapers he'd pre-folded in his bag. He recovered almost before we'd had time to scramble to the ground. He chased us, furiously vowing to rip off our limbs and beat us with them. Fortunately, they were our means of escape rather than the instruments of his retribution. He couldn't catch us. Oh, we thought we were clever gorillas!

I'd felt both terror and exhilaration as the cursing behemoth had rumbled after me. Escape made me feel invincible, but as I was to learn many times, invincibility is *only* a feeling. It doesn't really exist.

When my brother rounded the corner on his Schwin Red Flyer and pulled into the driveway of our house, it was my suggestion that he should be the objective of our next attack. Our success against the football player made Herk dwindle in the mind. Besides, I wanted to see the Golden Boy humbled.

12

Ever the tactician, Randy cleverly proposed that we approach our prey from opposite directions so that, in flight, Herk would have to choose which of his attackers to chase. Consequently, Randy circled around the back of our house and was in position to strike as Herkimer was jamming the kickstand of his bike into position. Randy's bright orange bomb exploded in the spokes as Herk started for the front porch. He whirled around in the direction from which the aggression had come, allowing me to launch my red grenade from behind. I hit him squarely between the shoulder blades, the balloon rupturing in a glorious spray of icy water.

It must have been ninety degrees that summer day, and Herk's thin shirt was already soaked through with sweat. Both my brother and I were inordinately sensitive to heat, so the unexpected shock of the frigid dousing made him gasp. Before I could rearm, he'd spun back and spotted me. He was wearing the kind of slip-on rubber clogs that you'd employ to protect your feet from fungus in a public shower, as if he'd been prepared for what had just happened to him. It's amazing, thinking back on it, how the choice of footwear on a particular day can so insidiously affect your life. He slipped out of them because they were no good for running and had closed half the distance between us before I could adequately savor my triumph.

I ran. In the blind confusion of my retreat, I foolishly led my brother past one of our ammunition dumps, where he paused momentarily to arm himself, then continued his barefoot pursuit. I managed to temporarily evade him by moving through the maze of drying bed sheets on the clothesline, but it was only a temporary reprieve. As I crossed the lawn into Ginny Gudsen's garden, a balloon exploded against the back of my head and sent me sprawling in a shivery spew of retaliation.

I don't know why I rolled to my feet and continued to flee. Herk had gotten me back. In his codebook of fraternal justice, that was enough. I expected to look back and see a vindictive leer of triumph on his face, but there was only empathy. It would have ended there had I not, inexplicably, shouted some taunting epithet and raised my middle finger in the obscene gesture so often employed by the defeated. I don't remember exactly what I said, but it had something to do with the masculine-sensitive topic of testosterone measurement, and it was enough for Herk to renew the pursuit with increased vigor and decreased sensitivity to inferior age and physique.

I never saw the rake, though it was lying right where I'd left it that morning after weeding the rows between the string beans to please Ginny. It had been abandoned for Randy's call to arms. It was lying there, prongs up, waiting to pierce. I never saw it. Herk didn't either. I initiated the chase. I forced its continuation. I left the rake there. Though I was the one wearing shoes, I must've leapt right over it. Odd how the Judge of Things chooses. It was Herk's destiny to be pierced. It was mine to carry guilt.

I'd just reached the concealing safety of the cornrows when I heard him cry out. Initially, I thought it was a ruse to draw me into the open. I moved deeper among the tall stalks which concealed me from the stalker. But the pursuit had ended, I knew. Herk's moaning was too real to ignore. He was never very good at deceit.

"Jim!" I heard him yell. "Jimmy, come back!" It was the passionate anguish in his voice that made me stop and turn around. It was only one of many calls he made to me that I couldn't ignore. Then I remembered the rake, and I knew. I went back, filled with the same dread my mother had felt as an Instrument of Wrong.

Herk's lanky frame, all six feet of it, (he'd grow another five inches before deciding he was close enough to Heaven), was twisted across several rows of trampled beans. His large head was pillowed on the mound of weeds I'd raked that morning as if they'd been arranged for that purpose. The unlaunched balloons lay nearby.

Like some bizarre prosthesis, the rake handle angled out from Herk's wounded foot. Three iron prongs, assisted by his weight and speed, had been driven entirely through his left foot and surfaced like horns on a goat's head on the top. He looked pale. His skin, when I touched his leg just above the ankle, was cold—despite his profuse sweating. There was no blood yet, as the prongs sealed the holes they'd made.

I must've said something like "I'm sorry", I don't really remember. My mind was clouded with fear and shame.

"It's okay, Jim," he said. There was no accusation there, no indictment. He grabbed my shirt. I looked down at his balled fist. I saw the white scar between his thumb and forefinger. I didn't know what to do. "It's okay," he repeated. "Just get Mom. Tell her to bring some towels and water." Calm urgency. "Get Mom."

By the time I came running back with her across the yard, Herk had removed the rake from his foot. I don't know how he did it. It must've been excruciating. There was a pool of blood in the dirt and his hands were sticky with it. With frantic intensity, Ginny washed the wound with water from the garden hose, then wrapped the purplish foot in a towel. Herk didn't cry or even moan. The expression I remember on his face was *impatience*. The piercing, like the rake itself, was taken in stride.

At the hospital, the trinity of holes was probed for dirt and rust particles. A needle and thread closed them. He was given a tetanus shot. More piercings.

My childish prank, whether born of malicious jealousy or an innate wickedness, cost my brother one summer of his life and a permanent limp from a fracture that was diagnosed a year after the incident and never healed properly. He spent most of his convalescence on the sofa, reading, his bandaged foot raised on a kitchen chair in front of him, while Randy and I raced about in the libertarian joy that is Children in Summer.

There were no words of recrimination from him then, or later. He never said, "I can't run because of you. I can't play football or baseball because you were careless." He knew, better than I ever would, though I knew it too, deep down where guilt lives, that I was no more to blame for his misfortune than are winter or the sea when they maim and kill. They're instruments, orchestrated and conducted by a Power that's beyond us. I wasn't the first of these, nor would I be the last. It was Herk's role that was primary. I told him many times how sorry I was, but never in a complete sentence. He would always stop me, wave it away. He said that a person couldn't have fault without intention—a notion that doesn't matter to most people, but would become a comfort to me, along with the knowledge that getting pierced would become habitual with my brother, and in these other piercings, I was never instrumental.

About a year after his encounter with the rake, once he was able to move around again without crutches or a cane, Herk was wounded by a submerged anchor while wading in Torch Lake. Torch is a beautiful inland lake, one of the largest in Michigan, located on the Leelenau Peninsula just a few miles off Grand Traverse Bay. Grandpa Watkins, Ginny's father and the only grandparent we knew, owned a cabin there. It served as a brief escape from our industrial birthplace.

In Saginaw, they knew Herkimer by name in the emergency room of Holy Cross Hospital. At one time or another, over the next five years, he was a visitor there at least once annually. He dropped a pair of pruning shears on the foot that had been spared the rake and anchor. He drove an awl through his hand while attempting to punch a hole through an old, leather belt. A cooking fork, camouflaged in dirty dishwater, found its way into his wrist. The neighbor's dog, a German Shepherd with the innocuous name of Heidi, bit his forearm to the bone when he tried to release it from the rope-leash in which it had become ensnarled. These were only a few.

The remarkable thing about them, other than their frequency, is that they were all *piercings*. I can't remember my brother ever suffering, as most of us do, from a burn, a sprain, or any cut or scratch that didn't drill a hole. I don't think that he was ever sick with the flu or ptomaine or even a cold. As Ginny and I sat with him in the emergency room during one of his innumerable visits, a young nurse who was new to Holy Cross went through a long questionnaire with him regarding his health history.

"High blood pressure?" she asked.

"No," he responded, as the blood from his latest wound dripped onto the tile floor.

"Ulcers?"

"No."

"Scarlet Fever? Mumps? Chicken Pox?"

"No."

"Measles? Pneumonia?"

"No."

"Mr. Gudsen." She addressed him that way even though he was still under eighteen. "Have you ever had *any* illnesses?"

Herk smiled at her in that way of his, that innocent way that made you want to strangle him and love him at the same time. "I guess I've been pretty lucky," was all he said. At the time, the physician on duty was extracting a ballpoint pen from his left hand, proving, in a most unique way, the inferiority of the sword.

The worst of these piercings, by far, occurred when Herk had just become a pastor. This one was so severe and so spectacular that it made the NBC Nightly News and the major newspapers throughout the country. Herk had been out for a walk. He and Meg lived on the outskirts of town in an old farmhouse they'd purchased. Herk loved to walk and, in spite of his limp, he managed a mile or two every day. The thick forest beyond the fallow fields that surrounded his house was the preferred site for his perambulations, and it was there that he almost died. It was December; Herk had virtually been living at the church, what with advent and other special holiday services. He'd told Meg that he really needed to get outside and be alone for awhile and that he wouldn't be long.

Meg got a call from Holy Cross about two hours later. After regaining her composure, she called and asked me to take her to the hospital. We picked up Ginny too. When we first saw him, I almost laughed. He looked ridiculous. How is it possible to look otherwise when you have an arrow embedded in your head? It wasn't an arrow, really, but what crossbow hunters call a 'bolt'. It's smaller than an arrow that's used with a longbow and it will only work with a crossbow. It's mostly used for shooting at targets. It went through his skull and his brain of course, the dulled point protruding through one side of his head, the feathered end visible on the other. He was sitting on one of those metal gurneys and smiling, apparently in full control of all his faculties. I swear, he looked like he was wearing one of those gag gifts you buy at a novelty shop, the kind that fits over the top of your head like ear muffs.

As we came in, he was trying to comfort his assailant, who'd been shooting at a target mounted on bales of hay. From what Herk could remember, he'd just turned back toward the house and was nearing the edge of the wood, where it opened onto what used to be a cornfield, when he saw the bales of hay, then heard a buzzing sound. After that, everything went black. The shooter had rushed to Herk and found him leaning against a birch tree, slowly regaining his consciousness. He told us that he'd helped Herk to his pickup truck and immediately brought him to the emergency room, not knowing that he lived just a few hundred yards away. The guy was in his early twenties, close to my age. He was damn near hysterical with fear over possible felony charges or litigation. With his yellow shirt and red face, he looked like a pacing campfire. His name was Auggie Two-River.

Herk had greater success in comforting Meg and Ginny, although he had to convince Ginny not to exact vengeance on the inept bowman who looked, increasingly, like prey. As for me, I was really convinced that he'd be okay. I honestly studied his head, looking for the tin band that connected, I was certain, the two ends of the bolt/arrow. There wasn't even any blood and Herk was calm and lucid.

He had to be flown by helicopter to the University of Michigan Medical Center in Ann Arbor to be examined by a team of the country's best neurosurgeons, hurriedly assembled for that purpose. Meg and I flew in the chopper with him. He never lost consciousness, never even complained of a headache. He kept his arm around Meg and whispered soothingly to her. One of the doctors flew in from Los Angeles, another from Providence, Rhode Island. Both had arrived shortly after we did. Herk pointed out the significance of the names of the cities. I hadn't noticed. That's how my brother is. Nothing escapes him.

He was in the OR for a couple of hours. The doctors told Meg and me that after cutting off the dummy point and the feathers, they'd decided to leave the shaft of the bolt where it was. To attempt to extract it would have been too much of a risk of brain damage. My brother was conscious throughout so that he could inform the surgeons of any sensory loss. They didn't anesthetize him until they had to make wider incisions at each wound in order to attach Teflon 'covers' over the holes in his skull, preventing any seepage of the precious fluid that keeps the brain floating inside the head.

The first EEG taken after Herk's return to consciousness revealed 'unusual' patterns, as the doctor from Providence termed it. The x-rays showed the bolt firmly embedded inside Herk's brain, but no evidence of interruption or aberration of skill, either motor, sensory, or behavioral ever appeared—unless, of course, you count the visions that would lead us all into a different life. But, of course, Herk never attributed his ability to hear the voice of God to accident.

Naturally, the media honed in on Herk and Meg with the sure and infantile determination of pups at a bitch's teats. Every radio and television station, all newspapers and tabloids were devoted, for many months, to what one dissenting journalist dubbed the 'William Tell Overdone' incident. It took Herk two weeks of constant refusals for interviews before the media finally left him alone.

At the time, none of us knew the real significance of this latest piercing—not even Herk. His recovery was miraculous, especially when you consider that he never allowed the doctors to follow up on their handiwork. He felt good and that was enough.

When God spoke to him, Herk never doubted that it was the penetrating, incisive voice of authenticity. The piercings, he believed, were both preparation and fulfillment, episodes in a continual suffering that would, if you'll excuse the pun, guide Herkimer Gudsen's uniquely holy life.

Chapter two

I f my brother hadn't married Megan Brocarde, *I* would have. I fell in love with her too. I was only eighteen when Herk brought her home to meet Ginny and, since she was very beautiful, I suppose some would attribute my being smitten to hormonal infatuation. Still, I *was* in love. Up until I met Minnie, if Meg had been inclined to dalliance, I'd have betrayed my brother in a minute for the chance to sleep with her, and I'd have been willing to mutilate anyone else who fostered the same, seditious thoughts.

People of both sexes, who'd met her, knew that there was an indefinable singularity about Megan that prompted idolatry. You couldn't help putting her on a pedestal. When she moved down the center aisle of Herkimer's church to her cushioned pew in front of the ornate pulpit where her husband spoke for God, you felt an uneasy apostasy, as if you were worshipping the wrong deity. Maybe that's why she was struck down. I don't know.

Herk met her in his senior year at Michigan State University, a year before his entrance into the seminary. She was then a sophomore, a nursing major volunteering at the campus infirmary where my brother, not surprisingly, was a frequent visitor. He met her after jabbing a screwdriver between his ribs. He'd borrowed the thing from a friend in another dorm to fix a desk leg in his room. He was riding across the commons area on his bike, screwdriver in hand, when he swerved to avoid another biker who was intent on waving to someone behind him. Herk went over his handlebars and landed directly on the screwdriver.

When Ginny told me about it, I could envision him well enough—staggering into the infirmary with that sheepish, apologetic expression on his pale, thin face, trying to explain to this beautiful girl how he'd managed to screw himself yet again. But meeting Megan would make up for all that. Being loved by her would have been adequate compensation, even for crucifixion.

This happened during finals week in the fall semester of Herk's senior year. He came home for Christmas break and, of course, to recuperate. Megan was all he could talk about. He didn't talk to me—there was too great a barrier there still, constructed of the raw materials of age and resentment—but Ginny got an earful. Consequently, I had no choice but to hear about her too.

"She's incredible, mom." I remember him using that adjective specifically. He never used the vernacular of his generation. I never heard him say that something was 'cool' or that a girl was a 'fox'. He was convalescing on the sofa and staring at the Christmas tree, his pale, blue eyes wide with the special fervor he normally displayed when speaking of God. His light brown hair, naturally streaked with patterns of gold and flecked at the temples with premature gray, was far too long, and he had to keep tossing it back off his forehead to keep it from interfering with his vision. Ginny would cut it for him while he was at home, of course, then he'd wait for the next trim until he saw her again in the spring. She sent *me* to the barber. She was careful to explain that Herk was injured and that's why she cut his hair at home, but the two hour drive from the university couldn't have been any less taxing than fifteen minutes in the barber's chair. Besides, he hadn't been injured when she'd cut it in September. I knew it, and she knew I knew it. What I didn't know yet, that she did, was who my brother was.

"What did you say her name was, Dear?" Ginny was lighting candles, the emerging pine scent contesting for dominance with the delicious aroma of the fatted veal roasting in the oven—a meal very different from our usual fare of hot dogs and beans or tuna-noodle casserole.

"Megan. She's wonderful, Mom. I've never met anyone like her." He winced as he shifted restlessly on the sofa. His hand went unconsciously to the wound in his side. "I think she likes me too."

I really hoped that this episode of *Leave it to Beaver* would come to an end. Herk had dropped more weight. He was always too thin. I remember thinking that perhaps he'd disappear altogether, and my guilt and envy with him, but I knew intuitively that that would only compound my weaknesses.

"Have you asked her out yet?" Ginny blew out the match before it burnt her fingers, then briefly noticed me. "Jimmy," she yelled, "don't turn the television on now, please! I'm trying to talk to your brother." I collapsed sullenly back into a chair, and blended again with the other furniture.

"No, not yet," Herk answered, "but I'm going to, as soon as I get back."

Ginny settled herself on the sofa next to him. *Here it comes*, I thought. She came in right on cue. "Do you think it's wise to get involved right now, Dear, when you're so close to graduation, I mean? Next year you'll be at the seminary and God knows where this girl will be." She said the word 'girl' in much the same way one might use the word 'vermin'. Sometimes it was advantageous to live in anonymity.

I'd lost my virginity, at age fifteen, to a cheerleader named Rhonda Reed. Ginny had no idea that lechery had become my hobby. She was just as oblivious to my current debauchery with Bethany Meyers, and my collection of Playboys concealed (once alongside Bethany) in my bedroom closet.

"I wouldn't classify asking a girl on a date as 'getting involved' mother." Herk got up, crossed the room with an accusatory limp, and took a Christmas cut-out cookie off a plate that Ginny had set out for us. He caused my resentment of him to be temporarily dismissed by guilt.

"I could have gotten that for you, Dear," Ginny said, rising to guide him back to the sofa. We all sat in reverent silence while Herk decapitated Santa Claus with a single bite.

"Want another?" I said, offering the plate.

"No, thanks Jim."

"I assume this girl is Lutheran?" our mother continued.

"I don't know, Mom. I didn't check her religious credentials. We only exchanged a few words." Santa's boots disappeared and Herk brushed the crumbs off his shirt.

"Of course. I don't mean to pry, Dear." She reached over and brushed the hair out of his eyes with her delicate fingers. I'd felt the therapeutic touch of those hands too in my life, but mostly in Herk's absence. Once, when I'd been feverish with some kind of flu virus, she'd sat by my bed and rubbed the sweat from my forehead for what seemed like hours. That was when I'd noticed that she didn't have any jewelry on her hands—no wedding band, no nothing. That was the last time I'd brought up the subject of our father. She'd told me, the first time I'd asked, that his name was Joe Gudsen and he'd just left one day, shortly after I was born, just before she'd joined St. Luke's Church. Even during that memorable, feverish moment, that was all I could ever get out of her, except that she didn't know where he was and didn't care. For a brief moment then, I'd felt a strange, emotional symbiosis with my mysterious sire.

"She told me that she hoped she'd see me again," Herk said. He spoke in that sanctuary voice and it kind of trailed off as he saw, again, what we couldn't.

In the spring, after graduation, he brought her for a visit. His letters and phone calls had been full of her and he'd done his best to describe her, but I'd seen enough pastors wives to know that men who served God generally didn't tend to voluptuousness in their women and voluptuous women weren't usually inclined to a life of church suppers and Sunday School teaching. But in this, as in so many of my impressions regarding my brother, I was wrong.

Megan was born to be noticed. She was *intensely* beautiful. Her hair was long and full and a striking auburn color that, in bright sunlight, could be mistaken for fire. There was fire in her eyes too, an emerald fire that smoldered unconsciously and captivated all who were, like me, injudicious enough to gaze directly into them. I doubt that she understood their effect on others. Her creamy skin flushed rose beneath her cheeks and she absently licked her full lips when she noticed someone gawking, making her beauty even more incendiary. Her body was almost indescribable in its perfection. Large breasts, a small waist, full hips and long legs could describe thousands of women, many of whom graced the pages of my cache of magazines in the closet, but she possessed those attributes in a combination that made them somehow superior to others in their fullness. All of these things united to create an aura of heat about her, a sense of fire and passion that her real innocence did nothing to assuage. As an adult, when I heard the next generation refer to someone as 'hot', I always thought of Megan.

Logically then, she was about as far removed from 'cool' as one could get. She was unaware of style, in both her wardrobe and her language. As luck (or fate) would have it, she'd been raised in a strict, Lutheran environment, (a factor that won instant approval from Ginny), and knew nothing of street life. In spite of her voluptuousness, I believed in her virginity—if such a thing ever required faith.

Much to my amazement, Ginny accepted her immediately, once she'd met her—even acquiescing when Megan and Herk decided to get married the summer *before* he went into the seminary. Ginny's only qualifier for her blessing was that they put off having children until Herk was ordained and they were settled in a congregation somewhere. As it turned out, avoiding the 'delicate condition' became no condition at all. Meg would eventually discover, among other things, that her husband was, at least initially, incapable of fathering a child.

She would come to understand, as we all would, that ours were lives connected to Herkimer Gudsen's and, as such, the natural must always be ancillary to the supernatural.

Megan set aside her own ambitions and gave up nursing school to follow her new husband to Concordia Seminary in Indiana. She took a job in a bookstore to pay the rent on their apartment. The plan was that she'd finish her medical training when they were settled somewhere, but it never happened, and I think they had both known it would never happen.

Herk graduated from the seminary in June of 1970. I remember the year, because I came back alive from Vietnam, an event, I suspect, which was secondary in Ginny's mind to my brother's ordination, although that might be an unfair assumption.

As God (or Ginny) would have it, Herk, after a short vicarage with a congregation in South Dakota, received a 'call' to become the pastor in the same church where we'd both been raised— St. Luke's, in Saginaw, Michigan. Ginny was ecstatic. She knew every one of the eight hundred communicant members of the congregation and now *her* son, her boy, would be shepherd to the flock. When old Pastor Doernhof decided to retire, Ginny had assisted God in His decision to choose Herkimer Gudsen as his replacement by browbeating every elder in the congregation and intimating that, as President of the Ladies' Guild, she could 'bring a sword' that would cause more trouble than the Trojan women ever dreamt possible or that another candidate would ever be worth.

Besides, Herkimer was well known and well liked among the parishioners. They had contributed money to his theological training, and most figured that they ought to have some kind of return on their investment. Many would come to regret their patronage, but a few would feel blessed.

I was there for Herk's installation, presided over by Pastor Doernhof in what was supposed to be his last public, pastoral performance. As Herk knelt in front of the old man to receive the benediction, Ginny and her entourage were weeping for joy, while most of their men were, like me, staring at Meg and allowing themselves the comfort of believing that their appreciation of her attributes was nothing more than the acceptance of God's will.

I didn't get a chance to talk to my brother until almost everyone had left Ladon Hall, where the reception for him and Meg had been held. Ginny and her votaries were still clanging dishes around, but everyone else had been cleared out. The herd of rams surrounding the new Shepherd and his wife had dissipated when Megan left her husband's side to fulfill her duty with the other ewes in the kitchen.

When he spotted me, I was sitting alone on one of several hundred metal folding chairs that Ginny and her adherents had purchased for the congregation through rummage sales or soup label collections, or some such fundraiser. He limped across the floor, his thin reflection preceding him in the white linoleum which Ginny's army kept sparkling. Still, like the women themselves, it was yellowing from too many coats of wax.

"How are you, Jim?" he said, collapsing into the chair next to me.

"Feeding frenzy over for now?"

He laughed. "For now. I expect they'll be back, after they sharpen their teeth a bit."

"No doubt."

There was a moment of silence between us then, which often happened and never felt awkward. Herk was the only person I knew who could enjoy someone's company without talking or making love.

When he finally *did* speak, it was in the semi-whisper that he used for conversation, a voice that contrasted dramatically with the powerful baritone that issued from the pulpit. "It must've been pretty bad over there," he said. I felt his pale eyes on me as I leaned my elbows on my knees and watched Ginny hand Meg dishes to dry behind the kitchen counter at the other end of Ladon Hall. This large reception area, named for the people who financed it, was attached, along with the kitchen, to the northern wall of the sanctuary.

"Yeah, it was."

"But you made it."

"Thanks for noticing."

"She's very grateful you're alive."

"Yeah."

"When were you discharged?"

"Two weeks ago."

He unbuttoned the white, clerical collar and slid a finger around his thin neck. He didn't like the fit. I could tell. I could've told him.

"Want to talk about it?"

"No. You don't need to counsel me, Pastor. Take the rest of the day off."

"Okay." That was how Ginny and Herk were different from me. They didn't get angry. They got hurt. I must've taken after the old man.

"What're you going to do now?"

"Kill time instead of people."

"They both diminish eternity."

I laughed. "Hate to trample on your aphorism, brother, but you can't diminish what doesn't exist. I don't believe in eternity."

"Why?"

"Because I really don't believe in time."

He smiled at me. It was Ginny's 'oh Jimmy, Jimmy, Jimmy' smile.

I continued. "Time is a rationale, an *invention* of life. It isn't something that has autonomous *being*. It's measurement."

"You've been reading philosophy."

"They had a pretty good library at Qua Trang."

"How does your idea affect eternity?"

"If there's really no such thing as Time, then there's no eternity, because Time defines limitations and limitations define the illimitable."

"Then there's no past?"

"Right. It's dead, gone."

"Then don't look so pained when I limp." He put his arm around my shoulders, then quickly kissed the side of my face. "I love you, brother," he whispered. "Come back to God and you may find time again—and perhaps a future."

He rose from his chair and stood in front of me. "You staying with mom?"

"Only for a few days," I answered, "but I'm sure that'll come as close to eternity as I'll ever get."

He frowned. "C'mon, Jim. You know she loves you."

I remember working hard not to raise my voice. I wanted to scream, to hurl bolts of epithets, like Zeus on Olympus. Instead, I said: "Ginny only has one son, brother. I'm just the defining factor—the limited for the illimitable, the bad for the good."

"That isn't true."

There was no winning with Herk. I didn't want to argue anymore and ruin his day. "We'd better go and rescue your wife," I said, nodding toward the kitchen where Ginny and Meg stood talking alone.

"You'll have to come out to our house, Jim. It's an old farmhouse, but it's perfect for what we need. I'll show you around the property. We have three acres and there's lots of state forest behind it. We'll have dinner, okay?"

"Sure."

"Promise?"

"I promise." I meant it. A night away from Ginny and spent with Meg—voyeurism sounded pretty good to me.

I didn't get around to it for about five weeks but, on a Saturday night in late July, I finally decided to accept what had become a weekly invitation and drove out to the Gudsen manse.

I was feeling almost euphoric that day. I'd found a job two weeks earlier, working as an orderly at Holy Cross Hospital. I didn't work anywhere near the emergency room, so no one associated me with my brother and, refreshingly, comparisons could not be drawn. I had no intention of making this a career, but the pay was decent and I'd cashed my first check a couple of hours before. Combined with my army severance pay, I had enough money to begin apartment hunting on Monday. I'd been accepted at Saginaw Valley State University and in September I'd be taking classes in philosophy and literature, courtesy of the government. In addition, the previous night, after a couple of drinks at the Amazon Club, I'd scored with one of the strippers. Her stage name was Hippolyta, but her real name, I think, was Madeline. Everyone called her Maddy. She nearly fucked me to death in the back of her Volkswagen van. The result of all this good fortune was that I was feeling independent, responsible and sated. I think it was the first time in my life I'd ever experienced all three of those feelings simultaneously.

I remember thinking, as the hot, late afternoon city air began to cool and become scented with mown hay, how Saginaw could change so quickly, from metropolitan downtown to suburbia to rolling farmland, in just a few minutes' drive.

I pulled off the potholed blacktop into Herk's gravel driveway promptly at six. I parked in the shade of a magnificent old oak whose thick, verdant canopy shaded the entire house and yard. I think the tree was older than the farm itself, probably by a century or more.

As I walked to the house, I noticed a big barn at the rear of the property. There was an old chicken coop near it, and in between was a building that, with its ancient chimney, might have served as a blacksmith's shop at one time. There was a two-story carriage house as well, which had been converted to a garage by the previous owners. That owner was not Doernhof, who occupied the congregation-owned house adjacent to the church, where he'd be allowed to live out his life as part of his retirement package. Because Herk had to shoulder the mortgage on this place, the elders had raised the pastoral salary a bit, and arranged for a low-interest mortgage through a banker who was a member at St. Luke's.

I couldn't help but think how fortunate Herk and Megan were to live here. Once I shut down the eight-track player and the harmony of *The Carpenters* died, there was such a worshipful *quiet*, like a sanctuary at midnight. There were birds crosscutting the air above me, but they were no more a disturbance to the evening stillness than the flickering of candle flames at an altar. Unlike my car, they were not intruders in this placid countryside, but its rightful occupants. They *belonged* in this pastoral place.

As I mounted the beaten step to the broad porch, I looked out across the open fields and saw, across the road, a dark-complexioned old man, in bib overalls, opening a dilapidated wire gate leading into a pasture. A dozen black and white dairy cows lifted their heads and left their grazing to greet him, apparently eager to return to the shelter of the barn and escape the descending damp and darkness. The sound of the bells around their necks did nothing to disturb the hush. It was noise, yes, but like the birds, so indigenous to the scene that it was no more invasive than the wind, the crickets, or the auscultative human heart.

"You've never seen cows before?" I turned to find Megan standing in the doorway behind me. She was wearing a pair of shorts made from old jeans that were cut off high, near the groin, and a blouse that was too tight. I'd had my first hard-on, that I could remember anyway, watching *Li'l Abner* on TV. Meg was the very image of Stupefyin' Jones. There was a voyeur's gap between two buttons that strained to maintain a tenuous grip against the unrelenting pressure of her breasts. I felt that pressure too, commanding my eyes, against their will, to find an alternative vista, but they were helplessly ensnared in cleavage. Peripherally, her auburn hair, fanned by the breeze, flamed around her head, and the sensation of heat, concentrated particularly in my loins, rose to intensity.

"Hi Meg," I managed to blurt. "I didn't hear you open the door."

"I guess we hear what we want to hear," she said, simplifying my earlier musings. "C'mon in, Jim. Herk's back in the kitchen, turning water into iced tea."

We also see what we want to see, I thought, as I studied the graceful seesaw motion of her retreating buttocks. I actually felt blinded, but she left an invisible trail of soap and perfume that eyeless Teiresias could have followed.

Herk was leaning against the kitchen counter by the sink. He was reading intently from a piece of paper in his hand and he looked annoyed. I could see that he'd just come from work because he was wearing the all-black uniform of his trade. A pile of unopened mail lay on the counter next to a carafe of freshly prepared tea. His scowl quickly evaporated, however, when we entered the room, though I think it was Megan who was responsible for the metamorphosis. "Jim," he said, switching the letter from his right hand to his left and extending the unencumbered one. "I'm so pleased you could finally come."

"Me too." I took his hand, that was crushingly warm, as always, and forced my eyes to abandon their attachment to Meg.

He sat down at the kitchen table and motioned for me to do the same. Meg was already filling glasses with tea.

"How's the new job?"

"It's okay. At least I can get my own place now."

"Great," he said, but I knew he was thinking about how Ginny would have to adjust to being alone again.

Meg brought over a tray with three glasses full of tea, each with its own wedge of lemon. She sat down next to her husband. Herk handed me one of the glasses and I took a long drink.

"Anything interesting?' Meg said. She pointed to the letter that was still firmly constricted in Herk's left hand.

"Larry Ladon again," Herk responded.

Meg's pleasant smile evaporated and she took a sip of her tea as if to conceal it.

"Who?" I said. It was none of my business, of course, but I felt a sudden need to throttle the author of so wicked an epistle that it could erase Meg's smile.

"Mr. Ladon is the Chairman of the Board of Elders at St. Luke's," Herk explained.

"And the self-appointed watchdog of virtue among his fellow believers," Meg added.

"Megan."

"It's true. You know it is." The emerald eyes were remorseless and riveted on Herk. He didn't turn to look at her, nor did I, and she may have felt ignored, though I believe, in both instances, aloofness was merely a device to prevent her beauty from muddling our thoughts and confounding our tongues. Physically, she was that remarkable.

"You mean that guy Ginny talks about all the time," I said, "the guy who owns the apple orchard on Sleepy Creek?"

"That's him," Meg replied, before Herk could stop her. "He's such an obdurate man. He's legalistic and condemning."

"As you are now, Meg?" Herk interjected.

I decided to pursue it, probably because I could see that my brother wanted to avoid the subject. "What's he writing to you for?"

"We get a letter from him about once a week," Meg offered, "usually criticizing someone else. I'll bet it says something about 'duty' in there," she said, pointing at the letter. "It's always his 'duty' to point out someone else's shortcomings. He strikes me as terribly rigid, pompous even."

I could see, very clearly, that Herk was aggravated. "When someone like Mr. Ladon," he said, "or even *you*, Megan, tell me that a person is this or that, I have enough sense to know that usually what they mean is that the object of their criticism *did* this or that—*acted* basely or unfairly. The evaluation of a person based upon a single act of meanness or cruelty, doesn't make anyone wicked."

I couldn't help entering the fray. "What about people whose whole lives have been continuous acts of cruelty?"

Herk turned to me and took a sip of his tea. "Like?"

"How about Hitler?"

"He committed horrible atrocities, yes—as a result of judging others." He smiled solemnly at Meg.

"Sorry, brother," I continued. "He was a cancer, a disease, a plague on humanity. He was wicked beyond redemption. You can't possibly equate your wife's indignation over an injustice with his psychopathy."

"Can't I?" He turned his pale blue eyes on me and I immediately felt like a child caught with a water balloon. "True evil can't be judged. You say Hitler was a cancer? A plague? How can you condemn a disease? Cancer doesn't have to be anybody's fault. It's inherently and indiscriminately wicked. It can only grow and kill. It has no loyalties, no love of country and no devotion to anyone or anything but itself. I can't think of a sane human being for whom that's true, not even Hitler—and he didn't act alone. The Holocaust came about because of the complicity of thousands of men and women who went to their jobs every day, whether as SS men at Auschwitz or secretaries in Berlin or laborers who fashioned the gas chambers at I.G. Farben or engineers who drove the trains. They went home at night and played with their children. These people, devoted to their families, their country, and even their religion, were not evil, but acted wickedly because they believed, as you do, in the evil of *others*. It's this…this, *banality*," he said, holding up the letter, "this petty judgment, that creates an environment in which cancer can grow, but it isn't the cancer itself."

"We're all born evil," Meg said.

"We're all born with the *tendency* to evil, but everything we do isn't evil—not for any of us."

"This letter was petty judgment," Meg continued.

"As was your reaction to it. But it doesn't make Larry Ladon, or you, evil."

"Then the worst we can do is aid and abet," I offered, smug in my apostasy.

"Unfortunately, yes," my brother agreed.

"Why unfortunately?"

"Because it's also the *best* we can do." The Reverend Gudsen seemed enormously saddened by this thought, and we sat in silence for a few minutes. I noticed that Megan put her hand on his arm, as if to comfort him, although why he needed comfort at that moment I still hadn't come to understand.

"What's the letter about?" I finally ventured, "or isn't it any of my business?"

Meg got up immediately. "I've got to tend to the pot roast. You guys go ahead and talk—but you've only got about fifteen minutes before I force you into congeniality." She kissed my brother on the top of his head as she walked behind him. He didn't seem to notice.

"Ladon takes great pride in his knowledge of Scripture. He told a mutual friend that he knew the Bible better than most pastors."

"Is that true?"

"Well, let's just say that he knows it well enough that I can't tell if it's idle boasting or not. Besides, it doesn't matter."

In spite of Herk's avowal of apathy, I believed that it *did* matter to him, somehow.

"Anyway, Ladon's teaching a Bible class, Sunday afternoons, on the Books of Moses. There's a man in that class, a young guy about your age," (my brother often forgot that he wasn't yet thirty himself). "His name is Baxter Bird. His great-grandfather, like Ladon's grandfather, was one of the charter members of St. Luke's. He's got a brother, Caleb, at the seminary right now. I had some classes with him."

He paused in another of those non-awkward moments of silence, then continued in his naturally soft-spoken tones: "Mr. Bird apparently took exception to a passage in Leviticus, the book they were studying last Sunday."

"What passage?"

"Chapter eighteen, verse twenty-two: 'Do not lie with a man as one lies with a woman; that is detestable'."

"Oh-oh."

"Mr. Bird, according to Mr. Ladon's letter, then proceeded to express his doubt about the origin of that passage—maintaining that it was not God-inspired. He argued that it was the cultural bias of the writer that led to its inclusion in the ancient manuscripts."

"I'll be damned, an unliteral Lutheran."

"They're not as rare as you might suppose."

"What about the prohibition against wearing clothes that are both wool and linen? I
think it's in that same book somewhere."

"Deuteronomy 22:11, actually. But that's ceremonial law, the law that Christ said
He'd overcome. This is *moral* law. It doesn't change."

"Who makes the distinction?"

"Between ceremonial and moral law?"

"Yes."

"The church."

"Which church?"

Herk smiled and sighed. "The Lutheran Church – Missouri Synod of course."

"Of course. So is this Bird guy homosexual?"

"I think so, but I don't know. His recent companion is a very effeminate man. Baxter

35

introduced him to me after church a few weeks ago. He's a member of St. Luke's too, but I can't remember his name. They're inseparable."

"So what does this Ladon guy want you to do about it?"

"From what I can make of it, he wants me to set Mr. Bird straight."

I couldn't help snickering. "And if you can't?"

"Then he wants him brought before the Board of Elders to explain his views."

"And Ladon is the Chairman of that board?"

"Yes."

"What're you going to do?"

He raised his voice to an exaggerated volume. "Eat some roast beef, I hope!"

Megan, potholders in hand, was opening the oven door. As she bent low to retrieve the roast, I turned away, heroically fending off my desire to abet the devil.

"Five minutes," she said. "I have to make the gravy."

I looked at my brother. I knew that beneath the serene exterior, his mind and soul were troubled. I, of course, was comfortable in my ignorance, like a little child trying to pet a cobra. I repeated my question.

"I don't know. Perhaps a sermon on tolerance," he said, "or a placating letter."

"Herk," Megan warbled from across the room. "Could you set the table service, please? Everything's ready. Jim, would you be kind enough to carve the roast?"

Herk stood and moved quickly to retrieve plates and cups from the cupboard. "How come he gets the fun job?" he whined in false petulance.

"Because you and sharp objects don't get along," she answered. We all laughed, but it was nervous laughter—like a person amused by someone who knocks on wood, but has done it himself when no one's around.

The meal, like its concoctor, was warm and sumptuous. Food had never tasted this good before and I was certain that it never would again. I was positively gluttonous.

The conversation was light and cheerful, carefully orchestrated by Meg, who would allow no interruption of the gaiety. It was, thanks to her skillful maneuvering, the first time my brother and I had enjoyed each other's company since we were children. It was the beginning of our reconciliation and my conversion. It's part of the reason that we both were willing to die for her.

As I slurped up a second helping of strawberry shortcake, the phone rang and Meg went to answer it. She returned almost immediately. "It's Lena Gossbach," she said. Herk's relaxed demeanor vanished as he rose from the table and shrugged his shoulders apologetically. "I'll take it in my study," he said, a phrase that would be repeated often in his life. Meg left to hang up the other phone, but was back in a couple of minutes.

"More coffee? she said.

"No, thanks. I couldn't swallow another thing. God, that was a great meal!"

"I'm sure He appreciates your gratitude."

"What?"

"God."

"Oh, jeez, I'm sorry."

"No, no. I wasn't correcting you. Really. It's possible to pray in a lot of different ways."

"Yeah, but I wasn't praying."

"Weren't you?"

She sat in Herk's chair, across from me, and smiled warmly. I was thanking God again—this time that humans weren't endowed with the ability to read each other's minds. "Who's Lena Gossbach?—or isn't it any of my business?"

"She calls here several times a week. We inherited her from Pastor Doernhof."

"Inherited her?"

"She's had a problem for years that needs continual pastoral counseling."

I didn't ask, but she offered the information without a qualm. I thought then, that I'd never violate that trust.

"She has religious OCD."

"What's that?"

"Obsessive-compulsive disorder. Are you familiar with it at all?"

Staring at the gap in her shirt, I believed I had some familiarity with the affliction. "It's a kind of maniacal attentiveness to something, isn't it? Like the woman who's so afraid of fire that she returns to her house twenty times a day to check and see if she turned off the stove?"

"Something like that, only with religious OCD, the victims of the disorder are so afraid of what they think God can do to them that they live their lives in this awful fearful kind of servility. Herk calls them 'God's toadies'. They pray constantly, continually, about everything. They kiss their crucifixes at certain times each day, pray on their knees at all hours, even wash their hands in a ritualized formula which, they believe, keeps them safe from God's bacterial wrath. They're obsessed with the idea of a Vengeful Deity and feel compelled to appease Him. Every detail of existence, for them, has to do with their fear of God."

"Are you sure that's what Mrs. Gossbach has?"

"It's Miss Gossbach. She never married. I'm not sure a husband could have coped with it all. Yeah, they're sure. She sees a psychiatrist regularly and she's gotten better—but she has her episodes, probably once a month, and then she needs to be reminded of God's forgiveness and mercy."

"She can't remember that by herself?"

"No." Megan smiled. "It's got to come right from the horse's mouth. Because Herk's a pastor, she sees him as God's agent. She was raised Catholic. If *he* says she's okay, then she's reassured—at least until the next episode. Somebody must've scared the hell out of her when she was a kid."

I was somewhat surprised that she would use the word hell, but I tried to appear as if I wasn't. "More likely scared it *into* her," I said.

38

There was a peculiar instant then. Megan was looking directly into my eyes. Her face had become serious. I looked back, mesmerized. It was like the moment in which two potential lovers must decide to kiss—intimate, exciting, anticipatory, and dangerous. I remember actually *leaning* toward her and I think she moved, ever so slightly, toward me. Then she straightened up, and the spell was broken. "Could I have one of your cigarettes?" she said, pointing at my shirt pocket.

"Sure." I pulled them out and lit one for her.

She took a long drag and exhaled with a hedonistic sigh. "Wonderful," she said. "You must not be terribly addicted. You haven't smoked since you've been here."

"I was trying to be polite."

"Well, don't. A pastor's wife doesn't get too many chances to feed an addiction. You must visit often and smoke continually, leaving your lit cigarette where your sister-in-law can sneak a puff now and then. It'll be fun. Besides, it's a rare opportunity to be deceitful. Deal?" She winked at me.

"Deal." At that moment, I began to admire Megan for more than her physical attributes.

The pleasure of that clandestine moment was broken by the sound of Herk's approaching footsteps on the wooden floor of the hallway. "Here!" she said, shoving the cigarette at me. She waved away the telltale cloud in front of her as my brother entered the kitchen.

"Let's get these dishes done," he said. "I'll wash. Jim, you dry. Megs gets to put 'em away."

A paring knife, tossed haphazardly (by me of course) into the soapy water, found Herk's hand and we ended our pleasant evening in the emergency room at Holy Cross.

If God demands, as Luther taught, that we must live in order to die and die in order to live, then surely the Almighty must have a sense of humor.

Chapter three

I found an apartment the next week. It wasn't much—a single, large room over a furniture store—but it was cheap, and Ginny didn't live there.

I saw my brother frequently. His work, like his propensity for injury, brought him often to St. Luke's, where he visited the sick and dying of his congregation. He would usually be carrying a silver box, containing the flesh and blood of God, while I wielded a mop or bedpan. We would speak, briefly, in the sterile hallway, then he would move on to comfort patients in his way, and I in mine. He never failed to invite me for dinner and I rarely declined. It was a chance to see Megan and feed her habit. As the weeks and months passed, Saturday night at the Gudsen manse became a ritual—along with Sunday mornings at St. Luke's.

I'm not sure yet how he got me to attend church. I'm not even certain it was he—more likely it was Meg. Either way, the sheep was brought into the fold. I began by sitting in the last pew so that I could make an innocuous escape if the pressure of Goodness proved too much for me, but at Meg's insistence I wound up next to her in front, craning my neck to watch my brother perform in the ornately carved pulpit above us. Ginny sat with us too, but that turned out to be profitable for me as well. I could claim a visit without ever having to listen to her. Ginny was a serious—and silent—worshipper.

I was constantly amazed at the power of my brother's voice, which was, in normal conversation, barely audible. His rich baritone floated over the heads of the faithful like tongues of fire, and his sermons, always inspirational and exhilarating, lifted the spirits of his flock. He armed them with an encouragement that would allow them to endure another week of quiet desperation.

He was the first pastor St. Luke's had ever had who didn't, in some way, mention the financial obligation of its members...ever. He refused to, even when pushed by Ladon and the other elders to exhort the membership to tithe. Worse, he eliminated the sacred tradition of pledging and relied entirely upon the Holy Spirit to inspire the faithful to generosity.

It worked. At the close of Herk's first fiscal year, the treasurer's report, required by charter to be read to the membership, declared that St. Luke's was operating, at least as far as its annual budget, in the black. Herk himself gave twenty-five percent of his meager remuneration. At that same meeting of the General Assembly, Baxter Bird motioned for a five percent raise for Pastor Gudsen. It was seconded several times and quickly approved by an overwhelming majority, despite Elder Ladon's objections. Herk refused it—as much, I think, to reduce factionalism as to set a noble example. Either way, it served to further endear him to his flock.

Ginny was sinfully proud. If pride was explosive, she would have been blown to Kingdom Come. Her popularity with her ladies was directly correlative to Herk's growing stature, and she basked in her son's light more audaciously than the Virgin herself might have with hers. She often spoke of my 'important studies' at the university and once I overheard her tell a friend about my 'ministry' among the sick at Holy Cross, but I think she was relieved not to have to invent superlatives for Herk.

Once a month, she'd be at the Saturday night gathering at the manse, but I really didn't mind it. She occupied Herk's full attention on such occasions, giving Meg and me a chance to enjoy each other's company.

One Saturday evening, in early October, just after a meal that would have sated the most zealous of gluttons, Megan suggested we all take a walk around the property to exorcise the demons of obesity and leave the clean-up until later. Ginny wouldn't hear of it. To her, dirty dishes represented a slovenliness that she couldn't abide and they had to be eradicated as soon after supper as possible. She urged the rest of us to go ahead without her. Herkimer volunteered to stay and help while encouraging me to escort his wife—another pastoral compromise for the sake of harmony. I needed no encouragement, and Megan and I were soon outside in the crisp, autumn air, strolling across an open meadow. It was a fine evening, so rare in Michigan, when there was no humidity and the temperature promoted neither perspiration nor gooseflesh. The slanting light crept across the golden field and struck the line of red, yellow and orange trees that marked the edge of the state forest. Nature seemed full of color and light and beauty. As its personification strolled quietly by my side, I felt a peace and contentment that rarely manifested itself in my anxious mind and covetous heart.

Megan too, seemed enamoured of it all and, uncharacteristically, was silent for the first few minutes of our walk. When she finally did speak, it was to ask for a cigarette, which I readily provided.

She inhaled deeply, then emitted a sigh that was much more than the simple expulsion of smoke.

"Why do you think it is, Jim," she said, "that our keenest pleasures are often designed to hurt us?"

"You mean like tobacco?"

"Tobacco, food, alcohol, you know."

"Maybe it's supposed to be a lesson in moderation."

She smiled, picked up a stone and threw it into the trees, which we were slowly approaching. "But moderation kills the *joy* of it. What person ever smoked just one cigarette and said 'ah, now I'm content. I'll never need another'? What happiness is there in a single slice of double cheese pizza or one glass of wine? The need continues. We're never completely *sated*."

"That's true, but if it weren't that way, there'd be no desire. Nothing would tantalize us. If you smoked one cigarette and it satisfied you, for life I mean, then you'd lose the longing, that *something* that promises enjoyment. You wouldn't fulfill a craving, you'd end it. You'd lose your appetite. You'd eliminate lust. What kind of a world would that be?"

She stopped walking. We'd just entered the edge of the forest on a path that must have been familiar to her, perhaps made by her. She looked at me the way she had on my first visit and I felt the sudden joy of deprivation.

"You want to kiss me, don't you Jim?"

The question so staggered me that I could do nothing but stand in awkward silence, staring at the full mouth that spoke those words.

"You do, don't you?"

"Yes."

"Why don't you?"

"I didn't think…" my voice trailed off, but the incomplete sentence was an adequate summation of my mental processes.

"You didn't think I'd let you? You didn't think I knew you're attracted to me? I'll let you, you know. Go ahead." She threw her cigarette away, closed her eyes, and leaned toward me.

I remember thinking, briefly, that I'd never be able to look my brother in the eye again, then I kissed her. I felt her tongue in my mouth. I pulled her roughly against me, felt her arms around my neck. I touched her breast, but her hand moved mine away and she stepped back, leaving me panting, trembling, my erection pressing painfully against my jeans.

"So you've had your kiss," she said. "Do you feel better? Does the fulfillment of your desire give you pleasure, or would it have been better not to have had it at all?"

I was feeling awkward, foolish, vulnerable, traitorous and, more than anything, pissed. "You mean to tell me that this was some twisted philosophical *experiment*? That was a shitty thing to do, Megan," I shouted. "What the hell's wrong with you?"

Then I saw her tears, and my anger, like my erection, faded.

"I'm so sorry," she cried. "So very sorry."

She ran out of the trees and back into the open meadow. I raced after her and, after a hundred yards or so, caught her arm and turned her around.

"Let me go!" she screamed and I glanced toward the house, afraid that her voice would bring retribution and, worse, the destruction of the delicate new harmony between my brother and me.

She finally quit struggling and fell to her knees, sobbing. I knelt by her.

"Herk found out yesterday," she said, fighting to collect herself.

"Found out what? What?"

"We were going to try artificial insemination, but he's sterile." Her hand was shaking as she tried to wipe away her tears and the strands of wet, auburn hair that matted her cheeks.

"I'm sorry Megan, but you've lost me. Who was Herk going to artificially inseminate if you didn't know until yesterday that he was sterile?"

"*Me!* We want to have children, but Herk can't...he can't...perform." She laughed out loud, but it was more bitter than funny. "What a ludicrous word," she said. "He's impotent. Might as well call it what it is."

I was so astounded I didn't know what to say at first. Eventually, my curiosity got the better of me. "How long has he...been this way?"

"Always, as far as I know. We've been married for over a year, Jim, and technically I'm still a virgin."

"You didn't, uh, experiment before you were married?"

"No. Oh I love him desperately, Jim, but my nights are filled with erotic dreams. I can't help it. I'm twenty-one. I'm healthy. I want so much to be a mom. This attraction between you and me, I didn't know where it was going, but your face is so like his I began to imagine that.... I'm sorry. You shouldn't have been drawn into this." She breathed deeply, gaining control. "Didn't know your brother married a slut, did you?"

I suddenly felt an enormous empathy for my sister-in-law. If ever a woman was intended to make babies, it was Megan. Not only was she a sexual magnet with birthing hips and breasts designed to feed but, as I came to know her, she was naturally maternal.

"I can't say I ever heard of a virgin slut. You're human, that's all."

"Thanks for that, Jim." She smiled weakly.

"Cigarette?" I held out the package.

"Oh please, please, please." She forced a broader smile, wiped away her remaining tears, and sat down in the tall grass. The sun was fading quickly, though a glance at my watch told me it was only a few minutes after seven.

"How's Herk handling all this?"

"He takes it in his stride, like everything else. He's so kind, Jim. He does everything he can to…to please me. We'll lie in bed, sometimes for hours, kissing, caressing. He seems to enjoy it immensely, but it's as if he has no feeling there, no sensation, nothing. I've never seen him with an erection. I thought for a long time that there was something wrong with me until I…saw you."

I knew then that a need for reassurance of her own desirability had prompted her earlier advances as much as my resemblance to my brother or her own deprivation.

She looked out at the dying sunlight that shadowed the meadow with descending cold and lit the top of the forest beyond in an illusion of fire. "He's like autumn," she said.

Even in the lowering gloom, she must've seen the question on my face.

"Passion without heat," she explained. Her mouth curved in a sad, apologetic smile. She turned her head so that the wind could brush her unruly hair from her face.

"How do they know he's sterile?"

"What?"

"How'd they get a…specimen?"

"Oh. They extracted it—with a needle."

I must have grimaced unconsciously, because I witnessed a genuine smile for the first time that evening. "This is your brother, remember? He's used to being pierced."

"Yeah, but there? Ugh."

She actually giggled, but her brief vivacity quickly faded to a gentle melancholy. She was reflective for a few moments, gently fingering her wedding ring. I waited for her to interrupt the silence. Somewhere off in the forest, a raven's raucous cry interrupted the serenity.

"May I have one more cigarette?" she said. "Then we should get back."

I got one out for her and lit it. She turned to look back at the house. The lights were on now in the kitchen and though we were within a few hundred feet of the house, the descending darkness undoubtedly hid us from view.

"I've prayed so hard about this," she said. "Do you think it could be a test of my faith?"

"You're asking the wrong person."

"I really am so sorry about tonight. I don't know what happened. I love your brother, more than my life, and I'd never leave him, never!"

"I believe you," I said, but I wasn't sure that I did—then. "What're you going to do?"

"Go on as we have, I guess—praying, hoping for the best."

"There are other ways, you know."

"Other ways?"

I immediately regretted my words. I thought, at the time, how strange it is that once spoken, they can never be retrieved. "To, uh, satisfy a woman."

She smiled again, I think, though the shadows were erasing her features. "I have this satanic urge," she said, "to make you explain. But I won't. I know what you mean. For my sake, Herk's tried, but his heart isn't in it. I think he perceives these other 'methods' as wrong. Although there's nothing in Scripture against them, I think he views them as unnatural and he's uncomfortable with it. Besides, they won't bring us children will they?"

"No."

She reached out and put her hand on mine. "Thanks for putting up with your crazy sister-in-law," she said. "I feel much better about this just by having someone to confide in. I don't have any family or close friends. I've struggled with this alone for almost a year. Now I don't feel so, so…solitary, and Jim, if I didn't love your brother so much, it would be, well, easy to love you."

"I'm used to coming in second, at least when competing with my brother." I tried not to look serious. "I'll always be here for you, Meg. I'm your friend." I had no idea, then, what that promise would entail.

"Yes," she whispered, "I believe you are."

When we got back to the house, we could hear Herk and Ginny conversing in the living room. My brother was saying something about rescheduling a dinner.

"I'm going to the bathroom," Meg confided. "Going to brush my teeth and swallow some mouthwash. Be back in a minute."

I walked into the living room. I sat down in a ragged, over-stuffed chair that looked like it had been rescued from the side of the road.

For the first time I could ever remember, Ginny turned her attention from a Herkian discourse to address me. "Well," she said, "you were gone for *quite* a while. Have a nice walk?"

"Lovely."

"Where's Megan?"

"She had to pee."

"Really, James! Must you be so vulgar?"

I didn't want to spoil the evening, so I acquiesced. "She had to visit the restroom."

"That's better."

Our mother could have easily passed for our grandmother— the tight, pinched expression; the gray hair pulled severely back into a bun; the wardrobe that included only dresses; the conversations about static cling. Only her youthful complexion and vigorous frame belied the supposition. I sensed that, with the right clothes and make-up, she could be beautiful.

"I didn't mean to interrupt," I told my impotent brother.

"Your presence is never an interruption," he said. I wondered then, if he would feel the same way if he knew the truth about what had just transpired between his wife and me. But then, what is the truth? "We were just trying to work out a scheduling problem, that's all."

"I'm telling you, Darling," Ginny said, turning back to her favored boy. "*I* can be flexible, but the other ladies aren't going to like it. We've *always* had the Swiss steak dinner on the third Saturday in October. A lot of the Ladies' Guild members plan their whole *year* around it. And you know how much revenue it brings in. Last year we profited almost *fifteen hundred dollars!* That's nothing to sneeze at."

Herk smiled his benevolent surrogate-husband smile. "You're right of course, Mother, but I can't be in two places at once. I'll just have to skip the dinner if we can't change it."

"Well *that's* out of the question," she said. "The pastor and his wife *always* attend. You'd offend too many people if you weren't there."

"What's the conflict?" I interjected, hoping to keep the lamb from slaughter.

"It's my fault," Herk was quick to say. "I inadvertently scheduled a wedding on the same day as the Ladies' Guild Swiss steak supper. It wasn't on the calendar, but growing up in this church, I should have remembered." He looked at Ginny in such a grievous manner that an outside observer might have suspected that he'd done something bestial, like screwing sheep. For some reason, that image made me smile.

"I assure you James," Ginny said, noticing my smirk, "this is no laughing matter."

I would have enjoyed telling her that nothing that had to do with her was, but I'd betrayed my brother enough for one evening. I ignored her. "Whose wedding?"

"Ben Tower's daughter," Herk responded.

"Skinny Minnie?"

"What?"

"Minnie Tower. I went to high school with her. We used to call her Skinny Minnie. She was practically a skeleton. She looked like that English model, what's her name?"

"Twiggy?" Megan said as she entered the room and sat on the beat-up sofa next to her husband.

"Twiggy, yeah. Her dad owns that bison ranch doesn't he? I remember reading about it. He thinks there's going to be a big market for buffalo meat."

"That's one of his enterprises, yes," Herk said. "His ranch is only a few miles north of here."

"He's one of the richest men in the Saginaw Valley," Ginny said. "He can afford to be eccentric."

"How come I've never seen Minnie in church? I mean if you're her pastor, she must go to St. Luke's."

"She doesn't attend regularly," Ginny offered. Mother Gudsen kept track of such things.

"I don't think you'd recognize her anymore brother," Herk said. "I guess she must've filled out since you saw her last. She's really a beautiful girl now."

"The Towers won't change the wedding date?" I was earnest in trying to find a solution, if for no other reason than to move the conversation to a more intriguing subject.

"It's only three weeks away," Megan said. Apparently she and Herk had discussed this before. "They've sent out their invitations, rented the hall—you know."

"How about if they had it in a different place?" I suggested.

"They already are," Herk answered. "It's going to be held in the groom's church over in Bay City. It's at four and the steak dinner doesn't begin until five. I could probably make it back by six, but many members of our congregation will be going to the reception and that would undermine our fundraiser considerably. I have no choice but to move the Swiss steak dinner to another night, Mom."

Ginny's lips became more pinched, her lemon-sucking expression more pronounced.

"Well that's fine," she said in a tone and manner that indicated that it wasn't, "but Mr. Ladon will be furious and you've already made an enemy of *him*."

"Well I can't help that," Herk said.

"Pastor Doernhof managed to stay in Mr. Ladon's good graces for twenty-odd years. You've managed to alienate him in a few months."

There was an uncomfortable silence as my brother, looking wounded, carefully weighed his response. There wasn't the slightest trace of anger in his demeanor. I, on the other hand, was prepared to knock over tables and clear the temple.

"Would you have me just comply with Mr. Ladon and ignore my conscience, Mother? God has placed me here to lead His people by love and example—not acquiescence. I will do my utmost to promote harmony in God's church, but not at the price of integrity. I won't be an impotent figurehead." His cheeks flushed at the realization of what he'd just said. He glanced quickly at Megan whose sympathetic expression only seemed to intensify his discomfort. I felt a great affection for my brother at that moment. His suffering then seemed, like so many experiences in his life, to be excruciating. It was the beginning of my devotion.

Only Ginny was unaware of her son's humiliation and, like her son, she had no intention of retreating. "Listen, I don't like Larry Ladon either," she said, but there was something fraudulent in her tone.

"He's a Philistine," Megan suggested, drawing a disapproving look from her spouse as he struggled to recover his composure.

"I suppose you could say that," Ginny continued, "but he's not wrong about this business of Baxter Bird. The man's a sodomite. He and his 'friend' are getting bolder too. Gertie Schmidt says she saw them holding hands during services!"

"Mother," Megan said, "with all due respect, there's a very big difference between holding hands and sodomy."

"Do you seriously think," Ginny continued, "that a man who holds hands with another man isn't homosexual?"

"It's not our place to judge, Mother. Besides," Herk said, "the issue here isn't Mr. Bird's sexuality. It's a doctrinal matter."

"How so?" I said, genuinely intrigued.

Herk turned his attention to me, the rosy flush in his face fading. "Mr. Bird has never said that he's homosexual. He might be better off if he had. Though the church—and Scripture—view homosexuality as a sin, it is, like all sins, (except for the denial of God), forgivable. What Mr. Bird has suggested is that the passages in Deuteronomy, Leviticus and Judges condemning the practice are mere cultural bias, as he puts it, and not the inspired Word of God. That position, not only according to Luther himself, but also by concord of the Lutheran Church, Missouri Synod in convocation, is heretical. Mr. Ladon would have Mr. Bird *and* his companion immediately expulsed—revoking their membership at St. Luke's."

"Which the church demands," Ginny said.

"Not demands, Mother. *Advises.* I would rather give it time, counsel with Mr. Bird, as I'm doing now. As far as his friend, well, he's done nothing except hold Baxter's hand—if that's even true. He's kept silent and—as Thomas More so aptly illustrated in his heresy trial—in ecclesiastical law, silence can only be interpreted as consent or agreement with the prevailing orthodoxy."

"The Big-Endians and the Little-Endians," I said.

Ginny looked at me as if I'd spoken Arabic. "What?"

"It's not that kind of petty factionalism," Herk said, although there was little conviction in his voice.

"Isn't it?"

"What *are* you two talking about?" Ginny said.

Megan explained. "It's an allusion to Swift's *Gulliver's Travels.* The Lilliputians, the tiny people in this fictional kingdom, have a war. It's caused by a controversy over whether an egg is properly broken at the big end, (the heretical view), or the little end, (the orthodox view). It's meant to satirize theological disputes that, in Swift's opinion, weren't important."

"Thank you," Ginny said, then turned on me. "You think that this is some silly thing like that, James?"

"Yes, I do."

"You're wrong," she said. "This argument has *great* meaning."

"Everything we do and say has meaning, but meaning doesn't necessarily indicate significance. Meaning simply refers to purpose. Purpose is not import," I replied.

"What God says isn't significant to you?" Herk said. He seemed very agitated, very disturbed.

"I'm afraid I have to agree with Baxter Bird here, brother. I'm not sure it's God who's speaking."

Ginny gasped and put her hand over her mouth as if she'd committed the blasphemy herself. I fully expected her to tear her dress momentarily. Herk shook his head, sadly, ever the man of sorrows. I'd crossed to the enemy camp and I knew that the little familial happiness I'd experienced over the past few months was about to evaporate, but I couldn't stop. Herk and I were two people that refused to make our lives easier with deception. We'd have to see this through. I don't know where Meg stood, and Ginny?— well, ignorance is bliss only insofar as self-doubt requires intelligence.

"Are you saying that the Holy Bible isn't the inspired Word of God?" Ginny asked this with a pleading tone, as if to beg me to provide the answer she wanted. Whoever said 'familiarity breeds contempt' must've meant 'family'.

"I think we need to think about it—a lot. Especially when it concerns removing someone from the company of his fellow believers."

"Which of you by taking thought can add one cubit to his stature?" Ginny proclaimed. "The Gospel according to St. Matthew, chapter six, verse twenty-seven."

"And this means that we shouldn't think or we won't get tall? C'mon." I was looking at Ginny, but I could *feel* Megan smiling.

"It means you can't gain eternal life by intellectualizing," Herkimer said. "You know what it means, Jim. Don't antagonize Mother. Say what you want, but dull the sword's edge a bit, okay?"

"Okay."

Ginny had tears in her eyes, which she did nothing to hide. They were meant to be weapons. They were sharper than my tongue and, with Herk at least, they were effective.

"After we talked about this a few weeks ago," I said to Herk, "I went home and did some reading. There's another passage in Deuteronomy, something about cross-dressing. Do you know it?"

Herk reached for a well-worn Bible that was on a coffee table in front of him. "I can find it pretty quickly," he said. He turned to it almost instantly. "Here it is. Deuteronomy twenty-two five: 'A woman must not wear men's clothing, nor a man wear women's clothing, for the Lord your God detests anyone who does this'. That what you were thinking of?"

"Yes, thanks. Now—"

"But Mr. Bird doesn't do *that*, James," Ginny said, apparently recovering. "I don't see what relevance—"

I ignored her and directed my full attention to my brother. "Ceremonial law or moral law?"

"Moral law."

"And we should take it literally?"

"Yes."

"Then Jack Lemmon and Tony Curtis are hated by God?"

"The actors?" Herk asked.

Megan laughed. "Some like it hot," she said.

Chapter four

My brother and I argued, or rather 'discussed' the
non-literal literalness of the Bible for several hours that evening. I
told him, at one point, that we should change the subject, that we
weren't getting anywhere and that God probably wasn't interested
in our arguments anyway. He answered that God was very interested, even present. He quoted a passage from Matthew: 'For where
two or three come together in my name, there am I with them.' I
told him that if he took that literally, then God wasn't really with
us that evening, because there were *four* of us, although Ginny had
fallen asleep, and perhaps a convocation of the LCMS might be required to determine if consciousness was necessary to enumeration.

And so it went, until Ginny woke sometime past midnight
and went home. I followed shortly after, suddenly realizing that
Herk had to preach in the morning. I promised to continue to
come to church and apologized for my flippancy.

I realized, while driving back to my apartment, that not once
during our 'discussion', as I ridiculed Herk's beliefs, had he raised
his voice or evidenced any anger. I also reflected upon the fact that
Megan had been responsible, to a great extent, for keeping the
peace. When tension had developed between my brother and me,
she'd been quick to interject some kind of humor—never taking
sides, but always a bit closer to the left. For example, Herk had
quoted a passage from Leviticus that instructed; 'Do not lie with a
man as one lies with a woman; that is detestable.' Megan had,

tongue in cheek, offered the suggestion that that particular passage would make a great placard for a Lesbian Alliance parade.

My brother had smiled. Fortunately, Ginny had been napping. I laughed out loud.

As I crawled wearily into bed, I wondered if Megan was attempting, at that moment, to get a different kind of rise from her husband. How long could she live a life of celibacy before she turned away from him and came to me? How *does* one pray to a virgin God with a virgin mother for the simple experience of orgasm?

Two weeks later, Herk received a letter from the LCMS Michigan District President. In it, the executive expressed his concern that Pastor Gudsen was alienating certain brethren in his congregation by refusing to 'take positive action' in a matter 'crucial to the sanctity of God's Holy Word.' The epistle further related that, at the request of his own Board of Elders, Pastor Gudsen's 'position' in the matter of an allegedly unrepentant homosexual named Baxter Bird would soon be evaluated by a delegation from the President's office. The letter assured Pastor Gudsen that the Reverend President did not necessarily believe the allegations brought forward by Chairman Ladon, but that Mr. Ladon's long history of good standing in the LCMS would indicate that he would not enter into such accusations lightly, nor was he likely to be guilty of 'casuistry'. Consequently, there must be some 'miscommunication' or 'misinterpretation' of the facts. A review, 'not uncommon in regard to first-year pastors' could only serve to defuse an 'unpleasant misunderstanding' so that the 'good work of the Gospel' could go forward 'unimpeded'. The Inquisitiors, as Megan furiously referred to the investigators, were expected to arrive in November, the week preceding Thanksgiving.

I saw the letter on a Saturday night in October, the weekend before Halloween. Herk showed it to me while we sat on his back porch, watching hamburgers sizzle on his rusty charcoal grill—undoubtedly another curbside acquisition. It had been a good day for me. My classes at the university were stimulating and so was

Bethany Meyers' younger sister Hannah who, despite the fact that
she was less than a year out of high school, had already accepted
more piercings from me than her agreeable sibling. Thus was I in a
magnanimous mood and had pledged myself to eschew any dispar-
aging remarks and keep the evening light and congenial. But when
I arrived, a bottle of good Merlot in hand, I could see that my
brother and Megan were both deeply depressed.

I knew, of course, of the controversies regarding Baxter Bird
and the developing aggression of Larry Ladon, but I didn't see
them as more than temporary trials that any pastor might encounter in the normal course of shepherding. After all, sheep are not the
brightest animals. I knew that Herk was deeply solicitous about the
situation, but then my brother often cared about things whose
worth didn't merit his devotion (including our parents).

So I took the matter lightly, even though I knew from Ginny
of the approaching 'investigation' by the office of the Michigan
District. I asked to see the letter and Herk fetched it for me, although he showed little interest in it and appeared to be preoccupied when I questioned him about it. I knew then that his melancholy had nothing to do with the advancing confrontation any
more than the smoke from the grill had to do with his tears. I heard
Megan banging utensils in the kitchen.

He put his scarred hands over his face and leaned forward,
his shoulders moving like the rolling clouds of that dark, sad day.

"Herk, what is it?" I said, unconsciously embracing him with
one arm as much to stop the frightening and unfamiliar motion of
his sobbing as to commiserate. I looked out at the leafless forest and
lifeless meadow and felt a stabbing terror.

"I can't bear this cross," he said, his soft voice muffled in his
palms. "Not *this* one."

I tried to be gentle and patient, but my mounting anxiety
was certainly palpable in the intensity of my voice. "What's the
matter?"

"She, she…" he sobbed, trying to choke back the constrictive
hold with which strong emotion can strangle the voice.

'She's decided to leave him', I thought, and a secret, wicked part of me rejoiced.

"She's got cancer," he said.

I was certain, only for a moment, that my brother had lied, to hurt me, to pay me for my cruelty to Ginny, for his everlasting limp, yet I knew him to be neither specious nor vengeful. Ginny couldn't have cancer, she seemed too cheerful, too full of the future. Then, I was suddenly sure that he wasn't talking about our mother.

"Who? Herk, who has cancer?" I think I shook him then, I don't remember.

"Megs."

It couldn't be, of course. She hadn't smoked a carton of cigarettes in her life. She'd just registered to vote for the first time. It couldn't be.

"There's got to be some mistake," I said, "a mix-up at some lab. She looks healthier than I do. There's a *mistake!*"

"She's got a year, maybe less." This was spoken so laconically that I wanted to punch my impotent, beloved of God, beloved of Ginny, beloved of Megan, brother. If he was able to fight me I would…. If he was Abel….I could raise Cain….

That was the last and only time I ever saw my brother lose heart. I don't mean that he never cried again or was distressed—I'd see that plenty in the coming months—but it was the single moment that I ever witnessed in him a lack of *direction*, a lapse in faith, a confusion about who he was and where he was going. I could literally see him gathering himself, marshaling whatever forces drove him. His posture, his facial expressions, his entire demeanor changed and he was calm again. It was as if he were putting on some kind of invisible armor, preparing for an invisible war—which, as it turned out, was exactly the case.

He stood up, went to the grill, and turned the hamburgers. "She was feeling some pain in her abdomen and she was getting really nauseous, especially after eating. She was developing some little lumps around her vagina and the small of her back. Finally, two weeks ago, I convinced her to see a doctor. They took tests.

They did x-rays. Doctor Herman told us that it's called carcinomatosis. She's got epithelial tumors."

"Skin cancer?" I said, recalling a high school biology quiz.

"The skin is epithelium, yes, but it's also the stuff that forms the coverings of most internal surfaces and organs as well. She's got tumors at many bodily sites, both internal and external. They're malignant."

"Maybe they made a mistake, Herk. It's possible isn't it? Maybe there was a mix-up in the lab or—"

"They did biopsies on six tumors. They've done all kinds of chemical tests. They've triple-checked. Dr. Herman is sending us to an oncologist in Ann Arbor, but they're sure."

"There's no cure?"

"No."

"Who knows about this?"

"Me, Megan, now you. I'm going to have to tell Mother, of course."

He turned to look at me, his eyes filled with tears. I stood up and embraced him, held on to him. Though I'm much shorter than he is, he *felt* fragile, if such a thing is possible. "I'm so sorry," I whispered.

"It's a test," he said.

"A test?"

"All things work together for good, for those who love God."

"Careful," Megan said, standing behind us, her face somewhat obscured by the dark screen of the outer door. "Larry Ladon might drive by, see you two in a clutch, and add more fuel to the fire."

I couldn't help smiling, as much in admiration as amusement.

"Bring those burgers in will you?" she said, "before you've charred away all the meat."

We sat in silence around the table, no one eating from appetite, but only to encourage the other two. Finally, Megan forced it. "I'm not dead yet," she said. "I don't want you two mooning around here. If you don't love me enough to try to keep me cheered up, then get the hell out!" She got up and began clearing the table.

"Megan," I stood up. "I'm so very—"

"Oh *please* don't tell me you're sorry," she said, turning to face me and leaning back against the sink. "A, it's not your fault and B, I don't want to be the object of pity. Let's just go on, shall we?" There were no tears.

Herk crossed the kitchen and stood next to her, but didn't touch her.

"What can I do?" I said, more to myself than anyone else.

"You can ask," she replied.

"Ask?"

"Matthew's gospel. Jesus said: 'Again, I tell you that if two of you on earth agree about anything you ask for, it will be done for you by my Father in heaven.'" She smiled. "Seems pretty straight-forward to me, literal or not. You and Herk think you can agree on what you want to ask for?"

I looked at my brother. "Yes," we said, simultaneously.

"Then get at it, okay?"

"Okay."

"Good. Shortcake anyone?"

Ginny, as could have been predicted, took it badly and, again pre-dictably, her major concern was with how Herk would deal with it all. I don't mean to suggest that she didn't care about Megan, I know she did. It's just that for thirty years her life's focus had been her oldest son, and a habit of that duration is hard to break. As al-ways, I left the burden of dealing with her to my brother.

I did the only thing I could for Megan, other than supplying her now again with a little tobacco—I prayed. I hadn't done that for a decade or more. (I think the last prayer I'd uttered was a plea that Bethany Meyers wouldn't be pregnant). That supplication hav-ing been answered to my satisfaction, I had thanked my Benefactor by cutting off all communication. I don't know why I quit talking to God—maybe it was just to see if He'd do anything about it, or maybe it was because I was uncomfortable with the idea of invisible fathers.

Anyway, I began asking again. Every morning and evening I got on my knees, by my bed, and I begged God to spare her. I knew from experience that the Creator was more conducive to justice than mercy and if a substitute was allowable, I offered to be it. God, perhaps justifiably, gave me the silent treatment.

I continued to go to church and keep Meg company, while her husband's sermons, more and more, featured the Book of Job. I even helped out at the Swiss steak supper that had been switched to the first Saturday in November so that Herk could officiate at Skinny Minnie's wedding. Ginny had a tough time getting help. Many of the ladies who'd been faithful workers for years used the changed date as a scheduling excuse, but I suspected that a large number of them were simply miffed about the change and sitting at home. The Ladies Guild took in only eight hundred dollars, their lowest profit in fifteen years.

Nobody said anything about Megan's cancer. She preferred to wait as long as possible. Eventually, the disease would announce itself, as Megan's wonderful fullness would begin to succumb to its emaciating rage. As is the case with all deceptions, Megan didn't want to explain until explanation was necessary. Surprisingly, Ginny was able to keep her mouth shut.

Autumn ended violently with an early blizzard on the fifteenth of November. It was one of those storms for which the city of Saginaw never seemed to be adequately prepared. There were never enough snowplows and salt.

The county road commission, on the other hand, had its shit together, and the rural roads, including Herk's, were always kept clean.

The power went out in my apartment at around midnight and I woke up in freezing darkness. I went to work unshowered and heavily deodorized. The storm dissipated by late afternoon, but half the city was still in darkness with no heat. The utilities companies used such crises to justify raising consumer prices, but they never seemed to be able to move any faster and this time was no exception. My apartment was still in darkness. I went back downstairs and walked to a corner payphone and got hold of Megan. She said that Ginny was fine and among the fortunate half of the population that had power. So did they. She invited me to come out to their house and spend the night, an offer that I happily accepted.

My all-weather tires had apparently been designed for all the weather in someplace like Arizona, because I had to enlist the aid of more than one burly Samaritan before I finally pulled into the driveway of the Gudsen manse. I grabbed my bag and waded through two feet of sodden whiteness, an effort that left me winded, and made me consider, yet again, the possibility of taking the Surgeon General's advice.

It felt so good to enter into the light and warmth of the house that, initially, I paid no attention to the faces that, once I noticed, appeared grim and austere.

"What is it?"

"I didn't want to talk about it over the phone," Megan said. "It's not something that concerns you directly anyway, but you should probably know about it."

I looked at my brother. I could see another cross had been added to his shoulders. He looked stooped, bowed, but not lost.

"Take your coat off," he said. "Let's have some hot coffee."

I was anxious to know what the trouble was, but I could see it had nothing to do with Megan's illness and she'd already assured me that Ginny was fine, so I didn't press.

Once we were seated in the kitchen, Herk began his narrative. He told me that Baxter Bird's father, a widower who worked the graveyard shift at one of the General Motors' plants in town, was on his way home that morning when he stopped at his son's apartment. Most likely, the visit was prompted by the storm. He'd probably heard on the radio that at least half of the town was out. He didn't know yet if his own place had power, since he'd been at work all night, and probably wanted to be reassured that the furnace in his son's building was functional before he went to bed for the day.

By the time he'd climbed the stairs to the second floor, it must have been apparent to him from the lights in the hallway and on the landing that the apartment building had escaped the outage, but he knew Baxter would be getting up soon to go to work and he probably decided to just stop in and say hello. The door to Baxter's apartment was unlocked and, perhaps fearful that his son might still be sleeping, he stepped inside and likely decided to wait for Baxter to get up. Sounds from the back of the apartment must have drawn his attention, and he crossed through the kitchen to the bedroom in back. There, he discovered his son.

I leaned forward, fearing the worst. "Well go on. Was he okay?"

"Baxter was kneeling on the floor in front of Robin Stym."

From Herk's perspective, that was the end of the story, but I didn't understand. "Who's she?" I asked.

"*He* is the guy that Baxter comes to church with all the time. They were both naked."

"Ouch."

"Exactly." Herk continued: "Baxter told me that he didn't know how long his father stood there, watching. He and Robin, to use his words, were 'pretty self-absorbed' and didn't notice him until they'd, uh…finished."

"The old man didn't know his son was gay?"

"Gay?"

"It's a new expression for homosexuality. It's what they prefer."

"Homosexual or not, that's one word I certainly would not associate with Baxter Bird today."

"So his father didn't know?"

"Until that moment, he hadn't had a clue. Baxter had done a pretty good job of hiding it, even to the point of introducing a lesbian acquaintance to his father as his 'girlfriend'. It must have been a terrible revelation for the old man, who was still deeply depressed over his wife's death, which was less than two years ago."

"So now you know for sure. Is that what all this is about? It makes it difficult for you to defend him against the delegation from the Michigan District, doesn't it? When are they coming?"

"Monday. But that's the least of it. Baxter's father didn't say a word. He just left the apartment, his naked son crying after him. He drove to his own dark, cold house and filled his bathtub with water. He ran several extension cords to the tub, cut the ends off, bared the wires and submerged them in the water. Then he got in himself, clothes and all, and waited for the power to come on."

"You're saying he's dead? But the power's still out," I said.

"On your side of town. They got it going at a little after ten this morning over there. Baxter found him. He went over to the old man's house on his lunch hour to try and smooth things over."

"Man, that's terrible."

"Baxter's a mess. I just got back from the hospital about an hour ago. Robin had taken him there because he was getting hysterical."

"Is he going to be okay?"

"I don't know. Naturally, he feels responsible for his father's death. They've sedated him and they're going to keep him overnight for observation. Robin is going to stay with him."

We talked through the evening about it, then retired early. The next morning, a Saturday, the suicide of Cornelius Bird shoved the earliest Michigan blizzard in a decade onto page two of *The Saginaw Times*. Baxter Bird had been hysterical enough to tell the truth about the whole business to the investigating officer. He, in turn, had relayed the sordid tale to a reporter he was acquainted with at the *Times*. The headline read:

DISCOVERY OF SON'S HOMOSEXUAL TRYST CAUSES FATHER
TO KILL HIMSELF

The article was in Larry Ladon's possession when the Board of Elders and Pastor Gudsen met with the Michigan District delegation on Monday evening. It was a typically Lutheran entourage that arrived from Lansing—three white men with white hair, white shirts, and conservative dark suits and ties.

I wasn't present of course, but I got the gist of it, later, from Herk.

Ladon was allowed to speak first on behalf of the church elders. Their position was relatively simple. Homosexuality was an 'abomination', according to Scripture. The newspaper left little doubt that two of Pastor Gudsen's congregation were practicing homosexuals. In a Bible class taught by Mr. Ladon, the two 'sodomites', as Ladon referred to them, took the stance that God's commands on this subject were not really God's, but the result of 'cultural bias'. Then Ladon administered the coup de grace. He quoted St. Paul's letter to the Corinthians. "But now I am writing you that you must not associate with anyone who calls himself a brother but is sexually immoral or greedy, an idolater or a slanderer, a drunkard or a swindler. With such a man do not even eat. What business is it of mine to judge those outside the church? Are you not to judge those inside? God will judge those outside. Expel the wicked man from among you."

Herkimer countered with the words of Jesus: "For if you forgive men when they sin against you, your heavenly Father will also forgive you. But if you do not forgive men their sins, your Father will not forgive your sins."

The leader of the delegation, a man named Gerald Ryan, insisted that forgiveness, even from God, required repentance, and we should require no less. Were Mr. Bird and Mr. Stym repentant? Did they see their 'aberrations' as the sin that Scripture names it? Did they plan to end their fornication?

Mr. Ladon said 'no' to each query. Herk said he wasn't certain, and suggested that, after a suitable lapse of time to allow Mr. Bird to recover from the trauma of his father's death, the three delegates should come back and ask Mr. Bird and Mr. Stym directly. Pastor Ryan, after consulting with his colleagues, agreed, and set a return date for January fifteenth, my birthday.

Things like this always seem to take place in January—at least in Michigan, at least with me. The setting must be appropriate to the mood and in this most depressing of months, fraternal condemnation comes naturally, like the suicidal urges of lemmings and sperm. One tiny flagellum, a survivor from my father, penetrated the assuredly reluctant ova of my mother so that I could be born in this month of the two-faced god, the guardian of beginnings—and endings. January is the natural time to begin to face the supernatural.

I'm getting ahead of myself—a pleasure literally shared by the Meyers' girls, but figuratively, only possible on paper.

Chapter five

n the day after Herk and Megan went to Ann Arbor to see the oncologist, Herk was shot through the head with the crossbow bolt.

As I've already related, it was in December, just before Christmas. The shooter was August Two-River II, a guy about my age, whose unusual name stemmed from the fact that his grandfather was full-blooded Ojibway and his grandmother, the Ojibway's wife, was a German immigrant. Their son, his father, was August Two-River I, and he owned a dairy farm called Auggie's Stables. Part of it was immediately adjacent to Herk's property and another thousand acres were directly across the road from the manse.

My brother had met the father and invited him to church, but August Two-River was a staunch pagan. He was the man I'd seen rounding up stray cows on the first of my Saturday night visits to Herk and Meg's place.

For some reason, August Two-River II had set up his bales of hay and his target at the corner of his father's farm where it abutted Herk's property. He was home on Christmas break from his agricultural studies at Michigan State University and, from sheer boredom, had decided to try shooting the crossbow that his grandmother had brought with her from Germany.

The target had been placed just outside of the forest's edge, where Herk had been taking a walk. Fortunately, he'd realized that he'd wandered off his own property and had just turned back when the bolt struck him. I say fortunately because if he hadn't turned at that moment, the bolt would've hit him directly between the eyes.

It happened shortly before five o'clock, which in a Michigan December, is twilight. Auggie Junior hadn't seen him at all, but had heard him cry out. He had not made the assumption that his victim might live in the farmhouse just a few hundred yards away, which was still visible in the gathering darkness. Instead of taking him home, he'd helped Herkimer into his pick-up truck and driven like a bat out of hell to Holy Cross.

I need not detail all that happened that night. Megan was called, she called me, and I picked up Ginny. We were all there in a matter of minutes. We went to Ann Arbor that night, where the decision was made to leave the bolt where it was and simply cover the holes made in Herk' skull.

By Christmas Day, he was home again. The pastor's flock held a prayer vigil for him and Pastor Emeritus Doernhof was temporarily ushered out of retirement to cover Herk's responsibilities until he was able to resume them. Larry Ladon must have thought his prayers were answered. He had no idea what was ahead of him.

August Two-River II was a daily visitor at the Gudsen manse, constantly expressing his gratitude that Herkimer had taken no action against him. He found it hard to believe that Herk bore him no ill will.

Ginny took up residence to assist Megan in caring for her husband (the pronoun 'her' being left intentionally ambiguous). Because of Megan's weakened state, Ginny did most of the cleaning, laundry and cooking, (although more food was brought to the manse than could ever possibly be consumed by dozens of people, let alone three).

December 25th was a somber event. Herk was doing exceptionally well, but we all knew that it was likely to be Megan's last Christmas. She'd refused any further treatment, knowing that medical science couldn't save her. The oncologist in Ann Arbor had told her as much.

I continued to beg God. I broke it off with the Meyers sisters. I even vowed a more general chastity until Meg returned to

health. I figured if you're going to ask, then you ought to be prepared to do something in return—a show of good faith. I see now,
how little I understood God.

By December 31ˢᵗ, Herk was well enough to deliver the New
Year's Eve sermon. He said little about his injury except to thank
his flock for their gifts and prayers. With his golden hair and white
frock, he looked angelic, high above us in the pulpit—the gauze
wrapped around his head serving as a halo.

He became a celebrity, and his waning popularity among the
members of Holy Cross was given a sudden boost through the simple device of notoriety. The *Times* had called his recovery 'miraculous' and the flock, so eager to find hope for themselves, believed.

After the service, looking exhausted and drawn, Herk asked
me if I'd like to come over the next day to watch the bowl games. I
declined, thinking that he and Meg could use some time alone.
Ginny had moved back to her own house that morning and it
would be, I knew, their first opportunity for a little privacy—
assuming the media and Auggie Two-River would leave them
alone.

But Meg, looking pale and thinner, had insisted. I don't
know where she found her strength. She was dying and her husband had just come close to doing the same, but she continued on,
refusing to waste her remaining months pouting. My admiration
for her, if possible, grew.

I got to the manse around noon. Meg was alone. Herk had
just run to the store to pick up some snack food. In America,
watching football, even for the normally righteous, is an exercise in
gluttony.

I was shocked to see the positive changes in my sister-in-law
from when I'd seen her the night before. Though she still looked
too thin, her color had returned and there was a spring in her step.
She looked radiantly beautiful. She greeted me with a spectacular
smile. She was *animated*, full of joy. It seemed incomprehensible.

"What's going on?" I said as she took my hand and pulled
me into the kitchen. She was *humming*, for God's sake.

"Light a cigarette will you?" She let go of my hand so I could do as she asked and while I fumbled in my pockets for my lighter, she kissed me lightly on the cheek. "You're a sweet man," she said, barely controlling an impulse to giggle.

I lit the Marlboro and handed it to her. "What the hell is up with you?" I said. "The cancer, is it—"

"Oh, it's got nothing to with *that*," she warbled, as if I were talking about a headache.

"For crying out loud, Meg, you're acting like a kid who's just been laid for the first—"

She nodded coyly, grinning stupidly like one of those drunken street people who live on the sidewalk downtown and have no reason, other than booze or just being alive, to do so.

"You mean you and Herk, you—"

She nodded again, the grin growing to Cheshire proportions. "Hope deferred makes the heart sick," she said, 'but when desire comes, it is a tree of life.'

"What?"

"Proverbs. Chapter thirteen, verse twelve."

"But how? How was Herk able to—"

"I don't know. Prayer, I think. Do you know what it feels like for two frustrated virgins to finally…well…you know. I hope I'm not embarrassing you, but I had to tell someone and you're the only person, other than the doctor, who knows about it."

"I'll be damned."

"No, you won't. If anybody makes it, you will." She hugged me and kissed me on the cheek again. "I just feel *wonderful!*" She took a long drag on the Marlboro.

"Meg, I'm not normally the voice of caution, but—"

"Five times."

"What?"

"I know what you're going to say. It was a fluke, some temporary 'juju'. You're wrong. We were up all night. I could hardly *walk* this morning."

"How can that be?"

"Have you ever seen your brother naked? He's pretty well-endowed."

"I don't mean *that*," I said, unable to stop myself from laughing with her. "I mean what caused his, uh, restoration."

She giggled at the word and butted out the cigarette. "You know what word came to my mind?'

"What?"

"Resurrection."

I started laughing again, almost uncontrollably. I choked on my own guffawing and doubled over, trying to catch my breath. Megan struck me on the back. "The dead have risen! Ahhhhhh ha ha ha." I was off again and Megan with me, until we collapsed into a paroxysm of hilarity on the kitchen floor.

When we were finally able to recapture our wayward wits, we climbed into a couple of chairs and wiped away the tears. I remember thinking how joy could cause tears as well as pain and God most certainly wouldn't resent them.

"Seriously now," I said, lighting another cigarette. "What do you think caused this…change?"

She took it from me. "Some people would attribute it to his injury, I'm sure."

"How so?"

"I don't know, but every part of the body is controlled by the brain. Maybe that arrow or bolt or whatever it was, prompted the change."

"But you don't believe that."

"No."

"What do *you* think caused it then?"

"God."

"Why?"

"Because I asked."

At that moment, Herk came through the door, weighted down with the devices of our corruption. "Jimmy!" he warbled. He set the grocery bags down on the Formica table. "Summer sausage, Gouda, pizza rolls, potato chips, French bread, bean dip, whatever you want!"

He kissed Megan on her cheek and the hollow of her neck. His back was toward me, but I could see Megan's face clearly. She smiled and raised her eyebrows in a kind of 'see what I mean' expression. I laughed.

He turned to me. "What? You've never seen a man in love with his wife?"

We watched game after game, stuffed ourselves, laughed a lot. Herkimer even caught Megan sneaking a puff, and didn't seem to care. Halfway through the Rose Bowl, I decided to leave, offering the lop-sided score as an excuse. No one objected. The real reason was that Herk and Meg were having a hard time keeping their hands off one another and I felt increasingly like a voyeur.

As I waded to my car, I watched the squares of light on the snow, thrown from the tall windows of the old house, disappear one by one. By the time I'd reached the end of the driveway, the house was completely dark. It seemed Herk wasn't going to watch the rest of the Rose Bowl either. Maybe he didn't believe in comebacks, but if anyone did, he should have.

That was a beginning but, as I mentioned before, Janus was a two-faced god. On January fifteenth, Herk, Baxter Bird, and Robin Stym faced the Inquisition. My brother had spent many hours counseling Baxter after the latter's father had exacted his terrible retribution, and the poor guy was barely keeping it together.

Herk asked me, going in, what I thought of it all. It was another first. I mean he was always interested in my point of view, but this time he was seeking advice. Had Ginny known, she would have been dumbfounded.

I told him that when I was in high school, we used to ridicule a kid that was gay. We called him a faggot, pushed him around, made his life a nightmare. To add to his misery, his name was actually Harry Cox. After gym class one day, my friends and I were in the locker room goofing around and snapping each other with towels. Harry came out of the shower. We redirected our aggression to him. A wet towel, properly applied, can leave a nasty welt. We whipped him until he was huddled, naked and crying, in a corner of the locker room. But the thing that left the deepest impression on me was that the PE instructor, Mr. Kenan, watched the whole thing and never said a word, never stepped forward to stop us. It scared me more than my own capacity for cruelty, because we'd been raised to believe that those in authority were our *protectors*. He should have helped this kid, but he just stood there, and I began to think that if he could be so callous with Harry, what if there was something he didn't like about *me*! I realized that what we were doing was *sanctioned* persecution, legitimized brutality. Authority should be *protective*, not join the mob—even if I'm part of the mob. After that, I tried to befriend Harry. It cost me some of my friends. It didn't work. Harry always hated me.

"So what are you telling me?" Herk said.

I told him that the delegation from the Michigan District was here to defend Larry Ladon's towel whipping; that they too, were sanctioning persecution. "I've seen enough death, enough hate, in Vietnam and elsewhere, to last me a lifetime," I said. "If two people love each other and they want to express that love physically, then more power to them. Besides, I'm just as guilty of 'sexual immorality' as they are. I'm not married and well, let's just say I'm not a virgin. I'm pretty much unrepentant about it too, but nobody's hunting me down—not yet anyway."

I don't know if what I told him had an impact or not. I think he'd made up his mind already about what he was going to do. But he'd listened, carefully, and I was grateful for that.

With the permission of the delegation, Pastor Gudsen taped the interrogation, so that in a matter of such importance, no one would be misquoted later on. Meg, Herk and myself sat listening to it later that evening in my brother's living room. After an opening prayer given by Pastor Ryan, thanking God for Pastor Gudsen's recovery and offering a plea for guidance, Robin Stym was asked directly by Pastor Ryan if he was a homosexual.

He said that he was.

Pastor Ryan asked him if he understood that homosexuality was a heinous sin.

"The Lutheran Church, Missouri Synod, unlike our brethren in the Roman Church," Herk interjected, "does not recognize degrees of sin. The use of the word 'heinous' infers that homosexuality is worse than other sins. I would hate to see *any* of us, in the course of this investigation, committing doctrinal errors."

As I listened to the tape of this catechizing, I began to understand why my brother had insisted on recording it. I wished I could see the expression on Pastor Ryan's face. I had to settle for the irritation in his voice. "Holy Scripture calls it an abomination."

"Scripture also refers to an altar to Zeus in the temple at Jerusalem as an abomination."

"Very well," Pastor Ryan said. "Do you, Mr. Stym, believe that homosexuality is sin?"

There was a long, silent lapse on the tape. "No," he said, finally.

"Then you believe you have done nothing that requires repentance? You have no intention of changing your lifestyle.

"I can't. I am who I am."

There was a general murmuring, then the interrogation switched to Baxter Bird.

"Mr. Bird," (again, Ryan's voice). "Do you regard the practice of homosexuality as sin?"

"I love God," was the soft response. "But I love Robin too."

Larry Ladon's deep voice suddenly interrupted. "Did you love your father?"

"Mr. Ladon!" Herk said. "You have no right to say such a thing! Pastor Ryan, I can't abide—"

"Quite right, Mr. Gudsen. Mr. Ladon, please refrain from such callous remarks."

"*Pastor* Gudsen," I heard Herk say.

"Forgive me, *Pastor* Gudsen. Now, Mr. Bird, do *you* regard homosexuality as sin?"

He said "no," in a barely discernible and shaky voice.

"Then you don't repent?"

"I repent of...my father...no. I don't."

"Thank you, Mr. Bird. You and Mr. Stym are excused."

I heard the shuffling of chairs and the closing of a heavy door.

"Well," Larry Ladon said. "You can see why I...why we, were concerned."

"Yes," Pastor Ryan agreed. "Pastor Gudsen, in the interest of harmony and unity of doctrine I would suggest, and I'm sure my fellow delegates would agree, that you sign the letters of expulsion for Mr. Bird and Mr. Stym that have been prepared by your Board of Elders. It always grieves me to see this sort of thing happen, but the protection of God's directives is our pastoral duty. Now if you'll excuse us, it *is* getting late and we have a bit of a drive ahead of us. Thank you for your time and may God—"

"I can't do that," Herk said.

"Excuse me?"

"I *won't* do that."

Meg and I looked at each other.

"Pastor Gudsen," Ryan said, "your signature is required for dismissal. The only alternative would be to have the Michigan District President sign the documents in your stead. I don't think you would want that. President Hoefmeier would want to know why you refused. Surely you wouldn't wish to defy God's Holy Word or those placed by Him in authority over you?"

Meg and I leaned toward the recorder as we waited for Herk's answer. He sat across from us in the living room, recently returned from the confrontation, his head leaning into his hand, his long legs sprawled in gangly disorder in front of him. The bandage/halo had been removed several days ago.

"I don't wish to defy anyone. I would only ask that we give this matter a bit more time. The fact that letters are already written suggests a hasty contumely on the part of Mr. Ladon that I find reprehensible—yet I freely forgive him. I'm sure he feels he's done nothing that I should forgive him for and is, therefore, unrepentant. Can't we extend such generosity of spirit to Mr. Bird and Mr. Stym too?"

"Well said," I mumbled.

"Shhh. Be quiet, Jim," Meg upbraided. "I want to hear this."

"Pastor Gudsen," Ryan began, "God's Word is very clear in this matter. 'Do you not know that the wicked will not inherit the kingdom of God? Do not be deceived: Neither the sexually immoral nor idolaters nor adulterers nor male prostitutes *nor homosexual offenders* nor thieves nor the greedy nor drunkards nor slanderers nor swindlers will inherit the kingdom of God.' First Corinthians, chapter six."

"Yes," Herk said, "but let's finish that passage. 'And that is what some of you were. But you were washed, you were sanctified, you were *justified* in the name of the Lord Jesus Christ and by the Spirit of our God.' Should we undo what God had done?"

Ryan was quick to respond. "It's neither within our province nor our power to undo anything that God has accomplished. But repentance is necessary for salvation, and repentance requires recognition of sin. We must turn yet again to St. Paul who writes: 'Therefore, since through God's mercy we have this ministry, we do not lose heart. Rather, we have renounced secret and shameful ways; we do not use deception, nor do we distort the word of God.' In our faith, Pastor Gudsen, as you know, there can be no gospel without the law. We are instructed, in the Epistle of James, to not merely listen to the word, but to do what it says."

"I'll say this for the old boy," I said. "He knows his Bible." Again, Meg chastised me.

"I'm not trying to distort God's Word, Pastor Ryan. But a sinner can't be brought to repentance if we turn him away from the means of Grace. I'd venture to say that every man, woman and child in this congregation sins daily. Many, perhaps most, do it knowingly, fully understanding, at the moment of transgression, that they have offended God. Do we bring them all into this conference room and examine them?"

"No. But if we did, if it was brought to our attention and we did, how many do you think would deny that what they had done was sin? You said it yourself and that's the point. Even if they do it, they still *see* it as wrong. That's not the case with these two men."

I suspected, at that moment, my brother was studying Larry Ladon's face, but I never asked him.

"Brethren," Herk's pleading voice said. "I'm not asking you to overlook what they've done. I only want a little time to help them to…come to repentance."

"Scripture clearly says—"

"Scripture is a *guide*, not a god!" It was the first time I'd heard my brother shout in anger.

Larry Ladon's voice: "In the beginning was the Word and the Word was with God, and the Word *was* God."

That was it. Someone had stopped the recorder. "What happened?" I said to Herk. He shook his head.

Megan went to him and sat on the arm of his chair. She put her arm around his shoulders. She kissed the side of his head, just above the shaved area where the circle of stitches could still be seen. "How did it end?" she asked.

"I took the recorder and left."

"Without saying anything?"

"I quoted the Lord."

Meg smiled, but I could read the concern. "What passage?"

"Matthew, chapter fifteen, verses six to nine."

This was, apparently, enough of an explanation for Meg. "Anyone for a sandwich?"

No one spoke of the visit from the Michigan District again that evening, but as soon as I got home, I looked up Herk's parting passage. In it, Jesus was rebuking the Pharisees. It read: "Thus you nullify the word of God for the sake of your tradition. You hypocrites! Isaiah was right when he prophesied about you: 'These people honor me with their lips, but their hearts are far from me. They worship me in vain; their teachings are but rules taught by men.'"

As I read on, I knew my brother was in serious trouble.

Chapter six

The Sunday following Herk's confrontation with Pastor Ryan and his own Board of Elders, my brother preached a sermon on the evils of intolerance. The text was the fifteenth chapter of the gospel according to St. Matthew. It was a magnificent oration, God-inspired I like to think and, as the congregation filed out, they seemed to be especially gracious to one another. "Wonderful sermon," I heard people say over and over as they lined up to shake his hand.

I'd watched Larry Ladon during this exhortation. He sat in back, with his sour-faced wife. He hadn't batted an eye. During the distribution of the Lord's Supper, the two of them had ducked out a side exit.

After the service, we all went over to Ginny's house to celebrate my twenty-third birthday. She'd made a German Chocolate cake, (Herk's favorite), and given me a leather satchel to carry my books and papers for school. Meg and Herk gave me a little book by C.S. Lewis called *Mere Christianity*. I looked upon it at first as a burden, because my brother would nag me to read it until I did, then would want to discuss it with me until I'd convinced him that I had. So, after I got back to my apartment and asked God for Meg's life, (more to honor my promise to her than a belief in its efficacy), I got in bed and opened the book.

I finished its hundred and something pages in a few hours. I was enthralled. What few books I'd read on religion were proselytizing appeals to a deep sense of obligation or guilt. *God created you, you owe Him. God gave His Son for you, you owe Him. Your parents want you to believe and you owe them.* But this was the first defense of the Christian religion I'd ever read or heard that was *philosophical* by argument. Step by step, Lewis *logically* justified his assertions. He wasn't asking me to believe what he believed. He wasn't, in fact, asking me to believe in anything. He just presented his case and asked me to think about it. He didn't say I was damned if I didn't go along with him.

The book changed me. It put a heretical thought in my head—maybe God inspired writers *after* John's *Revelations.* Perhaps the Bible wasn't the only book that God spoke through. Maybe he spoke through Lewis or Kierkegaard or Copernicus or even Darwin. It was my introduction to a larger view of a larger God.

Two days later, Herk received the expected letter from Dr. Hoefmeier and what I began to call the 'small-god people'. Meg called me and asked me to come over directly after work. I had a night class at the university on Tuesday evenings. It was a philosophy class on teleological ethics taught by Dr. Aristotle Mantus, unaffectionately known around campus as 'The Bore'. I was never entirely sure how that was spelled, because not only did he give the dullest lectures in the most monotonic fashion, but he also sported a ridiculous porcine snout above his white-whiskered chin which would have easily qualified him to be 'The Boar' as well. I decided to skip the class. Meg said that she and my brother needed me. That was enough. Escaping the narcolepsy-inducing lecture was merely a side benefit.

I didn't get to the manse until well after dark. The fierce January wind had blown the Gudsen's discarded Christmas tree across their driveway. As I watched it roll back and forth in my headlights, dead and brown, I felt a kind of sinking despondency. It had once been a thing cold, green and alive in the dead pale of winter. It had been cut from its life-giving roots, placed inside, and decorated with a façade of gaiety. Festooned with lights and the collective ornamentation of fading hope, then tossed aside to die a slow death, only a few stubborn needles and bits of tinsel to show that it had ever meant something. I believe Martin Luther had started the custom.

I had to get out and move it before I could park.

I let myself in, since Herk never locked the doors. He and Meg were sitting on the sofa, their arms around each other, a single lamp illuminating the winter's early darkness.

I sat down across from them and switched on another lamp. Herk smiled, but the smile barely moved his lips. I lit a cigarette. Meg got up and took it from me, then returned to her husband. Herk didn't seem to notice. He was looking at the letter on the coffee table in front of him. I never thought my brother could be pierced by a piece of paper, but the wound was open and apparent. "We began with such promise," he said.

"What did they say?"

"My Divine Call to St. Luke's has been prorogued until I've met with Dr. Hoefmeier. Pastor Doernhof has been induced out of retirement again, poor man, to replace me until, let's see, how did they put it?" He picked up the letter. "Until my, quote: 'adherence to the tenets of the Lutheran Church, Missouri Synod and the teachings of Holy Scripture have been thoroughly substantiated by the Michigan District Commission on Orthodoxy.' In other words, Jim, I'm to sign the letters expelling Bird and Stym or be defrocked."

"You think it's that serious?"

"I know it is."

"What're you going to do?"

"Baxter Bird called me this afternoon. He wanted to know if he was still a member of the church his great-grandfather had helped to build; where he'd been baptized, confirmed, and taken Christ's body and blood for his own."

"He put it that way?"

"Yes."

"Is he mad at you?"

"He was, until I explained that I'd refused to sign the expulsion letters. But I told him that I might yet be forced into doing it and even if I didn't, the Michigan District President would. I told him it was only a matter of time before he and Stym had their membership revoked."

"What did he say to that?"

"He told me to go ahead and sign them. He said we might as well keep martyrdom to a minimum."

"He sounds like a better man than Doctor President What's-His-Name," I said.

Herk forced a smile. "I asked him if he and Robin Stym could find a way to…to love each other without the physical side of it."

"You mean celibacy?"

"Yes. If they could do that and confess that their previous behavior was wrong, then there'd be no need for any of this."

I was pretty sure that Bird's answer to that proposition would have been something like 'go to hell', but I asked anyway. "What'd he say?"

"He asked a hypothetical question. If the situation were reversed, he said; that is, if the church condemned heterosexuality and demanded that I no longer make love to Meg, no longer live with her, and say that our relationship up to that time was sinful, in order to keep my membership at St. Luke's, would I do it?"

Having so recently been introduced to the raptures of carnal delectation himself and knowing that Death was in earnest pursuit of Meg, I knew Herk's answer.

"I told him no," Herk said. "He continued by saying that he loved Robin like that and couldn't believe that God would condemn it. He said, 'I will always love God, Pastor Gudsen, and I believe He will always love me. I've sacrificed a father, I guess I can sacrifice my church. But do you think that the price of loving someone should be this high?'" Herk looked first at Meg, then at me. "I can't sign those letters."

Meg squeezed his hand. She smiled at her husband with a satisfaction that reflected her deep confidence in his goodness.

"Not that it matters," I said, "but I think you're doing the right thing." I meant it.

"It *does* matter," he replied and I think *he* meant it.

"Thanks."

The phone rang. Meg answered it. "What?" she said. "I'm sorry, but you're going to have to slow down a bit, I can't understand...oh, Lena. Yes dear. No, no, it's all right; Pastor Gudsen's right here. Hold on. Yes, I'll get him right away." She held out the phone to Herk.

"Lena Gossbach?"

Megan nodded, sympathetically.

Herk got up. "I'll take it in the study."

I watched him leave the room. It seemed to me that he was limping less, but it was probably my imagination.

Meg listened until he picked up the extension, then she hung up.

"That the OCD lady?" I asked.

"That's her."

I lit a cigarette and offered it to her. For the first time, she declined, explaining that she felt a bit queasy. I asked her how she was doing.

"It's becoming a problem," she said. "I'm losing my appetite and I sleep way too much. I think it's beginning to take hold. I'm trying to fight it off, Jim, but it's not going to go away. We know that."

"I'm asking," was all I could manage.

"That's all we can do." She smiled, weakly. She was beginning to look too thin, like an obsessive jogger, but her color was good. I wasn't sure that even cancer could affect her beauty. I tried to change the subject.

"Is Herk still..."

"Oh yes," she said, "randy as a teen-aged colt. I always used to wonder about those women who have headaches all the time. I don't anymore. It's the only way I can get any sleep!" Her laughter indicated that she didn't mind not sleeping.

There was a brief silence between us then. We could hear Herk's voice making comforting assurances in the next room. *What will Lena Gossbach do when he's gone*, I thought. *What will a lot of people do?*

"I don't know how he's going to tell Ginny," Meg said, reading my mind. "Herk told me that she'd spent her whole life waiting for him to become a pastor. She said she always knew that he was *destined* to serve God. She takes such pride in it."

"Her life has been pretty well centered on him," I said.

"But not on you."

"No, but that's okay. Herk's different. He's always been different. Hell, we don't even look alike. Sometimes I wonder, really, if we have the same father."

"Herk never speaks of him. Neither do you."

"Our father?"

"Yes."

"What's to say? He left right after I was born. I never knew him. Herk would have been three, maybe four..He says he doesn't remember him."

"What about Ginny? Didn't she ever talk about him?"

"No. I asked her about him. I asked all the time when I was a kid. But she'd shrug it off, change the subject."

"We listened to Herk's still, small voice for a few seconds. It was soothing, narcotic. There was, indeed, something special about my brother. As yet, I didn't know how special.

"Both of my parents are gone," Meg said, interrupting my musings.

"I know. Ginny told me they died in some kind of accident?"

"It happened in my first month at Michigan State. MSU is a big place, and I wasn't, believe it or not, what they called a 'party girl'. I was really homesick. I didn't want to be there anymore. I decided to live at home and go to the local community college for a while. Mom and Dad were on their way to pick me up in East Lansing when their car was struck head-on by a drunk driver. The guy swerved into them from the other lane. I was told they died instantly."

"I'm so sorry," I said. What else do you say when you stand next to someone at the edge of a bad memory? "Do you have any brothers or sisters?"

"Nope. I'm an only child." She wiped away a tear that oddly enough, suggested strength, in much the same way that despair suggests the promise of hope. Like her husband, Megan was capable of a complete transcendence of self—the opposite of evil, a quality some would call faith.

"So you stayed at MSU because you had nowhere else to go?"

"I stayed because I was supposed to meet your brother."

"You *knew* that?"

"Not in a conscious way, no. I just couldn't leave. My parents had been prevented from taking me back. I was supposed to stay."

"A high price to pay for finding someone to love you," I said, paraphrasing Baxter Bird.

"Not just someone—Herk."

"And now you have this...this illness."

"It's called cancer."

"Forgive me for asking, but..." I stopped. A rare seizure of wisdom got the better of me.

"You were going to say that if Herk and I are supposed to be together, then why am I dying?"

I was stunned by her composure. My first private conversation with her had been so different from this. I remembered the tears, the anguish in her voice, and then she'd been facing only celibacy, not death. "Something like that, yes."

"Maybe I won't die," she said. She was calm, almost serene. "If I do, then it's supposed to happen. It has to do with him, you see. It all has to do with Herk."

"Bullshit."

She laughed. "You've been around him long enough to know what I mean, Jim. You can't deny it forever."

"And *you* have been spending way too much time with your mother-in-law."

"What're you talking about," Herk asked, as he entered the room. "Can't deny what?"

"The will of God," Meg answered.

"No doubt about that," he admitted. He wasn't duped, he simply understood that we didn't want to elaborate, and he let it go. He was one of the few people I knew who could do that.

"Say Jim," he said, "have you read that book by Lewis yet?"

I told him that I had and, after being subjected to the expected test of affirmation, I enjoyed a brief conversation that was much more stimulating than anything I would have experienced in Aristotle Mantus' classroom.

During a lull in our enthusiasm over the book, Meg directed the discourse back to the crisis at hand. "When are you going to tell your mother that you aren't going to be the pastor at St. Luke's anymore?" she said.

His blond hair looked gold in the glow of the lamp behind him. His face was masked in shadow, so I couldn't read his expression. "I don't know. Soon."

"It'll have to be before Sunday," Meg said. "She'll want to know why you aren't preaching."

"Yes, I know." He stood up and walked over to a window, turning his back to both of us. "Jim," he said, "I wanted both you and Megan to hear this, together, because you might be the only people who could believe me."

I looked at Meg for some hint of what might be forthcoming. She shrugged her shoulders to indicate her own ignorance. I lit a cigarette.

Still looking out at the barren landscape of winter, he said, "I'm to gather Twelve." I wasn't sure I'd heard him right. His naturally soft voice was further muffled against the window. I waited for him to explain. He said nothing else.

Finally, Meg broke the silence. "Twelve what?"

"People."

"To what purpose?" she said.

"I don't know yet."

I wanted to see his face, to see if there was a hint of capriciousness there. As if to accommodate me, he turned around and flicked on the switch of an overhead light before returning to his place next to Megan on the sofa. I saw nothing in his expression but a kind of mysterious euphoria.

"God spoke to me," he said, as if it were something that happened in the normal course of a day's activity.

I was used to Herk's 'sense' of God. He'd felt God's presence, moved to that inner voice, followed that intuitive and elusive Spirit all his life. "You had another dream?"

He smiled at me as, I'm sure, every man who believes that he has greater understanding has always smiled at those he thought did not. "It wasn't a dream, Jim," he said. "It was the actual voice of God, the spoken *voice!*"

I laughed. "You sure that metal bolt in your brain isn't picking up radio signals?"

He didn't seem offended, perhaps a bit saddened by my skepticism, but that's all.

Meg kissed his hand and held it, with both of hers, against her breast. "When?" she said. "When did you hear these voices?"

"*A* voice," Herk corrected. "*The* Voice. This morning. I got up early. I felt a need to pray. I came down to the kitchen and fixed a pot of coffee. You were still sleeping. I asked God, again, to spare your life. He said that He would."

I saw Meg's reaction—a glimmer of promise, something to hold onto. I thought then that it was a cruel thing to tell her, even if he believed it himself. Nothing is meaner than counterfeit hope. I told my brother as much.

"It *was* God, Jim. He said, 'I am. I am.'"

"It sounds more like Popeye the Sailor to me," I replied. I meant no humor and none was taken.

"There's no false hope with God. Megan will survive if…."

"If what?"

"If I do what I'm told to do."

"Gather your disciples."

"They're not mine. They're His."

"For what purpose?"

"I told you, I don't know yet."

Tears were caressing Meg's face. I envied them. I thought at that moment that she was weeping for her crazy husband, that she thought the same as I did—that my brother, about to lose his church, his career and his wife, had cracked under the strain. Either that or the bolt in his brain had done more damage that anyone imagined. I guess he had a rationale. The irrational always do.

But Meg's tears weren't sympathetic. They were the liquid measurement of a peculiar kind of joy. The slow realization crept into me that Megan was becoming my brother's first convert.

"Well," I said, "if that's all it takes to save Megan, to recruit twelve people, then sign me up."

Herk put his arm around Megan. "It's not that simple. *You* aren't supposed to be one of the Twelve. Neither is Meg, nor mother."

"Did God give you a list?"

"I know of three. The rest will be made known to me as God wills it."

"Well," I said, deciding for the moment to humor him, "who are they?"

"Two of them are Baxter Bird and Robin Stym."

"Makes sense," I said. "And the third?"

"Larry Ladon."

Chapter seven

I tried to get Herk to see a psychiatrist which, I suppose, tells you what I thought of the 'miracle'. He wouldn't. Then I tried to get him to return to Ann Arbor, get a checkup on his damaged brain, and just relate the story of his encounter with God to one of the neurologists there. There was this one guy, a doctor who had worked closely with the surgeons who'd treated Herk's wound, who might've been able to help him to understand that sometimes a person can hear voices when they aren't really there. Herk wouldn't go. He was convinced. Herk had always operated on the basis of faith. I guess there was no reason to expect that he'd be any different now.

He *did* tell Ginny. Meg and I went with him. I thought for sure she'd go to pieces when he explained that he was about to be kicked out of the church where she'd been a member since the Jurassic period—and all *that* for a couple of queers. She didn't. She was upset at first, but when he explained that God had spoken to him, she accepted it without protest. Uncharacteristically, she didn't even appear to harbor any antipathy toward her son's primary anatagonist, Larry Ladon. She said she'd known all his life that Herk was destined to be a special agent of God. (I immediately thought of the FBI training school at Quantico. *Special Agent of God, Herkimer Gudsen, Licensed to Save*). Ginny said that she had just assumed that in order for her son to fulfill his destiny, he'd have to be a pastor—and a Lutheran one at that.

Meg explained to her that St. Paul had been a Pharisee before he became the Great Apostle. Martin Luther had been a Roman Catholic monk. It was enough for Ginny. Instead of a life of pastoral obscurity, her son was now destined for greater things. Meg had just placed the darling boy in heady company, and that image, at least in Ginny's mind, would never go away.

Herk didn't even bother to go to Lansing. He wrote a letter to Dr. Hoefmeier instead, in which he explained that his conscience would not allow him to sign the expulsion letters of Baxter Bird and Robin Stym. Therefore he was resigning, effective immediately, as the pastor at St. Luke's. God, he wrote, had issued him another call. Copies were posted to Pastor Gerald Ryan and Larry Ladon.

Dr. Hoefmeier accepted Herk's resignation, but was alarmed by the 'another call' line. He assumed that some other LCMS congregation not aware of Pastor Gudsen's heretical stance had innocently offered a divine opportunity for employment elsewhere. In a panic, he contacted the Missouri Synod President, who promptly appointed a committee of inquiry. Within a month, Herk' ordination was rescinded and his membership in the LCMS terminated. His name, to them, became anathema.

Herkimer Gudsen became famous, or rather infamous, throughout the national network of LCMS colleges, churches and schools. His name was the topic of many discussions at the Seminary and some young seminarians, like Baxter Bird's brother, Caleb, saw him as a hero. But whether God's servant or Satan's, Herkimer Gudsen was no longer anonymous. Ginny's prophecy was fulfilled. Her son was a celebrity.

Herk wrote another letter, which was distributed to every communicant member at St. Luke's. The entire text of that letter, which was not very long, follows here.

Dear Brothers and Sisters in Christ:
As most of you are aware, two members of our congregation were recently involved in a situation that was headlined in *The Saginaw Times*. Our Board of

Elders saw its duty, as leaders of our church, to expel these members.

I asked the elders to be patient, allowing me more time to counsel the two brethren concerned, to bring them to repentance and thus to forgiveness and continued membership at St. Luke's. Unsatisfied with this response from me, the Board of Elders contacted the Michigan District of the LCMS, which then sent a delegation to investigate the controversy.

In a meeting with this delegation and our Board of Elders, the two young men in question refused to admit that their behavior was wrong. Their argument, put briefly, is that the Bible's admonition against what they did is cultural bias on the part of the human writers of those verses pertaining to the subject, and not really the will of God. In other words, they are of the opinion that certain passages, perhaps even all of Scripture, is open to interpretation and is not to be taken literally.

This position is directly contrary to the teachings of the Lutheran Church, Missouri Synod.

I have chosen to support these two men for the following reasons:

I feel that the action taken against these men was a 'rush to judgment' and more of a witch-hunt than the loving admonition appropriate to the family of Christ.

I have come to believe that the Bible is meant to *guide* us as children of God, not to be a means for acting out our prejudices, justifying our power, or as a vehicle for condemnation.

I have experienced a personal revelation from God, which has led me to resign as your pastor at St. Luke's and from the Lutheran Church, Missouri Synod at large.

On Sunday, February 3, 1972, I will be holding services for a new church at my home at 1517
Horizon Road at 9:00 A.M. All are welcome, but
please be aware that your attendance at this service
could jeopardize your standing and/or your membership at St. Luke's and with the LCMS.

I will pray for you that God may help you to
grow in the Christian faith and bring you, through
that faith, to abundant and everlasting life.

Still Your Brother In Jesus Christ,
Herkimer Gudsen

So began The Gospel Church of Faith and Revelation,
which is what Herk decided to call his little Sunday gatherings,
since its principles, as yet not fully defined, were based on those
words—that is gospel, faith and revelation. In the beginning, there
really was no charter, no constitution, and no creed. Herk said that
that would all come later when the new church was large enough to
define itself.

On that first Sunday, I helped Meg and Herk put up a few
folding chairs in their living room, in front of an old wooden music
stand which would serve as the pulpit.

Besides Herk, Meg, Ginny and I, three other people attended—Baxter Bird and Robin Stym, of course, were two of them.
The third was Lena Gossbach, whose fear of being without her pastor was larger than her fear of being without her church. It's hard to
call a church for comfort in the middle of the night when terror of
the Almighty has you wound up in a knot.

In the next few weeks, we all received letters of expulsion
both from St. Luke's and the LCMS for supporting, by our attendance at The Gospel Church of Faith and Revelation, something
called 'Montanist heresy'. Herk explained to us that Montanus had
been the leader of an early group of Christians around the middle
of the second century A.D. Montanus contended that the Holy
Spirit spoke to the church through him, just as it had through St.
Paul and the other apostles.

"How do you know that wasn't true?" I heard Baxter Bird say, after a Sunday service at the manse during the week when the seven members of the new church had all received their walking papers from the LCMS.

"The Council of Constantinople, in 381 A.D., declared that Montanism was pagan," Herk replied.

"You mean a bunch of guys who thought that *they* spoke for the church got together and condemned the teachings of this other guy who thought that *he* spoke for the church?" This came from quiet, effeminate little Robin Stym who, even without cross-dressing, (which he never did), was prettier than most girls.

"Yes," Herk said.

"So we're depending on some council to decide for the church? *They* could have been wrong, couldn't they? Maybe this Montanus guy was right. And if he wasn't, I mean if orthodox Christians are going to trust the church's so-called leaders to condemn those with a different point of view, then why do Lutherans follow Luther? *His* teachings were condemned by the church too. How do we know he was right and Montanus wasn't?"

All eyes turned to Herk for an answer, all except Baxter Bird's and mine. Baxter was holding Robin's delicate hand and looking at his lover with the swollen pride of an indulgent parent.

"This is what happens," Herk explained, "when there is too great a dependence on the ornate machinery of the church and a lack of reliance on the inspiration of the Holy Spirit. Church organization and the formulation of doctrine have supplanted the very real possibility of man's continued spiritual contact with God. One of the great, early church fathers, Tertullian, was a Montanist, and hundreds of other people believed what Montanus taught. In other words, Brother Stym, we don't *know* that he was wrong. It's part of the reason we're all here."

Discussions like this went on every week after Herk had delivered his sermons. He encouraged open discussion of whatever should be brought up. He didn't elaborate on his own revelation except to say that the new church was a part of it and that he was 'expecting further guidance' which, he told me privately, he believed would not come until Larry Ladon joined The Gospel Church of Faith and Revelation. In other words, when hell froze over.

He also continued to keep Meg's condition a secret but, to his credit, he was only following her wishes. She felt that any revelation of her illness might be construed as a plea for sympathy or pity. Meg had no intention of allowing her health to become an issue in any ecclesiastical struggle.

The eighth member of The Gospel Church of Faith and Revelation turned out to be Herk's neighbor, August Two-River II, the guy who'd almost killed him. I thought it appropriate, since I believed, at the time, that Auggie was more responsible for the voice in Herk's head, and thus the founding of The Gospel Church of Faith and Revelation, than God was.

Auggie's narrow escape from becoming a murderer led him to forego his second semester at MSU so that he could visit Herk, (which he frequently did) and follow the recuperative progress more closely, as much, I suspected, out of fear of litigation as concern for my brother's welfare.

Herk invited him to join us in a worship service, and suddenly one Sunday morning there he was. Auggie Two-River hadn't had much religious training. His old man, somewhere in his past, had had connections through the German side of the family with Lutheranism. But that connection had been severed long before Auggie II was born and *he'd* been raised pretty much without *any* kind of religion.

Auggie's mother had died shortly after he was born and the old man had raised his son by himself. Auggie told us, in one of those informal after-service, group counseling endeavors, that his father, like the half-Ojibway he was, believed in a form of nature worship, (Animism, Herk called it), augmented by ancestral worship. Auggie II had never liked his grandparents. The old, full-blooded Ojibway who was his grandfather and who had had the interesting name of Skunk Two-River, was an alcoholic. His disdain for water was both anomalistic to his surname and fitting to his given. He was always dirty and smelled badly, according to

Auggie. His German grandmother was a frightened little chubby woman who was abused by her husband, and took the regular beatings from the drunken Skunk with the dumb good humor of a loyal dog. Auggie remembered her always wearing sweat and grease-stained dresses that revealed her fat, hairy, varicose-veined legs. Though Lutheran, she was not allowed by Skunk to ever leave the homestead to go to church or anywhere else. To Auggie's knowledge, the only time she ever left the farm was when she died, sometime in her grandson's fifth or sixth year of elementary school. Skunk, a victim of cirrhosis, followed close on her heels.

These being the only ancestors (other than his dour sire) that Auggie II had ever known, it seemed no miracle to me that he would have little interest in his father's religious practices and would look elsewhere for inspiration. Across the street seemed as good a place as any, and more convenient than most.

Although no one, (least of all Auggie), knew it, he was destined to become one of the Twelve. But not, of course, before Larry Ladon joined the fold. Miraculous as that might seem, it *did* happen and it didn't take that long.

Shortly after Herk began a Sunday worship service in late February, Larry Ladon walked into Herk's living room and sat down on the folding chair closest to the door.

Since all eight of us were in our usual places, the addition of *any* person would have drawn our attention, but Larry Ladon's arrival was an idiosyncratic and bizarre phenomenon on a par with Rudolph Hess parachuting into England or Henry Fonda's daughter shaking hands with Ho Chi Minh.

Though Herk had seen him come in first, his blue eyes had betrayed no surprise, and he had gone on reading the passage he'd chosen for that day from the seventeenth chapter of Proverbs: "The crucible for silver and the furnace for gold, but the Lord tests the heart." He'd begun his sermon then, but all eyes were turned to the back and he knew that no one would listen to a word he said until some explanation of the enemy's presence was offered. So, in typical Herkimer fashion, he dealt with the problem directly.

He stopped in mid-sentence, looked directly at the intruder and said: "Mr. Ladon, it's so nice to have you here. Welcome. We've been expecting you." Herk's use of the pronoun 'we' must have been employed in the royal fashion because, judging from the number of gaping mouths and astonished faces, Herkimer Gudsen was a minority of one in this expectation.

"You have?" Larry Ladon said, adequately expressing all our amazement.

"Yes."

Of course Herk had told Meg and me that this would happen, as, he claimed, God had told him. But *I* hadn't believed it would happen, (hell must surely have gone cold), and *Meg*, though she believed, hadn't expected it so soon, so abruptly. So we were *all* astonished—except Herk, of course.

I had never seen anything but smug egotism on Larry Ladon's face before, but now there was only fear and uncertainty. The stiff pride with which he had held his back and neck so erect had gone flaccid. His shoulders slouched forward. His posture reminded me of a spent penis, the juices gone, head sagging downward. He began to cry when Herk welcomed him, *weep* might be a better word, as if mourning over his shriveled condition. He was a small man anyway, in his sixties, who until today had always seemed vigorous and filled with a kind of confident vitality. His dark hair was only slightly gray.

I knew very little about him. He was married, had been for many years, to the pinched-faced old termagant everyone referred to, even Ginny, as Mrs. Ladon. No one seemed to know her first name. I'd often wondered if Larry did. She was bigger than her husband, tougher and meaner too. Most people understood that when Mr. Ladon spoke, it was with Mrs. Ladon's voice.

They owned the apple orchard on Sleepy Creek, west of the city, and had turned it into a gold mine. They grew only Golden Delicious, an apple the color of my brother's hair, originally developed in California. When Larry had bought the trees, some twenty years ago, most of the apple growers in the area had thought he was crazy. But now he was the exclusive supplier of Golden Delicious in the Saginaw Valley. It was in great demand as an eating and juice apple, and Larry could provide it right here—no need to pay expensive shipping from California. Mr. and Mrs. Ladon were growing rich, while the Jonathan and MacIntosh growers fell behind.

The Ladons had three daughters who no one had seen in a couple of years. Ginny knew that the oldest, Hester, had graduated from Smith, married an alumnus of Cornell, and moved to New York or New Jersey. Herk had graduated with Hester, even asked her out once, but Mrs. Ladon had declared that Hester, at seventeen, was too young to date. Herk told me that Ginny, too, had seemed strangely upset with the idea and was relieved when Mrs. Ladon had squelched his advances. The second daughter, Rebecca, had graduated from Concordia Lutheran Teacher's College in Ann Arbor and 'taken a call' to teach somewhere out west. I remembered the third myself, because I'd had more than one dream about her. Her name was Rusha, and she was knockdown, drop-dead gorgeous. She had honey-blonde hair and wide blue eyes with lashes so long they looked artificial. She had a full, sensuous mouth and a body, (despite her mother's attempts to hide it), that rivaled Meg's, in a less statuesque way.

We'd graduated in the same year from Saginaw High. Rusha never dated, never went to the prom, never seemed to run with any crowd. After graduation, she disappeared.

None of the girls, apparently, ever came home—at least they were never seen publicly. Mr. and Mrs. Ladon always came to services at St. Luke's alone—even at Christmas and Easter, yet they appeared to be solidly and stoically content...until now.

Larry Ladon looked miserable and abject. His head, far too large for his physique, was stooped, his round face hidden in his hands. His shoulders heaved, forcing out muffled sobs between his stubby fingers. A diamond ring glittered in the slant of winter sun that shone only on him, like God's spotlight.

Herkimer left the makeshift pulpit, walked between the members of his paltry congregation and sat down next to the man who'd cost him his church. He put one arm around the sagging shoulders and whispered to him. I couldn't hear what he said, but

Ladon embraced him and nodded as if in agreement. Then he looked at the rest of us, wiped the moisture off his scarlet cheeks, and spoke to us. "I…I don't know how to say this," he began. "I've always liked to think that I was in control of things." He sighed deeply, as if his heart had stopped and he was trying to get it started again. "But I'm not. I'm not." He took a moment to collect himself again, then continued. "I'm here," he said, "because…well, Mrs. Ladon…she, passed away last night. It was her heart you see…" His eyes remained dry, but his voice wavered. "I don't know why I'm *here*, really." He glanced at my mother. It looked like she actually *smiled* at him. I dismissed it as imagination.

"God has brought you here," Herk said, softly.

Robin Stym said, "Amen."

I was still too astonished to say anything. I looked over at Meg. Her eyes were alive with hope. She had believed from the beginning, but her faith had just improved—as had mine. We've become accustomed to thinking of degrees as indicators of intellect, but they also measure heat, commitment—even belief. Coincidentally, they can also delineate their opposites. You could *feel* it heating up and, if there had been a thermometer for faith in that room, it would have exploded.

"I guess so," Larry Ladon said.

Herk squeezed his shoulder.

"I've been up all night with her…with Mrs. Ladon, at Holy Cross. I have to make arrangements. I was on my way home and…I came here." He looked over at Baxter Bird and Robin Stym, who were clutching each other as if Beelzebub had just noticed them. "I need your forgiveness," he said to them. "I was convinced that I was right about your…'situation'. Mrs. Ladon too was insistent…well. I know now that I was wrong. I'd take it back if I could."

It got a little warmer for me, as if someone had just lit twenty campfires in the closed room.

"It's okay," Robin Stym said immediately.

Baxter Bird said nothing until Robin whispered something in his ear. Then he said, "I forgive you. I'm sorry to hear about your wife. It's a difficult thing to give up someone you love." It didn't sound convincing and the tone of accusation was there, but it pleased Robin, who ran his fingers through Baxter's thick hair and pridefully patted his shoulder.

Ladon didn't seem to notice. He turned to my brother. "Herki...excuse me, *Pastor*, I've wronged you too."

"You were doing what you were *supposed* to do," he answered. "Nothing to forgive."

Larry Ladon shook his head as if he understood, although I don't think he did yet—not like we were beginning to.

Long ago, I'd known that there was something different about my brother, but every time I began to admit his uniqueness, my own jealousy would surface and that childish envy invariably led to denial. I understood Auggie Two-River's guilt—and Larry Ladon's. When you crossed Herk—and he'd been crossed a lot—you *knew* that you were fighting a force way beyond you. Identifying that force as God took some time for me, but that's what, or rather Who, it was.

There was no more denial for me after Larry Ladon walked into Herk's living room on that wintry Sunday morning in February. There would continue to be doubt, of course. The follower never believes like the leader—that's why he follows—but there was no question anymore, in my mind, that there was a God, that Herk was somehow led by Him, and that wherever he was leading us, we were on the right path.

As Herk returned to the music stand and continued his sermon, Ginny went to Larry Ladon, sat down next to him, took his hand in hers, and helped him through the service. *Her* behavior had me completely perplexed, but Goliath was in the fold. The Philistines, the small-god people, had lost their leader.

At the conclusion of the sermon, Herk praised God for Larry Ladon's presence among us, then ended his prayer with the request:

"*We humbly beseech you, Heavenly Father, to return your beloved child, Rusha Ladon, to her earthly father. We know you have brought him among us to this purpose. May we not fail him in this, so that his faith may grow and his role in your new church may be ful-*

filled according to Your Holy Will and direction. We ask this, dear Father, in the name of our crucified and triumphant Lord, Jesus Christ. Amen."

Larry Ladon's face resembled, in my mind, what St. Peter's must have looked like when Jesus strolled across the sea to meet him.

It was clear that he'd said nothing to Herk about his daughter. He'd had a purpose in coming here after all, though he hadn't known it at the time. God's spotlight was still on him, and he spoke. "Yesterday," he began, still holding Ginny's supportive hand, "I received a large manila envelope in the mail. It was addressed to only me—not to Mrs. Ladon too—and there was no return address, although the postmark indicated that it had been mailed in Saginaw."

Why any of those details should be important, none of us would know until much later, and we waited impatiently for him to continue. This revelation, or confession, or whatever it was, was obviously a battle he was determined to win.

"When I opened it," he continued, "I was appalled. It was a...a pornographic magazine, the worst kind, depicting men and women and..." here he sobbed and glanced at Baxter Bird, "...and women with women, in all kinds of lewd, sexual poses. My first inclination was to throw it away, attributing the mailing to some kind of prank. But then, I saw my Rusha..."

Here he broke down again, sobbing, his eyes haunted by the image now reenacted in his mind. Meg rushed to his other side to assist Ginny in comforting the broken man. I almost got up myself, but I'd not yet been empowered with empathetic spontaneity.

"I couldn't believe it, of course. Rusha...we hadn't heard from Rusha for some time, perhaps two months. But we knew she was living in Los Angeles, and she wrote fairly regularly. She...she told us she was working as a secretary in a law office out there. I knew something was wrong. Big city lawyers don't hire kids just out of high school as secretaries. She wrote that her phone was out of order, but that she'd call us soon. We hadn't heard her voice in six months."

Herk handed him a glass of water. He sipped it, then quickly reattached himself to Ginny, as if she could keep him from drowning in his own pain. Ginny, who'd expressed such bitterness regarding Larry Ladon, was now his chief comforter. The world was becoming surreal and, suddenly, too unsteady.

"I looked at the pictures again. I forced myself. I couldn't believe what I saw. But it *was* her. It was. I showed the magazine to my wife. She took it from me and threw it in the trashcan. She said it wasn't Rusha, couldn't be, but someone who resembled her, that's all, and the magazine had probably been sent by one of you people here—for revenge, she said. But I knew that it was Rusha. My sweet little girl!"

He collapsed again, this time with such pitiable weeping that I was afraid he might die. But in a few minutes, he found the strength to continue. "Last night, before...before..." he gripped Ginny's hand, then went on, "I got a call from Pastor Ryan in Lansing. Someone had sent him the same magazine, identifying Rusha as my daughter. He asked me if I knew about it—if it was true. I told him it was. He expressed his sympathy, but said that since Rusha was still a communicant member of St. Luke's, an investigation into her 'depravity', as he called it, was warranted."

Robespierre, I thought, *meet Dr. Guillotine.*

"Three hours later, Mrs. Ladon collapsed on the kitchen floor. She died in the ambulance on the way to the hospital. This morning, I came here. I think it was because I knew this was the way for me to find my Rusha, my baby. I think I was right to come. Pastor," he said, looking earnestly at my brother, "you *knew*, without me telling you, you *knew*."

Herkimer, standing close to his fallen enemy, glass of water in hand, smiled. "Yes," he said. "God will guide us to bring her home."

How *that* promise would ever be kept, I didn't know, but I didn't doubt that it would happen.

The next morning, I was standing in a third floor waiting room at Holy Cross, smoking a cigarette as I took a break from mopping the hallway. I looked down at the snow-covered street, absently ruminating about yesterday's epiphanies, when I saw my sister-in-law exit the building across the street. My first inclination was to shout, my second to wave, but she wouldn't have heard or seen either gesture. So I just watched her graceful motions as she walked toward the parking ramp a block away. As she disappeared, I looked back across the street, and an uneasy feeling rose from somewhere in my previously tranquil mind. It was the feeling you get when you up the ante with a bluff hand. The sign on the building from which she'd emerged read: Holy Cross Obstetrics and Gynecology Center.

I felt intuitively, perhaps spiritually, certainly ominously, that the saving of Meg's life had now become doubly important.

Chapter eight

Herk told Robin Stym, Baxter Bird and Larry Ladon of his revelation about 'the Twelve' and that they were the first three of this inner circle. He told them that God had called them by name. None of them ever questioned the authenticity of Herk's visions. They took their positions as if they were the original apostles—with the devotion and zeal of the sons of Zebedee.

I had expected Larry Ladon's 'conversion' to be a temporary lapse into traumatic regret, like some men occasionally lapse into evil. I was, again, mistaken. He never missed a service, just as he had never missed one at St. Luke's, but this time his impeccable attendance was accompanied by kindness, understanding, and a liberality that went beyond many of us. He was always the first to donate his time and money to the new church. It was a conversion worthy of the Damascus road. He never looked back. He became a pillar nonetheless.

The Sunday following his public confession, the membership of the Gospel Church of Faith and Revelation doubled. Ben Tower, (the owner of the buffalo ranch and father of 'Skinny Minnie') came into the fold along with his wife, Sylvia. Herk had recently officiated at their daughter's wedding, causing the infamous Swiss Steak Supper debacle. Minerva, or Minnie, would eventually come with them, but only after separating from her new husband, whose special talent, she learned too late, was beating the shit out of those he professed to love. As Herk had observed,

Minnie had filled out admirably and once the bruises faded and the wire brace was removed from around her broken jaw, she turned out to be a remarkably beautiful woman. She certainly was no longer the anorexic teen I remembered from high school.

If memory serves, the old busybody Gertie Schmidt and her obedient husband, Oscar, also showed up that week. Larry Ladon's fellow elder, Herman Goetsh, his wife, and three daughters joined the week after that. Herk performed his first baptism as pastor of the new church on Herman's granddaughter, Isabelle. He told me it was good to have kids around. It promised a future. I remember wondering when he was going to tell me about Megan's visit to the obstetric clinic at Holy Cross, or if he even knew.

The congregation was not drawn entirely from St. Luke's, or even the Lutheran Church. There were people who came from the wider world as well. Caleb Bird, Baxter's brother, drove up from the seminary in Indiana and took up residence in his father's house, although he had the bathtub removed and a shower installed in its stead. After the old man's suicide, Baxter hadn't had the stomach to live in the house and had retained his apartment. He and Caleb were joint inheritors and had decided to sell the place, before the latter's rebellion against the LCMS, spurred by my brother's defense of his sibling, had resulted in an inglorious end to his theological studies. Caleb had quickly joined the Gospel Church and become a sort of vicar to assist Herkimer in his ever-expanding duties. He brought with him six other former seminarians who were intrigued by the stories of Herk's revelations, and were anxious to witness for themselves the strange man who'd caused such a stir throughout the LCMS. Caleb, unlike his brother, was strongly self-assured and, at times, even a bit arrogant. Also unlike his brother, Caleb Baxter possessed a penchant for the opposite sex—an appetite that was not easily sated, and equaled, at least, my own. I suspect that this addiction, perhaps as much as his adherence to unorthodox theology, was responsible for his expulsion from the seminary.

Ginny proselytized for the church tirelessly and her efforts bore fruit. Her hairdresser, a guy named Sammy Epstein, converted from lapsed Judaism and quickly closeted with 'The Birds'. (This being the sobriquet attached by some members of the congregation to Robin Stym and Baxter Bird, appropriate as much for their virtually married relationship as their respective names).

Another of Ginny's non-Lutheran converts was her next-door neighbor, Seamus O'Connor, (father of the balloon-throwing Randy who was then in medical school). Seamus attributed his triumph over alcohol to Ginny's diligent prayers as well as her advice to his wife Fiona that she should leave him. Fiona did leave, and that shock certainly played no small part in his reclamation. She came back when he dried out. Seamus and Fiona left St. Joseph's Parish, whose priest, an alcoholic himself, had been more a drinking buddy to Seamus than a confessor. The O'Connors became regular communicants at the Gospel Church of Faith and Revelation where they were allowed to partake of the Lord's blood through the less tempting medium of Welch's Grape Juice.

It always amazed me how little all these people cared about theology. They were good people with weaknesses. They didn't want to feel condemned, that's all. They wanted to believe in a God who accepted them, who loved them, who saw the worth beneath the dirt, like any good parent.

By the first of March, the congregation was becoming too large to fit in Herk and Meg's living room anymore. During one of the after-service open discussions, Larry Ladon came forward with the idea of converting the old barn in the back yard of the manse to a 'proper church'. Ginny, who had never abrogated her seat next to the old apple grower, declared it to be a wonderful suggestion. She beamed at Ladon with a pride which had previously been reserved only for Herkimer, and she patted Ladon's knee familiarly. I wondered at how swiftly Larry Ladon had recuperated from his wife's death, since she had not been gone a week yet. Nevertheless, the Birds chirruped a hearty second and by St. Patrick's Day, serious planning was underway.

Somehow, money never was an obstacle. Ben Tower was especially generous, and wrote a check for ten thousand dollars to begin the renovation of the barn. Meg's inheritance was enough to provide a year or two's salary for Herk, and the normal collection for a month of Sundays was adequate to foot the mortgage payment on the manse.

As the Spring of 1972 approached, the future of the Gospel Church of Faith and Revelation seemed assured, but such an optimistic prophesy evaded my sister-in-law.

Meg began to look increasingly gaunt and hollow-eyed. Her lovely skin had taken on a listless yellow hue, like old wax on linoleum. The rigidity in her spine appeared to give, like a sapling under the weight of wet snow, and she slumped in her chair, too weak to concern herself with posture. Although she smiled often, it was more the evidence of her courage than her joy. The sparkle was gone from her eyes. Even her fiery hair seemed to have flattened out and cooled, like the last embers in a forgotten hearth.

Strangely, her appetite remained, but it took on an exotic character. She developed a penchant for peanut butter and green olive sandwiches. She couldn't get enough sardines and she took to eating tablespoons of mayonnaise right from the jar. She devoured bags of M and M's. Still, her weight continued to plummet.

On Good Friday, she stayed in bed all day, but struggled downstairs to attend the evening worship service. When she failed to appear on Easter morning, Herk was finally forced to reveal her illness to the concerned assemblage. He also assured them of God's promise to save her, but omitted the condition about gathering the Twelve. God had not yet directed him about the other nine, and Meg was obviously dying. I kept asking, though I knew the deal had been struck.

In May, the church was moved outdoors to accommodate the latest converts. Every day there was the frenetic sound of hammers and power saws as the barn slowly metamorphosed into a new sanctuary. Larry Ladon, who had the luxury of owning a business that pretty much ran itself, was the most avid of the builders, working many days from dawn to dusk. Caleb Bird and Herk were constants as well. Most of the other men of the Gospel Church, including myself, had to continue in their regular employment, but our evenings and weekends were spent crawling over the surface of the old barn like a colony of termites.

Ginny moved back into the spare bedroom of the manse to attend to Meg and cook the enormous meals that were required to keep the builders energized. She delivered Larry Ladon's meals to him personally. She had a lot of help from Gertie Schmidt, Lena Gossbach and Robin; Mr. Stym preferring the gentler occupation of the kitchen to the aggressive and noisy labor outside.

On June 8th, Megan had to be hospitalized, and it was then that my brother finally told me that she was, as I had suspected but had been unable to believe, pregnant. "She's in her second trimester," he said, as we stood, alone, in the visitor's waiting room near the Cancer Treatment Center doors on the fifth floor of Holy Cross. It was unusually deserted. I passed that room frequently in the course of my day, and it was normally filled with visitors, taking a break from death.

"How long have you known?" I asked. I must have looked angry to him, because he looked back in a way that suggested more of the sheep than the shepherd.

"Quite a while. Months."

"Look," I told him, "I know I'm not one of your precious Twelve, but—"

"I haven't told anyone else. Not even mother. Just you."

"Then why such a damned secret?"

"Because Meg was diagnosed with cancer *before* she became pregnant," he said. "We would appear to be so...so *irresponsible*, uncaring, I don't know."

"Why? Because of what Meg would have to go through, you mean?"

"She could die before she comes to term," he said. My brother didn't take his eyes from mine. Damn him, he always faced the truth head-on, when a little evasion or denial would allow those of us who were weaker a little respite from pain.

"Why *weren't* you using birth control?" I asked. It was a cruel question, to which I already knew the answer, but something in me wanted to see my brother helpless, not self-assured. I wanted very much to see him squirm. As always, he turned it back on me, as always, unintentionally.

"I was told by Doctor Herman," he said, "that we couldn't have children, that I was sterile." It was hard for him to continue. He put his fingers to the scar on the right side of his head where the bolt had pierced him, as if he could draw some kind of courage from the memory. "I should have trusted God," he said. "I should have trusted Meg. I should have trusted *you*, Jim. Forgive me."

"Me?"

"When Meg told me she was pregnant, I knew I couldn't have been the father. I've seen the way you look at her. She always confided in you. You've had a lot of experience with women. I just thought...well, I was wrong, Jim. I'm sorry."

I didn't know what to say. Meg and I had come close enough for me to feel guilty. Even my imagination was enough to make me wince a bit. "It's okay, Herk," I managed.

He had tears in his eyes. He embraced me, smothering me momentarily in his chest. "Jealousy is a terrible thing," he said. "It's covetous and possessive. It's, it's *wrong thinking!*" Herkimer Gudsen jealous of James. Maybe miracles really do happen.

His blue eyes penetrated me. I suffered a terrible moment where all I wanted was to confess. I wanted to tell him that I *did* kiss his wife. I touched her breast. If she'd let me, I would have taken advantage of her desperation and had her pants off in a minute. I never would have given him a thought. I wish she *was* carrying my child. I wish I *was* the father, the favored son of Ginny, the man who had God's ear and heard God's voice. But I only said: "Then how did she get pregnant?"

"God restored me."

"What?"

"I went back to see Doctor Herman. I asked him to test me again. It was a weakness of my faith, but I did it anyway. I *insisted.* He refused at first, said there was no point to it, but I pressured him and he finally agreed."

"And?"

"And I'm okay. My sperm are healthy. God restored me, Jim. I'm the father. Meg was telling me the truth and I doubted her. I doubted God. I won't doubt again. This was supposed to happen." He stared past my shoulder for a moment as if he were looking at someone behind me—an absence I'd grown used to.

"How did Doctor Herman explain it?" I said, calling him back.

"What?" He was still in that place beyond me, beyond almost everyone. Then suddenly he was back. "Oh, he said they must've made a mistake before, on the first test. He said that because they didn't have to use a needle this time that perhaps...." He stopped. His face reddened. He would tell me the truth if I pushed it, of course, but his eyes begged me to ignore his slip.

I did. I don't know why, but I missed my chance. Herk is an exceptional man and exceptions have to be made. "So you think God gave you your sperm back?" I said.

He smiled. "And more."

That was it. I don't think he ever knew that I was aware of his double reclamation.

I changed the subject. "What do the doctors here say about the baby? Do they know? The cancer guys I mean."

"Yes." Herk's voice dropped to a barely audible whisper. "They know. They're recommending an abortion."

He said that last word with the disgust and disdain that the LCMS had taught him. With the possible exceptions of the Vatican and the Bible belt Baptists, no Christian denomination condemned abortion more than Missouri Synod Lutherans.

"That's not legal is it?"

"It is in cases like this, but it's a moot point. I told them that it was impossible. They said the pregnancy would hasten Meg's death and the baby probably wouldn't make it. We refused anyway. I think they see me as a monster."

"This is how Meg feels too?"

"That I'm a monster?"

"No. That she should continue the pregnancy."

"Yes."

"You think God will save them."

"Against all hope, Abraham in hope believed and so became the father of many nations, just as it had been said to him 'So shall your offspring be.' Without weakening in his faith, he faced the fact that his body was as good as dead—since he was about a hundred years old—and that Sarah's womb was also dead. Yet he did not waver through unbelief regarding the promise of God, but was strengthened in his faith and gave glory to God, being fully persuaded that God had power to do what he had promised."

I always marveled at my brother's ability to quote Scripture. I still think he has the whole thing memorized. "I thought you'd moved to more direct communication, Herk. Why do you still keep spouting that shit? Those stories can't save Meg."

His face darkened with anger. There was in it a gorgon's ugly rage. Something old and primal moved his flesh, extinguished the light. "*Stories?*" he shouted. I remember backing away from him. I felt the weight of water-filled balloons. "The Bible is the *Word of God!* Don't you *ever* be flippant about it—ever!"

I gathered my retreating courage. I stood firm, but couldn't look at the snake-face. "Don't yell at me you pompous son of a bitch," I shouted. I might have been able to take him, but it never occurred to me to try. He was the only father I'd ever known and fathers don't have to be strong to defeat you.

But his anger dissipated as quickly as it had come. The exposed teeth disappeared beneath the uncurling lips. The feral eyes went calm. "I'm sorry, Jim," he said, his voice returning to its normal half-whisper. "I'm sorry. I love you, you know that. But don't suppose that because I've left the Lutheran Church that I've abandoned the Word. It *is* God's holy book. It *is* Truth."

"Okay," I said, "but isn't all this about whether it's truth or not?"

"No. It's about the *interpretation* of that Truth. It's about finding God's Truth in other ways too. It's about continual revelation. It's about faith over law. It's about love over condemnation. But it's *not* about denying the Truth God's already given us." He came across the waiting room and embraced me again. "I'm not Christ, Jimmy. I'm not a Messiah. I'm weak. I don't have all the answers. I only know that God has chosen me for something and that I love Him above all else—even Meg. 'All things work together for good for those who love God.' *That* is Scripture. That is real Truth. I believe it as much as I believe God's voice when He tells me He will save Meg."

"But there's a condition."

"Only to save her for *me*."

"But you want that."

"More than my life." A tear formed in one eye and ran down his bony cheek.

"I didn't mean it," I said. "The thing about being pompous."

He laughed. "I know. As for the reflection on my parentage, I might remind you that we're brothers."

I wanted to tell him that sometimes I needed that reminder, but I just laughed with him.

We went in to see Meg. She looked terrible, but we both lied—at least I did. I think she may have still looked beautiful to Herk. She would have to stay for a while, was all she said.

Sitting in Herk's beat-up old Chrysler, I felt sad, even morbid. My naivete or faith or love was not as strong as Herk's. I stared out the window at dust rising from tractors as they cruised the open fields. The smell of manure was heavy in the air. Still, the dirt and cowshit were welcome changes from the polluted city. They were natural smells. They were real. I lit a cigarette out of habit and immediately threw it away. It didn't belong to the moment.

"When do you start finding the others?" I asked. "Time is…short."

"You through with classes for the summer?" he said.

"Yeah."

Herk turned onto Horizon Road and was approaching the Two-River farm. "Can you get some time off from work?"

"I guess so," I said. "Why?"

"We have to go somewhere."

"Where?"

"I'm not sure."

"For how long?"

"I don't know that either."

"You and me?"

"Yes."

"Why me?"

He sighed, as adults do when children ask them impossible questions. What does God look like? What's a virgin? Why are people mean? "I don't know," he finally responded. "You're supposed to help me."

"Help you what?"

"Find Rusha Ladon. She's number three. And she'll lead us to number four. That's all I know. Will you go with me?"

Sometimes a prophet *is* honored in his own country.

Chapter nine

I expected that Herk would want to go to Los Angeles right away. That was where Rusha's last communication with her parents had come from and if we had to scour *that* city, I thought we'd better get at it. But Herk just told me to be patient. Where and when we had to go, we'd discover—*I'd* discover.

I watched Meg deteriorate each day and my impatience turned to anxiety. I felt an increasing pressure to *do* something. I think most desperate people desire action precisely when there's no action to be taken.

My brother assured me that God would show me the way. I asked Him to hurry. I asked Him to give me patience. I begged Him to save Meg. Unfortunately, God and I have always had a party line. I knew He was there, He knew I was here, but it was always hard getting through. In the last week, I'd felt like the line was dead altogether, the connection severed.

Typically, I'd stop by Meg's room after my shift, and just visit for a while. One day she'd be almost like her old self—bright, alert, cheerful. The next, she'd be in and out of some other world, sent there by the drugs that dulled her pain.

While her face and arms thinned dramatically, the little mound under the white sheets grew larger, allying with its mother's enemy to eat away at her remaining strength. I didn't hate the child, but I looked upon my potential niece or nephew with the disdain and resentment one reserves for matricidal creatures. Raw survival can be a very selfish proposition.

Once in a while I'd run into Herk while visiting Meg, but mostly he came to see her in the mornings, knowing I'd be there in the late afternoon and Ginny would take the night shift, often accompanied by Larry Ladon. There was a constant flow of visitors from the congregation at all hours, so Meg was seldom without company during the solitary process of dying.

Two weeks went by and, finally convinced that God had no intention of ever conversing with me, I spitefully decided to abandon my celibacy and headed for the Amazon Club downtown. I conveniently attributed my frustration to being horny and I had every intention of looking up Maddy, my strip-teasing pal, and getting laid.

Hippolyta, Queen of the Amazons, was still receiving primary billing on the marquee outside, but I didn't know if Hippolyta was still Maddy or not. I doubted it. I don't know why.

It was around eleven when I entered the club. Except for the dimmed stage lights and the colored lamps over the bar, the place was pretty dark. There were some empty tables, but it was a large crowd for a Tuesday. At that point no one was performing, so it was quiet except for the subdued conversations of a few businessmen who were entertaining their clients or simply discussing strategies for some capitalist venture or other. The Amazon was a gentleman's club and any raucous hayseeds quickly found themselves on the pavement, dispatched by the heavily-muscled black giant of a bouncer named Atlas Johnson. He claimed to have been an offensive tackle for the Detroit Lions, back when they were always battling the Bears for the NFL Championship, but only he knew for sure. No one remembers the guys who open the holes, he'd tell me later—only the ones who go through them. He was sitting in his usual chair by the door, reading. I nodded as I went by. I don't know if he remembered me or not, but he nodded back.

I found Maddy at the bar. She must have just recently performed, because she was wearing a silk kimono that she always used to cover up between shows. I sat on the cushioned stool next to her.

She didn't notice me at first. She was staring into her drink, and knowing Maddy, it wasn't her first.

"Hey Mad," I said.

She turned and the dull expression disappeared. "Jimmy!" She put her arms around my neck and gave me a long, wet kiss. No one had gone that far into my throat since I'd had my tonsils extracted. When she finally pulled away, I gasped for breath. She put one hand on the bulge in my pants. "Nope," she said, "you haven't gone queer on me. You must've got religion."

"What makes you say that?" I said. I laughed, but it was unconvincing.

"Isn't your brother the guy who got shot in the head with an arrow?"

"A crossbow bolt."

"Yeah. I read about him. He was a priest or somethin' and he got fired—opened his own church. It was in the papers. You got religion, Jimmy?"

I shrugged.

"I thought so. Only God can keep 'em away once they've had a piece of Maddy pie."

Maddy's face was never good enough to marry. It was angular. The eyes were remarkable, but set deeply, and her jaw protruded too much. Her cheekbones were high and pronounced. She wasn't homely exactly, but she lacked the symmetry and softness of classical beauty. She reminded me of a female Jack Palance—unusual face, great body. It didn't matter. Few people paid much attention to her above the neck anyway.

"So how you been, Mad?" I was trying to keep my brother and Meg and Ginny and God and jealousy and death outside, and I wasn't being successful.

"Oh, you know," she said. "I dance, I drink, I pay the rent." She took another sip of her Manhattan and munched absently on the Maraschino cherry she'd retrieved from the bottom of the glass. The bartender interrupted for a moment. I ordered a gin and tonic and a refill for Maddy. "I'm gonna be doing some acting too," she said.

"Really?"

"Yeah. The new girl put me onto this guy who does stag films. It's pretty good money—better'n stripping anyway, and it could lead to bigger shit, you know?"

"Sure."

She smiled. We both knew we weren't talking about an Oscar.

"Anyway, Hippie says I got a real future—"

"Hippie? Is that a name or a description?"

"Hippolyta, the *new* Queen of the Amazons. Her real name's Rita, but she likes to be called Hippolyta. I got pissed off when she came here. I figured I been around long enough to be the headliner, but Lance, he's the manager here, he said I couldn't be Hippolyta anymore. I wasn't drawing big enough crowds. I hated her at first, but she's been nice to me and she got me into this movie thing. We're cool now."

A spotlight appeared on the red curtain at the end of the runway, and the announcer's voice filled the club, booming his introduction over what I recognized as the musical score to *Spartacus*: "Ladies and gentlemen...for your delectation and titillation...all the way from the jungles of Los Angeles...the warrior woman...the ball-busting giantess...the Supreme Dominatrix...the Queen of the Amazons...please welcome, HIPP-O-LY-TA!"

"I gotta go," Maddy said. "I'm on in a minute. Wait for me?"

I nodded and she was gone, disappearing through a curtained opening at the end of the bar. All conversation had ceased and 'Hippolyta' was greeted with enthusiastic applause as the curtain opened and she stepped onto the runway. I could see instantly why she'd replaced Maddy. By law, she had to be twenty-one to do what she was doing, but she didn't look old enough to vote. She was very beautiful. Her mouth and cheeks were childishly full, as if she hadn't yet lost all her baby fat, yet the heavily mascaraed eyes, half-concealed below her long lashes, were strong—even cruel. Her hair was a deep ebony, so black that it had to have been dyed. The fierce blue eyes supported that assumption. She was very tall, perhaps five-nine or ten, even without the spiked three inch heels. She wore some kind of plate armor on the shins of her long legs, and on her forearms. A wicked-looking knife in a metal sheath was strapped by leather thongs to her left thigh. Around her hips, she sported some kind of chastity belt composed of metal and thick leather. An old padlock dangled from the strategic center. Her full breasts bulged over the restrictive borders of a metal bra. Spikes protruded from it like jeopardous nipples. On her head was a bulky tiara of metal and fake jewels, making her look even taller. She looked vaguely familiar to me.

She strutted down the runway, a sensuous enigma of incongruous metal and flesh, gyrating to the bump and grind saxophone that had replaced the epical opening. She stopped just short of the end of the stage, moving her hands up and down her naked torso. Her self-stimulation appeared to excite her so fiercely that she attempted, again and again, to force her fingers under the leather and metal barricade that guarded her loins from invasion. She shivered in masturbatory anticipation at her own caresses, but the treasure was secure in its tomb, a citadel against her groping hands. Rebuffed, she began to fondle the hard metal encasing her breasts. She reached behind her back with both hands, attempting to release her bosom from its confinement. The men cheered, encouraging her, but the spiked bra was also padlocked and she writhed in simulated frustration as the onlookers moaned with her.

I picked up my drink and walked over to an empty table by the runway. Being human, I was excited by this woman—she had me wishing I was a locksmith. I was enthralled, but something else brought me closer too, something I knew—a recognition. Herk used to say that God could be found anywhere except hell, because He goes where we go. I know now that that's true.

As soon as I sat down, the Queen of the Amazons minced back toward the larger stage, away from me. At the curtain's edge, she turned back to the crowd and grinned seductively, as if she'd remembered a solution to her dilemma. The white shirt and tie executives at the next table began to yell. "Do it, Baby! Bring her on!" Apparently they'd seen the act before.

This was the new Queen of the Amazons. She reached into the split between the curtains, pulled out a chain, and began sauntering down the runway again. The chain was attached to Maddy, or rather a heavy-looking manacle that circled Maddy's neck. She looked afraid as she was pulled, roughly, onstage. I knew it was an act. Maddy had been around the block enough times that fear wasn't an emotion she felt on a regular basis.

She was dressed only in a rough, ragged loincloth. Attached to the leather strap that held it in place was a large, metal ring from which dangled a variety of over-sized keys.

Hippolyta pulled her along, never looking back and often jerking hard enough on the chain attached to her slave that Maddy appeared to stumble.

Through all this, the new Queen didn't lose a single beat. Her feet, indeed her whole body, was never out of synchronization with the music. It must've been difficult for Maddy to abdicate her crown and play the pawn to this younger woman, but I detected no resentment. Maddy was a true pro. The new Hippolyta stopped directly in front of me, ignoring the clamoring businessmen who were trying to lure her further on with dollar bills extended into the runway lights. She looked right into my eyes and smiled. It was a lascivious grin. I think if she had refused to continue I might have jumped onstage and offered my services.

She yanked the chain again and Maddy was drawn close. The Queen ran her hand along her slave's neck, across the taut breasts, down the lovely curve of her torso, and then pulled at the loose knot that held the meager covering. She deftly clutched the key ring as the garment fell to the floor of the runway. Maddy wore a small, sequined g-string underneath—otherwise, except for the manacle around her neck, she was entirely naked.

Hippolyta grabbed Maddy's hair and pulled back roughly, forcing Maddy's face upward. She kissed her, passionately. The men below cheered.

When the Queen let her go, Maddy looked confused and embarrassed, though I was sure the kiss hadn't bothered her at all.

Maddy wasn't a lesbian, but she loved being on stage. Like I said, she was a pro.

Hippolyta handed Maddy the keys, turned her back to her, and bundled up her long hair on her head to give Maddy access to the lock on her back. Maddy appeared to fumble with the keys, then the spiked bra loosened and the Amazon wriggled out of the constrictive metal. It dropped, one spike neatly embedded in the wooden floor. Hippolyta reached behind her, eyes riveted on mine, and brought Maddy's arms around her body, placing Maddy's hands on her liberated breasts, keyring still dangling from her wrist.

The Queen stared at me, licking her lips and grinding her backside against her slave-lover as she appeared to revel in Maddy's caresses. She didn't close her eyes, or throw her head back, but kept up a steady gaze. It seemed to me as if her eyes were disembodied. They were passionless, devoid of emotion or excitement—almost predatory. If dragons ever existed, they must've had eyes like that. I don't mean they were reptilian, not structurally anyway. They were cold, like the glass eyes in a hunting trophy that seem to follow you around a room—even when you know they can't.

I know that Maddy 'unlocked' the chastity belt and slipped it off, but I don't remember that part of it. I was imprisoned too, and Maddy couldn't help me. There was something in those eyes— a memory—something.

I didn't recover my senses until the two women were already retreating behind the curtain and the music died. The businessmen were hooting and whistling like schoolboys but that noise, too, quickly subsided. A balding little man with the stub of a wet cigar in his mouth came out on the darkened runway and recovered the girls' discarded costumes as inconspicuously as he could.

I felt myself beginning to calm. I wanted very much to leave, but I couldn't. I'd promised Maddy I'd wait for her, but that was only an excuse. Something else held me. I wasn't smitten with Hippolyta either. I'd been bewitched, bothered and bewildered, as the old song goes, and the Amazon had certainly wound my gears pretty tight, but I really had no longing to see her, now that she was out of sight.

I ordered another gin and tonic. A new entertainer, a striking blonde woman, began her act. I barely looked up. I was occupied with an interior seduction of a very different variety.

Finally, Maddy showed up. She was wearing jeans and a tight-fitting pink blouse that matched her pink stiletto heels. "Whew! Sorry I took so long, Jimmy," she said. "That shower just felt so good. How'd you like the show?"

I didn't really know what to say. I told her that I thought she did a great job of acting.

She put her hand on my cheek. "You're always so sweet, Jimmy, thanks. It's not easy for me, you know. The slave-girl thing was Rita's idea and Lance loves it. So, we do it, but I'm really not into women."

"I know."

"You should." She laughed. "Buy me a drink?"

"Sure."

We watched Atlas 'escort' a drunken patron out the door. The guy must have been close to six feet tall, but his feet dangled off the floor.

"Hippie practically gave you a private show. I wanted to get over by those guys," she nodded in the direction of the business-men who had waved the money at them, "but Rita stayed right in front of you. You were drooling, Babe." I detected a hint of re-sentment in her voice. "I've never seen her do that before. She *always* goes for the money. She told me she wanted to meet you. That okay? I told her I'd introduce you."

"When?"

Maddy gestured toward the end of the bar. "Here she comes now."

Like Maddy, the Amazon was in casual street clothes and probably done for the night too. She looked very different without the heavy make-up and exotic costume. She seemed smaller, younger, less intimidating. She gave me a warm smile and moved to the opposite side of the table from me, nearer to Maddy.

"This is Jim," Maddy said to her. "He's an old friend of mine."

"I know." The Queen produced a wry smile and offered her hand. I took it. It was cold, in spite of the heat that always seemed to permeate this place. It was perpetually summer in the Amazon Club. "You liked the act?" she said, as she withdrew her hand and sat down.

"Loved it."

She smiled. "My name's Rita, but everyone here calls me Hippie."

I said: "You aren't you know." For just an instant, she seemed angry, defensive.

"Aren't what?"

"Hippy."

She laughed then and relaxed. I ordered her a drink. "I suppose it's not the most flattering nickname. Maddy's the one who started it. I prefer Hippolyta."

"What's wrong with Rita?"

She looked up at the stage, at the blonde who was lolling, upside down, in a wooden chair. She didn't answer me.

"You're from California?"

"Yeah."

"What in hell made you come to Saginaw, Michigan of all places?"

"Yuri insisted. I really didn't want to come…here."

"Who's Yuri?"

"Oh, he owns all the Amazon Clubs. There are over a hundred, you know, across the country. Anyway, I was working at the club in L.A. and he wanted me to kind of 'revitalize' this place. It's been losing money." I looked over at Maddy. She was studying her drink. "I go to Detroit in a couple of days, then to Miami. I'm kind of on tour, you know? Maddy's coming back to L.A. with me in the fall to do a film, aren't you Sugar?" She brushed a strand of hair from Maddy's face and winked at her. "We're pretty good together, Maddy and me. We'll be even better on film. Did you know Maddy was going to be in a film?"

"I heard," I said.

I thought the dragon eyes were blue before, but it must have been the lights. They looked gray now, or maybe green. The long lashes I'd assumed to be artificial were, apparently, her own. She really was a remarkable beauty.

"There must be three hundred people in here," Maddy said, looking around, "and on a week night too. Last weekend there was standing room only. Can you believe it, Jimmy?"

The blonde was on the floor now, in front of the business-men, who were joyfully adorning her g-string with dollar bills. "That's great Mad," I said. I turned my attention back to Rita. "Who's going to be Hippolyta when you leave?"

She sipped her bourbon. "Yuri's sending over another girl from a club in Chicago. I think she'll be the permanent one here, at least for awhile. She could see Maddy's dejection. "It doesn't matter who the Queen is anyway. The act isn't anything without the slave girl. Maddy's the real star."

Maddy beamed. "You think so?" Maddy was at least eight to ten years older than Rita, but the latter was unquestionably in charge.

"No doubt, Sugar. You've got the best ass and legs in the business. You're a good actress too, that's why I want you to go back to L.A. with me. Yuri knows some Hollywood people. You never know." Rita turned to me. "She's straight, you know, but you'd never guess it when she's on stage."

She knew, of course, that when she was performing no one paid attention to the 'slave girl', but it was a kind ruse and Maddy swallowed it. Maddy wasn't the sharpest knife in the drawer.

Rita finished her drink and whatever evaluation of me she'd had in mind. She stood up. "Gotta go," she said. "I'm meeting a friend back at the Holiday Inn. Nice to meet you, Jim."

"The pleasure was all mine," I said, and she was gone.

Maddy wanted me to go back to her apartment with her and indeed that had been, I'd thought, my reason for coming to the Amazon in the first place. But now I was overwhelmed with an in-tense desire to be gone, as if I'd accomplished what I came for and now was supposed to be somewhere else. It's hard to describe, but I felt *satisfied*, I guess, even sated—though my appetite for Maddy, especially after that dance, was very much intact.

I begged off with some poor excuse that Maddy saw through in a second, but she didn't push it. She was half in the bag anyway.

I like to think that I kept my promise to God that night, but I really didn't have much to do with it. It kept itself.

On the way back to my apartment, I passed St. Luke's and counted the rows of windows to the fifth floor. I wondered if Meg felt the child inside her. Did she feel the cancer spreading? Did she really believe that her strange, remarkable husband would meet God's deadline? Was she even sure that God was talking to him, that it wasn't some kind of ESP he'd picked up from a bolt in the brain? It wasn't much to bet your life on. But Larry Ladon *had* come to us, and for the first time, I felt guided, on course. I'd always believed that I was a bit player in the story of my own life. I'd always seen the loveliness of life, the beauty of its composition, but I couldn't ever create it for myself. My artistic inclination always devolved into puns. Like the dead Beethoven, I'd been decomposing for years. I believed a lot of things, but I'd never really *known* the truth of anything. I sensed that all of that was changing.

At the top of the hill, a couple of blocks from home, there was a large church. It was a massive concrete structure, resembling a mausoleum more than a place of worship. I'd passed it many times before, only really noticing it now. The bold black letters across the front could still be seen by the pale light of the summer moon: WORDS OF HOPE CHAPEL.

On a yellow marquee, on the lawn in front, a message illuminated the paved entrance. Moths flickered about it, drawn to this small light out of the universal darkness.

NO MASK WILL HIDE YOUR SINS FROM GOD

This, I thought, is where religion has always failed. Christ came to teach us, but we always get it wrong. Something always gets in the way. The Church has held out hope so many times, then crushed believers' hearts with a hammer of condemnation. God was starting over—again. Herk was the new voice. Maybe not the only correct one, but the new one. Where would it all go? I know I was beginning to believe in Time—maybe even eternity.

I was glad to be away from Maddy and the Amazon Queen and the sad, useless idolatry of the physical.

I was brushing my teeth when I realized it, when that sense of familiarity overwhelmed me. God *had* led me. Rusha Ladon had come home.

Chapter ten

I stopped in to see Meg the following day after punching out. She was too drugged to know I was there. I headed out to Horizon Road to meet with Herk.

As always, there were many people around. Several of them were talking and laughing in the kitchen, but most were outside working on the barn-church. My brother and I had the former chapel to ourselves—a rarity. Herk and Meg's home was beginning, more and more, to resemble one of those hippie communes from the sixties—minus the teepees and the LSD.

It was terribly hot, even for July. Temperatures had soared between ninety and ninety-five and stayed there all week. The matching humidity made it difficult to stay dry and clean.

Herk and I had always hated the heat, which we both defined as any temperature in excess of seventy-five degrees. We could never understand why so many older people moved to Florida and Arizona to retire. Herk once quipped that they were probably all atheists and were likely trying to get accustomed to hell. Even the extremes of January were preferable to these awful dog days. It was worth a Michigan winter to have those few, cool, clear weeks of autumn when you were comfortable all the time and the sun was a friend.

"Are you sure it was her?" Herk said, over the obnoxious but necessary whirring of a fan.

"No, I'm not," I told him, "but when I saw her, I had this sense of recognition. Later on, back at home, it sort of came to me. I remembered her from high school, especially her eyes. They're weird, Herk. Cold. They always seem to be changing color."

"She wasn't at her mother's funeral," Herk said, "and she was right here in town?"

"She probably wasn't aware of it. How would you know she wasn't there anyway? Did you go?"

"Yes."

"It was at St. Luke's?"

"I didn't go to the church, just the interment, at the cemetery, to support Larry."

"That must have been fun."

He wiped the sweat off his expanding forehead and shook the moisture away in a gesture of disgust. "I remembered her sister, Hester. I had asked her to the prom when we were both seniors in high school. Her parents wouldn't let her date—me or anyone else. It was mostly her mother though. I suspect that Larry didn't make too many decisions in that household. Mom didn't want me to date Hester either. When I told her what I had in mind, she fussed and fumed about it for days. She wouldn't leave me alone about it until I finally told her that the Ladons wouldn't allow it. She never objected that vehemently to any of the other girls I dated—not more than usual anyway. I think she must have really hated the Ladons."

"Ironic isn't it?" I said.

"What do you mean?"

"That she's so cozy with Larry now."

"I suppose so, yes." He got up and adjusted the fan a bit, so that it was aimed more directly at us. "Did Rusha ever date anyone in high school?"

"I think the 'no dating of the Ladon girls rule' had been pretty well established by then. The second girl, Becky I think her name was, was pretty plain. No one was interested in her, so there wasn't much of a problem there. But Rusha was damn beautiful. I remember she was taller than most of the guys. She wore frumpy, baggy clothes, but you could still see that she had a terrific body. *That* couldn't have been disguised if she'd worn a tent."

"But she didn't date either?"

"Not that I knew of. There were rumors that she got around, but I never saw her with anyone—not even the other girls. She was kind of a loner."

"She's a blonde?"

"She was—in high school."

"Not now?"

"Not if she's this Rita person. *Her* hair is jet-black, so black that it looks like it's dyed, you know? It looks unnatural."

"I don't think it's her," Herk said.

I was baffled, disappointed and angry. I'd told him where I had been led, and he wouldn't accept it. 'We're all God's children', Herk had said in his most recent sermon, but apparently He only conversed with one of us. I'd accomplished nothing. My visit to the Amazon Club had been futile, without purpose. God had no intention of acting through me and I'd missed my chance to have some fun. "Look," I said. "She told me she had come here from Los Angeles. The announcer at the club said it too. That's where Larry said Rusha's last letter was mailed from, and when I asked her why she'd come to Saginaw, she hesitated. I think she was going to say 'back here' or 'back to Saginaw', like she'd been here before. I keep replaying it. She's got those strange eyes like Rusha had. I think it's her."

"You think who's who?" Ginny entered the room. Larry Ladon was right behind her. I'd never seen our mother look so attractive, so happy. She radiated joy, like a young bride. Her hair was no longer in a bun, but lounged around her neck and shoulders in hedonistic freedom. Her face had lost its pinched look, as if releasing her hair had loosened her face as well. Larry Ladon seemed pretty contented too. I remember thinking that he might have been a pretty handsome man thirty years ago. At any rate, the aging process, in both of them, appeared to have run into a brick wall and shifted sharply into reverse.

"Who're you two talking about?" Ginny repeated. Larry seemed interested as well and I knew Ginny wouldn't let it pass. She'd always been one of those people that you're forced to lie to. It was up to me to formulate the falsehood. It was one area where I had the edge on my brother. "We were trying to decide who the actress was in *Butch Cassidy and the Sundance Kid*," I said. "I'm pretty sure it was Natalie Wood, but Herk thinks it was Ali McGraw."

"You're both wrong," Larry Ladon said. "It was Katherine Ross."

"You're sure?"

"Positive." Larry said.

I looked over at Herk. "Never thought I'd see the day," I said, "when my brother was as wrong as I was." He was struggling not to laugh.

"Anyway," Ginny said, "Larry and I are going to run up to see Meg, Darling."

Neither of us had any doubt as to whom she was addressing. "All right, Mom," Herk replied. "Give her my love will you, and tell her I'll see her in the morning."

"Of course, Dear. Bye Jimmy."

I'd turned my back to her, but I waved a hand to signal my farewell. I could read Ginny's disappointment on Herk's face. "You could have been more pleasant," he said, after they were gone.

"I could've been born the 'darling' or the 'dear', but I wasn't. We all have our crosses, Brother."

I lit a cigarette and looked about for an ashtray. Herk got up from his chair and found one on the television. As far as I knew, holding ashtrays was its primary function. I don't think it had been switched on since the bowl games over six months ago. I wondered if it even worked anymore. He gave me the ashtray and limped back to his chair.

"You think the old girl's sleeping with him?"

"Mom and Larry? They're *friends*, Jim. Judas Priest!"

The juxtaposing of the name of Iscariot the traitor and the title of Caiaphas, his patron, was about as strong a weapon as my brother carried in his limited arsenal of epithets—an indicator that a return to the subject at hand would be in order.

"Okay, I'm sorry. Now, what do we do about Rita Whoever-She-Is? If she isn't Rusha Ladon, then my trip to the Amazon Club was a waste."

"Was it?" When my brother stared at me, as he was then, I always felt like a lab rat who was getting dumber—Algernon at the end of the play.

"Yes."

"Your interest was entirely centered on this, uh, Rita?"

"Once I got there, yeah. I didn't know she was going to be there, Herk."

"Then why did you go?"

I put out my cigarette and lit another. My stomach grumbled from neglect, but it was too hot to eat. It felt like the temperature was actually *rising* with the setting sun.

"To see a friend of mine," I explained, "a woman named Maddy."

"A stripper?"

"The former Hippolyta."

"Oh. You just went there to visit?"

"No. I was looking to get laid. That what you wanted to hear?"

"I want to hear the truth." Suddenly, Herk's face twisted in pain. He raised his hand and pressed two fingers against the left side of his head, just above the temple, where the bolt had gone in. He reacted as if he'd been shot a second time. He looked surprised, as the color drained from his cheeks. He slumped forward, emitting a long moan that frightened me.

"*Herk!*" I yelled, reaching out to prevent him from pitching headlong onto the floor. "You okay?"

He managed to pull himself back. He rested his elbows on his knees and folded his hands together, the white scars on them especially noticeable against his tanned skin. "I'm okay," he said, speaking to the floor. "Just a bad headache." Beads of sweat dripped on the worn carpet.

"Headache my ass," I said.

"It happens like this," he whispered.

"What happens?"

"The voice of God."

"Your hear it now? Because I can't hear it, Herk. You said it wasn't in your head. You said you could hear it out loud."

"Be still." He looked beyond me to another place where he saw nothing—or everything. His hands gripped mine hard enough to interrupt blood circulation. The fierce look of pain on his thin face melted into euphoria. He quit perspiring. His lips quivered. He smiled. His eyes were wide, unmoving, full of light—wild, yet strangely *absent*. I'd seen that look only one other time in my life, in the eyes of a guy named Jeremiah, just before he died in the wet mud of the Mekong Delta.

My brother's hands loosened, his eyes focused again. He let me go.

"Herk? You okay?"

"Yes. Did you hear Him, Jim? Did you?"

I could see that he wanted very much for me to say that I had—not because he needed affirmation, but because he wanted me to share the experience.

"No, brother, I didn't."

"I heard His voice, Jim. It was all around us."

"No, Herk. It was just you. I didn't hear it. No one came running from the kitchen. It was inside your head."

"But it was real."

I shrugged.

"It *was* real, Jim." He pressed his fingers against his head again. The gesture reminded me of a sports commentator having trouble with his earphone.

"You kept your promise," he said. That, of course, was the proof. "I don't know what the promise was, but He knows you kept it. Does that make sense to you?"

I must have nodded or said yes. I don't remember. Every time I tried to walk away, I got yanked back again. I was not to be allowed the liberty of unbelief.

There was more. "Rita *is* Rusha. I didn't think so before, because I was sure that we had to travel somewhere to find her. But Rusha is only going to tell us how to find the fourth person. *That* will be our journey."

I got angry. I don't know why. Maybe it was because God, even God, favored my brother over me. I *sensed* guidance. Herk got it first hand. "Why all this bullshit, Herk? Why all the rigmarole? Why do we have to play this *game*? Why doesn't God just save Meg? Better yet, why let her get cancer in the first place? Huh? Why not just reveal it all and leave us alone! Shit! I need a drink." I got up and went to the door. Then Herk's hand was on my shoulder and I knew I wasn't going anywhere.

I turned around and looked up at him. Even at six feet, I had to look up.

"If we didn't have to make choices, Jim, we'd be nothing more than rats on a pile of garbage."

I shook him away, but I went back to my chair. I lit a cigarette. "I feel like a pawn," I said.

"You're not." Herk's voice was soft, calming. "God set up the board, created each figure, gave them their own importance, set the rules—but, unlike the pawns on a chessboard, *we* make the moves. There are a million variations, but we *choose!*"

"Why even *have* the game?"

He sat down and put a scarred hand on my knee. "God's a creator, Jim. Do you think a writer would construct a great novel, and then put it in a drawer? Did Beethoven hide his symphonies? Creators want to see how their creations work. So they give them to the world and they say 'test it, go ahead, tear it apart, study it, choose how you want to use it, but the glory is mine because I made it. Now, you have to remember me. Now...I'm not alone.'"

"That doesn't explain it all."

"Of course not. We're meant to wonder."

A third voice, decidedly not God's, interrupted us. "Excuse me, Pastor Gudsen, but supper's ready," she said. She was standing in the archway that separated the living room from the kitchen. She smiled pleasantly at me, wiping her hands on an apron fastened around her slim waist. "I have orders from Virginia. She told me I'm to make sure you eat," she said to Herk, although her eyes were on me. "She says you're getting too thin."

"We'll be there in a minute," Herk said. She smiled at me again, then turned and went back into the kitchen.

I watched her retreat, enjoying the full hips and long, shapely legs that the apron had partially obscured. I'd never heard anyone refer to Ginny by her given name before. The 'too thin' remark sparked a recognition. "Is that Minnie Tower?" I said to Herk, more for confirmation than information.

"Yes. She joined us on Monday. Beautiful girl, isn't she?"

"She sure doesn't look like Twiggy anymore."

Herk laughed. "I guess not."

"She's married, right? You did the ceremony."

"She was. She just got her brace off a week ago."

"Brace? What kind of brace?"

"Her ex-husband broke her jaw."

"Sounds like a swell fellow."

"She seems to like you."

"What do you mean?"

"Well she never looked at *me*, not even when she was talking to me. I doubt she was admiring the furniture."

"Get thee behind me Satan," I said.

Herk laughed. "First time I've ever been called *that*. Don't tell the LCMS, they might believe you." He stood up and patted his stomach, what little there was of it. "I *am* getting pretty hungry."

I followed. Outside I saw the workers gathering around the forty-foot long table they'd built out of old doors to accommodate everyone. It was spread out under the giant oak in the yard. Long, homemade benches bordered either side. But for the clothes and the absence of Indians, (Auggie Two-River excepted), it might have been the Plymouth puritans settling down to a Thanksgiving feast. As we went through the kitchen, Minnie Tower was heading for the screen door that led to the yard, struggling with a large platter, piled high with fried chicken. I opened the door for her. She flashed another smile at me, then hurried down the porch steps and across the shaded yard. Suddenly, I understood what Wordsworth meant when he said his heart 'leapt up'. It was the first time any woman had caused that sensation in any part of me other than my penis.

I started to go after her, but a feminine voice behind me called my name. I turned around. It was Robin Stym. "Phone for you, Jim," he said and held it out to me.

"They say who they were?"

"No. It's a woman, though, I think."

Sammy Epstein drew Robin's attention. "Binnie," he shouted, "can you *please* help me with these mashed potatoes, dear?"

The phone had one of those long cords on it and I found a quiet corner.

"This is Jim."

"Oh Jimmy, I'm so glad I got hold of you. I tried to call your apartment, but there was no answer. I looked up the only other Gudsen in the book. Hiram or something."

"Herkimer. He's my brother." I recognized Maddy's voice. She sounded unstable, panicky.

"What's wrong, Mad?"

"They've closed the club, can you believe it? I've been arrested!"

"Who closed it?"

"The police! Who else? They came in, kicked all the customers out and arrested Lance and Atlas and all the girls." I could hear the commotion of mixed voices in the background and that slight echoing that stone walls produce. "I'm scared shitless, Jimmy. They're treating us like we're *criminals* or something. I never hurt nobody in my life! I haven't done nothing. What's the matter with them?"

"I don't know, Mad. There are obscenity laws. Some zealous politicians probably decided to enforce..."

"Obscenity? Do you think what I do is obscene?"

"I didn't have you arrested, Mad."

"I'm a *dancer*," she shouted, "an *artist!*"

"Calm down, Mad." She was beginning to sound hysterical. "Do you have bail money?"

"Lance is working it out. He says he'll have us out of here in a couple of hours, but I think they're going to shut us down for good. I don't know what I'm going to do Jimmy, dancing is all I know."

"What do you want me to do?" I saw Minnie come back through the screen door with her empty platter. She didn't see me.

"I'm worried about Rita. They raided the club at about six. She doesn't come in until nine. I'm afraid she'll get arrested too if she tries to come to work."

"I don't think they'd hang around, Mad. They have to catch you in the act. They wouldn't even know who she is."

"I know it sounds silly, Jimmy, but I'm worried. Would you go over to her motel and tell her what's happened, just so she doesn't get all pissed off or scared? She's over at the Holiday Inn by the expressway. I'd consider it a huge favor." Her voice took on a kind of little girl coyness. "You know how *grateful* I can be." I was watching Minnie as she held out her platter and Isabelle Goetsh slowly heaped chicken on it.

"I'll take care of it, Mad. You okay?"

"I'll be all right. Atlas is here too. He isn't letting anyone look at us cross-eyed. You know what a sweet man he is."

I remembered the six-foot drunk with his feet dangling in the air. "You're in good hands."

"You'll see Rita then?"

"I will."

"Tell her to call the other late shift girls too, will ya? Charisse and Roxanne, oh, and Cherry too. She'll know."

"Okay."

"You're an angel, Jimmy. I'll call you in a coupla days to let you know about the club. They took down the names of all the customers. Even if we open again, they'll be scared to come back. Can you believe it? In *America*, for God's sake!"

Maddy didn't know that in Europe they'd gotten over trying to enforce the Old Testament a half-century ago.

"I gotta go," she said. "There's a long line. Love ya Babe."

I hung up the phone and headed out to the yard to let Herk know where I was going. I thought he might want to come along. Minnie was at the door again and she smiled at me. "You seem to be at the right place at the right time for me," she quipped. I didn't understand then, and nor did she, how appropriate that remark was.

"Always happy to assist a beautiful woman," I said.

She blushed. I felt that leaping sensation. The door banged behind us, a sound heard hundreds of times a day at the manse. We stood on the porch. "Can I take that for you?" I said, indicating the platter of chicken. Why did I feel like I was in the third grade again?

"I've got it," she said. She lowered her eyes for a moment, then looked up at me again. "I'm Minnie."

"I know." Brilliant repartee, James, brilliant.

"You're Jim Gudsen. We went to school together. I had a crush on you and you didn't know I was alive." She laughed.

I'm surprised I didn't say 'I know.'

"Bethany Meyers got most of your attention as I recall."

"I was more concerned with quantity than quality then." Another superlative witticism. Was there no limit? I was on a roll. What I meant, of course, was that I'd dated many girls—none of them as extraordinary as her, but as soon as it was out of my mouth, I realized that the former 'Skinny Minnie' might have thought I was comparing her directly to Busty Bethany. "Listen," I said, trying to correct myself. When in hell did I become so fumble-tongued? "What I meant was—"

"I know what you meant," she said. Her smile indicated that she really did.

"Do you mind if I call you sometime? Maybe we could go out for dinner or something."

"I'm divorced. Did you know that?"

"Yes."

"Does it make a difference?"

"No."

"I live with my parents. Ben Tower is my father." She pointed toward the table where he was sitting, talking with Auggie Two-River. "He's in the book," she said.

"Okay."

She smiled again. I swallowed, forcing my heart back into its cool, dark cave as I watched Minnie hurry across the lawn.

Herk had just finished the table prayers and, amid the clatter of dishes and boisterous conversation, I pulled him aside and told him about Maddy's call. I asked him if he wanted to go with me.

"You handle it," he said.

"You want me to tell her we know who she is? *Do* we know?"

"You handle it, Jim."

"You trust me here?"

"God does."

As I turned to go, he grabbed my arm. "I do too," he said.

It was getting close to eight by the time I reached the Holiday Inn, and I was afraid Rita might have left for the Amazon Club already. It took me a while to find her room because I didn't know what last name she was going by. It turned out to be a very unoriginal 'Smith'. I only knocked once before she answered the door. She was obviously on her way out.

"Well, hello," she said. "I was just leaving to go to work. If you want to hook up later—"

"You can't go to work." I told her about Maddy's phone call and the closing of the club. She didn't appear to be too concerned.

"C'mon in," she said. "I guess we have some time after all." She looked me up and down, appraising. Apparently, I passed. "Would you like a drink? All I have is bourbon."

I sat in a chair next to the air conditioner. It was wonderfully cool in the room and free of the awful humidity—an artificial autumn.

"No thanks."

She filled one glass and sat down on the edge of the bed. She was wearing a black leather mini skirt and black nylons with some sort of elaborate pattern in them. She smiled as she crossed her legs, knowing they had drawn my attention. I looked up, realizing I'd been caught, and was immediately captured by her eyes. It was very difficult not to look at her. She dominated the room.

"Maddy wants you to call the other girls on the late shift," I said.

"Okay." She pulled a little notebook out of her purse that, apparently, contained the numbers. She talked to two of them while I browsed through the only reading material around, a TV Guide. Cherry had already left for the club. "Hope she doesn't get too spaced about it," Rita said after hanging up. "This kind of thing happen often around here?"

I told her I didn't know.

"California's a little more enlightened," she said.

"You lived there long?"

"I was born there." The answer came too readily, too rehearsed. I was going to try to call her on it, but a person will give in on a point when he's not sure, and defend it to the death if he *knows* he's wrong. "I guess I'd better be going," I said, pretty convinced that Herk knew when to come along and when to stay away.

She put her drink down and stood in front of the short hallway that led to the door, effectively blocking my exit. "What's your hurry?" she said. "This may be the last time we get to see each other. With the club closed, I'm probably going to leave for Detroit tomorrow, but we could have a little fun tonight."

She stepped forward and slid her arms around my neck. With her heels on, we were about at eye level, giving her a decided advantage. I think one of the things that was so remarkable about her eyes, besides their indefinable color, the long lashes and their coldness, was that they always appeared to be half-closed, as if she were in a swoon. They looked closed as she brought her face close to mine, but I'm pretty sure they weren't.

We were locked in a drenching kiss before I knew what I was doing. I pulled away and buried my face in her neck, trying to find a way to hold together. I remember now the scent of apples and my hands fumbling with the buttons on her blouse as she struggled with my belt.

I knew the only way that I could break this off would be to make her do it for me. I moved my mouth to her ear. "Rusha," I whispered. She pushed against my chest and stepped back. Somehow, I didn't feel at all clever.

"What? What did you call me?"

"Rusha. You're Rusha Ladon."

"What the fuck are you talking about?" I wasn't sure, of course. I was mostly *not* sure. If this next thing didn't work, I was really going to feel foolish and the evening would likely end with a broken promise. "I recognize you," I said, still trying to catch my breath. I laughed. "We went to school together at Saginaw High."

She relaxed a little. "You remember me?" That was the first time that I was sure that Rita Smith a.k.a. Hippolyta a.k.a. The Queen of the Amazons, was Rusha Ladon.

"You're not easy to forget, though the dark hair threw me for awhile."

She smiled. "I remember you too. Some girl used to rant on in the showers after gym class about what a big cock Jim Gudsen had. Becky or Betsy or something."

"Bethany?"

"That sounds like it, yeah. Dumb as a box of rocks."

I laughed. "You sound like you didn't like her."

"I call it the way I see it." She began to unbutton her blouse and I knew the crisis hadn't passed. "Did *she*?"

"Did she what?"

"Bethany. Did *she* call it the way she saw it?" I felt her hand on my groin. I was beginning to wander around somewhere under those long lashes, getting lost in the smoky breath of the dragon.

"M-m-m-m, I guess so," she whispered.

To this day, I don't know where the words came from or why I said them. I believe now, that Minnie had something to do with it. Anyway, my promise just kept on keeping itself. "Your father wants you to come home," is what I said.

Rusha pulled away as if I'd struck her. "My father!"

"He saw you in a magazine someone sent him. It crushed him, Rusha. It tore him apart. He wants you back, to come home."

"Jesus!"

"He just wants to talk to you."

"He sent you?"

"No. He doesn't know you're here, in Michigan. He doesn't know about any of this."

Tears were melting her mascara and dark rivulets ran from her eyes. It was the first time, I think, that I'd seen them wide open. They were no longer cold. They were full of passion, of dragon rage. "Fuck you and fuck him!" she yelled. "Get the fuck outta here!" She began pushing me toward the door. I let myself be shoved against it so it couldn't be opened. "Get out, you *asshole!*" She swung at me and struck a glancing blow off the side of my head. It stunned me momentarily. I recovered just in time enough to interrupt Rusha's knee from colliding with the object of Bethany Meyers' admiration.

I curled both arms around her waist, buried my face in the apple smell of her bosom, (more for protection than eroticism), and lifted her off the floor. I carried her to the bed, her arms and legs flailing, fell on top of her, and pinned her arms.

"Get off me you motherfucker!" she screamed, and spit in my face.

'You handle it, Jim', Herk had said. Right. I could see now why he hadn't wanted any part of this.

"Listen, Rusha. *Will you just listen for a minute!*" I yelled. "*Hear me out, and I'll leave!*"

She seemed to calm a bit then, but I continued to hold her upper limbs, having gained a new appreciation as to why certain weapons of destruction were called 'arms'.

"I won't see them," she said. "Have your say, then go fuck yourself."

"Not *them*. Just your father."

She laughed. "That old bitch wouldn't let him take a piss without her permission."

"She doesn't know about this. She's dead Rusha. She died a few days ago."

She stopped struggling. She stared at me. Her body relaxed. I released my grip and stood up, waiting for the renewed assault that never came. She sat up slowly and leaned against the wall. "She's dead?" she said. The ferocity had left her voice.

I proceeded to tell her, as succinctly as I could, about what had happened—about my brother's struggle with her father, about the new church, about his vision, about Larry's conversion, about my involvement. She listened intently, stopping me occasionally to ask a question. When I finished, she went into the bathroom and washed her face. She looked very different without the heavy make-up, better I think. She hadn't shed a tear.

I spent the next two hours listening. I hadn't asked her to tell me anything about her past, but once she began, I was too appalled to even think about interrupting. Mrs. Ladon did have a first name—it was Monster. Rusha told me such gruesome stories about her mother that I actually began to be glad that Ginny was mine. At the age of eight, Rusha had been tied to an apple tree in the Ladon orchard and left there all night, gagged so she wouldn't yell, for vomiting on the living room carpet. She had been sick, she said, because her mother had forced her to eat a quart of strawberries that she had forgotten to put in the refrigerator. The berries had gone bad and she was being punished for her 'wastefulness'. She had nearly died when the gag had caused her to smother in her vomit. At thirteen, when Rusha left traces of menstrual blood on her sheets, Mrs. Ladon pushed her face into it, and forced her to clean it off with her tongue. There were too many stories that filled that two hours—enough to compose a lifetime of nightmares.

The abuse always happened when her father was away— gone to California, to negotiate the purchase of more apple trees or to visit some buyer, or to Elder's meetings at St. Luke's.

Rusha said she could never tell him because she was never alone with him, and if he suspected, he never let on. It got worse after the older girls were gone. Rusha became the lone target. She was never sure if Hester, the oldest daughter, had ever been abused at all, but she knew that Rebecca had, and once Rebecca left for college, Rusha bore the brunt of her mother's perverse and sadistic temperament.

"When I got to high school," she said, "when I got big enough to defend myself, it got a little better. But if dad was gone overnight, I laid awake in my room until dawn, afraid that she'd murder me in my sleep. I couldn't be vulnerable. I wouldn't eat any food she prepared for fear that it was poisoned. I took a wooden chair into the bathroom after I saw the movie *Psycho*. I wedged it under the doorknob so I could feel safe while I took a shower."

I wanted to say something, like 'I'm sorry', but it hadn't been me who had done those things to her. It seemed like *someone* should, just because of the terrible *wrongness* of it. But you can't apologize for another person. You certainly can't apologize for a monster. There is too much of *self* in monsters. Hell is not paved with good intentions—it's paved with excuses.

"The day after graduation, I lit out. I did what I had to do. I'm still alive." She said that with the same pride that a scholar might have in making it through Harvard or an athlete would feel when winning an Olympic medal. For Rusha, having been raised by a demon who never missed a church service, mere survival was just such an accomplishment.

"Maybe now would be the time to talk to your dad," I suggested, "to tell him what you went through."

"She must have been sick," Rusha said. "She *had* to have been. Why didn't he get her to a doctor? Why did he do whatever she said? Why didn't he *see?*"

"You could ask him. You could get it out in the open. You could, maybe, have *one* parent back. He's very different now, Rusha, and I know he loves you."

"I won't ever see her again. She's gone..." She was looking beyond me, at some other face. "I wanted to kill her so many times. She can't get to me anymore."

"Never again."

"Where is he? At the house?"

I looked at my watch. It was after ten. "He could still be at my brother's place. He hangs around there a lot."

"Why?"

"I told you, he's part of the new church. He's a close friend to my brother now. Besides...."

"What?"

"He's pretty interested in Ginny."

"Who's Ginny? You mean he's got another woman?"

"I think you might like her, most people do."

"But not you?"

"She's *my* mother."

Rusha Ladon took another shot of bourbon, directly from the bottle. Then she laughed. "Well, fuck me."

"I almost did."

She kissed my cheek. "It would have happened if you hadn't pissed me off." She straightened my hair. "I didn't mean to hurt you."

"I'm okay."

"You could've just fucked me and said good-bye. I would've never known. Why didn't you?"

"I wanted to, believe me. I still do—but I'm keeping a promise."

"To my father?"

"He doesn't know I'm here. He doesn't know *you're* here."

"To who, then?"

"To mine."

She looked puzzled, but she didn't pursue it.

Ten minutes later, in the old Chrysler, we turned onto Horizon Road.

Chapter eleven

W hen we pulled up under the oak tree, Larry Ladon's car was still there. I started to get out.

"Wait," she said. "Can we just sit here for a minute?"

"Okay."

The air conditioner in the Chrysler had never worked, so the windows were down. The night breeze drifting across the field made whispering sounds in the cornstalks like intruders in a rich man's house. The heat of the day lingered in spite of it. Rusha absently examined some of my eight-track tapes while she smoked a cigarette. She looked very different than she had a few hours earlier. She was wearing jeans, tennis shoes, and a light sweatshirt that was a couple of sizes too big.

"Were you really born in California?" I asked.

"No."

"You're good."

"A good liar, you mean?"

"Yes."

"You tell it enough, it comes natural."

"Rusha."

"Yeah?"

"I'm really sorry you had to go through all that."

"Thanks." She put her hand on my knee and gave me a weak smile. "Me too." I really wanted her to move that hand a little farther north, or just take it away, but I didn't tell her that.

"What are you going to say?"

"I don't know yet. I guess I'll play it by ear. You're sure *she's* not in there?" She pointed at the house. "You're not playing some trick on me?"

"No. We can leave right now if you want to." I don't know why I said that, except that I was pretty sure she wouldn't go. She didn't answer me. She was biting her fingernails, which, I could see, had been chewed almost to the cuticles. She must have worn fake ones for her act. I remembered her hand, with long, red fingernails, sliding sinuously across Maddy's bosom. I couldn't figure out how this insecure and frightened little girl could be the Queen of the Amazons.

"You want me to go in first—kind of break the ice?" I recalled using that expression in a conversation in Vietnam with a guy named Jeremiah. He was the guy I left behind in the red mud of the Mekong. He hadn't understood it, had never heard it before. He was from the South. Apparently, it was a Great Lakes metaphor.

Rusha pulled up on the door handle. "No," she said, "let's just go in and get it over with before I lose my nerve."

We crossed the yard and entered the kitchen—now dark and quiet. Mounds of drying pots and pans littered the counter. I was careful not to let the screen door slam. I thought of Minnie. "Wait here," I whispered

Ginny and Larry were sitting on the sofa. Herk was in the old chair across from them where I normally sat.

"Jim!" Herk said, standing up. He was always the first to notice anything. "We've got some great news—"

I ignored him. "Larry," I began. He turned toward me, smiling.

Then Rusha stepped through the dark archway and into the light.

At first, there was still just the pleasant smile of sociability on Larry's round face—a preparation for introduction. I think the black hair threw him off, but only for a second. The artificial pleasantness quickly evaporated and was replaced by an expression that was amazement, reverence, terror, wonder—all the ingredients of awe you'd see in the face of the true believer facing the unbelievable.

"Rusha?" He whispered the word in the same way that a timid student might respond to his teacher's question when he had no idea what the right answer might be.

He stood up. Ginny stood with him, as much, I think, for physical support as moral. He had turned deadly pale and looked as though he might collapse. If he had died just then, it would have been from happiness. The fear was gone, driven away by an all-encompassing euphoria.

"Rusha," he said again as if by speaking her name he could accept her reality. This time, however, the name was spoken confidently, loudly. It wasn't a question.

"Hi, Daddy," she said. It sounded strange, like she'd just returned from summer camp.

"My baby, my Rusha," he mumbled, and then he came apart in wrenching, pitiable sobs. He cried, I think, because he'd become accustomed to sorrow. It's always difficult to say good-bye to something with which you have been intimate, even if it's cruel. When he covered his face, I could see how badly his hands were trembling. The lamplight glittered off his diamond ring.

Rusha stepped forward and embraced him. He was shorter than his daughter was. He laid his head on her shoulder. He gripped her around her slim waist, hanging on with the passion of the damned, reprieved at God's feet.

Rusha laid the side of her face against the top of her father's large head. She had her arms around him too, and she gently rubbed his back as if she could physically smooth away the terrible sobs, like the wrinkles in his shirt. "Sh-h-h," she whispered. "It's okay, Daddy. It's okay."

It was hard for me to remember that Larry Ladon had ever been an arrogant, self-righteous son of a bitch, but the picture was still there—Mr. and Monster Ladon, sitting in the back pew, singing *A Mighty Fortress is Our God.*

Herk looked at me and smiled. I *had* handled it. He'd known I would.

Ginny quietly excused herself to make a pot of coffee. On her way to the kitchen, she did a very curious thing. She passed Herkimer without even looking at him. She stopped next to me, tears running down her face, and peered directly into my eyes. She stood on her toes and kissed my cheek. "Thank you son," she whispered.

More than one prodigal came home that night.

I don't know how long they stood there, father and daughter, in that constricting embrace. It must have only been a few minutes, but it seemed more like an hour as Herk and I watched them like helpless voyeurs. We could have gone with Ginny, but I think we were both afraid that Larry Ladon might faint. His sobs were inhuman in their intensity and resonance—the exorcism of demonic pain. They argued for our continued superintendence.

Finally, Rusha was able to get her father to sit down, but he continued to hold on to her, perhaps afraid that she would vanish again. Visions, after all, have to be grasped in order to be retained.

She sat next to him, his arm through hers, wiping away tears from those strange eyes that had become definably blue, definitely warm.

Gradually, Larry Ladon began to collect the scattered pieces of his psyche. When Ginny returned with a mug of hot coffee, he flashed a grateful smile at her. Rusha took it from his quivering fingers and placed it on the table in front of them, the table that was always littered with everything *except* the beverage from which it drew its name.

Ginny handed mugs to the rest of us as well, then took her accustomed place next to Larry Ladon, on the side opposite from Rusha.

"How…how long have you been back?" Larry managed.

"A couple of weeks, Dad," she answered.

"Why? I mean what made you come to Saginaw?"

Rusha looked over at me.

"Only the truth," I said to her. "It's something you have to give if you want it back."

She nodded. "I came here to work for a couple of weeks. I hadn't planned to see you, Dad. I was going to Florida and then back to L.A."

"Work?"

"At the Amazon Club."

"The place they closed down today?" he said, hoping, I'm sure, that she meant something else. "Ginny and I, we heard it on the radio."

"That's it, yes. Jim told me it had been closed down as I was leaving to go to work. I was going to catch a flight to Miami tomorrow. Jim asked me to come here." Larry Ladon looked at me. He didn't say anything, but there was more than gratitude in his expression. Pride, I thought, maybe even affection. He didn't ask how I knew her.

He turned to Rusha and placed his hands on her cheeks. "My sweet girl," he said. His thumbs wiped away her tears. "I don't care about what you've done. I don't care about any of it. It doesn't matter. I just want you to come home. Can that happen, Sweetheart?"

"I need to know something, Dad."

"She's gone, Rusha," he said. "She's never coming back."

"Jim told me," she said. "I need to know the rest."

Larry turned away from her and let go. He folded his hands in his lap. He looked down at them enviously, perhaps wishing that he had, like them, no mouth to speak, no eyes to see, no soul.

"I *need* to know, Daddy," Rusha repeated.

"Maybe we should leave you two alone," I suggested.

"No," Ginny said.

I looked at Herk. He shrugged, but he didn't get up, so I stayed too.

Rusha ignored us. "Why did she do it, Daddy?"

"Did...did she hurt you, Baby?"

Rusha looked at him in disbelief. "Hurt me? She damn near *destroyed* me Dad! How could you let her?"

"I didn't know," he cried. Then he covered his face, trying to crawl into a space that was too small to hide in. "I didn't *want* to know."

Rusha's eyes had gone gray again. They'd gone cold. Dragon eyes. "Why did she do it?" Her voice was steady. There were no tears. "Why did she do it?"

"You…were my favorite." Larry spoke into his hands. "You were always my favorite. It wasn't you she hated, Rusha, it was *me!* She wanted to hurt what I loved." Ginny put her arm around his shoulders. I don't think he knew it was there. He pulled his face from his hands, but he just looked down at the carpet. "At first, I thought it wasn't so bad. She was strict with all of you girls, but Hester was okay. Becky was doing all right. I thought you'd be okay too. We'd just get through it. It would go away. God forgive me. She was crazy, I know. I see it now. I should have seen it then. But I couldn't challenge her. I *owed* her."

Rusha forced him to look at her. "What did you owe her, Dad? Why did she hate you?"

Larry tried to look away, but she wouldn't let him. He tried to form the words, but they wouldn't come. He just stared at her, at the gray, cold eyes of the dragon.

"Because he was in love with someone else," Ginny said.

I looked at my mother. Her mouth was set in that pinched determination that I knew so well. She must have been closer with Ladon than I'd supposed, for him to have shared *that* with her. I looked over at my brother. He was rapt in a slow dawning. I'd have to wait until high noon.

"You mean you were cheating on mother?" Rusha said.

"At first, yes." Larry finally managed. "I was in love with another woman. I wanted to leave Theda, but Hester was just beginning to walk. I couldn't abandon her."

So, Mrs. Ladon *did* have a first name, Theda. Apparently this was no surprise to anyone but me.

"Theda was pregnant with Rebecca too," Larry continued. "The orchard was starting to turn a profit. I'd worked hard to build that business. Theda warned me that if I divorced her, she'd force

me to sell the orchard to get her share. I didn't have the money to
buy her out. I held a position of leadership at St. Luke's—that
would have been ruined too. I stayed with Theda for all the wrong
reasons, I know. I didn't love her. I cheated on her. She hated me
for it. Oh, what a mess I made of everything!"

"Dad. Look at me Dad!" Rusha forced his eyes to see hers.
"Why did you marry her in the *first place?*" She voiced the question
that I was sure everyone in the room was thinking.

"When she was young, your mother was a beautiful woman.
She came from a prominent family, a powerful family in the
church. Your grandfather had many business connections. He was
willing to loan me the money to buy the golden delicious trees
from California. At the time, it all seemed logical. Besides, I hadn't
met..." He stopped. We waited for him to go on. He didn't.

"Grandpa Sturm?" Rusha said. "The one who died of cancer
when I was little? He paid for the orchard?"

"You never knew his wife, your grandmother. She died before you were born. She died in Ypsilanti State Hospital."

"That's a hospital for the mentally ill?" I asked, knowing full
well that it was.

"Theda's father left us a large inheritance. I knew you girls
would be set for life."

"So you settled," Rusha said.

He touched her face, as one might touch the surface of an
original Van Gogh—partially in awe, partially to see if it was real.
It didn't change her eyes. "I tried to...I wanted to.... Yes, I settled."

Rusha nodded. "If you hated each other so much, how was I
conceived?"

He looked at the gray eyes. I think he began to believe that
no more damage could be done. "We...we hadn't been...intimate
for a long time. I came home one night..."

"From seeing your mistress?" The cold voice matched the
eyes.

"Yes. Theda was sitting on the porch in that old wicker chair
that she liked. There was a suitcase on the floor next to her. I

thought she was leaving me, that she was only waiting to say good-bye. She told me to put the suitcase in the car and she got in her-self. She told me to drive. I asked her where Hester and Rebecca were. She told me they were inside the house, with a sitter. She seemed too calm, too sure. I was afraid for the girls, but when I checked, the sitter *was* there. She was feeding Becky a bottle and Hester was watching cartoons on the television. I came back out and got in the car. I thought, *It's going to happen. She's going to leave me and we'll all be free.* I was sure I was taking her to the airport or the train station. I didn't want to ask any questions. I was afraid she might change her mind. She had me drive out to the old Motel Six, the one they tore down a few years ago to build the downtown access off Interstate 75. We stopped at the desk. She got a room. When I drove up to the door, she told me to get her suitcase and come in. When I asked her why, she said she was going to 'revive' our marriage. I told her I didn't want to."

Ginny had placed both her hands on his back, since he was facing away from her, toward the dragon. She didn't move her hands. They just lay there, as if she were holding him together.

"Go on," Rusha said.

"She took a gun out of her purse. It was an old gun. I think it had come from her father's collection, but I was sure that it worked. She told me we were going inside together or we were go-ing to die together in that car. I knew then that something had snapped inside her. We went in."

"Are you trying to tell me that I was conceived at gunpoint?" Rusha said, "but why? Why would she want *that* if she hated you so much?"

Larry sighed. I could see that the memory of it was crushing him, but after living with lies for so long, he wasn't going to make bad choices anymore—not even under duress.

"She held the gun at my head the whole time. I know it sounds ridiculous that a man could 'perform' under such threats, but she...she used her mouth, her hands, anything she could to – stimulate me. We finished. She waited awhile. She watched a movie. Then she forced it again. It went on all night. She told me that I was going to make her pregnant again, that my 'whore' was going to see that I still loved my wife."

"No wonder she hated me," Rusha said.

"When you were born, she refused to nurse you," Larry said. "You hadn't done what you were supposed to do. You hadn't brought us together. She wanted to name you Jezebel."

The cold dragon fell apart. Rusha cried. It's a hard thing to know that you were brought into the world for spite.

"But *I* loved you, Darling," Larry said. "I named you Rusha. I fed you your bottles of Similac. I changed your diapers. I bathed you. I saw you through the measles and the chicken pox and your first day of school. I *loved* you, as I do now. You were special to me because you were *only* mine, really…only mine." His voice died in the whirring of the fan.

Rusha looked at her father. I think she didn't know whether to embrace him or hit him. She did neither.

"As you grew older, Theda seemed to warm to you a bit, enough to help you with your clothes, make sure you brushed your teeth, got you through your first period."

"Yes," Rusha said, looking at me, "I remember *that*."

"It seemed okay for awhile. I knew you were becoming afraid of her, but she always denied that she ever hurt you. There were never any marks—"

"Not on the outside," Rusha corrected. "When did you break it off? With this other woman, I mean."

He turned and took Ginny's hand. I'd never seen her look so happy. For me, the sun was finally beginning to rise though it was still dark outside.

"Our mother?" I shouted. "You fucked *our mother?*" When Ginny didn't correct my language, I knew it was true. I looked at Herk. I wanted an ally in my outrage. He was silent, composed.

"Did you know about this?" I said to him.

"No."

"*This* is what drove our father away," I yelled. "It wasn't me at all, Mom—*it was you!*"

Ginny looked at me. "That's the first time you've called me mom since you were a little boy," she said. Her voice quivered, but she was getting tensed, coiled, *ready.*

"Where did you get the name?" Herk asked, in his usual whisper. He seemed calm, even relaxed.

Ginny smiled at him. She was uncoiling, happy to let the danger embrace her, even destroy her. It was high noon.

"Alex Gudsen was a character in a little book I read as a child. It's a Swedish name. It means 'good son,' at least that's what the writer said. It was appropriate—for *both* of my boys."

"What the hell are you talking about?" Rusha said.

Larry Ladon looked first at her, then at me. "Your father never went away, Jim. He's always been proud of you and Herkimer. He…I, love you both." He glanced back at Rusha.

"The silver cord is loosed…." Herk whispered. I had no idea what *that* meant.

"You're our *father?*" I remember saying to Larry Ladon. "But you fought us! You did everything you could to *hurt* my brother's ministry. You—"

Herk stood up. "God *used* him," he said to me, "to lead us to *this* ministry, to show us the way." He limped across the room and embraced Larry. He turned to me. "Jim," he said, "it's all happening the way it's supposed to happen."

"The way it's *supposed* to happen?" I was shouting, I think, I don't remember. "You mean we were *supposed* to grow up without a father, even though he only lived a few miles away? You mean Rusha was *supposed* to be abused by that old harpy? What kind of a god would orchestrate that shit?"

"It wasn't God who walked away from us, Jim. God didn't lift a hand against Rusha. We make our own choices."

"He could have interfered anytime. You, of all people, ought to know *that!* He could have made it different. He only butts in when He *wants* to."

"No, Jim. When He *needs* to, for our benefit, when we can't make the choice, when we can't keep the promise—or won't. Listen to you. You blame God for not having a father. Well, he's here

Jim, standing in front of you. Who do you blame for that? No one ever said *you* caused any of it, Brother, that it was your choice!" He glanced at Rusha. Her blue eyes warmed him. "God guided us to find our sister," he said, "but *you* made the choice to bring her here. *She* made the choice to come. That's how it works."

I was wrong. I guess I thought that growing up without a father, always feeling secondary to my brother, being lied to about who I was, somehow entitled me to a measure of vindictiveness.

Herk would have no part of it. To be fair to myself, he knew what was going on and I didn't. I'd almost been seduced by our sister, and he hadn't. But there would be no excuses with Herk—for himself, or anyone else. There would also be no recrimination. We would 'play the game out' as he put it, together. "We aren't rats on a trash heap," he said.

We talked through the night. There were more arguments, more accusations, but Herk would always steer us away from judgment.

When the first roseate haze of dawn lit the fields outside, we had all changed—forever. I had a father. Both Rusha and I had gained a mother—the same one. My sister and I would talk later, privately, of what had passed between us. We would even laugh about it—but we'd come perilously close, and we knew it. I guess God had needed to step in.

Rusha didn't leave for Detroit. She checked out of the Holiday Inn that afternoon and moved in with her father—with *our* father. She hated the house in the orchard. It housed too many ghosts. So, after a few days, she and Larry moved, with Ginny, into our old house in town. Turns out Larry owned it anyway. I would call him Larry for a long time, though Herk started calling him 'Dad' that same morning. Old habits, at least with me, die hard.

With Theda's death, Larry now had full possession of Ladon Orchards and the house. He signed the deeds over to the Gospel Church of Faith and Revelation.

The greatest miracle of that night went unmentioned until well after the sun began its heated assault on the summer world and I was dozing, nodding in my chair. Rusha was already asleep on the sofa and mom had gone to the bathroom to rid herself of the effects of too many cups of coffee.

"Tell him, Son," Larry Ladon said to my brother. The word 'son' sounded foreign, silly and ridiculously good.

"Jim," Herk whispered. He nudged my arm. I forced my eyes open.

"What?"

"Meg is coming home. The cancer is in remission, Jim. She's coming home."

Of course, I thought, and I closed my eyes again. Larry Ladon is my father. My sister is the Queen of the Amazons and I think I'm in love with Skinny Minnie. Of course Meg is coming home. All you have to do is ask. What a dream—what a bizarre and beautiful dream.

Chapter twelve

Her doctors didn't know what to make of Meg. One of them told us that it was a pretty safe bet that her name would soon be appearing in medical journals. There was just no *reason* for the cancer's remission. Meg had refused any treatments. Radiation and chemotherapy, she believed, would have harmed the developing life inside her. She would never have traded uncertain life for certain death. Besides, she knew that she wouldn't die. In science, reasons are necessary, but faith is excused from logic.

My brother, however, was close enough to God to know that He could—and would—allow death. Herk would have to do what he was guided to do, or Meg would die. I know theologians argue that God doesn't make deals, but the Bible's full of them. Ask Abraham or Noah or Moses or Job or Paul if He does or not. Ask me. I don't know how Christians could debate for centuries over the meaning of bread and wine and still deny the Creator's enjoyment of a good wager. What, in fact, is Christ's life and crucifixion but a renegotiation with humanity? Believe, repent, and be saved. A deal's a deal.

So Herk knew it wasn't over. He was certain the cancer would reappear or something else would replace it. In his mind, Meg's life was still on the line. He believed that God was giving us some time—that's all.

In August, Meg came home. Now in her third trimester, she was bulging and beautiful. She'd put on some weight since I'd seen her less than a week earlier. She looked healthy again and she had her natural energy back. Like most pregnant women, she looked radiant, full of the future. I still thought that she was the most beautiful woman I'd ever seen, but I wasn't in love with her anymore. She didn't have her former cravings either, (she'd given up cigarettes), and that would always make a difference. It made me feel strangely unnecessary.

Rusha called the owner of the Amazon Clubs in Los Angeles and told him she was getting out of the business. She said later that the guy was 'extremely pissed', to quote her, and threatened to sue, but in that line of work, at least in 1972, there were no contracts. Commitment to the dark, as to the Light, was pretty much based on faith. By the time Meg came home, Rusha was becoming a blonde again. Her eyes would remain blue.

She attended services with Ginny and Larry, but she usually sat by Meg. She became a member of the developing commune, but her faith in God was a long time coming. It was the sense of *family* that kept her with us. For the first time in her short life, she said, she didn't feel afraid.

Rusha and Meg became inseparable. It made sense I guess. They were about the same age, and Meg—an only child—was delighted to have a sister. They were constantly whispering and giggling like a couple of bobby soxers, and I had a feeling that Rusha was learning far too much about her stepbrothers. They worked diligently, doing whatever they could, both indoors and out, (Rusha had surprising carpentry skills and the kind of energy that is dictatorial to the less ambitious), but they were never far apart. I felt a kind of burgeoning jealousy, though I'm not sure at whom it was directed. I realize now that it was my gradual displacement by my halfsister that caused me to suffer, in part, that sense of obsolescence.

As each week passed, the property on Horizon Road, more and more, took on the character of a small village. Except for the forty hours a week I spent at Holy Cross I was there continuously. I didn't realize I *lived* there until I woke up one morning in my apartment and discovered that all my clothes were in the spare bedroom at the manse. I told Herk that I wouldn't mind paying my rent to the church if I could live there. He thought it was an excellent idea, but he would only take half of what I'd been paying and my checks were made out to the church, never to him.

Meg and Rusha, of course, knew that Minnie was the real cause of my relocation, and they laughed when I made the suggestion. To my chagrin, neither of them displayed any jealousy about Minnie—only mild amusement.

Minnie would generally be at the manse before I left for work, (by this time, the church was serving breakfast for a dozen or more workers every morning), and she would be at the manse when I came home. She left only to go back to her parents' ranch each night to sleep. One evening, after the communal meal under the oak had been accomplished and the many volunteers lounged in its shade to digest the feast before returning to their labor, I asked Minnie if she wanted to walk with me. She was busy helping to clear away the carnage left after a supper for fifty, but when she looked at Ginny, who was unofficially in charge of the clean-up, my mother smiled at her and urged her to go. Ginny actually winked at me. She knew what it meant to love. She certainly understood devotion.

Minnie and I walked in silence for awhile, side by side, across the open field toward the forest. Even in mid-August, some of the trees were beginning to turn, as if—like a woman in love—they were anxious to change into gaudier garments before the anticipated nudity of a cold lover's embrace.

When we were far enough away from the house to be unheard, we stopped for a moment, while I lit a cigarette.

"Is there something between us, Jim?" she said. It was a question typical of her—direct, honest, uncomplicated.

I threw away the cigarette and put my hands on either side of her waist. I remember how my thumbs rested along the bony projection of her lower ribs, starkly contrasting with the wonderful curve of warm flesh below. She was wearing a light sweater over a silk blouse. I don't believe I'd ever felt such delicacy. Minnie, as her name suggested, was extremely small. I don't mean in terms of height. She was probably five-five or five-six, but she was delicate, fragile, and almost childish. She had a woman's curves, but they were subtle and easily disguised. She would never be called voluptuous, but for me, that was a strong part of her appeal.

She looked at me with raised brows above her dark and serious eyes. Her black, intensely curly hair cascaded from her high forehead to the small of her back, framing her face and accentuating the pale, delicate skin.

Her thin hands rested on my arms and held tightly to my loose shirt. She waited, looking up at me with an expression that can only be described as confident apprehension.

"I've been with a lot of women, Minnie," I said.

"I know."

"But I never really loved any of them. I don't think I understood what love was."

I wanted her to interrupt, to help me through it, but she just held my shirt and waited.

"I think I know now," I said.

She smiled, exposing her fine, white teeth. Her cheeks flowered when she did, her wide mouth forcing them up and out in rosy abundance on either side of her small, sharp nose. Her face, like her body, was almost childish, but just as her breasts and hips betrayed the impression of adolescence, so did her mouth and eyes reveal the woman behind the precocious façade.

"I think I love you Jim," she said. It was a simple, direct statement, like a little girl who loudly and unabashedly declares, in a crowd, her need to find a restroom. I knew I loved her too, as much for that uncomplicated *honesty* as anything else.

Throughout that first private encounter with Minnie Tower, my heart leapt about like a wounded rabbit—unsure of direction, full of adrenaline and fear, trying hard to avoid the hunger that both pursued it and drew it on.

We walked on for a while, as the sun's intensity mellowed and its light filtered through the trees beyond in shafts of golden luminosity that no artist had ever captured—or ever could. Beauty of such rarity is as much mood as eye. At the forest's edge, we kissed. We sat there in the dry grass, holding each other, ignoring the insects that cried for our attention like spoiled children. We were content in that.

The bell that Herkimer had mounted on the oak tree as a call to worship and our communal meals broke our reverie.

"It's almost dark," Minnie said. Her small head was resting on my chest. Perhaps her ear was wondering where my heart had gone. She lazily brushed a mosquito from my arm. It came apart and left a wake of my own blood. She didn't notice. "That's probably my parents," she said, "wanting to get home."

"I guess we should head back then," I said. It was a reluctant suggestion.

"I don't want to go, Jim. I could die right here, right now, and I'd be happy." I stroked her luxuriant hair. It was so thick and curly that it added another dimension of incongruity to her. I remember thinking that someone with that kind of hair, man or woman, would have to have a proportionate fullness elsewhere on the body, but the opposite was true of Minnie. Her skin was smooth and bald. There was no peach fuzz—not even the hint of a shadow. Even her arms were bare and pale. I learned, later, that the trait was comprehensive.

"I wanted to die once," I said, "but not now. Not unless you go with me."

I felt her thin arms tighten around my waist. She kissed the palm of my hand as it quit playing with her hair and touched her cheek.

"Why?" she whispered. "Why did you want to die?"

"I was in Vietnam. It seemed like the most natural thing to do."

She sat up and pulled her hair back, holding it off her face. She was frowning. "You're being flippant. Don't be that way with me."

"You're right. I'm sorry. Force of habit."

"Will you tell me why?"

"Not now." The bell rang again. "We should get back."

"That's convenient."

"It seems that way, but I *will* tell you about it." I wanted to add something like 'then we'll see if you can still love me', but I didn't.

We strolled back, her child's hand in mine. Neither of us wanted to go.

"You didn't try anything," she said.

I laughed. "What do you mean by that?"

"You have a reputation," she said. "You didn't even touch my breasts." She sounded petulant, even disappointed. "I would have let you, you know. I would have had sex with you, even if it's wrong."

"Wrong in whose eyes?"

"God's."

"I don't think He was watching."

She stopped and turned me to face her.

"Nothing that lovely is possible without Him."

"I wasn't mocking, Minnie."

"Then why?"

"I'm keeping a promise."

"To Reverend Gudsen?"

"To God."

"You mean you've sworn off it, so to speak?"

"Yes."

"Until you marry?"

"No, that doesn't have anything to do with it." I lit a cigarette. I was looking everywhere but at her, so we began to walk again. No one was in the yard, so we sat down on one of the long benches under the oak. "Minnie?"

"Yes?"

"It'd very easy to break that promise—with you I mean."

She smiled. "I can wait as long as you can."

I could see that the lights were on in the house. People were still moving around in the kitchen. We could hear the clatter of dishes and the opening and closing of cupboard doors through the open screen door. I caught a glimpse of Meg.

"Your brother is a very special man," Minnie said.

"I know."

"Do you believe that God speaks to him? Everyone says it's true."

"It is."

"How do you know?"

"Because everything he says will happen, happens."

She shrugged. "Maybe he's just intuitive."

"If you believed that, you wouldn't be here."

"I have a friend at St. Luke's," she said. "Her name is Sibyl Springbok. Did you know her when you were there?"

I searched my memory. The name had struck me before. "Was she the woman who joined St. Luke's when Herk first got there? The one Herk baptized along with her child?"

"Yes."

It wasn't difficult to remember her—not only because she was the first black Lutheran I'd ever seen, but also because her cocoa beauty made her quite unforgettable. I remembered her sitting with the Towers after Minnie had gotten married and moved on to her husband's church. Sibyl's baby was always with her, but no one had ever seen its father. "What about her?"

"She called me a couple of days ago. She said that things are falling apart at St. Luke's since Reverend Gudsen left. Attendance is way down at services.

"Some have come here of course, but mostly she says people are just tired of the same old stuff. She says the church is two centuries behind society. She still draws stares and whispers all the time because of her race and the fact that she has a baby and no husband. She says that's proof enough."

"Why didn't she come here, with you and your parents? She has to feel really isolated now."

"I've talked to her about it. I know she'd love it here. Everyone loves it here."

I watched her smile, brushing her curly tresses behind a delicate ear. I swallowed hard, trying to focus on what she said. It's still so easy for me to get lost in what she *is*. "So why doesn't she join us?"

"She always gives me this strange answer, and she won't explain beyond it. I don't understand really."

"What does she say?"

"She says she's waiting. It isn't time, she says. I ask her what she's waiting for, she says she doesn't know. That's odd, don't you think?"

"Maybe."

"*Minnie?*" Sylvia Tower appeared at the kitchen door.

"I'm right here, Mom."

"Oh." Mrs. Tower squinted into the shadows. "Is James still with you, Dear?"

"Don't worry, Mom. We're behaving."

"Of course you are." She smiled pleasantly in my direction, though I was sure she couldn't see either of us. "Your father needs to get home, Honey. They're doing a slaughtering tomorrow, as you know. He's tried to be patient but, well, we really *must* go."

"Okay." Minnie stood up and kissed me quickly then headed for the house.

"Will I see you tomorrow?" I called after her.

"Not tomorrow." She kept talking to me while she walked backwards. "I have to help Dad. He's got a big meat order for a guy in Wisconsin and we're processing five or six bulls. We'll be back Friday though."

Somehow I couldn't see Minnie butchering buffalo. She'd grown up on that ranch, so she probably knew every facet of its operation. Since her separation from her husband, she'd been living with her parents again, recuperating from the beating her husband had given her. My love for her brought new hate into my life. Who was this guy? How could he hit her? I wondered if their divorce was final. There was so much I still had to learn about Minnie.

"I'll be here on Friday," I shouted after her as she disappeared inside the house. I smoked another cigarette. They left by the front entrance but I could see Minnie wave to me by the light from the porch.

When the car pulled away, I went inside. Lena Gossbach was the last to clear out of the kitchen, probably because she had to keep checking to see if everything had been turned off. I said good-night to her but she didn't respond as she hurried past me out the door. Herk and Meg and Rusha were sitting in the living room.

"Somebody's been having a good time this evening," Rusha said as I entered the room. She was getting into the sister thing a little too quickly for me. Meg laughed. Herk seemed preoccupied.

"Good clean fun," I said.

"Uh huh." Rusha winked at Meg.

I rolled my eyes and looked to my brother for help. He was oblivious.

"We're sorry, Jim," Meg said. "We just can't help it. You're so *obviously* smitten."

"Smitten?" Rusha said. "Did you say *smitten*? Who uses a word like that anymore?"

"What word would you use?" Meg asked.

"Puh-lease," Rusha quipped. "Not in front of the Reverend."

They both giggled again. I suddenly decided that I was in need of sleep, though it wasn't ten o'clock yet. I headed for my room upstairs.

"We have to go to California tomorrow," Herk said. I stopped. The snickering stopped too.

I turned around. "What?" I thought I hadn't heard him right.

"You remember Jim, when I asked you if you could get some time off from work? I thought then that we'd have to go some-where. I thought it would be to get Rusha, but that obviously wasn't the case. We have to go now."

"Why?"

He looked at me for the first time since I'd come in. He gave me that sad, man of sorrows, smile.

"You don't know," I answered for him.

"Right."

"Been getting headaches?"

"Yes."

"What *do* you know?"

He shook his head, like a dog might, to try to rid itself of the weight of water. *His* burden, however, was not so easily dismissed. "This was different, Jim. I don't think there was a voice this time."

"You don't *think* there was?" I said. "You mean you couldn't tell?" Rusha's face was filled with skepticism. I noticed that she glanced first at me, then Meg, as if she expected us to affirm her doubt. Instead, she found only the expectant patience of faith.

"It was more like a dream or vision, but I was fully awake."

"Are you sure?" I said.

"I was in the shower. I just kept seeing the same things over and over. They were images, shapes, some clearly defined, some not. Eventually, I was able to see what they all were."

"Well, what were they?"

"Images of you and me…and Rusha."

Our stepsister raised her eyebrows and looked at Meg, but the latter's attention was entirely on her husband. She was waiting, tensely.

"I know this sounds crazy, but we were standing on something that looked like a putting green, only it wasn't round and it wasn't grass. Maybe it was just the color. It had an irregular shape, longer than it was wide, and *angular*. Each of us was holding a leash or strap of some kind, attached to an animal. Rusha's was a lion, a male with a large mane. Jim, yours was attached to a pig."

Rusha laughed, but everyone ignored her.

"Not a domestic pig," Herk continued, as if that made a difference to the comic image. His forehead was furrowed in concentration, as if trying to recapture the image. "It was a wild one, with shaggy thin hair—and tusks."

"Like a boar," I suggested.

"Exactly," Herk answered. "A wild boar."

"And you?" I said. "What was yours?"

"A crab. A huge, white crab—the size of a card table. It had dozens of legs and large pincer-like claws."

"You must have been half-asleep when you got in the shower," the former Queen of the Amazons said. "It was a dream."

"It was in the middle of the day," Herk whispered, trying to be patient with our neophyte sister. "I'd just come in from working on the new church building this afternoon. I was wide awake."

"He sees what we don't see," Meg said. Rusha didn't understand yet. She didn't know that Herk wasn't like the rest of us. She was about to learn, if she didn't let skepticism drive her away.

"Why California, Brother?" I said. "How do you know that? And why visions instead of the directness of speech?"

"I didn't figure out California until a few minutes ago. That green stuff that we were all standing on—I kept trying to think what it meant. My mistake was concentrating on the material itself. It was some sort of wood, painted grass-green. When I focused on the *shape* it was like looking at a kid's wooden puzzle of the United States. We had one Jim, do you remember it? Each piece was a state."

"Michigan was blue," I said, recalling it vividly.

"Right. And California was green. It was the same shape, same color. That's what the three of us were standing on."

"That's what makes you think we should go to California? The image of a puzzle piece?" Rusha laughed. "Holy shit. What have I gotten mixed up in?"

"I knew we had to travel before," Herk said, ignoring her. His voice was much calmer than mine would have been. "God has revealed the destination, that's all. It *is* California."

"Crabs on leashes?" Rusha shook her head. "Sounds like Looney Tunes to me."

"I called the airline an hour ago," Herk said, ignoring her. "We have a ten o'clock flight in the morning."

"What?" Minnie's image was foremost in my mind, but after the earlier ribbing, I avoided the subject. "What about my job?"

"You'll have to call someone tonight, let them know you'll be gone for a while," Herk responded.

I wanted to ask him for how long, but I knew he didn't know. Instead, I said: "Who's going to run things here?"

"I've already talked to Caleb Bird. He's going to run services."

There was a long silence. Finally, Herk said: "I don't want to go either, Jim." He looked at his pregnant wife. She returned an adoring smile.

"I'll be okay," she said, reading his thoughts.

"We're still running the race, Jim."

"I'm not going," Rusha said. "Things are fine right here. I'm just beginning to have a little happiness in my life and I'm not going to fuck it up over some crazy dream."

Meg took her hand and patted it affectionately. She whispered something that I couldn't hear.

"I'm not going to force anyone," Herk said. He rubbed the white scars on his hands. "But I'm leaving in the morning." He got up, wished us all good night, and limped from the room.

I went to the phone and called Minnie.

In the end, Rusha went too.

Chapter thirteen

Herk slept through the entire flight. He'd been up most of the night, trying to comfort Lena Gossbach through another crisis. For Lena at least, God always became threatening at night.

Rusha and I talked quietly in the seats directly behind him. Meg had tried to explain all this to her, but it's difficult to accept as only improbable that which living has taught as impossible. Rusha's mother had raised a solid realist.

We landed in Los Angeles only because, Herk said, Rusha had come from there. He wasn't sure that it was our destination; he only knew that we were in the right state. He certainly had no idea what we were looking for in L.A. or where to start.

The three hour time change, booking a couple of rooms and unpacking and getting something to eat put us well into evening. Herk called Meg to let her know exactly where we were and she promised to inform Minnie. She told us that Auggie Two-River's father had been taken by ambulance earlier in the day to Holy Cross. It was, she said, an apparent heart attack. He was still alive, but in intensive care. She assured us that Caleb Bird was with Auggie as well as a number of other friends from the Gospel Church. She'd keep us informed.

When Herk hung up, we looked at each other like children who had the freedom of summer before them and no idea what to play.

Rusha paced, chain-smoking cigarettes and occasionally looking at her half-brothers as though she'd just come upon a pair of gorillas on a jungle trail. There was surprise and confusion in her expression—even admiration—but mostly fear.

"Well," she said, "what now? We just sit here and wait for another vision, or does God expect us to figure it out?"

Herk limped over and put an arm around her. I thought she'd get angry and shrug him off, but she didn't. She seemed to calm, and she sat down when he led her to a chair. He hadn't said a word.

"I don't want to be here, Herk," she said. Her eyes were moist, but she set her jaw. "Where the hell did you get a name like Herkimer anyway?" That, we would learn, was Rusha. When besieged, she'd attack.

Herk laughed. "I wondered about that too, especially as a kid. Mother told me my father had chosen it. He was a military history buff, she said. Nicholas Herkimer was an American general in the War for Independence. He was killed in the Mohawk Valley in New York. Larry told me about him when we became friends—before I knew he was my, our—dad. He went on and on about the guy, knew every detail of his life. When it all came out—that first night you came to us—I knew it was true. Larry Ladon had given me my name. You can blame your father."

I hadn't known and I wished I hadn't learned. I guess it was because it made my brother's quick acceptance of Larry as our father less mysterious—less *spiritual.*

"Why Los Angeles?" Rusha said. She appeared unamused by the story. "California's a big state."

Herk got up and limped over to the sliding glass doors that led to a small balcony. We were several floors up and the glass provided a panoramic view of the lights of the City of Angels.

"I don't know," he said. His back was to us, but somehow we could still hear his soft voice. "I thought maybe *you* could tell us."

"Me?" Rusha said. "God doesn't speak to me."

"You know this town," Herk reasoned, turning to face her. "You came from here. You're part of the vision. It seemed logical. Jim and I have never been to California."

"What do you think the lion thing could mean, Roosh?" I asked. Her name is pronounced 'Roosha', and I'd taken to eliminating the 'a' as a more sisterly nickname. It sounded a bit like Ruth. She liked it, I think.

"I don't have any idea," she said.

"You never used anything like that in one of your acts?" I could envision the Queen of the Amazons in her leather girdle and spiked bra, leading a lion by a tether. I would have bet that the lion would have been, like the slave girl, completely cowed.

"No," she said. "You saw it, Jim. Maddy was at the end of my leash. I've never worked with animals." She didn't seem aggravated or embarrassed by the memory, but she certainly wasn't wistful. "Besides, Yuri's got a thing about cats. He hates them. One of the girls brought a kitten in one time that she found rummaging in the dumpster in the alley behind the club. Yuri threw a fit, threatened to fire her if she didn't get rid of it." She laughed at the recollection.

"What?" I said.

"Nothing." Rusha was still grinning and looking at our brother. "It was just a joke among all the girls."

"Tell us."

"It's not something you share with your pastor."

Herk laughed. "You can't clean out the barn if you're afraid of getting shit on your boots," he said. "I'm not a prude. Go ahead."

Rusha looked at me. I nodded encouragement. "Well, the girls used to say it didn't make sense that Yuri should be so turned off by pussy when he made his living parading it down a runway."

I laughed. Herk was smiling.

Rusha bummed a cigarette from me and sat in a chair. I watched her cross her wonderful legs and I remembered that kiss in her room at the Holiday Inn. I could still see her hand on my groin. I wondered if Rusha had told Meg how very close we'd come to turning the natural into the unnatural. Only the supernatural had prevented it. Rusha saw me gawking and I felt like a horny teenager who'd just been caught rummaging through his older sister's underwear drawer.

"Tell me more about this guy, the owner of the Amazon Club," Herk said. If he'd seen what passed between his brother and sister, he didn't show it.

"I don't know that much about him," Rusha responded. "His name is Yuri Theus. He talks with a heavy accent—Eastern European I think, maybe Polish. He always said he was a football player. He told me that that's where he got the money to start the clubs, but he looks way too little to me to have been an athlete."

Herk appeared to be stunned. He had that revelatory look on his thin face, but he didn't seem to be in pain. He wasn't rubbing his temples. "That's it!" he said.

"What's it?" Rusha looked as puzzled as I was.

"Jim, you have to remember Yuri Theus. He was that Yugoslavian field goal kicker—an All-American at Michigan State. One of the first to use the soccer-style kick, remember?"

"Yeah. Back in the early fifties." It was coming to me. "This is *that* guy? He was one of the greatest kickers to ever play the game! He was all-pro too."

"And who did he play for, Jim—in the pros I mean?"

"Detroit, Herk, you know that. He bled silver and blue. He was a Lion through his whole…."

When the ball finally sailed between the goalposts, Herk and Rusha were already at the door.

By the time we were able to hail a cab and get to the Amazon Club, it was close to eleven. I warned Herk as we went in that this experience might be something he wasn't used to, but he laughed, perhaps because the naivete that I thought was his was really my own.

For a while, Rusha was anonymous. It was due, I'm sure, to her newly blonde hair and more conservative clothing, as well as her desire to blend with the background. We took a table in a dark corner and just sat for a few minutes. None of us wanted one, but we ordered drinks because it was required. The club was overflow-ing with people. They were mostly men, but there were several dozen women among the clientele as well. We would never have found a table had we cared anything about seeing the show. The tables around the stage and runway were all packed and many peo-ple were standing by the bar, leaning against the walls. The heat and smoke and noise drifted through the place in about equal thickness.

"Have you seen him yet?" I shouted to Rusha.

"No, but he's here. He practically lives here. He'll probably find us."

The public address squeaked on and the announcer intro-duced, in typically grandiloquent style, the new Queen of the Ama-zons. The curtain opened and as the epical music, (possibly from *Ben Hur* this time), assaulted our helpless ears, Rusha's replacement appeared onstage. We could only catch occasional glimpses of her because of the crowds around the runway, but she was wearing the same headdress, the same metal plates of armor, (on her arms at least), the same spiked bra and leather girdle. The dark heads of her adoring fans obscured her from the waist down. She was a beautiful woman, but very young. She had a child's face that was both confi-dent and sad.

I looked over at my brother, who was watching with great interest, yet seemed neither excited nor awed by her. His expression spoke more of helpless sympathy, like one I'd seen on his face when our childhood pet, a cocker spaniel named Lucky, had not lived up to his name and been struck by a car.

When her leash yanked the slave girl onstage, Rusha nudged me. "Look," she said in a kind of bellowing whisper, "it's Maddy."

Apparently, Maddy had done what she'd said she would do. She still wore her chains. The major difference in this act, however, was that the new Queen was not nearly as cruel as Rusha had ap-peared. Her kisses were hesitant. Her slaps were simulated and quickly followed by sympathetic caresses. Maddy had to fake being pulled to her knees. The Queen thrust her hips forward at the slave girl, but there was little of eroticism in it. The Queen was inexperienced and awkward. The customers loved it.

Herk continued to watch, but I could see the empathy, the sorrow he felt over the indignation before him. It smothered my own lust and made me feel ashamed of it.

"Holy shit!" Rusha said.

"What?" I'd barely been able to hear her exclamation over the noise.

"That's Teena!"

"Sheena? Who's she?"

"*Teena,*" Rusha shouted in my ear. "The Queen of the Amazons—that's Athena Theus, Yuri's daughter. She practically grew up around here. We all called her Teena. She's just a fucking *kid!*"

"Are you sure that's who it is?"

"Yeah, that's her. That son of a bitch has got his own kid up there. She can't be more than eighteen, nineteen at most."

"How do you know that? I mean she *looks* pretty young, but I thought you did too."

"Yuri threw her a high school graduation party at the club—three months ago. I was there. She was getting ready to go to college. When I quit, he said he didn't have anybody to replace me. That's Tina all right. What an asshole!"

Rusha got up suddenly. I grabbed her arm. "Where you going?" The girls were strutting off the runway to the accompaniment of raucous cheering.

She pulled away from me without answering and began shouldering her way through the crowd. I got up and followed. I'm not sure Herk had heard any of it, because of the noise, but he was gamely limping after us. We caught up with her at the entrance to a hallway that led to the back rooms of the place. A gigantic black man whom I immediately recognized as Atlas Johnson blocked her progress. Like Maddy, he'd apparently found employment in California.

"Man, I'm sorry Rita," he was saying when Herk and I caught up. "I didn't recognize you at first. You dye your hair or somethin'?"

David Turrill

"Yeah," she answered. "Listen Honey, me and my brothers just want to see Maddy, okay? Can you let us through?"

"Sure, Rita," he answered. "You never shoulda quit strippin', Babe. You were the best." Then he caught sight of me. "Jim?"

"Yeah." Rusha was already past him and on her way down the dark corridor.

I suppose he remembered me drooling over Rusha at the Amazon Club in Saginaw. *Brothers? Man, that's kinky,*" he exclaimed, as Herk and I passed.

Some opportunistic drunk tried to follow us, but the former lineman blocked his way in pass protection mode.

At the end of the hall, Rusha burst through a door. The light from inside flooded the passage. There was a long row of mirrors against the back wall, bordered with bare light bulbs. Costume racks covered another wall. There were three shower stalls against a third.

Maddy was sitting on a bench in her silk kimono, talking with the under-aged Queen. The expression on her face, when she saw me, was pure happiness. "Jimmy!" she shouted. She ran right past Rusha, embracing me with arms and legs and smothering me with a long kiss. When she finally let go, and put her feet on the ground, I was gasping for breath. I could feel my brother's eyes on the back of my head. Two other half-naked dancers stared at the scene after emerging from what must have been a bathroom by the showers.

"Maddy?" Rusha said.

Maddy looked at her, looked at me, looked back again. "Hippie?"

Maddy generally had two facial expressions to share with the world—ecstasy and confusion. This anger thing was a first.

"Oh I get it," she said. "The handsome prince rescues the damsel. Jim shows up one night, you quit the business and go off with *my* man. Nice."

She turned away from us and went back to Teena.

Rusha followed, talking to her as she retreated. "You've got it wrong, Maddy. I left because of Jim, but not because I'm in love with him. He's my brother."

"Your brother? C'mon," Maddy said. The familiar look of confusion returned with an added hint of derision.

"It's true, Mad," I said.

"Rita?" Teena stood up.

"It's Rusha, Teena. My real name's Rusha Ladon and what the hell do you think you're doing?"

"Whaddya mean?"

"You're too damn young for this. You could be arrested. You know that?"

"I'm old enough to—"

"You're not old enough to *feed* yourself," Rusha shouted. "What the hell's wrong with your father?"

Teena burst into tears, covering her youthful face with her hands. Maddy put her arm around the girl's shoulder protectively.

"Leave her alone," she said.

"You're supposed to be at UCLA this fall Teena! Marine Biology, right?"

"You don't know," Teena cried. "You don't know everything. You deserted him. He needed you and you left. *I* decided, not him. He's got a problem, he's he's…." She collapsed in another spasm of tears.

"Where is he?" Rusha demanded.

Maddy looked up. "He's in his office."

Rusha whirled around and left the room. I followed. About halfway down the corridor, she stopped in front of a door with the single word OFFICE on it. A couple of strippers shuffled past us on the way to the dressing room we'd just left, wearing only g-strings and heavy make-up. I looked behind me to see Herk's reaction. He wasn't there.

Rusha thrust the door open and walked in. A huge bronze-coated desk dominated the center of the room. The dark green walls were plastered with photos of football players. One bookshelf was littered with trophies. A blue and silver jersey with the number

10 and the letters THEUS embroidered on it was mounted in a lighted, glass case. There were no windows in the room.

A small, balding man sat behind the desk. A rubber strap was wrapped around his bare arm. He was pulling it tight with his teeth. The veins in his arm bulged with the pressure. The whole arm was black and blue. It looked like Atlas Johnson had jumped up and down on it in football cleats. In his free hand he held a syringe which he was obviously about to use.

"You fucking bastard," Rusha said.

Suddenly, Herk was there. He moved past us and stood in front of Yuri Theus.

"Put it down," he said to the Lion.

Theus looked dopily up at my brother through clouded eyes. He dropped the syringe.

Herkimer Gudsen laid Hippolyta's leather girdle and spiked bra on the desk. The man stared dumbly at them as tears welled in his distant and absent eyes.

"Come with me," Herk said. His voice was soft but authoritative. He turned and left the room as abruptly as he'd entered it.

Yuri Theus stood up and stumbled weakly to the front of his desk. Rusha offered her hand. He took it. We left the Amazon Club a few minutes later—Rusha with her Lion in tow.

Chapter fourteen

I t was miraculous of course. After Los Angeles, Herkimer
Gudsen became more than my brother. In fact, I rarely viewed him
as a relative anymore. Not because I didn't feel close to him—the
opposite actually—it's just that fraternal love became too small a
definition for my devotion. Perhaps disciple would be a better
word.

It really wasn't difficult to define who *we* were; the problem
was in defining Herk. When we arrived back in Saginaw and word
got around about what had transpired in Los Angeles, people began
using words like 'prophet' and even 'messiah'.

Herk didn't like any of the definitions. He was, he said, simply a servant of God like the rest of us, but we all knew that he was
different. His humility wasn't false, just inaccurate.

Yuri Theus and his daughter, Athena, came back with us. He
would tell us later that he didn't know why, except that from the
first moment he saw Herk, his addiction to heroin left him and he
became a man again. He would have followed my brother anywhere.

I know the cynics will always dismiss what happened, attributing Theus's instantaneous conversion to some powerful inner
desire to save himself and his daughter. They'd maintain that Herk
was merely a catalyst, an excuse if you will. But none of those people saw Yuri Theus. He wasn't on the verge of sobriety—if anything, that dose he was about to administer to himself would have

been the *coup de grace* that would have ended his slavery in a very different way.

But the real miracle was in the way he *stayed* clean. There was no padded room, no vomiting, no hysterics, no fever, no convulsions—none of the very physical symptoms associated with withdrawal from that most lethally addictive of drugs. Yuri never showed *any* desire to touch the stuff again. His cure, like his conversion, was immediate and permanent—like the fishermen of Galilee.

I pointed out to Herk, on the flight home, that his vision had only been a third fulfilled. The menagerie was short two creatures. He didn't need to be reminded of course. He sensed, he said, that we would find them elsewhere. Besides, he felt a pressing need to return home.

Teena also accepted Herk's call without protestation. Perhaps it was because any life would have been preferable to the one she'd been forced into. Perhaps she just saw it as a way for her miserable father to get clean. I like to believe that she knew who Herk was—that she recognized intuitively that God was leading. Teena later told me, when she began her classes that fall at Saginaw Valley University, that Herk carried God with him like a mysterious and rare cologne. You didn't know what the aroma was, but it smelled so good that you wanted to be close. In her long life, Teena Theus would never stray very far from the smell of God.

Rusha had tried to convince Maddy to come with us, but Maddy's sense of the Infinite was somehow directly correlative to her intelligence. I'm not suggesting that you have to be bright to follow God—Lord knows there were some real cretins among us—perhaps *awareness* would be a better word. Maddy couldn't see beyond the possible.

So, along with Robin Stym, Baxter Bird, and Rusha and Larry, Yuri Theus joined the Twelve. I wasn't sure then why their status was higher than any of the others who'd come to the Gospel Church, but I trusted my brother.

"We have five now," I observed.

"Only four," he corrected. "The Birds are one. They go together." There was no point, of course, in asking him how he knew. He just did. I began to question less and pray more. The idea of 'why' began to matter less and less. I was glad to be back. Contentment began to replace curiosity. When you're happy, the world really doesn't have to make sense.

Minnie and I spent all our spare time together. All my life I will remember those early autumn days after L.A. There weren't many. It wasn't long before all hell would break loose, but those few idyllic days would carry me a long way. Minnie and I ambled across gold fields at dusk, breathing in the cool, clear breath of autumn that filled our lungs and hearts with freshness like the leaves filled the sky, a bit of brilliance at a time, in the summer's slow undressing.

We kissed and touched and played, like children who revel merely in exploration, always postponing the inevitable fulfillment to keep the dream of it alive. Our bliss wasn't the satyr's rutting lust, but the agony of Tantalus, 'forever panting, forever young'. Minnie believed I was moral, but I was only keeping a promise to God.

During our sojourn in California, Auggie Two-River Sr. had died. Auggie Jr. handled it well, especially after Herk's eulogy which, typically, was sensitive and beautiful and left judgment to God. The old man had scorned religion all his life and he'd taken no part in the church which his son had accepted with such enthusiasm. But Herkimer assured the grieving son that salvation was personal and God never ceased to love. To hear my brother speak, one would tend to believe that hell had few occupants.

Auggie took Yuri and Teena Theus into his home. It was an old five-bedroom farmhouse, and he had more room than he could ever use by himself. Like Larry Ladon, he would, eventually, deed the property to the Gospel Church. It became an additional barracks to house new members, and its location—across from the manse—was ideal. The hundred head of beef and dairy cows became a major source of sustenance to the growing commune, as did the fields of potatoes and corn.

The ex-football player, drug addict and strip club owner became a competent farmer. His arm and heart healed. He sold the Amazon Clubs, put away enough money for Teena's delayed education, and gave the balance to our church.

Money was becoming another cross for Herk to bear. The man who never preached a sermon on any subject remotely fiscal found his church swimming in a sea of currency and deeds. Ever since the original split from St. Luke's, Robin Stym had been in charge of the new church's books, but the donated properties and enormous cash flow had become too complex even for his orderly mind. Herman Goetsh, the former colleague of Larry's on the Board of Elders at St. Luke's whose granddaughter had been the first child baptized into the Gospel Church, was a retired accountant. He volunteered his services to straighten out the financial mess, and with Herk's approval, Robin happily stepped aside. Within a month, the old man had straightened it all out, establishing a system of bookkeeping that kept it all in order. In September, he reported to the Council of Twelve, (really Four), that the church's assets exceeded the million dollar mark.

Herk met with the Council every week on Sunday, after services. Caleb Bird, our associate pastor, was also allowed access, as was Herman Goetsh. Herkimer convinced me to quit my job at Holy Cross, (a mop and bucket career that took little consideration to abandon), and created the position of First Counselor, for which I would be paid a small remuneration superior to my previous employment, and by which I would serve as an *ex officio* member of the Council.

It amazed me how our newfound father, critical and pompous as he'd always appeared, had become such a loving example of humility and grace. This Pharisee, the gay lovers, the stripper and dope addict, thrown together by God and Herkimer Gudsen, became tireless and pious disciples, and slowly began to operate the bulky machinery of church administration

There were many problems that deserved our immediate attention. The new church building required completion before winter set in. Workers were needed to help operate both Ladon's Orchard, (which was approaching its picking season), and the newly acquired Two-River property. The Council needed to determine a budget and salaries for Herk, Caleb Bird and now, myself. It was decided that a barracks should be constructed for the many people who virtually lived on the property. The Gospel Church of Faith and Revelation was becoming, in many respects, a small town. Officials at St. Luke's referred to us as a cult and warned their members of the evils associated with that word, but each week more of their number increased ours.

In my brother's mind there was no greater urgency than completing the Council of Twelve. No further communication from God was forthcoming—presumably because the last He had sent had not yet been fully realized.

The images had befuddled my brother and me. We were constantly alert to possibilities, examining new members as they came into the fold, believing, perhaps, that one of them might fit the vision. But we also were certain that the 'leashes' in the vision indicated who was to find the new members of the Twelve. Rusha had led us to the Lion. Herk must find the crab. I had to discover the boar. Who were they? Megan looked pale again and she needed to sleep a great deal. She was swollen with child, but it was a false impression of the future. Herk was convinced that time was running out.

Then, shortly after Labor Day, we found them.

In the process of assisting Athena Theus in choosing her classes at Saginaw Valley U., I decided to take another philosophy course. We were poring over the catalog and a particular title intrigued me—*Theanthropism: The Personification of the Ideal Hero in Myth and Faith.* Even though the soporific and monotonic Professor Mantus would have to be endured a second time, I felt that the content of the course would be worth the torment. Dr. Mantus, tedious as his delivery might be, knew his stuff.

It wasn't until the night of my first class that I finally caught on. It was one of those three-hour marathons from seven to ten. Dr. Mantus had introduced himself then, typically, droned on for an hour and a half at which time he gave us a short break. I was in

the dark hallway, stretching my legs and feeding my tobacco demons—my mind circling round the image of Minnie Tower—
when I overheard a couple of co-eds chatting by the coffee machine
a few yards away.

"God," said the taller of the two, "I can see why they call
him The Bore. I can hardly keep my eyes open."

"I'd like to shut mine," the short one added, "just so I don't
have to look at him. God, that nose! I can understand why he's not
wearing a wedding band. Have you ever seen anything like it? It's
so *big* and kind of squashed up into his face."

The taller one laughed. "Being fat doesn't help either," she
said. "He looks just like Porky Pig! Bi-dib, bi-dib, bi-dib—that's all
folks!"

These models of tolerance burst into hysterical giggling, the
taller one spilling her coffee on the tiled floor. Only the appearance
of the object of their amusement emerging from the restroom down
the hall quieted them.

They continued to smile and whisper to one another as Dr.
Mantus walked past and reentered the classroom. He appeared to
notice nothing. Perhaps he really didn't, but I suspected that a lifetime of teasing and ridicule had taught him to wear a mask of
oblivion.

To my mind, he was a man of great dignity and erudition.
Unfortunately, it had been his fate to earn a living by publicly dis-
pensing his wisdom to superficial dullards—a task for which he
possessed little talent. Still, it took the co-eds' cruelty for me to finally recognize who the Boar, or Bore, was in Herk's vision. Dr.
Mantus *had* to be my part of it. Not only did his homonymic nickname fit, but his incredible nose and generally porcine appearance
conformed to the presentment as well.

I found it even more difficult to sit through the second half
of his lecture than usual. I was eager for the end of the class so that
I might speak to him. I didn't really listen to a word he said in that
hour or so. The two girls continued their whispering silliness in the
second row down from me, but Dr. Mantus took no notice. He
droned on like an automaton. I wanted to stand up and yell at the

brats, to tell them to show some respect for one of God's Chosen, but I knew how preposterous that would sound to those outside the church, and I kept my silence.

At five minutes to ten, he dismissed us and the students quickly headed for the exit, the two gigglers leading the exodus. Dr. Mantus was gathering his notes and stuffing them haphazardly into his leather folio as I approached.

I took him by surprise. Clearly, he was not used to his students hanging around, and he looked uncomfortable. His small green eyes, tucked into the crevices created by his fat cheeks and bulbous nose, looked nervously away, avoiding contact with mine. He squinted from behind thick glasses.

"Dr. Mantus?" I said. I had no idea how to go about this. How do you tell someone that he's supposed to join a religious sect because your brother had a dream about him? "My name is—"

"You're James Gudsen," he said. "You're the first student at this university to take two of my classes consecutively. Usually one is enough to drive them away."

He continued to nose about his papers nervously. I swear I even heard him grunting.

"I prefer Jim," I said, not knowing what else to say.

"What can I do for you?" His voice was nervous, with an edge of irritation.

"I thought perhaps…I…well…there's this church I belong to."

"Yes? Has my lecture offended you in some way?"

"Oh no, no, not at all. I just thought you might…enjoy it. I'm really no good at this."

"You're proseletyzing, is that it? I'm not a religious man, Mr. Gudsen. Now if you'll excuse me…." He bunched the folio under his arm and waited for me to get out of his way. I wasn't sure if he could see me through those bottlebottom glasses.

"I'm not either—or I wasn't. My brother has started this new church. He had this vision about you. I can't really explain it, but…."

Dr. Mantus put his folio on his desk. Although he still avoided eye contact, his interest was growing. I could see it. He knew something too.

"Do I know your brother?"

"No, I don't think so."

"What kind of vision?" he asked.

I wanted to avoid the offending specifics of it. "I think I'm supposed to bring you into our church. I know this is all pretty crazy. I apologize, but I was sort of…compelled to say something. I'm not very good at this. Could you give me five or ten minutes of your time, let me explain what's going on? Then I'll never say anything about it again."

For the first time, he looked straight at me. His tiny eyes were nervous and feral. It was difficult not to stare at his upturned nose. Little wiry hairs protruded and I could see deeply into the wide nostrils.

"There's a little restaurant across from the campus on the other side of Bay Road," he said. "It's in that little mall. It's open until midnight. I noticed you smoking during the break. I still have the vice too. We could meet there in, say, ten minutes or so, and have a cigarette with some coffee. How would that be?"

I couldn't believe he'd agreed. I wouldn't have in his position. I'd shut the door on more than one Jehovah's Witness in my lifetime. I'd never been fond of evangelizing—it always smacked of egotism, even elitism. I don't think God is Lutheran or Methodist or Roman Catholic. I'm pretty sure He doesn't carry a membership card. I accepted the professor's invitation with gratitude and hurried to my car.

I got there first and found a booth that afforded some privacy, although I didn't believe that it was all that necessary. The only other customer in the place was a trucker whose semi found easy parking in the deserted mall lot. Fifteen minutes went by. I was sure I'd been stood up and I'd decided to leave when I spotted Dr. Mantus through the window, waddling toward the front door.

He found me without difficulty and forced his chubby figure into the booth. "Sorry it took me so long," he said. The short walk from his car had left him winded and he spoke with difficulty. "I had to go back to my office and pick up some papers."

"That's fine," I assured him. "I haven't been here long."

We ordered coffee. He had two slices of apple pie. I half-expected him to plunge his upturned nose into the food, but he cut each slice into tiny forkfuls and consumed them with the same cautious monotony that characterized his lectures.

I began by telling him about Herk's brush with death when Auggie Two-River shot him. He remembered reading about it in the newspapers. I related the events surrounding our expulsion from St. Luke's and Herk's defense of the Birds. I told him of Herk's sterility and Meg's pregnancy, (omitting the impotency business), Meg's cancer and its remission, and the rapid growth of the Gospel Church. Then I carefully told him of the calling of The Twelve, Larry and Rusha's conversions and, finally, Herk's latest vision that had led us to California and resulted in Yuri Theus's conversion and rehabilitation.

He listened politely as he steadily ingested his pie, sipped his coffee, and kept his eyes focused on his placemat. He listened as dispassionately as he spoke, and there were several moments during my narrative when I suspected that he'd not heard me at all.

When my story was done, I lit a cigarette and waited for him to either scoff at me or excuse himself in embarrassed haste. He did neither. He simply sat there, a cigarette wedged between his pudgy fingers, weighing my summation with the intensity of a prudent juror.

"I think you should know, Mr. Gudsen," he finally said, in the most casual manner, "that I had planned to go home tonight and kill myself." He didn't look to see my reaction. He hadn't said it for that reason. A single tear escaped his eye and created a tiny circle on the white placemat. It was the only blemish on it.

"Dr. Mantus…" I began. But he raised one stubby hand.

"I'm not looking for sympathy. I've found very little of that in my life and I've become accustomed to doing without it. I was just telling you the truth, as I think you're telling me what you believe is the truth. I don't think I'll do it now, though. You've intrigued me."

The waitress interrupted us with refills on the coffee. When she left, I decided to keep quiet and wait for him to continue. After an awkward silence, he did. "I'm an ugly man, Mr. Gudsen. I've been an object of ridicule and amusement all my life, just like with those two young ladies tonight, in my class, who thought I was oblivious to their scorn. My father died when I was a boy. My mother passed away last fall, almost a year ago now. I've never been kissed or embraced by anyone but her. It was...difficult to lose her." I thought for a moment that he would break down, but he kept his composure. "I don't have friends either—not real friends. I'm confiding in you because I know you as well as anyone." The dreary, level voice droned on, tempering his passionate story with the steely edge of despairing apathy. Here was a man who believed that life had shown him the best that he was going to see. "I've always prided myself on analyzing the world and my place in it with absolute clarity and dispassion. Ugly people, Mr. Gudsen, are the subject of ridicule. It's something the sensible man learns to accept. I've adapted to it, as well as to loneliness, forced celibacy, and isolation."

I opened my mouth to object, but he stopped me.

"Two things have kept me from destroying myself," he continued. "A belief in something beyond this life, and academic curiosity. I've recently lost my interest in both. Cessation of the consequent ennui seemed the next logical step. I have been, in short, literally bored to the brink of death. Fortunately, you have resurrected my curiosity and I should like to see where it leads. When may I meet this brother of yours?"

I didn't know what to say. "Whenever. Now if you like."

He glanced at his watch. "It's a bit late. Perhaps this weekend? The anticipation would give me something to enjoy."

"Sure. We have services at nine on Sunday mornings. If you came then, you could meet some of the other members too."

"The other ones, The Twelve you spoke of. They'll be there?"

"Yes. They meet right after. Herk would welcome you, I'm sure."

"That would be good then. Yes, I think so." He stubbed out his cigarette and raised the corners of his mouth in the semblance of a smile, although it was difficult to tell if he actually was smiling—the grotesque nose so dominated all his other features.

I wrote down the address of the manse and pushed it across to him. "You'll be there, then? For sure?"

He knew I was concerned about his earlier reference to suicide. "Don't worry," he said. "I'm not hysterical and I'm certainly not crazy. As I told you, I'm bored. This promises to be amusing, at least. I'll be there."

I saw him to his car and watched him drive off. The cool air of early autumn was invigorating. On the way back to Horizon Road I left the windows down and relished the sensation of shivering. I could hardly wait to tell my brother that I'd found the second of the three characters of his vision. When I arrived, it was almost eleven, but the lights were still on in the house. I found Herk sitting at the kitchen table with Ginny, Larry and Caleb Bird.

Ginny was sitting close to the Prophet, her right arm encircling his thin shoulders. She looked up at me with a pained, tearstained face as I entered, and I knew something had gone terribly wrong.

"It's Meg," she said, without me asking. "She vomited blood today. We took her to Holy Cross. The cancer's back."

Herk looked up at me. His face was strained and sallow. He looked exhausted.

I placed a hand on his shoulder. "You all right?"

"I knew it was coming," he said. "I knew." He put his scarred hand over mine and squeezed it hard. Knowing, apparently, was not the same as acquiescence. There was fear in his grip.

Faith isn't always stronger than fear—probably because we have so much more experience with the latter. Herk loved God, even more than he loved Meg, but he was afraid of Him too. "We are fearfully and wonderfully made," he once quoted in a sermon, explaining that it was as much a description of what fills us as to how we are constructed. I saw his point.

"What about the baby?" I said.

"It's doing well," he answered, but his voice sounded detached, disinterested. Ginny frowned a little and shook her head, indicating it was not a subject to be pursued.

"Then there's Lena to deal with too," Ginny said.

"What? What's wrong with her now?"

Ginny looked at Caleb Bird as if to prompt him. "She came here looking for Herk," Caleb said. "I told her they were all at the hospital, that they'd taken Meg to Holy Cross."

"Yeah?"

"She just about went nuts. She said she had to see Herk. *Had* to. I told her I could help her. She wouldn't hear of it. She started screaming and throwing everything she could lay her hands on. I finally had to escort her out the door and into her car. She calmed down after a little while, but I've never seen anyone so hysterical. She really needs some professional help."

"I'll see her soon," Herk said. He sighed. "I've found two more," he said wearily.

I knew what he was referring to, and talons of doubt tore at my insides. Two? Was I wrong about Dr. Mantus? Were we only seeing what we wanted to see? Wasn't I supposed to bring one of them?

"I met Meg's attending nurse tonight," he said. "She had been Meg's friend before, the first time. She was the night nurse though, so I'd never met her. She...she's the one who's supposed to see her through to...to the end." He hung his golden head and pressed his hands against his temples as if trying to contain the explosive pressure of his mind's eye. Ginny tightened her arm around his shoulders. "Her name is Judy Crabbe."

I nodded. "Your part of the vision?"

"Yes."

He lifted his head and looked at me with his suffering blue eyes. He seemed hollow, delicate. I thought then that God might be requiring too much—that the Prophet might not live out his martyrdom. The raptor of skepticism kept ripping my soul and I was afraid.

"Do you know what the constellation of the crab is, Jim? What the astrological sign is called?"

I shrugged. "No, I never paid much attention to—"

"Cancer." He said the word with all the disgust and hatred that a man reserves for the thing that destroys his happiness and preys on his security.

He was silent for a moment, then he said: "I've asked Auggie Two-River to join the Council of Twelve."

"Auggie?"

"Yes."

"You think he's the other one? In the vision I mean? I thought *I* was supposed—"

"No, no. It doesn't have anything to do with that. I was just told. I felt it, you know?"

Of course I *did* know. Hold on. Keep the faith. The talons let go.

Herk shook his head, as if to clear it. "We still need to find *him*," he said.

"No, brother," I said. He must have read my grin.

He smiled back at me. I think it was because he didn't feel so alone anymore.

Chapter fifteen

W hen I went to visit Meg the following day, I barely recognized her. She was so thin and pale, so weak, that she found it difficult to raise her hand above the rail of the bed to hold mine. That wonderful *fullness* of hers was gone. It was as if all her ripeness had been funneled into her mid-section, which swelled in a white and incongruous mound beneath the hospital sheet. Even her usually bounteous auburn hair was sullenly lackluster, clinging in oleaginous flatness to her emaciated cheeks.

Though I tried to hide it, she saw the pity in my face. Her response was a thinly courageous smile.

The nurse, Judy Crabbe, was omnipresent. She merited her name, presenting herself as a termagant of such irascible temperament that it was difficult not to hate her. She literally pushed me away from the bed, defending her charge like Dickens' Pross, a bulwark through which no enemy could penetrate. Unfortunately, Meg's hydra was internal, and much of its work, I could see, was done.

Nurse Crabbe was one of the largest women I'd ever seen. Getting a leash on her, even a figurative one, would be no small task. I sensed that God would have his hands full with Judy Crabbe. She was at least six feet tall, perhaps more. Her girth was half that, forming her into a rough rectangle that presented an imposing figure to the most determined visitor. She was a caricature of femininity, like a large man in drag, even though I was convinced, somehow, that she was female. She was perhaps thirty-five or so, but she acted as though she was much older. The severity of her dress and manner fostered the impression. Still, there was a singular kind of beauty about her—something indefinable.

I think, as was the case with almost everyone who knew Meg, that Nurse Crabbe was in love with her. I don't mean that romantically. It's just that Meg, I think, was meant to draw people to her—both physically and emotionally.

I didn't stay long. Nurse Crabbe wouldn't allow it—and rightfully so. Megan didn't have the strength to sustain even this tenuous façade for more than a few minutes, before drifting back into a drug-induced and therefore less formidable consciousness.

Nurse Crabbe ushered me out with little aplomb. I told her that I was looking forward to seeing her at church on Sunday. She only grunted in a kind of grudging recognition of the promise she'd made to Meg that she would attend.

I prayed in the elevator, because I was alone, and because I wanted so desperately for Meg to live. I reminded God that I was keeping my promise. I suppose He didn't need my memorandum.

Perhaps to prove myself, I drove out to the Tower Ranch to see Minnie. Another culling was scheduled for that day and she would be busy helping her father, but I needed to see her, touch her—an affirmation of life and reality, I guess. Also, I was bored. A First Counselor can't counsel for eight hours a day, and our parents had been doing most of that in any case. I thought I might be of some help to Ben. The slaughtering, as so many in history, was on behalf of the church. Days earlier, we'd had a walk-in freezer installed in one of the outbuildings on Horizon Road. It'd been donated by one of our newer members, purchased from a private school that had gone bankrupt. Ben Tower had promised to fill it with meat.

When I turned onto the dirt road that led to the Tower Ranch, I'd managed to hide the nightmarish image of my dying sister-in-law somewhere in that censorious grotto that conceals exiled images from conscious contemplation. I've often marveled at the ability of many to ignore what they don't wish to see, crediting their proficiency in this to their own shallowness. But the desire to be happy, the avoidance of pain, can expurgate even the reality of the *danse macabre* and that desire works in the deepest of minds, the noblest of souls.

As I drove along the fenced pastures, I saw the shaggy beasts, grazing placidly in the open meadow. They still seemed to me to be so out of place in the meager clearings of Michigan forests. I expected to see Dakota or Cheyenne appear at any moment on painted ponies over the rise beyond, bows taut, ready to give chase. These buffalo were animals that did not belong to fences, but I suppose at some point in history, someone had thought that of cows and sheep too.

When I pulled into the corraling area near the house, I spotted Minnie. She was on horseback, maneuvering her agile mount among the snorting, frightened brutes, deftly isolating single animals and directing them into a fenced channel that funneled the beasts, single file, into a large barn. Her long curly black hair bounced as she rode, but the rest of her lean figure was firm in the saddle.

I got out of the car and stood by the corral fence. Minnie saw me and waved, but immediately returned her attention to her work. Ben Tower was on horseback as well, along with two other men. They had what looked like the more dangerous job of separating the bulls from the cows and calves. The big males, with their massive heads and horns, were being culled from the larger herd in an outer corral and guided into Minnie's area where, now segregated from their harems, the monsters appeared to settle into docility and accept the bitter destiny to which we all are guided.

I had to admire Ben. He must've been close to fifty, but the lean, rigid frame he'd passed to his daughter looked better in the saddle than did those of his youthful assistants. His thick grey hair, hidden under a Stetson, didn't betray this image. He was the very portrait of the work and weather-hardened cowboy. He orchestrated the bulls' movements with a virtuosity that made me forget that some of these animals weighed a ton or more and that their fear or anger could result in lethal rebellion.

"Hi Jim." I was startled by the woman's voice. I'd been lost in my own musings. Sylvia Tower put her hand on my shoulder and leaned against the corral fence next to me. "What brings you here?" she said, laughing. "As if I didn't know."

Like her husband and daughter, she wore tight jeans, a simple shirt, and pointed high-heeled boots. Unlike them, she had a harder time packing her fuller figure into them. I don't mean she was overweight—merely voluptuous. Her straight, short hair still showed no gray, though I was certain that *that* was a magic, like the deceptive jinn, that had come from a bottle.

I pointed toward Minnie. "She's really good. I didn't know she could ride like that."

"She's a natural," Sylvia said. I could see the pride in her expression. "She took to it the first time she rode. She was only eight, I think."

A wild, eerie bellowing began as the first of the bulls exited the corral and disappeared inside a large tin-roofed barn.

"What's that for?" I asked.

"The killing," Sylvia said. "The slaughtering goes on in there. Want to see?"

"I'll pass. Thanks. You don't send them to a meat-packing place?"

"Not for these few, no. We butcher them here, ourselves, then transport the meat to the new freezer over at the church. It'll feed a lot of people—for months."

"The meat doesn't spoil in transport?"

She pointed at a large truck near the barn. *Tower Farms* was painted on the side, together with the rough image of a buffalo. "Refrigerated," she said. "Ben's pride and joy. He bought it a couple of years ago."

She turned her head back to look at her husband and her pleasant smile disappeared. "Ben's found a stubborn one," she said, pointing to the far end of the larger corral.

A massive bull was blocking the opening into the inner corral where Minnie was waiting to receive the rest of the doomed animals and guide them to the chute. The beast was turned outward, his hindquarters toward the intended path. It was clear that he had no intention of 'going gentle'. Ben was actually bumping the brute with the flank of his mare, trying to nudge it in the proper direction.

"Be careful Ben," Sylvia whispered, "don't be foolish."

As if he could hear her, Ben reined his horse back. The bull stood his ground, snorting streams of warm breath into the cool autumn air and digging holes in the soft earth with his hooves as if to entrench himself. The animal's posture was defiant. Behind Ben, the herd began to disperse and rumble away toward the larger pasture, keeping the other two riders occupied in blocking their retreat. The bawling of the frightened calves and the bellowing of the adults was deafening.

Minnie had emptied her smaller corral, and seeing the difficulty that her father was facing, reined her horse in the direction of the bottleneck.

"What's she doing?" I asked Sylvia.

"I think she's going to try to distract the bull. Maybe she can get him to turn around, then Ben can force him through from the back."

I fumbled in my pockets for a cigarette, then remembered I'd left them in the car. "Is this something that happens a lot?"

Sylvia shook her head, nervously. "Not that I've ever seen."

The ploy appeared to work. When Minnie approached, yelling and waving one arm dramatically, the bull turned lazily toward her.

Then he charged.

"*Oh my God!*" Sylvia cried out. I held my breath.

Minnie reined in her horse and tried to reverse her direction, but the bull was already at a gallop. The speed and acceleration of such a colossus amazed me.

It struck Minnie's horse a vicious blow in the haunches, just as the panicked mare had almost completed its turn. It went down hard into the soft mud, whinnying hysterically. Dark blood oozed over her white flank.

"*Minnie!*" Sylvia screamed.

Fortunately, the impact had been so forceful that Minnie had been thrown clear and not been pinned under her fallen mount, but she was dazed and sluggish as she attempted to rise from the mud.

The mare whinnied grotesquely as the bison rammed it again, vindictively goring it—this time in its soft, exposed belly. A third charge and the screaming mare quieted. It lay dying, eviscerated, its life's blood, along with its intestines, seeping languidly onto the ground.

"Pilar!" Minnie yelled the doomed mare's name as she collected her senses. The bull pulled back then rammed its gory head into the horse again. The mare didn't move.

"Pilar," Minnie sobbed. "My sweet Pilar." Her cries drew the attention of the beast as he circled round the dead mare and he lowered his head, preparing to charge the sound of Minnie's voice. He was so preoccupied that he didn't see or hear Ben Tower galloping at him from behind—nor did he notice me. I scrambled over the corral fence and rushed toward Minnie. Sylvia yelled at me to stop, but I was already inside, pausing only long enough to grab a rock and hurl it at the beast. The rock struck its hump, but had no more injurious effect than a water balloon. It *did* cause the bull to turn briefly away from Minnie in my direction.

I'll never be sure, and Minnie has never blamed me, but I believe now that my untrained intervention contributed to the tragedy—perhaps because it was meant to. The shaggy goliath merely turned, and in that movement, one wild and rolling eye caught a glimpse of another horse, a second antagonist. The panicked beast threw all its massive weight against the vision and Ben's horse thudded to the ground, its left foreleg splintered. The equine shriek sent chills coursing through me. So anguished was its whinnying that my initial fears were only for the poor beast. But then I saw Ben Tower on his hands and knees behind the mare, reduced, like the other beasts in this gladiatorial arena, to a primordial struggle for life. Without the inventive weapons of human ingenuity, without his domesticated allies, Ben was at an extreme disadvantage. The bull, his mammoth head and shoulders soaked in blood and foam, the snot from his ponderous snout dripping in his beard, knew his rare advantage. He thundered across to attack the real tormentor of his kind.

I pushed Minnie over the corral fence and into the safety of the reaching arms of her mother. I turned back for Ben. I was too late. The approaching riders from the outer corral were too late. The slaughterers, emerging now from the barn with rifles in their hands, were too late.

The mountainous bull lowered his gigantic head and rammed the stunned man, crushing the side of Ben's head against the unforgiving earth as an argument for the still possible triumph of raw emotion over thought.

I saw Ben raise one arm in a feeble attempt to ward off his attacker. The arm was snapped backward at a grotesque angle before disappearing, with the rest of his body, beneath the bull's amazing bulk.

Desperate to do something, I threw another stone, barely conscious of the women's screams behind me. The bull slowly turned in my direction. I remember shouting at it, but I don't remember what words I used. What do words signify anyway, when you're yelling at Death?

The bull started toward me, and my mind recalled another place, a river, with different corpses strewn in foreign mud. I survived *that*, was my fleeting thought, only to die here, still young, in different killing fields?

As the buffalo charged, I heard the guns, three shots I think. The bull's legs wobbled. It fell. I felt the earth tremble. Two more shots and it lay still, the heat of its steamy rage clashing with the autumnal air and surrounding the placid carcass with surreal mist.

I could only stand there, staring in bewildered gratitude, as the rogue snorted his last breath at us. The ranch hands rushed to Ben Tower. Minnie and Sylvia were pushing the corral gate open. "He's alive!" someone shouted. "Call 911!" Mother and daughter were on their knees in the mud. Minnie had removed her blouse and wrapped it around her father's broken head. She cradled him against her small bosom. Her bra was quickly crimsoned with his blood.

I remember the shame I felt at yet another failure to divert death from its sure course, and also my envy of Ben Tower, broken as he was, nestled on the tender chest of his child.

The ambulance arrived within fifteen minutes, during which time Minnie tried to comfort her stricken father and frantic mother. I found her some towels and another shirt in the house where, having never been inside before, I felt like an intruding thief.

The ranch hands used chains and a tractor to pull the fallen bull from the arena to the barn—his struggle for naught, as saws and knives turned his body into subdued meat—sustenance for his enemies. I thought later that he should have been buried. He'd shown himself close enough to man in his desire to protect himself and his kind that there was an earned nobility there. Demonstrating this courage, the bull should have been allowed to rot, rather than be devoured and excreted as human shit in a porcelain bowl. I never ate buffalo meat again.

Ben's horse had to be shot. It, and Minnie's beloved Pilar were given proper internment later on—reward for their loyalty. An hour after the ambulance arrived at the hospital, the doctor emerged from the operating room. I noticed dark spots of blood on the cloth footies that covered his shoes as he stood before us in the waiting room and gave us the news.

Ben Tower would live. Sylvia burst into joyous tears, but Minnie knew more was coming. She waited for the surgeon to finish his report. I kept looking around for my brother. I'd told Pete, the foreman at the Tower Ranch, to call him. He should have been here by now.

"There will be some brain damage," the doctor was saying. "How extensive, we don't know yet. Most of the trauma was to his head. His arm was broken in two places and that was the only other real damage, but his head…."

Minnie's dark eyes searched the physician's stoic features for clues. She couldn't depend only on what he chose to say. I'm sure she could read the severity of her father's injuries in his stooped shoulders and the way his capped head moved slowly from left to right. "What about his head?" she asked.

"The left side of his skull was badly damaged," the doctor continued. "It wasn't just fractured, it was crushed, caved in. The brain itself, well, it's been damaged. There's even some tissue loss. We have another couple of hours of surgery ahead of us. We've cleaned the wound and stopped the bleeding. We'll have to reconstruct the skull, using an artificial wall. Fortunately, Mr. Tower's motor skills don't seem impaired. He won't be paralyzed. I'll get back with you, Mrs. Tower, as soon as possible."

He left abruptly, his rubber shoes squeaking like frightened mice on the shiny tile as he retreated.

"Mr. Gudsen?" I turned to see a young girl, a high school volunteer, scanning the heavily populated waiting room. She wore a uniform that looked like a candy cane.

"That's me," I said.

"If you'd come with me, Sir," she said sweetly, "there's a phone call for you."

I looked at Minnie. She motioned for me to go as she held her mother.

"I'll be right back," I said.

I followed the girl to a nurse's station. She went behind the counter and handed the phone across to me, smiling too pleasantly. I suspected that I could have her if I wanted. I tried to put it out of my mind.

"Hello?"

"Jim?"

"Herk! Where are you? The Towers could use a little help right now and I thought—"

"How's Ben doing?"

"He's hurt pretty badly. They tell us he's going to make it, but in what condition, they don't know." I heard shouting on the other end of the line—and sirens. "Herk, what's going on? Where are you?"

"I'm at the house. Jim, somebody set the church on fire."

"*What?*"

"The church. It's burning right now. There are fire engines here. They're trying to put it out, but it was too fast. The wind spread it quickly and they used a lot of gasoline."

"They? Who's they?"

"We don't know yet. The flames have spread to most of the other outbuildings and some trees. They're hosing down the house to keep it from spreading here. I think they're getting it contained." He was shouting into the receiver as people often do when they're excited—not for the benefit of the listener, but in reaction to what was going on around him. I remember thinking that it was so much like the rest of life—we believe everyone lives, or should live, in our particular world, especially at moments of tragedy.

"You're sure it's arson, Herk?"

"There was a gas can on the lawn and…."

"What?"

"There's a note too. Larry, Dad, found it on the windshield wiper blade of his car."

"What'd it say?"

"False prophets burn."

I knew how that must've pained him. "Nobody saw them?"

"Everyone had gone home, Jim. I was at Holy Cross with Meg. Rusha and mom and dad had gone out to Cinema Six to see that mafia movie."

"*The Godfather?*"

"Yeah. Rusha thought they could all use a little down time and mom did too. They insisted."

"Herk, did anybody get hurt?"

"Not badly, no. Auggie discovered the fire, but he didn't see anyone. He and Yuri called the fire department, then tried to fight it themselves. Yuri burnt his hands a little, nothing serious."

Herk was interrupted by someone then. I heard him say: "Are you sure?" The rest of it was garbled.

"Jim."

"Yeah?"

"The file cabinets in my office have been rifled. A bunch of stuff is missing."

"What?"

"Mostly financial files I think. I'll have to have Herman go through it."

"They broke in?"

"We never lock the house. You know that. We're never gone either. There's always someone here."

"Until tonight."

"Until tonight."

"You know what that means?"

"There's a Judas."

I thought about who it could be. I had no clue. Someone had been shrinking God again. "What do you want me to do?"

"Stay there. We're getting things under control. Minnie needs you more than we do right now. I won't be able to get away from here for a while. The police have a lot of questions. Check on Meg, will you?"

"If I can get past the Crabbe, sure."

He laughed. "Explain to Sylvia why I can't come right now?"

"Sure."

"I'll send Caleb. Keep me posted. I'll see you later."

"Right. Bye."

"Bye."

I wasn't sure that I should tell Minnie and Sylvia what was going on, but I had no other reason for Herk not to be there and the truth, however painful, is usually better, I think.

They were appalled of course. By midnight, Minnie and Sylvia and Caleb Bird and I were alone in the waiting room. Caleb had shown up within half an hour of my conversation with Herk. As I listened to him pray for Ben's recovery and for the church, I was struck again by the differences between him and his brother. Robin was so tentative, so sensitive. Caleb was, like his voice, strong and sure and utterly masculine—cocky even—which I guess is the same as masculine. He knew how to enlarge himself and crow for the comfort of the hens and chicks. He knew, of course, like his ornithological counterpart, that greater creatures controlled the world, but in *this* barnyard he could strut in cocksure dependency.

When Minnie fell asleep, around two in the morning, I excused myself to Sybil, who was listening intently to Caleb's diatribe on eternal life, and took the elevator to the Oncology ICU.

When the doors opened to reveal the nurses' station on that floor, I was relieved to find that no one was there. Judy Crabbe must actually *have* a home, I thought, though I suspected that, like my position as First Counselor, it wasn't useful enough to warrant the payments.

I knew from my visit that morning, (was it only *that* morning?), that Megan's room was at the far end of the hall. I moved stealthily through the shadows in that direction, expecting at any moment to be accosted by a watchful nurse who would tell me that discovering the condition of a dying relative could only be done during visiting hours. But the guerrillas never materialized and I continued down the corridor unimpeded. As I drew near to Meg's room, I discovered the reason for their negligence. Light poured into the dark passageway from Meg's room, and white-clad nurses moved in and out of the doorway in anxious haste. Something was wrong, and I prayed again, a silent and personal petition to God, for Meg's life, and the life of her child.

I grabbed the arm of one of the nurses who emerged from the room. Alarm monitors were beeping obnoxiously behind her and I heard the whispered concern in the hushed voices of those who were still with Meg. The woman looked at me in horror, as though I must be the cause of whatever crisis she was dealing with.

"I'm Meg Gudsen's brother-in-law," I said. "What's wrong? What's going on?"

"You shouldn't be—"

I tightened my grip on her arm. It pained me to see her wince, but I wasn't going to be subjected to a lecture. "What's the matter with her? Tell me!"

"I'm sorry," she said, "But I'm not allowed—"

"Listen. If you don't tell me, you're going to need one of these beds yourself! Do you understand me?" I'm sure she was con-

vinced, from my voice and the expression on my face, that I meant
it. I think I did. I'm glad that I didn't have to find out.

"She...Mrs. Gudsen...has gone into a coma. We're trying to
attend to her and the child. Please, let me go!"

I released her arm and apologized. She didn't seem to care.

I hung around the entrance to Meg's room for an hour,
standing in the dark hallway, praying, listening to the groans of the
other dying patients. No groans came from Meg's room. She was
past that.

Finally, a kinder nurse took pity. "Mr. Gudsen," she whispered. "Your wife is—"

"She's my sister-in-law, my brother's wife."

"Mrs. Gudsen is in a coma, but her vital signs have stabi-
lized. The baby seems to be okay. Why don't you go home for a
while and we'll call you if there's any change. How would that be?"

"Will she come back?" I mumbled. "The coma, I mean. Can
she come out of it?"

Sympathy. Her face held sympathy. Sympathy always means
'no'. "I think they'll take the baby soon," she said, looking at her
watch. "You should call your brother."

"Yes. I'll do that. Thank you." She went back into the room
where God presided. I wasn't allowed in.

I went back to Minnie and told her. She held me. Some of
her father's blood rubbed off on my jacket. I called Herk. The fire
was out. He'd be there soon. He was calm. Faith can sometimes
turn people away from their expected humanity. I thought he
ought to cry.

When I returned, the women were alone. Caleb had gone for
coffee.

Sylvia seemed to have gathered some strength. "Jim," she
said, "Dad's going to live. They feel very certain about it now. The
doctor was just here."

"That's wonderful news, Sylvia." I forced a smile.

"We saw him. He looks good, doesn't he Min?"

"Yes, Mom, he does." Her voice lacked enthusiasm.

"Why don't you take Minnie home, Jim? She can put some clean clothes on, take a shower. Look at you too. You're covered in mud. Then you can come back right away. Pastor Bird's here. I'll be fine."

"I'll stay, Mom."

"No, Dear. You can come right back, then I'll go. Please."

Minnie looked at me. "It makes sense," I said.

"I won't be long." She kissed her mother tenderly.

When we were in the car, Minnie said: "He won't be the same. They think he's going to be..."—she forced tears away—"...limited."

"Limited?"

"Retarded."

"Oh. You don't know, about brain injuries, I mean. My brother—"

"Your brother is special."

"So is your father."

"To me though, and my mother—not to the world."

"Let God make that decision."

"I think he has."

When we got to the ranch, everything was dark except where the harvest moon illuminated the earlier scene of carnage. Minnie briefly glanced that way, then hurried into the house. She went down the hall to her room while I turned on several lamps. She returned only a few minutes later, wearing a robe.

"You showered already?" I said.

"No." She slipped out of her robe and let it fall. She was naked. I could see a deep bruise on her left hip. She held out her hands. "We can get clean together."

"Oh, Minnie."

"I know. I need you though. I need to be loved. I want to be touched and held and penetrated. I want to feel alive! Make love to me, Jim. Take it all away."

There was no help for it. It was a broken day.

Broken faith.

Broken bodies.

Broken dreams.

Broken promises.

When it all comes apart, it seems to be perfectly logical to heal the soul with the body.

Chapter sixteen

Meg was unaware of the birth of her son. They took him by caesarian operation the morning following Ben Tower's accident and the burning of the church.

He was a healthy boy, almost nine pounds at birth. He had his father's golden hair.

Meg looked as delicate and white as an eggshell cast aside by its former tenant, broken and forgotten by the little life it had nurtured. The doctors gave us no reason to hope. Time, they said, was running out. Herk said that it was the only thing that time could do.

He did not forget Meg. Judy Crabbe didn't forget. Neither did I, but I'd betrayed her and wished that I could. Rusha, the former Queen of the Amazons, became our nephew's surrogate mother. It was amazing to me how maternal my sister looked and acted when she fed the child his bottle or changed his diaper.

Herk and I had discussed changing our name to Ladon, since no one named Gudsen had ever really existed in our lives, but tradition is a strong force and we decided to keep the name our mother had given us. Herk felt it would be too confusing for the members of the church. Besides, it was no less given than our given names and no more an invention than we were. Dad understood. So the new child was named Benjamin Ladon Gudsen.

He was baptized the first Sunday after his birth. It was a beautiful October day, close to seventy degrees. The service had to be held on the lawn again. It was difficult to look at the still-smoldering ashes of all our labor as we sang A *Mighty Fortress is Our God.*

Herk gave a riveting sermon about adversity and the eventual triumph of all who trusted Jesus. He preached mercy and God's all-encompassing forgiveness. I thought of Minnie. She was with her father. We had not talked about what had happened between us, but I had become afraid of justice. Herk ended the sermon with the final verse from Luther's great Reformation hymn:

> *Take they our life,*
> *Goods, fame, child and wife*
> *Let these all be gone*
> *They have yet nothing won,*
> *The Kingdom ours remaineth.*

I saw him falter over the second line. He glanced over at his son in his grandmother's arms. Then he straightened, stiffened actually, and went on. At its conclusion, many in the growing congregation wept. Some shouted *Amen!*

I wondered what the kingdom was worth, if all we loved was gone.

The Council of Twelve, really still Seven, met immediately following the service to address the obvious problems of rebuilding the church and how we were going to shelter the worshippers against the approaching winter. There was also the pressing need to find the remaining members of The Twelve, although I feared that that was not going to save Meg. I was convinced, like most believers, that my broken promise to God was more important than His ultimate purpose. We are an egotistical bunch, we God-lovers. Religion would reduce Him to a denomination. I would, that morning, reduce Him still further. Herk kept the wider vision.

Judy Crabbe, despite occasional sour glances in my direction, appeared to accept Herk's explanation of her role as one of The Twelve. He told her of his vision and though she wasn't flattered by the image, she believed it, especially after Yuri's stirring account of his conversion and Rusha's documentation of her own reclamation. Still, I think Judy's approbation stemmed more from an earnest desire to be Meg's protector than any sublime epiphany.

Doctor Mantus was a harder case. He agreed to attend the council meetings, but he told us flatly that he didn't believe that what we were doing was divinely commissioned. He confessed that academic curiosity was his motivation for coming to us that day— that, and what he referred to as enlightened self-interest, would have to suffice as a substitute for faith. Herk, who was the first person I'd ever seen who could look Aristotle Mantus straight in the face without revealing some hint of distaste or amusement, agreed that it would be enough for now. I think, really, that he'd won the professor earlier though, with a fraternal hug, at their introduction. The welcome was sincere. Doctor Mantus, despite his theological reservations, had found something entirely unique to his life's experience—genuine acceptance. I sensed that we wouldn't lose him. By the end of the meeting of the Council, I was certain.

We gathered in the kitchen immediately after the service. After an opening prayer by Caleb Bird, Herman Goetsh reported that our financial situation was, to use his term, 'disrupted'. The ledgers, bankbooks, property deeds, accounts, receipts, etc. had been stolen by the arsonists. Herman had spent the entire day after the fire visiting the various banks where the church's accounts were maintained, changing access numbers and transferring cash to secured amenities. It did not appear, he reported, that the thieves were interested in money, since no attempts had been made, (though they possessed the codes), to access our accounts. Still, it was a mess, and it would take considerable time before he would be able to give us an accurate accounting. He was more concerned, he said, about the deeds to the Ladon and Two-River properties as well as the records regarding the sale of the Amazon Clubs. Those documents would have to be reviewed by the Registrar of Deeds from their originals, and Herman would need Auggie and Yuri and Larry to assist him in that effort—which they readily consented to do. The business records were gone, and in that area at least, he would have to start from scratch.

Herk sat impatiently through all this accounting, which consumed the better part of an hour. Money truly meant nothing to him and I know he was anxious to get to Holy Cross to see Meg. When Herman finally sat down, Herk appeared to focus again.

"We need to clean our stables," Auggie Two-River said as Herk prepared to address the next item on the agenda.

"What do you mean?" Herk asked.

"I think you know what he means," Robin Stym said. "Somebody in this church burned our new sanctuary. We need to find out who it is."

"Why?"

"Why?" Rusha said. "Because they could do it again. We have to be prepared to fight our enemies don't we?"

"No, Sister," Herk said quietly. "We have to be prepared to love them."

"You're right," Larry said. "You're right, Son. God knows I needed it. But we live in a real world where—"

Herk turned quickly in his direction. "Reality is what humanity has made it. We're seeking something greater than that. I won't answer violence with violence. I'm not interested in retribution."

"Ve have ta vatch ourself, Pastor, yah?" Yuri added in his thickly accented voice. "Dey von't stop, but ve make 'em."

"We can tighten security, yes. We won't leave things unattended. We'll lock things up. We can be practical in that regard, but our goal is prevention, not vengeance."

"I think we should try to find out who did it," Rusha said. "We need to get rid of the Judas."

Everyone in the circle nodded their agreement.

"I *know* who it was," Herk said.

There was a disquieting silence.

"Who?" Baxter Bird asked.

"I'll handle it myself."

That was it. We let it go. It was testimony to his authority, a measure of the confidence that his councilors had in him, or perhaps it was the realization of no viable alternatives. At any rate, there was no real argument.

"We've begun clearing the rubble already," Herk continued, gesturing toward the screen door where the sounds of tractors and trucks and human voices drifted inside. "The concrete foundation is still good. We've ordered new lumber. We'll have to work day and night, but I think we can get it done before winter.

"In a month?" I said.

"Yes."

"What about the completion of the Council?" Rusha said. "Have you any idea who—"

"No!" Herk's answer was flatly decisive. I heard a hint of irritated frustration, which he was obviously struggling to conquer. "I'm sorry, Rusha," he said. His weak smile was forced, but genuinely remorseful. "I didn't mean to be short with you. It's just that this whole thing weighs on me. My Meg...." His voice broke, momentarily. Rusha reached across the table and took his hand. He recomposed himself and continued explaining the urgency of the completion of The Twelve to those newer members of the Council.

Throughout the meeting, Professor Mantus had been busily jotting notes on a legal pad. He was, I was discovering, almost blind. His piggish nose was virtually even with his hand as he scribbled continuously with an expensive pen he grasped in his pudgy fingers. He seemed oblivious to the rest of us. Once or twice during the meeting I got up to refresh my coffee and tried looking over his shoulder to get a look at his notes, but his weak eyes caused him to hunch over his work so assiduously that his head and back thwarted any glimpse of its contents. I don't think he was making any conscious attempt to be clandestine.

"How can God expect us to do what he demands, if He won't show us how to get there?" Baxter said. He looked at Robin for approval and, as always, found it.

"In His own time," Herk said.

"But time is a luxury He doesn't seem to be affording us," Judy Crabbe unnecessarily reminded him.

Herk was about to respond when Doctor Mantus sat upright in his chair and softly said: "We have what we need." He had mumbled it, really, still squinting intently at his notes, although he held them up now, and no one except Larry Ladon and myself who sat next to him, had even been sure it was he who had spoken.

"I'm sorry," Herk said. He was staring intently at the chubby little man. "Did you say something Doctor Manus?"

"Mantus," I whispered at Herk's right hand.

"Doctor Man*tus*," Herk corrected.

It was really amazing to me how the professor stared so confidently at my brother. He looked so comfortable and uninhibited. Herk was equally unabashed. He literally took no notice of Aristotle Mantus's porcine features. He never indicated the slightest disgust or revulsion at his deformities. He never stole secret glances. But then, Herk wasn't ever interested in the physical. Meg was the only person I knew who moved him at all in that way.

"I said," Professor Mantus repeated, squinting at his copious notes, "that I think we have what we need."

"What do you mean?" Herk said. "What we need for…what purpose?"

"The purpose of completing your Council of Twelve."

Herk studied the little man carefully. The rest of us were deathly silent as we watched, with varying degrees of disdain, Doctor Mantus rooting about his papers like a hog at a corncrib.

"Have you ever read much about mythology?" he finally said to Herk. "Greek mythology?"

"A little. Not much though, and only insofar as it applied to the history of the early church. I'm afraid I'm no authority. Why? What does it matter?"

"I find it fascinating myself. It was the vehicle by which I became interested in philosophy. James told you at our introduction a few hours ago, it is my area of expertise, what I teach at the university."

"Doctor Mantus," Rusha said, "I'm sure this is all very—"

The little man raised his chubby hand in her direction, but avoided any contact with her alluring and consuming eyes.

212

"Please," he whispered. His voice was shaky and nervous as he addressed her. "Hear me out, Miss Ladon. I think you'll find what I have to say of relevance here."

Rusha accepted his mild remonstrance, but I found myself, as I had at many of his lectures, screaming *spit it out!* (Within, of course, the safely territorial limits of my own mind).

"I've always been aware of my own, uh, appearance," he continued. "As a child, I was likened by my schoolmates to Porky Pig, the animated figure from the Warner Brother's cartoons. I even stuttered like him when I was little. Even now, my students call me The Bore, which is, of course, homonymically associated with the word 'Boar'. In short, I've always been associated with pigs. That's why I'm here, in fact, Pastor Gudsen, isn't it? Your vision, I mean."

I was listening intently now, too absorbed to see Herk's reaction. I heard him utter a simple "Yes."

"As a teen-ager I came across the legend of The Boar of Erymanthus. My mother must have felt, even as I lay in her womb, her son's proclivity for philosophy, because she named me Aristotle." He snorted a little at this observation and Rusha turned her face away from him as he did so. "That would be the metaphysical interpretation of course. More rationalistic thinkers would say, perhaps, that I unconsciously chose a profession that matched my name. In either case—"

"Doctor Mantus," Larry Ladon said, "if you could get to the—"

"Yes, yes," he grunted. "Forgive me. Digression is the vice of those who must lecture for a living. To the point—I was always called Ari. Ari Mantus."

Most of us waited for him to continue, but Robin Stym caught it right away. "Ari Mantus," he said. "It sounds very much like Erymanthus, the Boar of Erymanthus."

"Indeed," said the professor, beaming triumphantly at his new student.

"But what's it mean?" Baxter protested. "What relevance does your story have to this Council, other than it brought you to us?"

"It brought all of you," Doctor Mantus said. There was an immediate murmuring around the table, an undertone of muddled confusion.

"We've been brought together by Divine intervention, Professor," Herk said.

"That may be, that may be, though I'm not much on miracles," the little professor responded, "but there is a pattern nonetheless. It's as plain as, well,"—and here he snorted happily—"the nose on my face."

"Perhaps you'd care to enlighten the rest of us?" Judy Crabbe said. I could see her anger rising by the second. She wanted to leave to attend to Meg, and this ugly little man was interfering. She was cross, and she did nothing to disguise it.

"Of course," Doctor Mantus said, "please forgive me. The Boar of Erymanthus is one of the *Twelve* Labors of Hercules. Without undue extrapolation, another involves Hippolyta, the Queen of the Amazons, a character that *you*, Miss Ladon,"—he twisted his face shrewdly and glanced hurriedly at Rusha—"must be familiar with."

Rusha crimsoned for a moment.

"Miss Crabbe, you are a nurse at St. Luke's? You are tending to Mrs. Gudsen I believe. It seems you fit the story of the Hydra of Lerna. How, I'm not exactly certain, but the hydra was a monster with many heads." Baxter Bird giggled. "No, no," the doctor hurried to correct, "*you* aren't the monster. The cancer is the hydra, I think. You cut off one of its heads and two more appear, just as the disease so often seems to be conquered, then reasserts itself. Cut out one tumor, two more take its place. No, a crab was sent by Hera, Queen of the Gods, to unwittingly assist the hydra. Hera hated Heracles, her namesake. Heracles, or Hercules, crushed the crab underfoot and Hera placed its image in the sky as the constellation, Cancer."

Judy Crabbe stood up. "I would never harm Mrs. Gudsen!" she shouted.

Doctor Mantus shriveled in the face of her fury and hid his face among his papers.

"Judy, please!" Herk said. "We know you'd never hurt Meg. He's only telling us about some legends. Please sit down. I think we need to hear the rest of this."

Caleb Bird went to her and put a soothing hand on her shoulder. She sat down again, but the malevolent expression on her face would have, I think, frightened a real hydra.

"Vat 'bout me?" Yuri Theus asked. He was sitting next to Rusha. Since getting clean, he'd developed a nervous habit of rubbing the little white scars on his arms and then running his fingers through the wisps of hair that had survived, in very small numbers, on the surface of his balding pate. He did so now as he continued to speak in his thickly accented and timid voice. "I know I'm da lion from da Pasture's vision and all dat. But dis an't joost a part of some mydology. I been raised from bad tings." He rubbed the scars again. "Vas a meeracle, dat's so."

"Perhaps," Doctor Mantus said, keeping a close eye on Judy Crabbe.

"No. No perhaps," Yuri firmly answered.

"The lion, the *Nemean* lion, was the first of the Twelve Labors of Hercules," the professor said. "You have an accent Mr. Theus. Eastern European, I should think. Where do you come from?"

"I was boy in Belgrade, but I was baby in Greece—Corind."

"Corinth?"

"Yah."

"The ruins of the ancient Greek city of Nemea are just west of Corinth. Did you know that?"

Again there were many exclamations of surprise and wonder among the councilors.

"No."

"The king, the man who ordered Heracles to kill the lion. His name was Eurystheus. Sound familiar?"

Yuri Theus rubbed both hands across the glistening surface of his head. They came away wet, and he wiped them on his pants. "Does someone half a ceegrette?"

I lit one and handed it to him.

"Auggie Two-River," I said. "The Augean Stables. Heracles diverted two rivers in order to clean the stables, am I right?"

"Excellent, James," the professor chirped. He was obviously delighted with this game. His ugly features were as pleasantly arranged as good humor would allow, rather like a gleeful warthog.

"Now," Professor Mantus said, slapping his knee, "to the Birds of Stymphalus. *Robin.* is the name of a bird, the state bird of Michigan, actually. Baxter *Bird.* Need I elaborate? Robin's last name, of course, fit with the first part of Stymphalus. The second syllable, phalus, is like phallus which…well, I think that everyone here is aware of the meaning of that word, though how it connects to Mr. Stym and Mr. Bird, I don't know, other than the fact that they both possess one."

Baxter Bird began to cry, perhaps recalling his father's discovery of his appetite for that particular article of human flesh. He rushed from the room, with Robin close at his heels.

Doctor Mantus seemed utterly surprised. "Did I say something inappropriate?" he asked. "I really didn't mean to upset anyone. Dear me!"

Herk smiled. "No," he said, gently. "It's not anything you did." He turned to Caleb. "Would you check on your brother, Pastor Bird?" Caleb nodded and, reluctantly I think, left the room.

Dad looked at Doctor Mantus. "You've accounted for everyone except—"

"Yes, well, I'll admit I'm baffled there, Mr. Gudsen—"

"Ladon."

Some epiphany was dawning on Aristotle Mantus' piggish face. "Your name is Ladon? But Pastor Gudsen introduced you as his father, so I naturally assumed—"

"I *am* his father."

"And Miss Ladon's also?" he said, nodding toward Rusha.

"Yes."

"But then—"

"It's a long story, Professor," I interjected

"I did wonder," Doctor Mantus said, "about the child—the baptism this morning."

"My son has both names," Herk said.

The professor shuffled through his notes again, and then looked at our father in a studious sort of way, as though he was analyzing bacteria under a microscope.

"This is going to sound like a strange question, Mr. Ladon," he said, "but do you have any connection with...apples?"

I looked at Herk. He caught my eye and smiled.

"Why yes," Larry answered. "I own, did own, an orchard. I deeded it to the church."

Doctor Mantus snorted a tenuous giggle. "I thought so. The Apples of the Hesperides, the golden apples of immortality. They were guarded by a dragon. The dragon's name was Ladon."

Dad laughed aloud. "A dragon! Well, I'm less reformed than I suspected."

"Personally, I'd have given that moniker to my mother," Rusha quipped.

"This is ridiculous!" Auggie exclaimed. He'd been fairly quiet, but he looked angry as he stood up. "You're suggesting that this holy and righteous man," he said, gesturing toward Herk, "has somehow been gathering people because their names or histories or whatever have some connection to fairy tales? Herkimer Gudsen is a real man of God! God speaks through him!"

"I don't think Professor Mantus is saying anything against that, Auggie." It was my own voice, but it seemed strangely foreign. It wasn't until later that I realized it sounded very much like Larry Ladon's.

"I don't think so either," Herk agreed. "In fact, I believe Doctor Mantus understands that I only made these connections now, as he pointed them out. I don't believe he's accusing me of any falsity, are you?"

"No, of course not," the professor said.

Auggie, his sense of orthodoxy satisfied for the moment, sat down.

The Birds reentered the room at the same time, and quietly resumed their places, Caleb standing solidly at Herk's left hand.

"I don't think Doctor Mantus has come here to interfere with the church or belittle our faith. On the contrary, he's heaven-sent. He's the map by which we are to find our way, whether he believes that or not."

"Well, I don't know…"

"What are the missing labors, Doctor Mantus?" Herk said. "How do we find the others?"

The professor smiled, emphasizing his snout. I could tell that he was having a hell of a good time. "Are we to assume," he asked, "that the birds are one character—excuse me, one councilor?"

Herk had always, intuitively, made the assumption. I looked at my brother with renewed admiration. He nodded.

"Then there are five labors left," the professor said. He squinted at his notes. "The Hind of Ceryneia, the Cretan Bull, the Horses of Diomedes, the Oxen of Geryon and the Capture of Cerberus."

"How in the hell are we supposed to find them?" Rusha cried. "*Five* people in what, a few days? I don't want to be cruel, but I don't think Meg has even *that* much time and I don't even know what a hind is."

Aristotle Mantus offered an explanation. "A hind is an antelope—or was, in the original story. I think your experience in this business, however, had indicated that it could be something else. The boar can be a philosophy professor; the lion, a football player and so on. It's a challenge, really. We have to figure out the code."

Auggie Two-River shook his head as he stood again to speak. "It seems to me that it's very petty of God to create such a silly game at the risk of human life. Why isn't simple prayer, simple faith, good enough?"

"Is that how you operate your relationship with Him, Auggie?" Herk said. "Communication and trust are enough? You don't really expect Him to *do* anything? You are straightforward with *Him*? We have to labor. We have to strive with mind and body Auggie, to find Him, as He has done to redeem us. If nothing is required of us, then there is no failure, but neither is there any victory. He doesn't give us anything we can't handle. He's given us Doctor Mantus here, to help us. Do you see?"

I don't think Auggie was entirely convinced, but he sat down again.

"Please continue, Doctor Mantus," Herk said.

"Well, of course I can't comment on the theology," he mumbled, "but I do enjoy a good puzzle." He rifled through his notes again. "A hind is also a rustic, a country bumpkin if you will. It can be a reference to one's posterior or part of a name. The hind of Ceryneia was gold-antlered and bronze-hoofed. It was sacred to Artemis, or Diana by her Roman name, the goddess of chastity, hunting and the moon. Any of these things, as far as I can determine, might come into play when trying to identify this person. The Cretan Bull was from the island of Crete but 'creta', in Greek, is the word 'earth' from which we have developed the geologic adjective, 'cretaceous'. Then again, it could be a closely related word, such as cretin, an idiot, or the French word 'crestin' for Christian. Cretinism is also, I believe, another term for myxoedema, a skin disease. Who knows? I think we have to watch for all of them and perhaps one or two I'm not aware of."

Herk was busily jotting all this on paper.

"What about the horses?" I said.

"The Horses of Diomedes," Doctor Mantus said. "They were wild mares who were fed human flesh by King Diomedes. Heracles killed this wicked king and fed the horses *his* flesh, which tamed them."

"And the oxen thing?" Larry said.

"Heracles was sent to the island of Erytheia to fetch the golden cattle there, which belonged to a monster named Geryon. Geryon had three bodies, three heads and six hands. Challenged to battle by the creature, Heracles ran to Geryon's flank and shot him through all three bodies with a single arrow. Then he took the cattle back to Eurystheus, sailing across the Mediterranean in a golden goblet shaped like a water lily."

"Well *he*, at least, ought to be easy to spot," Judy said, drolly.

"An't der one more?" Yuri asked.

"Yes," Doctor Mantus said, "the most difficult, really. Heracles had to go to Hades and bring back the horrible three-headed dog, Cerberus, that guarded the entrance to the Land of the Dead in the mythological underworld."

"He descended into hell," Caleb Bird mumbled.

"In a manner of speaking," Doctor Mantus responded, "yes."

"So we're supposed to find five people who represent these creatures?" Larry said.

"More the 'labor', I think, than the creatures in them," I said. "That seems to have been the pattern thus far."

"I agree," Herk said.

"And if we find them?" Rusha said.

"Bring them here, if you can. At the very least, let me know, so I can deal with it," Herk said.

"Why you, Herk?" I asked.

"Because," Professor Mantus answered, "he represents the figure of Heracles, I think. The similarities in the names, Heracles and Herkimer, are too much to be overlooked and he is the one who is being...guided."

Caleb lit a cigarette and pulled at his starchy collar. He never, to my mind, looked comfortable in his clerical clothes. "What caused Hercules to be sent on these labors in the first place, Professor?" he said.

Doctor Mantus focused on his notes as he answered, characteristically avoiding any eye contact. "In a fit of madness put upon him by Hera, the Queen of the Gods, he killed his wife and children. The labors, it's said, were his punishment."

"Who was his wife?" Caleb asked.

Doctor Mantus's innocent reply chilled us all. "She was King Creon's eldest daughter. Her name was Megara."

Chapter seventeen

After the meeting, Herk and Rusha and Judy Crabbe hurried off to Holy Cross to be with Meg. I confess I was just as anxious to get to the hospital. I wanted very much to know how Meg was doing too, since I believed, with a terrible foreboding, that my broken promise to God would bring a reckoning. *A deal's a deal.* I had betrayed God and Meg, but the loveliness of that single moment with Minnie Tower might have been worth the double-cross. It might have been worth hell. Reassurance of *that* magnitude required the touch of her hand, her physical nearness.

In spite of that, I stayed behind for a while to speak with Doctor Mantus. I had a couple of reasons. First, I think I was genuinely concerned about him. He'd spoken quite frankly, of suicidal leanings that no one knew about except me. My quixotic sense of morality forced an obligation on me to make sure it didn't happen. Secondly, I really wanted to know what he thought about all that had transpired. Certainly he couldn't deny that the forming of The Twelve and the founding of the Gospel Church bordered on the miraculous. I respected his wisdom and I guess I really wanted to know, more than anything else, what his opinion of my brother was. He knew nothing of Herk's earlier years, the piercings, the superior insight, the loving and sinless child. I wanted to tell him, to convince him, to *be* convinced.

I found him in the yard, sitting in the shade of the oak and smoking a cigarette, as he watched several dozen people, Yuri, Auggie and Larry Ladon among them, clearing charred timbers from the ruins of the new church.

"James!" he said as I approached him. "What a good day to be alive!"

"I'm glad to hear you say that," I told him, "considering that just a few days ago you were ...looking at life differently."

"Ah," he chuckled. "You mean the consideration of my own demise. Well yes, I suppose so, although I believe most people think about it on a regular basis. It's just that I'm willing to do something about it, you see."

"You wouldn't really want to end your own life, I'm sure. It's wrong. You know that."

"Well," he said, scratching his bristly chin, "probabilism is a wonderful concept. When there is doubt as to the moral rectitude of an action, the opinion that favors liberty may be followed, provided of course, that it is solidly probable, even though the contrary may be equally, or even more, probable. It's a Catholic concept, actually, and one that is marvelously handy. I think it probable that death could be liberating, don't you?"

I thought about it for a moment as I sat down on the lawn next to him. I felt the dampness of the leaves beneath me where the sun hadn't yet penetrated through the malingerers to burn away the night's heavy breath. "If there's a hell, I'm not sure it would be liberating."

Doctor Mantus laughed in his snorting way. "Ah, my boy, you're making assumptions."

"You mean about the existence of hell?"

"No. About the nature of God."

"God is just."

"Now *that* is an assumption. Do you fear justice?"

"Yes," I said. "I guess so."

"No," he said, studying my face. "You fear retribution."

I lit a cigarette and watched my sister in her tight jeans helping our father force a charred timber onto the back of Auggie Two-River's pick-up truck.

"Don't worry, James," the professor said. "I'm too deeply intrigued right now to go to hell or anywhere else. I've agreed to be on the Council. I'll see it through, at least until its completion."

We sat there silently for a while, watching people and leaves skitter around the yard in orchestrated mayhem, each to its own purpose. The October sun found an opening in the dying foliage above and warmed my back. An acorn struck my shoulder.

"Doctor Mantus," I said.

"Um?" I could see that he, like myself, had drifted off for a moment. He was following the flight of a particularly brilliant leaf.

"You think we're a bunch of crackpots and bullshitters, don't you?"

He smiled widely, raising his nostrils even further and exposing his large front teeth. It was one of his many oddities that, when serious, he appeared to be smiling. When he actually did grin, he looked feral, like a dog baring its fangs.

"Not at all," he said, but I sensed he was lying in order not to offend me and I told him so. "You're not crackpots, no. But I'm fairly certain I don't believe in the 'miracles' you told me about."

"But then how do you explain—"

"Oh there are *always* explanations, James. Always."

"We haven't lied about any of it."

"I'm sure of that. If *you* believe it, then it *is* truth, for you at least."

"What I've seen can't be explained by science or psychology," I told him.

"Maybe. What are your miracles? Larry Ladon's sudden conversion? Twenty-five years of longing to be with your mother, to reveal himself as your father, to save his daughter? Your brother's voices and dreams that appeared only after severe trauma to his brain? Auggie Two-River's guilt and fear about almost killing your brother causes him to want to be near him, to serve him, even, and atone for his error? Rusha and Yuri are provided with excuses to abandon lifestyles they hated? The Birds can love each other freely in this new church? I have an excuse not to kill myself and Judy Crabbe can exercise her custodial and loving nature freely without dropping that necessary façade of irascibility? These are your miracles?"

"But the names, the people—they fit the visions."

"They fit a story—a very old and well-known story. If the story is available, the characters can be easily fitted to it. Ask any writer."

I didn't agree. I'd tried to write seriously once or twice and even though I knew *what* I wanted to write, the *who* of it always got in the way. But I didn't contest the point. "That's all you think this is?"

"I don't know. I'm reserving judgment. I'm simply telling you that what you have isn't enough. Faith is never quite enough for me—or for most people. Most miracles, perhaps all, are never *really* miraculous." He shuffled his feet in the drying leaves.

"My brother was sterile," I said. "He was tested." I pointed at Ginny holding her grandson on the steps of the porch. "Now he has a son."

Doctor Mantus shrugged. "Mistakes in labs are common. Even men who've had vasectomies are known to have fathered children when the little tubes reconnect themselves. Miracle? Accident? Force of life? I don't know. I'm just telling you that I don't *know*, and I have to know. *Belief* won't do it for me."

"You'll help us?" I said.

"As much as I can, yes." He leaned toward me a little and put his hand on my shoulder. "Don't be surprised though James, if your brother's wife doesn't make it."

"She *has* to," I remember saying, "or there isn't a purpose to any of this."

"Oh life and death always have a purpose. It may just be too simple, too boring for us, that's all. Maybe a life is spent merely to procreate. Perhaps death is for paltry fertilization. I don't pretend to know."

I knew that if that was true, then I was as valuable to the world as my brother was and though I'd yearned for *that* recognition my whole life, the idea suddenly seemed very unappealing. I think that was when I began to realize that my life, the value of it, was inexorably tied to his.

"I have to get up to Holy Cross," I said, rising from the dead leaves.

Doctor Mantus stood up too as he grabbed my arm. "Thank you, James," he said.

"For what?"

"For this," he swung his free arm in a circular motion, indicating the manse and its environs. "This sense of community, this new interest."

"Miraculous?" I said.

"Preventative," he answered.

When I got to the hospital, I went directly to Ben Tower's room on the third floor. He'd been transferred from the intensive care unit to a 'regular' room that morning, so it took me awhile to locate him.

Minnie embraced me fiercely when I entered the room. I could see Sylvia over Minnie's shoulder, smiling approvingly at us as she held her husband's limp hand.

"How is he?" I asked Minnie, when she released me.

"He's going to make it, Jim. There's really bad damage to his head, but he's going to *survive!* Right now, that's all we care about, right Mom?" She said this last in a demanding way, as if there was only one acceptable answer.

Sylvia responded matronizingly. "Yes, of course, Dear."

As I approached the bed, I could see why discussion was limited to only hope. Ben's head was wrapped tightly in white gauze and bandages. What little I could see of his face had a purplish tint. His one exposed eye was closed, but his chest rose and fell in a healthy rhythm.

Minnie went to him, and whispered in his one, unwrapped, ear. "Daddy? Jim's here. Can you hear me, Daddy?"

The one eye flickered a bit, then opened. It looked dull and glassy—uncomprehending. His dry, swollen lips formed a single word: "Jimb?"

"Jim Gudsen," Minnie said.

"Jimb, uh, good son," he mumbled, and closed his eye.

Minnie's cheeks crimsoned a little at the error. Sylvia smiled at me. "Yes Dear," she said, lightly kissing her husband's bruised face, "he is."

"He's talked a little," Minnie explained, "but it's garbled and confused. He doesn't remember anything that happened." She pulled me over to one corner of the room. "They've done brain scans," she whispered. "There's damage…extensive damage. Doctor Mudeez told us…." Tears welled in her beautiful eyes. "He told us that dad will likely be…no…*is*, impaired. His thinking is slow and child-like. It isn't likely to change. Dr. Mudeez doesn't think that he'll ever be normal again."

"Who's Doctor Mudeez?" was all I could say.

Minnie forced herself to hold together. "He's the attending neurologist. He's Pakistani, I think he told us. When we went up to see Meg yesterday, that big nurse there—"

"Judy Crabbe?"

"Yes, Judy, she told us that Mudeez was one of the best neurologists in the country. We'll just have to wait to see how well dad responds when he gets a bit stronger."

She slid her arms around my waist. It was a good feeling, non-erotic and affectionate. "Oh Jim," she cried softly, "he's going to *live*, that's all I care about. I was so afraid to lose him. We prayed so hard and God has answered."

"Yeah." I kissed her dark curls. Her hair smelled like nature—nothing specific, not like the artificial odors of the hospital.

"Sybil?" Minnie was looking past me, toward the doorway of her father's room. "Sybil Springbok?"

She released me and rushed in that direction. I turned to see her embrace a stunningly beautiful black woman who was peering tentatively into the shadowy room from the bright hallway.

Minnie finally released her, then pulled her into the room. Sybil Springbok could easily have been a fashion model although, as I would discover, she'd never tried it. Later generations would rave over the dark skinned charms of Naomi Campbell and Tyra

Banks (my teen-aged son would have them both as part of his bed-room's décor), but they would have nothing on Sybil.

"Don't you dare look at her like that, Jim," Minnie scolded in mock jealousy. I must've been gawking and she knew it. I reddened. "It's all right," she laughed, "Sybil has that effect on people."

The woman smiled shyly, revealing perfect, white teeth. Indeed, physically at least, she was the embodiment of perfection. Perhaps that was what was so disturbing about her. People are used to finding mistakes in one another, and the discovery of a single flaw puts us at ease, perhaps because it's then easier to accept our own. I guessed that no one was ever completely at ease with Sybil Springbok.

She wore a colorful blouse, tucked into a short skirt from which emerged sinuous legs. Her arms, too, were very long. In her high-heeled shoes, she looked down at me. I could envision those drawn-out limbs enveloping a lover in a serpentine embrace and I suspect that no man would object to being constricted by them—even as prey. Her curly hair was trimmed close to her head, perhaps to diminish her imposing height. Her cheeks, her nose, her neck, were all symmetrically proportional to the longitudinal splendor of her torso and limbs. Her eyes were wide and doe-like, with long lashes. They gazed, rather than looked, at those around her with a kind of innocent cupidity.

She extended her hand to me as Minnie introduced us. The thin brown fingers enveloped my hand in a delicate kind of netting.

"Jim," Minnie said, "this is Sybil Springbok. We were roomies in college. I told you about her, remember?" I nodded. "Sybil almost qualified for the Olympics. She was one of the fastest women in the country in the 200 meter hurdles."

I mumbled something polite. I don't remember what, exactly. I was too intimidated by the woman's size and beauty.

"I *did* qualify actually," she said in a softly confident voice, "but the Committee isn't big on pregnant athletes."

"Where's *is* Jamal?" Minnie asked her.

"He's with his grandmum. I read about the accident in the paper," she said, nodding toward Ben Tower's prone figure. "You should've called me. I'd have been here sooner. I'm so sorry, Min." In two or three long strides she was next to the bed, embracing Sylvia and offering her condolences again. Sylvia accepted her warmly, like a second daughter.

"I'm going to leave you to visit with your friend for a few minutes," I whispered to Minnie. "I'm gonna run up to the fifth floor and see how Meg's doing. I'll be back in a few minutes. Okay?"

She kissed my cheek in a gesture of approval and turned back to huddle with Sybil and Sylvia over her uncomprehending sire.

Five minutes later, I was confronted by Judy Crabbe, who had effectively wedged her bulk into the doorframe of Meg's room—a bastion against unwarranted intrusion. The nurse had come to accept me as she might a nagging kidney stone and, painfully, she let me pass.

Herk was sitting in a chair by the bed. His back was to me. He didn't hear me enter. He was praying, his golden head bowed toward his dying wife, his words muffled in the sheets.

It's terrifying, even now, to think of that moment. Meg's beautiful hair, normally full and colorful, like a tree in autumn, now clung to her pillow in gnarled, ebony, shiny branches—the dying arms of winter raised, pleading, to the white and empty sky. Her hospital gown hung on her emaciated arms and shoulders like the tattered rags of a scarecrow too long abandoned in a harvested field.

I couldn't bear to look at her. Justice, I thought then, is too petty a device for anything that is worthy of worship. Death is too great a price.

"Dear Father," I heard my brother whisper. "I have tried so hard to do Your will all my life. Take this cup from me." His voice was pathetic, pleading, absent of all confidence and courage. It was the wheedling, uncertain cry of the utterly impotent. I had never heard it before. "Save her, Dear God," I heard him whisper. "Take me, if you will. I have always been yours. Save her!"

His golden head burrowed into the gathered sheets. He broke into sobs, a kind of self-indulgent blubbering that hammered at the specter of death like dried leaves against a fallen log.

"Save her! Save her!" Herkimer Gudsen cried. It was the only time I ever saw him desperate. "*Eloi, Eloi, lama sabachthani!*"

I felt a soft hand on my shoulder. It made me start. It was our sister, Rusha. She held a Styrofoam cup in her other hand, filled with coffee. She placed it on the eating tray that sat unused next to Meg's bed and then wrapped both her arms around Herk, laying her head gently on his back. I embraced them both and we held that awkward position, we three children of Larry Ladon, begging God for exemption, for expiation, for an 'ex gratia' dismissal of the law.

I was the first to let go. I sat down in a chair in a shadowed corner and watched Rusha help our brother to sit up. She wiped away his tears with the edge of her blouse. She fed him coffee, though it was too bitter. Herk liked sugar. She kissed him lightly on the top of his golden head.

When she let him go, finally, he sat in his chair and stared at Meg's cadaverous frame. It was an uncomprehending stare, a look of utter futility. I could see, in those sad eyes, what I knew to be true—that the bag of wasted bones on the bed was now only an icon, a trinket saved from one already departed.

"It's my doing," I said aloud as Rusha took a chair by the window. They both looked over at me, surprised, I think, as much by a non-whispered sentence as by its content.

"What?" Rusha said.

"Meg. It's my fault she's so sick. I promised God that if He would save her I would...or rather wouldn't...do something—and I failed."

Shafts of shadowy light, sneaking through the half-closed blinds, cast prison bars across Meg's sheeted form.

"God doesn't make bargains," Rusha said.

I looked at Herk. He'd just offered God one. He knew better.

"What was it?" he said.

"The deal?"

"Yes."

"I think I know," Rusha said. "Jim promised God to give up his favorite hobby, didn't you?" She looked coyly at me. I thought I saw the dragon, just for a second.

Herk's face twisted into a single, interrogative frown. "His hobby?"

"Sex," Rusha explained. "He made God an out-of-season Lenten promise, didn't you, Brother? Celibacy in exchange for Meg's life."

I crimsoned. Herk looked at Rusha. "How would *you* know that?" he asked her.

She smiled, mischievously, I think. "Because no one had ever turned *me* down before. I tried to seduce him, before I knew we were children of the same father—in the hotel room where he came to get me. I'm pretty sure it was the first time in his life he had ever refused a sexual advance. It made me lose my confidence—for a minute."

Our brother was unabashed. "True?" he said to me.

I nodded affirmatively.

"But you broke your promise?"

"Yes."

"You must really love Minnie," Rusha said, quietly. I looked over at her. She was surprised to see that she was right. She had suspected the abettor of my failure, but she hadn't known. Herk *had* known. I never could quite understand how a man who was so absorbed by Divinity could see, so well, the corporeal.

"You aren't responsible for Meg, Jim," he said. "You're a good man. Your promise kept you from incest, that's all. God was looking after you."

"Good men," I whispered, "don't do evil things."

He smiled. "There's a difference between being wrong and being evil," he said, "just like there's a difference between being right and being good. Good men do wrong things, but they're not evil. You love Minnie?"

"Yes," I answered. My voice was declarative. It sounded like it came from somewhere else.

"You made love to her because of that?"

"Yes."

"In God's mind intent is everything, Jim."

"But if God is just—"

"Then we're all doomed. God is a great, loving Being. He's merciful."

"You offered your life for Meg's," I said.

Herk smiled again, that sad grin of irony. "It's desperation, Jim. He will do what He will do."

The machines that kept Meg alive cried out against his argument. Where was mercy for her? Was I more deserving than Ben Tower? More deserving than those terrible corpses embedded in the mud of the Mekong Delta?

Judy Crabbe rushed into the room as one of the machines issued a protest against Meg's destiny.

"You have to leave now," she said. "All of you."

"What is it?" Herk said. There was a deep anxiety in his normally steady voice.

"She's all right for now," the nurse explained, "but I have to clean her. I'll stay with her. I'll call you, Pastor Gudsen, if there's any change."

Herk didn't want to let go of Meg's bony fingers, but Judy Crabbe shouldered him out of the way. He placed his large hand on Judy's bullish arm. "Keep her alive," he said. "Keep her alive, even if there seems to be no reason. Still, keep her alive!"

"I understand," Judy answered. "Go find them."

In the hallway, I said good-bye to my siblings. They were going to return to Horizon Road. I told them I would be there soon, but I had to see Minnie before I left. We embraced, I remember, the three of us, as the machine went silent in the room behind us.

It was hard for me to remember a time when Rusha had not been our sister.

When I entered Ben Tower's room, it had already grown dark outside. Minnie and Sybil Springbok were sitting next to one another, their heads close, conversing quietly. Sylvia wasn't there. I stood there looking at them for a while from the shadowed doorway, amazed to discover that my longing was for the plainer girl, my Minnie. For the first time in my life, the lust in me wasn't motivated entirely by the physical. Oh, I could easily desire Sybil. I could imagine my hands on her, but there was no comfort in that idea, no sanctuary. To fuck Sybil would be the momentary alleviation of desire. To enter Minnie was its perpetuation.

"Oh, Jim," she said, rising from her chair. "You're back. How's your brother?"

It seemed an odd question until I realized that, like the rest of us, Minnie knew that Meg was already gone. Better to concentrate on the living.

"He's doing the best he can. He and Rusha went home. Judy's keeping a close eye on Meg."

"I'm so sorry about your sister-in-law," Sybil said, rising from her chair. Her long legs flexed athletic muscles beneath the tawny skin. "Minnie was telling me about her. The baby's doing well?"

"Quite well, yes. Thank you." I hadn't thought about my nephew since his baptism that morning. "Would you ladies care to sample the gourmet cuisine in the cafeteria downstairs? I understand the macaroni and cheese is renowned throughout the culinary world."

"Sounds great," Minnie enthused. "I'm starving."

"Me too," Sybil concurred.

Doctor Mantus and Auggie Two-River found us an hour later, just as we were leaving the cafeteria to go back upstairs.

"Jim! Thank God!" Auggie said, breathlessly. The look of white terror on his face scared me. "I thought you might have left."

"What is it? Is Meg—"

"No. Meg's the same."

"Then what the—"

"Pastor Gudsen, your brother—"

"What?"

He began to sob and covered his face. I grabbed his shoulders and tried to shake it out of him. Doctor Mantus continued for him. "Your brother's been stabbed," he said calmly. "Some crazy woman tried to kill him."

A deal's a deal, brother, a deal's a deal.

Chapter eighteen

Herk had been stabbed three times with a butcher knife from his own kitchen drawer. When he and Rusha had returned to the manse after their long day with Meg at the hospital, it was already dark, though it was only 7:00 P.M. The house was all lit up as they pulled into the driveway. Ginny and Larry were inside along with Doctor Mantus, the Birds and Sammy Epstein, clearing up the mess from the communal evening meal. Auggie Two-River, Yuri and Teena Theus, Seamus O'Connor and many others were still milling about in the yard, taking care of tools and hauling away the last of the debris from the burned-out church, operating by the illumination from the single headlight of Auggie's tractor. The scene must have seemed comforting, non-threatening to my exhausted siblings.

Rusha had just mounted the stairs to the kitchen porch, I overheard her tell the police. The ER's attending physician was suturing a nasty gash in her right forearm as she talked. She said she'd noticed a rustling movement in the thick bushes adjacent to the porch, but it hadn't alarmed her because the wind had picked up and often struck the old farmhouse heavily after sweeping across the harvested fields.

Then, immediately behind her, Herk had cried out in distress.

The first thrust had penetrated his shoulder and glanced off his scapula. The second had sliced through his arm, as he must have turned toward his assailant. The third had been a frontal thrust. It had met with no resistance and deeply invaded his chest cavity, piercing a lung. The next had encountered Rusha's protective arm, explaining her ugly wound. After that, Rusha said, the would-be assassin had been buried beneath an avalanche of rescuers and subdued.

Lena Gossbach had been desperately trying to reach her pastor throughout the day. She'd been up all of Saturday night, haunted by voices that whispered to her of her sin, reminded her of her filthy condition, warned her of the demons that were determined to have her soul. She had said a hundred rosaries, read Luther's catechism over and over, tried every artifice to drive away the sensation of impending doom that tormented her mind and tortured her soul.

Herk had been her balm in Gilead, but she had promised not to call him in the middle of the night anymore. She had pledged, after that scene with Caleb Bird in the kitchen of the manse, that she would deal with it, face her fears, get past her terror of God and only summon her rescuer as a last resort, during reasonable, rescuing hours.

She had fainted from dread, she told the police, and had awakened on her living room carpet at noon on Sunday, to the realization that she'd missed the Sabbath services. The voices had told her to burn the church, to take the papers. They told her she should never have left the 'real' church. Now the Pastor ignored her. He'd gone over to Satan.

She had come to the manse, she confessed, directed by the voices that would not allow her respite. She had to listen. She had no choice. If fire would not draw his attention, then it must be blood.

But Herk had just left for the hospital, following our revelatory meeting of the Council of Twelve. Ginny had spoken to Lena Gossbach, trying to ease the bedeviled woman's anxiety and pacify her. Lena had appeared to be mollified. She had spent part of the day assisting with the meal. Fiona O'Connor had told the police that Lena had helped them to dry the dishes, though she'd been ominously silent and aloof.

As darkness had settled over the compound, Ginny had asked if anyone had seen Lena. Robin Stym said he'd last seen her by the kitchen door putting her coat on, as if to leave. A few minutes later, Herk and Rusha had come home.

My brother's condition was critical. I hadn't been able to see him. He'd been whisked into the OR before I could reach him. Rusha, her wounded arm heavily bandaged, refused to be put into a bed or to go home to rest. In the overflowing waiting room, she sat on one side of Ginny and Larry Ladon sat on the other, both trying to console our distraught mother. There was such great terror in Ginny's face.

Minnie and Sybil had, of course, been with me when Auggie and Doctor Mantus found us in the cafeteria, and they stayed with us. Minnie was constantly at my side, her reassuring hand in mine, her sweet voice whispering a soft confidence that I couldn't feel.

The room was packed and grew to overflowing within the first hour of our vigil. All the council members were there except Judy Crabbe who continued her watch several floors up. Many other members of the Gospel Church had been there as well, but were driven off by an aggressive RN who justly reprimanded them for getting in the way. Led by Caleb Bird, they went to the hospital chapel to pray for the life of their Shepherd.

I remembered thinking how much I hated this place, this Holy Cross, the scene of so much suffering in my life and in the lives of so many others. It was aptly named, an iconic relic of human agony. I'd come here often as a boy and a young man to wait, as I did now, upon my brother's courage and endurance—to see if this time, God might finally kill him. Here, I'd emptied steel pans of the waste of humanity and mopped up their blood. I'd spread disinfectant around to fight off the million microscopic enemies of our kind, which was as effective, no doubt, as spraying deodorizer to conceal the rank odor of shit. Here, Meg lay dying, her gore-covered child ripped from her skeletal figure. Here, Ben Tower was saved, so that he might stare stupidly at a world he would now understand even less. Here, a man who loved God above all else, lay pierced again—perhaps his final crucifixion. Holy Cross—an instrument of human torture made sacred in bloody pain and sacrifice, a deal for humanity. Holy Cross—the everlasting cross, all the horror and hate and envy and sin—all this continual punishment for the sake of broken promises, for the satisfaction of a little curiosity. Holy, holy, holy cross.

So we sat there, a dozen people or more, praying, each in their own way, for the deliverance of Herkimer Gudsen. They were selfish prayers, because we all knew that what we had become was due to Herkimer, or to God working through him. No one wanted to go back and we knew we would if the Reason was taken away. Our *own* faith would fail us. Our natures would return as surely as winter. We, like the changed leaves, still clung to the tree.

Different doctors came to see us at intervals through the night. At midnight, one told us that a team of surgeons had closed Herk's lung and sutured the wounds. Several pints of blood had had to be transfused. Herk was critical, but improving. At 2:00 A.M., they told us there'd been a crisis. Herk's heart had stopped. At that moment, our collective heart did too. But the surgeons had managed, they'd said, to shock it into cadence again. For some reason, I thought of my Drill Instructor in Basic Training, perhaps because he'd had that same ability. At 5:00 A.M., they told us he was 'stable', and they'd moved him into a room upstairs in the ICU, conveniently, as it turned out, only a few doors from Ben Tower.

Like obedient children, we gathered our paraphernalia and, without exception, journeyed to our new station, the waiting room on the fifth floor. No one went home.

The family was allowed to see him shortly after that. Ginny and Larry first, as his parents, Rusha and I an hour later. He regained consciousness during our visit. The first image he saw, he told us later, was Rusha's face.

"Not yet, I guess," he murmured, smiling weakly.

"No," Rusha said, "not yet," then she burst into tears.

To me he said one word: "Meg," and then he returned to the unfeeling comfort of oblivion.

When we returned to the waiting room, most of the anxious parishioners were gathered around Larry and Ginny, eagerly interrogating them about Herk's condition. Rusha joined them and shared the latest revelation of his brief return to consciousness. Minnie was among them.

I noticed her friend, Sybil, closeted in a corner of the room with Doctor Mantus—Beauty and the Beast. I decided that joining them would be the least demanding of my options. I sat down and lit a cigarette after retrieving my Styrofoam cup of cold coffee.

"How is he?" Doctor Mantus said.

"He regained consciousness for a couple of minutes. He spoke to us."

"Wonderful!" The professor grinned in his porcine way, emphasizing his hideous snout. Sybil didn't appear to mind his appearance at all. She smiled affectionately in his direction.

"I'm so happy for you," she said to me. "Minnie's told me what a great person your brother is. I can't understand why anyone would want to hurt him."

"I guess Lena Gossbach let her fear of God get the better of her. Apparently, she took a dive into the deep end. I'm told she kept saying that 'voices' ordered her to do it."

"Who is she?" Sybil asked.

"She's a member of our church, an obsessive-compulsive. My brother had been ministering to her for quite a while. I don't know how many times he rushed to her house in the middle of the night to try to calm her down and comfort her."

"What was she afraid of?" Doctor Mantus said.

"God's vengeance, I think. She never quite understood the concept of forgiveness."

"As if anyone does," the professor reflected, and I changed the subject because I didn't like being reminded of Lena Gossbach. I wanted to kill her.

"Minnie's told me," I said, addressing Sybil, "that you've often thought about coming to the Gospel Church. If I'm not too prying, why haven't you?"

Her expression changed from calm concern to the wide-eyed confusion of a doe caught in headlights. "I'm not sure," she said. "Doctor Mantus and I were discussing that when you came over. I don't like it at St. Luke's. Jamal and I—Jamal's my son—have always felt disapproving eyes on us, whenever we entered the place. Whether that was because we're black or Jamal was born out of wedlock, I don't know, but I'm sure it's not my imagination. Minnie's been trying to get us to come to Pastor Gudsen's church for months and...well, I really thought we should too. I came to St. Luke's because Minnie and Ben and Sylvia were there. When *they* left, it seemed natural that I should too, since they were my only friends there. But...something held me back. I really can't explain it. I even drove out toward your place on Horizon Road a couple of Sundays ago, but I turned back and went to St. Luke's instead. I don't really know why. Silly, isn't it?"

"And now?" Doctor Mantus said.

"Pardon?"

"*This* week I mean. Did you worship at St. Luke's yesterday?"

Sybil seemed a bit uncomfortable. "No."

"May I ask why?"

She looked at me. I tried to smile some encouragement. "It's going to seem ridiculous to you, I know, but...I had a dream. Please understand, I don't usually put much credence in such things. I'm not a mystic by nature, but it seemed so...so...*real*."

"What was it about, if you don't mind me asking?"

"It was probably some unconscious memory of my childhood. I was born in South Africa you know. My parents came here when I was about three or four years old. Anyway, the dream was about a gazelle being chased by a big cat, a lion I think. The gazelle was caught unaware. It had a fawn with it. The lion was almost on them. There were two paths, two ways to run. One was toward a wadi, a dry gully, which seemed the best way. The other was toward high ground, in the open, where the sun was setting. There was a cross there, black against the sunset. The gazelle wanted the shadowed gully, but the lion cut her off, directed her toward the

horizon. She and the fawn escaped. I don't remember much else."
Sybil laughed. "I don't think there's anything to it. The only reason
I mention it at all is that I felt compelled the next morning to go to
your church. I didn't, but I didn't go to St. Luke's either. I just
stayed at home."

"But you came here," I corrected, "to visit Ben Tower."

"Yes. I read in the paper about his accident, but there was no
mention as to which hospital he'd been taken to. So I decided to
take Jamal to my mother's, then I drove into town, thinking I'd
stop first at Holy Cross. If Ben wasn't there, I'd go over to Saginaw
General. I had to go by Horizon Road. I'd been by it before, seen
the new church going up. I'd read about the arson. I thought I
might get a glimpse of the burned-out church. There were dozens
of people working in the yard. It occurred to me that one of them
might know which hospital Ben Tower was in, so I stopped for a
minute. A short, balding guy, who spoke with some kind of foreign
accent, told me that Minnie and Sylvia were here, at Holy Cross,
with Ben. So I came here. That was yesterday afternoon? Seems like
a week."

Doctor Mantus was grinning his feral, toothy grin. "The
man who told you which hospital Ben was at—is that him, over
there?" The professor pointed at Yuri Theus who was, with his
daughter Athena, listening attentively to Larry and Ginny's description of their visit to Pastor Gudsen.

"Yes," she said. "I hadn't really noticed him before in all the
confusion. Yeah, that's him."

Professor Mantus looked back at me and raised his eyebrows.
"So, Miss Springbok was guided toward Holy Cross Hospital by
Yuri Theus," he said.

I shrugged.

He was irritated by my nonchalance. "The lion."

"You mean her dream? What makes you think the dream
was about her?"

"*Antidorcas marsupialis.* The nurses have a dictionary which
they were kind enough to let me borrow a little while ago when I
first met this lovely lady." He smiled at Sybil in his grotesque fash-

ion. She returned his smile, once again apparently unaffected by his
ugliness. "*Antidorcas marsupialis* is a white and brown gazelle found
predominantly in Southern Africa. It has great leaping ability." He
turned to Sybil again. "Miss Tower said, when she introduced us,
that you were a hurdler in college."

Sybil nodded, but she was obviously confused by the professor's monologue.

"Okay," I said, "but that still doesn't—"

"The common name for *antidorcas marsupialis* is Springbok,
James. *She* is the Golden Hind of Ceryneia. Oh dear," he chuckled,
"this is all so…*stimulating*. I love it!" He grabbed my hand. "Would
you mind if I explained it to her?"

"Somebody please *do*," Sybil said.

I was perfectly content in my acquiescence. It will go on, I
thought. It will be played out. We are little men on a checkerboard,
moved by an infinite Hand. But if human behavior arises from celestial design, does it have any meaning—especially moral meaning?
Sybil Springbok, I knew, would join us. She had no choice, anymore than Lena Gossbach—or Judas Iscariot.

Suddenly I wanted, quite desperately, to be close to Minnie.
The crowd had thinned around our parents. Rusha, sitting next to
Ginny, was offering what comfort she could to my distraught
mother. Minnie was standing nearby. I went to her and slipped my
arm around her waist. She kissed my cheek. I noticed Sylvia smile
approvingly at us from a corner of the room where she was conversing quietly with the Theuses and Auggie Two-River. Baxter Bird
was asleep in a chair, his head resting comfortably in the crook of
Robin Stym's arm.

"Jimmy," my mother said, interrupting my musings and my
brief comfort. "Will he be okay? Do you think so, Son? Will your
brother be all right?"

"Yeah, I think he will, Mom." I took her outstretched hand
and squeezed it. She smiled at me, but there was a warning in that
smile. It said that I'd better be right.

I felt a shadow fall upon me. Initially, I thought it was God's—perhaps because of guilt, perhaps because I thought no one else could have that large a shadow. I was wrong on both counts.

"Johnny!" I heard Yuri and Teena shout simultaneously, echoed shortly after by my sister, who rose from her chair. The three embraced the behemoth that stood behind us, blocking the light. Then, I too, recognized him.

It was Atlas Johnson, the bouncer at the Amazon Club who had gone out to L.A. when the club in Saginaw had closed. Atlas Johnson, the former pro football lineman, a teammate of Yuri Theus, turned doting protector of strippers.

He grinned broadly as he lifted Yuri off the floor with one arm and Athena with the other, while Rusha hugged him about his torso, her head resting in the approximate area of his navel.

"What in hale you doin' here, Yonny?" Yuri exclaimed, as Atlas placed him on the floor again. 'Johnny' was a nickname used by all of Atlas' many friends, but Yuri had trouble pronouncing his j's.

"I been told," Atlas said in a deep baritone voice that seemed to shake the floor, "that you were clean and livin' right. This little girl," he shook Athena like a rag doll until I thought he'd accidentally kill her, "wrote me a couple of times and told me how great you guys were doin' here. She really loves this new church of yours. She says you all are livin' good lives." His dark eyes turned moist, I thought. "I really wanted to see you all again, but it wasn't the only reason I came. I'm sick of the damn club too. The guy you sold it to Yuri, is a real prick. Anyway, I hated California—too damn hot. Besides, I got some business here to attend to. So I came home. Thought I'd check you out."

Throughout this soliloquy, Athena's feet never touched the ground. When he finally put her down, she gasped for breath, but smiled happily.

"Damn, Rita," he continued, addressing my sister. "You look great, Woman!"

"When did you get here Johnny?" Athena said, still recovering from his crushing affection.

"Teena, you're a young girl again. My mama always said clean livin' showed on a person but damn, I never thought it showed as much as I see it on you three. *Damn!*"

Athena giggled. I remembered the first time I'd seen her, and Atlas was right. There'd been a profound change in all of us I suppose. We'd just been too close to see it. I'd recently read another book by C.S. Lewis called *God in the Dock*. The other book by Lewis had been so fascinating I'd had to buy this one. It was just published the year before. In it, Lewis wrote about the miracles of Jesus as being nothing more than the larger, 'wholesale activity' of God that goes on around us every day. God creates the vine, makes it draw up water by its roots, and uses the sun to turn the water into juice that ferments. That common process is never considered preternatural. But let God perform the same function on a smaller scale and in less time, at the wedding of Caana for example, and it's heralded as miraculous and, therefore, less believable. It's perspective, I think. So Atlas's innocuous comment reminded me of the difference between small and large God people and he helped, for a while at least, to hold up my increasingly weighty world.

"You didn't answer me," Athena said to him.

"When did I get in? Hell, I guess a couple of hours ago. Flew into Tri-City, then took a cab out to the address that was on your letters. Wasn't anybody there, darker than goddamned hell at midnight. There was a lot of excitement across the road though—cop cars and a crowd. I went over and asked a fella there if he knew where you might be. He told me about the preacher." Atlas looked at me. "Sorry Jim, hope he's okay."

"He's doing better," I said, surprised that the big man remembered me. "He'll make it."

"That's damned good news." He turned back to Yuri. "I had the cabbie drop me here. The kind folks at the desk downstairs directed me up here and Bingo! Damned if I don't find you all in one goddamned place." He laughed heartily, as if he believed that we were all here by coincidence. I guess he did.

"Yonny," Yuri said, "you stay wiz us, yah? We go home pretty soon. You stay for a while."

"Great!" Atlas boomed. "Damned if that doesn't sound good to me."

I felt a tug at my jacket and found myself looking down into the piggish face of Doctor Mantus. He pulled me aside. "I've found another," he whispered. The delight on his hideous countenance twisted his features to preposterous proportions. I was getting used to him, I guess, like a med student who adapts to cadavers in his anatomy class. It was strange that Sybil had never had to.

"Another?" I said. "Besides Sybil?"

"Yes, yes."

"Who?"

"The Minotaur's father, the Cretan Bull."

"What? Atlas you mean?" I nodded toward the black giant, surrounded now by other members of the Gospel Church. Athena and Yuri were making introductions.

"That's an interesting name," the professor said, "but no." He seemed preoccupied for a moment, then turned his attention back to me. "Minnie Tower, Minotaur. See the resemblance? A buffalo, a *bull* buffalo, injured her father. Sybil tells me the doctors have said he'll be, well, simple-minded, if you'll excuse my crassness. Forgive my bluntness, but—"

"A cretin."

"Yes."

Another placement on the checkered board. Another move in humanity's checkered career. The hand of God at work.

"That's nine," the professor said. "We're getting close."

"To what?" I said.

"To completion of the Council, of course."

"Then what?"

"Then we ask your brother."

"If he lives."

"Yes, if he lives."

Doctor Mantus lit a cigarette. "I've told Miss Springbok about it all. She's agreed to meet with us. *You* must speak with your...with Miss Tower. I think we have to meet soon, before next Sunday, even. I don't know how much time we have left. Now, would you be kind enough to introduce me to your gargantuan friend?"

Man, I have come to believe, is not the measure of all things and God, in spite of us, is wonderfully intrusive.

Chapter nineteen

Doctor Mantus made the arrangements for a meeting of the Council of Twelve for the following evening, which, as I recall, was a Tuesday. He cancelled his night class in order to be free to attend. I don't believe I'd ever seen anyone so enthused about anything. It was hard to believe that a man who had been contemplating suicide only a few days ago was now so full of *joie de vivre*.

It was agreed that we would arrange for trusted members of the church to stand vigil over Herk. Auggie Two-River, in spite of the fact that he'd been there throughout the whole of Sunday night, volunteered to stay through the day on Monday. Ginny and Larry, after catching some sleep, would return to relieve him.

Auggie would have done anything for my brother, I think, and it wasn't just guilt stemming from the errant bolt of his crossbow. I believe he, like so many members of the new church, *loved* his pastor. Auggie had taken in Yuri and Athena at Herk's mildest suggestion. He was just as amenable to Atlas Johnson's presence in his home, even though Yuri had never consulted him before extending hospitality to the giant. He told me that if we refused his offer to take the first shift, he would stay anyway. His life, he said, was God's now, and Herkimer Gudsen was his connection. Disciple was a term I always associated with Auggie.

Judy Crabbe slept and ate at the hospital in order to be close to Meg twenty-four hours a day. Her devotion went beyond discipleship. There was little change in my sister-in-law. I went in to see her before I left. It was ironic, I thought at the time, that she had no idea that two floors away her husband was also struggling to survive. Dying is a deceptive art.

Ben Tower was conscious when we went in to see him. He talked with Minnie and Sylvia, though he had little knowledge of what had happened to him. He spoke in a child's sentences. He knew that he was a father and a husband but, like so many healthy men, he really didn't understand what that meant. He cried when they told him they had to go home and get some rest, but was quickly placated by a nurse who had discovered his new passion for Wile E. Coyote and chocolate.

I offered Minnie and Sylvia a ride. When we left Holy Cross, at about noon on Monday, the thin icing of snow had melted and the sun was shining brilliantly in a cobalt-blue sky.

Sylvia had been strong throughout her ordeal, but the recent image of her husband's regression into childhood, coupled with the shock of her pastor's near-murder, finally overwhelmed her and reduced her to exhausted whimpering on the drive to the Tower Ranch. Once there, Minnie took her inside and forced her to lie down. Fatigue, they say, is the best narcotic. The poor woman was asleep in a few minutes.

Minnie, however, refused to do the same, despite my protestations. She quickly showered, changed her clothes, and went on with me to the manse on Horizon Road.

In spite of the fact that most of the members of the Gospel Church of Faith and Revelation had had no sleep the night before, many were industriously continuing the process of clearing the site for construction, which was scheduled to go forward the next day. Caleb Bird appeared to be running things.

As we pulled in the driveway, we could see Yuri Theus, Athena, and Atlas Johnson on the front porch of Auggie Two-River's place across the road, fumbling with unfamiliar keys to let themselves in. Teena waved and Minnie returned the salutation as they disappeared inside, Atlas having to duck down to clear the doorway.

I parked the car, and Minnie and I went over to talk to Caleb Bird.

"Hey Jim!" he said. He smiled broadly, but his face was covered with dirt and he looked exhausted. His denim work shirt was stained with sweat in spite of the cool temperatures.

"I would've thought you'd be sleeping, Cal," I said.

"Like you?" He laughed.

"Yeah, like me."

"How is he?"

"He talked to me. I think he's going to be okay, but it's going to be a long recovery process."

"Thank the Lord."

"Amen."

"What happens now?"

"The Council is going to meet tomorrow night. We'll have to decide what to do then."

He nodded. "What about them?" He pointed toward the kitchen door, which was cordoned off with yellow plastic that had the black words 'Crime scene, keep out', printed all over it. Two plain-clothes policemen were standing nearby, talking with a huge uniformed cop. They were writing in notebooks.

"What're they supposed to be doing?"

"I don't know. They've been poking around for the last hour, taking pictures, and asking questions. Guess they want to be sure they've got all the evidence, although it seems pretty open and shut to me. Oh-oh, looks like you're next." Caleb pointed in the direction of the house. The two plain-clothes guys were crossing the yard to where we stood.

The one who was leading was a very handsome man, I thought. I was never much of a judge of my own sex, physically or otherwise, but I could tell by the way that Minnie stared at him that my assumption was correct. I felt a stab of jealousy.

The Adonis extended his hand to me as he approached. "I'm Detective Yonger of the Saginaw Police," he said, smiling disarmingly. This is also Detective Yonger." He pointed to his companion, whose features were identical to his own, but arranged in a kind of corruption of the ideal, like a distorted mirror at a carnival. "We're brothers," he said, anticipating what must have been a frequent question. I couldn't get over how much they looked alike and how the characteristics of their faces, in distribution, could produce such polar results. It was like looking at two portraits of the same man—one by Gilbert Stuart and the other by Picasso—neither ugly, but one created along classical lines and thus more readily admired by an unsophisticated audience that doesn't comprehend the abstract.

I introduced myself and Minnie. Caleb wandered off to rejoin the workforce, having already been subjected to the Yongers' interrogations.

"You're the victim's brother, I'm told?" The question was asked by Adonis. As with so many attractive people, he appeared to have been blessed with confidence as well.

"That's right," I answered. "Herkimer is my brother."

"May I ask about his condition?"

I looked at Minnie who was, at that moment, unaware of my presence. Again I sensed a piercing jealousy which, I'm certain, manifested itself in the irritation in my voice.

"He's doing fine."

"Good, good." Adonis said. His light-blue eyes rested on Minnie. "And this is?" His cavelier attentions to her made me want to punch him. His brother nodded in her direction as well. They were both blond, but the spokesman's hair was fine and full and consistent in its flaxen beauty. His antitropic brother's hair, on the contrary, was thinning, and the various clumps of it against his pinkish head resembled the dried running of old wax.

"*This* is my girlfriend," I warned. "Her name is Minnie."

"You're a lucky man," Adonis said, capturing Minnie's hand and gently shaking it. Her countenance reddened and I was reminded of the cheeky faces of those teen-aged girls who drooled over Paul McCartney and Mick Jagger in hormonal idolatry. Minnie finally became cognizant of my disapproving frown and pulled her hand away, as if she'd been caught holding some other extension of his anatomy.

The brother, like me apparently accustomed to this fraternal antibiosis, merely smiled drably and waited for the real substance of the interrogation to begin.

"I'm told," Adonis said, "that you know the suspect, Lena Gossbach?"

"Yes." I had my hands in my pockets and I felt Minnie's arm curl around mine in sinuous apology.

"Were you aware that that isn't her real name?"

"What?" I felt my jealousy supplanted by curiosity. "I don't see how that could be," I said. "My mother's known her for probably fifteen or twenty years."

"Seventeen years, actually," the other Yonger said, speaking for the first time while consulting his notes. Even his froggy voice was the counter to his brother's dulcet and princely intonations. "We spoke with Virginia Gudsen just before we came here."

"And?"

"She said that 'Gossbach' was the accused's married name."

"The problem, you see," Adonis interrupted, "is that this woman never was married. We've interviewed twenty people, including your mother, who've known her for a long time, but none of them have ever met her 'husband'. There's no marriage certificate, no evidence that any guy by that name ever had any connection to our suspect. When we booked her, she gave her name as Rhea Theomastix." He said it slowly as he read from his notes. "*That* confused us of course, because all our witnesses, including your half-sister, were telling us that her name was Lena Gossbach. We thought that maybe she was just, well, 'out to lunch' so to speak. She was ranting about voices and the devil and such, and initially we just assumed that she was incoherent—but then we checked it. Turns out that the name she gave us is the one she was born with. 'Lena Gossbach' is an alias, although why she thought she needed one, we don't know."

"How'd you find out which name she used was real?" I said. Minnie's arm tightened around mine and I knew what she was saying. I squeezed back, but kept my eyes on the cop whose crop of yellow hair blended into the field of dried corn stalks behind him.

"We went through her house on a warrant," he answered. "We were there most of last night. We found her birth certificate and other documents in a cardboard box in the basement, shoved up an old coal chute in the wall. Looked like she was hiding the stuff, but to what purpose, we don't know."

"She was born in Greece," the plainer one told us. "Came here with her parents when she was about nine years old. They're both gone. Their death certificates are in the box. They died in a house fire when Rhea was sixteen. She had an older brother who was almost thirty at the time. There's no official record of what happened to him, although the newspapers said that authorities assumed he died in the fire as well. She's been by herself ever since, I guess."

Adonis looked irritated by his brother's words though I wasn't sure if it was because of what he said or because he stole the spotlight for a moment. Either way, his alter-image sensed his aggravation and returned to anonymity.

"Rhea Theomastix has a record," Adonis said. "She was arrested twice before she was twenty, in Detroit, on charges of solicitation."

"Solicitation?" Minnie said.

"Prostitution."

"Oh."

"Lena Gossbach?" I said. "You're sure we're talking about the same person?"

"Well," Minnie said, "it would explain the alias—if she was moving here, trying to start a new life."

"Yeah, but Lena? Judas Priest! I can't imagine her being a whore. She's about as innocuous and naïve as they come."

"Too naïve to attempt murder?" Adonis said, lifting one eyebrow. "You had a fire here just recently. It was arson I'm told."

"Yeah," I said, "that's what they told us."

"Well, Lena—that is Rhea—has admitted to it."

"*What! She* set the fire?"

"Apparently. Sometimes people who are carrying around guilt like she is will confess to things they really haven't done. But we know that's not the case here."

"How?"

"That box we found, in the coal chute? It contained all the papers that were reported missing from your brother's files."

I was dumbfounded and, as I recall, suddenly very frightened too. "Where are the papers now?" I asked, thinking out loud.

"We have them. They're evidence. I'm afraid we'll have to hold on to them for a while."

"Has she told you why she did these things?"

"Yes."

"And?"

"She babbles a lot. It's hard to follow her. She's usually incoherent. Our psychologist interviewed her. He says she's full of hate and fear—so consumed by them, in fact, that she can no longer function. We know she's obsessive-compulsive, but he maintains that she's also psychotic. Several psychiatrists are evaluating her this week. She keeps saying that she has to stop 'him'. We presume she means your brother, since she attacked him…"

"Allegedly," the brother corrected.

"*Allegedly* attacked him," Adonis continued, a hint of irritation in his voice. "Do you have any idea what she means?"

I looked at Minnie. "The only thing she would be 'stopping' by hurting Pastor Gudsen would be the Lord's work," she said.

"She hasn't referred to anyone else?" I asked. "Are you sure that the *him* she mentions is my brother?"

"No. We aren't really sure of anything at this point."

"She hasn't mentioned anyone else?"

Adonis glanced at his brother, then back to me. "She says the voice comes from The Boatman."

"The Boatman? Who's that?"

"We were hoping *you* could tell *us*."

"No." I looked to Minnie. She shrugged and shook her head.

"I see," Adonis said. "Well, thanks for your help. We appreciate it. Our best to your brother."

"Thanks."

They turned to leave, but then Adonis turned back. He flipped a page of his notebook and held it out for me to see.

"Any idea what this means?" he said.

Written in large characters on a blank page was the following:

καθῆκον

"It's Greek to me."

"That's exactly what it is."

"What?"

"It *is* Greek. It's a single word. It means 'Labors'. Rhea Theomastix wrote it on the walls of her cell last night, several times. Any idea as to what that means?"

I looked at Minnie. She smiled at me. It took me a moment to remember that she wouldn't know. She wasn't part of the Council and I'd never told her about what was so deeply affecting so many of us. I'm not sure why I lied to the detectives. Perhaps I was afraid they'd interfere—more likely I was concerned that they might think me crazy. Anyway, I said "no." Adonis seemed to accept it, but his brother stared at me suspiciously. I averted my eyes—an obvious indication of deception that any Psych 101 student would recognize. I upbraided myself for my stupidity and wondered again why I was hiding something that might be of interest to these men whose job it was to build a case against my brother's assailant.

"What did she use to write with?" I asked, as much to relieve my own tension as to satisfy my curiosity.

"What?"

"What'd she use to write the words on her cell walls? You'd confiscate anything like a pen or even a crayon, wouldn't you?"

The alter-image Yonger grinned. It was a satyr's smile. "Blood," he answered. "She used the broken end of a plastic spoon from her dinner tray to cut her leg. She used her own blood."

"I told you," Adonis said. "She's a few cards short of a full deck. Listen, we have to get back to the station. Thanks for your cooperation." He pulled out a business card and handed it to me. "Here's my number. If you think of anything that might help us, give me a call." He looked at Minnie. "Nice to meet you *both.*"

"Raphael?" I said, grinning at the card.

He remained unfazed. "Our mother was an aficionado of the Italian Rennaissance," Adonis said. "I prefer Rafe, myself. Call if you think of anything. Have a pleasant day."

With that, Rafe Yonger and his lieutenant left us, the former strolling across the yard to his car in confidant strides while his Caliban shuffled after him.

"That's an interesting couple," Minnie said, once they were safely out of earshot.

"Seems to me that your interest pretty well centered on *one* of them."

Her cheeks crimsoned except for the little white scar on her upper jaw, a keepsake from her possessive ex-husband. The observation of this cruel memento made my own jealousy seem petty and ungenerous. I quickly repented. "I'm sorry, Min. I don't own you."

"He's just pretty, that's all." She kissed my cheek. "A trinket to look at. You *do* own me, by the way."

I kissed her. "I'd like to own you right now."

She laughed. "Maybe we should go inside."

"Good idea."

We headed for the house, but stopped where the yellow tape cordoned off the back porch. Three uniformed police were still there. Two of them were making a plaster cast of what I assumed were Lena Gossbach's footprints in the soft earth. A third, a huge ox of a man whose uniform fit too snugly, was taking down the tape.

"About finished?" I said to the big one. He almost equaled Atlas Johnson in bulk and might have even had an inch or two on him in height. He turned toward us and I was shocked again, this time by his remarkable resemblance, in yet another way, to the two men I'd just been talking to. He wasn't nearly as handsome as Adonis or as abstractly homely as the brother, but there was no mistaking, despite his size, that he swam in the same gene pool. I looked at his nametag. It read: YONGER.

"Almost," he said, pleasantly. "Just wrapping it up."

I pointed to his identification. "Does everyone in the Saginaw Police Department have the same name?"

He laughed. "The two detectives you were talking to are my older brothers, Rafe and Mike." He extended his hand and I shook it. "I'm Donny. Our dad was a cop too. So were his father and his uncle. My brothers are the first Yongers to make detective though. I'm hoping to make it too, but that'll be a while. I'm only a year out of the Academy."

"Have you found anything?" Minnie asked, diverting him from the Yonger family history.

"Not much to puzzle over," the younger Yonger said. "The evidence pretty much jives with what everyone's told us, including the accused. From what I know of it, it seems pretty open and shut."

"Let us know if you need anything," I said as I anxiously pulled Minnie toward the front of the house.

"Thanks," Donny answered. "We're about done here. Hope your brother's okay."

"Thanks."

The house was, remarkably, deserted. We went up to my room. We lay on the bed with every intention of violating my oath, our belief, and each other. It was a hungry, greedy, self-interested kind of sex, with each paying little heed to the needs of the other, which were met by the sheer generalities of our passion. It was deeply satisfying and guilt inducing—like a starving person who's just filled his stomach with human flesh.

Gradually our gasping evolved into panting, the panting to even breath, and the even breath to the barely discernible respiration of the moribund.

We didn't get up until late afternoon. Caleb woke us, shouting my name up the stairwell.

"What is it?" I yelled back, as Minnie struggled out of the entangling sheets and rushed into the bathroom.

"It's Auggie, Jim. He's just come from Holy Cross. He wants to talk to you," Caleb yelled, his voice echoing in the empty hall.

"Be right there."

When we came down a few minutes later Minnie and I had managed, I think, to look fairly inculpable although our entrance into the living room together certainly fostered the notion of guilt by association. Fortunately, Auggie Two-River was too exhilarated to notice. He was marching back and forth at a frenetic pace and he rushed to me the moment he realized I was there.

Caleb stood by the window, watching the activity outside.

"Jim! Oh Jim!" Auggie clutched my shirt. My heart leapt in my chest like it had when Minnie first looked at me, but this leaping was not joy. It was the horrific vaulting of fear, fleeing from pain.

"Herk?"

"He's all right," Auggie quickly reassured us. "He's *more* than all right."

"Slow down, Auggie. Take a breath. What's wrong?"

"*Nothing's* wrong. That's what I'm trying to tell you!" He brushed his shiny ebony hair out of his face. His white teeth shone brightly from out of his dark face. "Pastor Gudsen's sitting up in bed. He's alert. The doctors looked at his wounds just a little while ago...." Unconscious tears ran down Auggie's cheek. His voice broke. "His wounds are healing at an incredible rate. The doctors can't explain it. He's been there less than twenty-four hours and they said his wounds were healing as if they were made a week ago. I saw them myself. They should be raw and red and moist yet, you know—fresh. But they aren't. They're dry and...closing. I saw him move his shoulder, the one that's fractured. He was twisting it around like he was warming up to pitch, getting the stiffness out. My sweet Jesus! The man's not *human!*"

"Auggie," I said, trying to calm him with the level tone of my voice, "you must be mistaken."

"What you're saying isn't possible Auggie," Minnie said.

Auggie stared at her, his forehead deeply furrowed in thought. "Like resurrection? Like resurrection is impossible?"

"That was God, Auggie," I reminded him.

"Lazarus wasn't God," he answered.

I knew I couldn't argue with him. I'd seen the miraculous in my brother more than once. It was like trying to convince yourself not to have hope. "Who's there with him now?"

"His parents...your parents. Ginny and Larry."

"What about Meg? Has anybody checked on Meg?"

"It's the first thing he wanted when he woke up, so I went up and talked to Judy. She's not good," Auggie said. His dark eyes glistened again with moisture. "Judy wouldn't let me in, but she says Meg is just taking one breath every few minutes. She's relying entirely on the machines now."

"Did you tell Herk?"

"He knows, yes. He wanted to go to her, but the doctors wouldn't let him. They gave him some kind of drugs to relax him. He was sleeping when I left."

"The lumber's here," Caleb said from the window. "I'd better go outside and see to the unloading." He smiled happily, as if to say that God was paying attention.

"My father?" Minnie said.

"He's asking for you. He's okay. Not much change."

She looked at me. "Are you going back to the hospital?"

It was an innocuous question, but it bothered me for some reason. I thought that I *should* go, yet something told me not to, that I should stay at the house. I don't know yet why I felt like that. It was like trying to explain how you remembered the name of a kindergarten classmate you'd long forgotten or why you threw water balloons and broke solemn promises. It really had nothing to do with yourself. It came from *outside* you, and you knew it.

I took my car keys out of my jeans and gave them to Minnie. "I have to stay here. Take my car, pick up your mother and go visit your dad. Come back here when you're done. Okay?"

I could see that she wanted to interrogate me, but I think she understood that my choice to stay had nothing to do with her or my concern for Ben. I walked her to the car, as Auggie left and drove across Horizon Road to his makeshift hotel.

"I'll be back in a few hours," Minnie said, kissing me tenderly on my cheek. "I love you."

"Call me if I need to come."

"I will."

She turned to get in the old Chrysler.

"Minnie?"

"Yes?"

"I want you to be with me for the rest of my life."

She put her thin fingers on my face, and brushed the bangs from my forehead. "I want that too," she said, "even more than my father's life." I knew that was the strongest oath she could take.

"God willing," I whispered, as she drove away, "we can have both."

I didn't really know what to do then, so I helped unload the lumber for the new church from the back of the lumberyard's flatbed truck.

Darkness was descending when the others disbanded and I sat down on the kitchen porch steps, now washed clean of my brother's blood. I watched thousands of leaves flying sorties through the cold air and ramble across the wide lawn in confused landings as if guided by a drunken air traffic controller. Most of the brown leaves of the mammoth oak, however, held firm against the approaching winter. Like all life-loving things, they struggled to hang on...hang on...for a few minutes or hours more...hang on to hope that the natural can be overcome by the supernatural...that a different kind of miracle could occur. The approach of Professor Mantus's car interrupted my musings. He parked and ambled across the lawn, standing in front of me by the steps.

"Any more insights?" I said as he greeted me, then lit a cigarette.

"No," he answered.

"You look exhausted."

"I went home to rest, but couldn't sleep." He offered a weak, piggish smile. "I've become obsessed with finding these last Three, but I'm having no luck at all." He took a long drag on his cigarette and blew the smoke out of his huge nostrils. It reminded me of the snorting bull at the Tower ranch, just before it charged Ben. "How is Pastor Gudsen?"

"Remarkably well," I said, "even miraculously well, if I'm to believe Auggie Two-River. He was here a little while ago. He says Herk's wounds are almost healed and that he's lucid. The doctors don't know what to make of it."

Professor Mantus didn't seem surprised. "And what do you make of it?" he said.

"I don't know."

"Have you seen him? Since we all left, I mean?"

"No."

"Why not?"

"I...I just felt I ought to be here."

"To what purpose?"

"I wish I knew."

Two dragonflies buzzed drunkenly in front of us, ending their summer dance. I knew the cold would kill them soon.

"Two hundred and fifty million years those insects have survived," Professor Mantus observed.

"Not those two," I said.

"No. Their species, I meant. Does it matter?"

"It matters to those two."

"I suppose so."

The porch light at Auggie's house went on, as did several interior lights.

"Doctor Mantus?"

"Yes, James."

"I thought you oughta know. The same person who attacked my brother started the fire that burned down the new church, the one we were building here." I nodded toward the cleared area where the cement base, now completely cleared of ashen rubble, was visible. "She's also the one who rifled Herk's files. They found the stolen documents in her home."

Professor Mantus looked animated for the first time since he'd entered the yard. For some reason, I thought of Napoleon—the Orwellian pig, not the French Emperor—seated at the head of Farmer Jones' kitchen table. "You mean the woman," he said, "that Lena Grospeak?"

"Gossbach," I corrected, "but that isn't right either. The detective who was here earlier told Minnie and me that her real name is Rhea, Rhea Theomastix."

The professor ingested these latest feedings eagerly, like a hog at a trough, then appeared to process them in a kind of pleasurable, mental, mud-wallowing. "Theomastix? T-H-E-O-M-A-S-T-I-X?"

"I don't know. He didn't spell it for me. Why? Is it important?"

"It's Greek," Doctor Mantus said.

"It sounds Greek. The detective said Lena was born in Greece."

"But do you know what it means, Jim? In ancient Athens, it was a word applied to anyone sent by the gods to punish mortals. Literally, theomastix means 'God's punisher'."

I'd been thinking of my hand on the soft curve of Minnie's hip. But with this explanation, he gained my full attention as he continued. "The name 'Rhea' is consequential as well. In Greek mythology, Rhea was one of the Titans, the wife and sister of Cronus. She was the mother of Zeus and Hera and other Olympian gods and goddesses. Rhea is also an anagram of 'Hera', the Queen of the gods. She was the terrible enemy of Heracles because Zeus, her brother and husband, had conceived Heracles with another woman. She tried to kill the child in his cradle, with deadly snakes. Heracles, (Hercules in Latin), means 'glory of Hera'. I think perhaps the name was meant to appease the jealous wife or, possibly, to antagonize her."

I was appalled. "Are you telling me that Rhea is supposed to be one of The Twelve?"

"No, no I don't think so. Her profile doesn't fit any of the remaining Three. But she's a player. By that, I mean she's involved in some way. Maybe she's supposed to lead us to one of them. I don't know."

I felt a sudden chill sweep across the empty yard. I zipped up my jacket. "She hears voices," I said. "She told the cops that some voice commanded her to kill Herk." I saw Atlas' huge form in the headlights of a passing car as he waited to cross Horizon Road to our side. The last light of day behind him seemed to sit on his dark, massive shoulders.

Doctor Mantus put his hand on my arm to draw me back. "Did the police say anything else? Is there anything you haven't told me?"

I thought about it for a moment as I watched Atlas meander up the driveway.

"She wrote a word, in Greek characters, all over the walls of her cell—in her own blood, the detective said."

"What word?"

"Labors."

Professor Mantus' hairy nostrils were turned upward by the animation of his smile. "The Labors of Hercules," he whispered. "Is there any way we can get in to visit this woman, James?"

"Are you kidding? Her lawyer's probably the only person who's allowed to see her, maybe her shrink—certainly not the brother or friends of the man she tried to kill. They'd be a little concerned about vengeance, I would think." I lit a cigarette as I watched Atlas approach us across the lawn. "There's something else too, Professor. They said Rhea kept talking about somebody called the Boatman. He, it, seems to be the source of the voice she keeps hearing."

"The Boatman?" It was Atlas Johnson's deep baritone. "You know him?"

"Him?" I said. "The Boatman's a real person?"

"Sure." He extended a huge paw toward the professor. "Saw you up at the hospital, but I don't believe we've been introduced. Name's Atlas Johnson."

"Aristotle Mantus," the professor rejoined, wincing from Atlas' vice-like grip.

"Charlie and me go way back. Known him since I was a kid." He pulled what looked in the night shadows like a gold coin from his jean pocket. It turned out to be one of those flat, circular chocolates wrapped in gold foil. He peeled off the covering and popped the morsel into his cavernous mouth. "I love these damn things," he said, extracting another. He offered it to both of us and, when we declined, sent it rapidly after its predecessor.

"Excuse me," Professor Mantus said. "Who is Charlie?"

"Charlie Sticks? I thought that's who we were talkin' about."

With patient exasperation, Doctor Mantus pursued. "Who is Charlie Sticks?"

Atlas shrugged. "Why, The Boatman of course."

I opened my mouth to speak, but the professor held up a hand to stop me. It was clear that he wanted to do the questioning. I didn't take offense. I'd come to trust the doctor's knowledge and puzzle-solving acumen.

"Why is he called The Boatman, Mr. Johnson?"

"Call me Atlas, if ya don't mind—or Johnny. The last person to call me Mr. Johnson was a kid who was trying to get my autograph when I played for the Lions."

The professor looked at me with a querulous expression.

"Atlas played professional football in Detroit—on the same team with Yuri Theus."

The professor nodded. The connection didn't seem to surprise him.

"Yeah. Hey, Yuri looks great doesn't he?" He's clean as a whistle. Jim, your brother saved that sonofabitch. We been talkin' all afternoon. I think he'd die for Herkimer Gudsen."

"Atlas," Professor Mantus said. "Why is Charlie Sticks called The Boatman?"

"Oh, yeah, sorry. I get sidetracked. Well, Charlie lives in Purgatory see—"

"What?"

"Purgatory Swamp," I interjected, seeing the professor's confusion. "If you'd grown up here, you'd know it. It's a huge marshland out east of town."

"That's it," Atlas agreed, the brilliant white teeth of his Cheshire smile suspended solitarily in the night air. "The only way you can move from place to place out there is by boat. Charlie's got this kind of flat-bottomed little barge that he gets around in. He's got a long pole he uses to push the thing. He's lived out there most of his adult life, I think, and he ain't no spring chicken. People call him The Boatman."

"But his name is Charlie Sticks?"

"Yup."

"And you know him?"

"I told ya, since I was a kid."

Professor Mantus frowned. It was a grimace I'd learned, that indicated confusion. "How would you know him?" the professor asked. "If he lives in this swamp, I mean."

"The old hermit saved my ass once, a long time ago."

"Could you tell us about it?" the professor said.

"Sure," the floating grin answered, "but you better sit down there, Mr. Mantus, it's a long story."

The professor, apparently not offended by the absence of his proper title, took up a spot on the steps next to me and lit a cigarette.

"We, that is my mama and me, was livin' over on Farwell Street, on the East Side. Farwell Street was smack in the middle of the First Ward then. People'd call it a ghetto now, though most of it's been leveled to build a park, I think. In those days all the white folks lived on the West Side and the black folks lived on the East Side, the old part of town. The First Ward was the worst area of the east side—gangs, drugs, pimps, you know.

"My old man lit out right after I was born, and mama worked as a cleaning lady for a white family. She'd take the bus over to the West Side and work like a dog all day just to put food on the table. First thing I did when I signed with the Lions was to buy her a house on the West Side, just down the street from the people she used to work for.

"Anyway, one day I got myself in some trouble at school. I was, I dunno, maybe twelve or thirteen. Got into this fight with another kid. I got suspended for two days. When the principal called mama, she damned near beat me to death. Told me she wasn't workin' so hard to raise no delinquent. Anyway, point is I got pissed off and decided to light out myself, thinkin' maybe the old man had done the smart thing. I just started walkin'. I was a good eight or ten miles out of town before I thought about what I was doin'. I was fumin' so bad I just got on the main road, Washington Street it was, and kept goin'. I never looked up again until I realized it was quiet and there wasn't no traffic. I cut across a big waste dump, you know Jim, the one close to the river on that dirt road off 13?" I nodded. "It was getting' dark, so I walked across a wide field behind the dump, lookin' for some place to spend the night.

"It wasn't until my shoes started stickin' in the muck that I figured I was right on the edge of Purgatory. That's also when I realized I was bein' followed."

"By Charlie Sticks?" Professor Mantus asked. The anxious tone of his voice indicated that he wasn't enjoying Atlas' personal history as much as I was.

"Naw, it was that little prick, Wendell Jackson, the kid I had the fight with that day. I'd won, by the way. Beat the shit outta the fucker. Trouble was, his older brother was in a gang called the Black Knights. These boys was bad. I mean they *killed* people. Wendell and his brother and three or four of these Knights had been followin' me, probably waitin' for me to get somewhere isolated so they could jump me. Well, I obliged 'em all right—real good. I was suddenly in the middle of nowhere and there was Wendell and the boys climbin' over the chain link fence at the back of the dump and startin' across the field to where I was standin' with my jaw draggin' in the mud.

"I knew I was dead if I didn't get outta there. The only escape seemed to be a rusted out abandoned car that sat on flat tires in the mud about fifty yards to my right. It looked like all the windows was still solid and I thought if I could get inside I might be able to lock myself in. They'd be able to bust in of course, but it would buy me some damn time. There was nuthin' else to do.

They were blockin' the way back and there was only swamp behind me.

"Turns out it didn't make no damn difference. They caught me before I could get there. Wendell's brother knocked me down, pulled a blade, and was about to stick me when this old white guy shows up outta nowhere and brains him with his boatin' pole. He sent that kid dancin', I can tell ya. When another one of the Knights tried to charge him, the old guy jams that long pole right in the fucker's balls and the kid folds up like an accordion. In a couple of minutes, the Black Knights were runnin' for their lives, back the way they came, and I met Charlie Sticks for the first time."

"He just appeared there?" I said.

"It sure as hell seemed that way," Atlas answered, "but his boat was there, so I'm assuming that in the shadows and fog nobody noticed him. He scared the shit outta me too, at first. His hair was hangin' on his shoulders and he had a beard that reached the middle of his chest. His clothes were in rags and he was *so* fuckin' skinny. He looked like somethin' that had just worked its way outta its grave."

"What happened then?" Professor Mantus said, apparently with renewed interest.

"He offered to take me back to his 'house', as he called it. It was just a fuckin' shack. There's an island, it's the only high ground, in the middle of the swamp. Charlie's place is there. The damned hut is only fit for rats and snakes, but Charlie likes it.

"I figured the Knights might be layin' an ambush for me if I headed home right then and I couldn't see how Charlie would save my life only to kill me later. So I went with him. I spent the night, then lit out for home the next morning. Mama damned near killed me for worryin' her."

"Did you ever see The Boatman again?"

"Hell yes, on a regular basis. Got to know him probly better'n anyone. I used to go out there once or twice a month—take him food and stuff. Even got him a generator so he could listen to baseball on the radio. Charlie loves baseball."

"Why does he live out there, did he ever tell you that?"

"He come from a pretty rough background. His folks was immigrants. He's got a sister, maybe ten years younger'n him. Their old man used to beat the shit outta him. The old man raped the girl, regularly, Charlie said. One night, he tried to stand up to the old bastard, protect his sister. Charlie was in high school then, I think. The sonofabitch hit him in the head with a tire iron. He ain't been quite right in the head since. That's when Charlie started livin' in Purgatory. I guess it was a step up from the hell he'd been raised in."

Atlas grinned, apparently pleased with his own *equivoque*.

"He's still out there?" I asked.

"Yup."

"Still lives alone?"

"Yup. Well, unless you figure in Full Count."

"Who?"

"Full Count. That's Charlie's dog. I gave it to him. Found it in the junkyard when it was a pup. That was about ten years ago when I was playin' college ball. I was home for the summer and I was on my way out to see 'em and I found the little shit in a drain-pipe, whining like a fuckin' banshee. I figured it was perfect for Charlie 'cause no one else'd want it. The thing was cross-eyed as hell. It's got triple vision. You drop a piece of meat on the ground and it sees three of 'em. It always goes after the wrong one too. Charlie trained him to attack strangers, but it don't do much good. Full Count sees three of 'em and almost always charges one of the two that isn't really there. He goes left or right of the real thing. That's why Charlie's pretty sure the mutt sees three of everything. It'd be kind of funny to watch if it wasn't so sad."

"What breed of dog is he?" the professor asked.

"I dunno. I think he's got some pit bull in 'im, but he's all black, like a Lab. But I don't think he's got any Lab, really, 'cause he had a long tail at one time. When I found him, someone had cut it off. The thing was layin' just outside the drainpipe. Poor thing had nothing but a bloody stump. Whoever done it had jammed him in that pipe to die. He would have, too, if I hadn't happened along when I did. Charlie took to the thing right away. They been together ever since."

"Why the name?" I said. "Why Full Count?"

Atlas laughed. "Well," he chuckled, "as if bein' cross-eyed and havin' no tail wasn't enough, the damned thing—I'm tellin' the truth here now—the damned thing has three testicles. Charlie, who's a real baseball fan, like I told ya, said the mutt was born with three balls and two strikes against 'im—a Full Count. Makes sense, don't ya think?"

"It does," I answered, unable to suppress a childish snicker. Atlas pulled another chocolate coin from his jeans, examined it, and put it back. "I better slow down on these things," he said, "or there won't be any left for Charlie. I bought a coupla bags and one of 'em's already gone."

"You're going to be seeing him soon, The Boatman?"

"Yeah. I'm goin' out there in the morning."

"Do you think we might go along?" the professor said. The enthusiasm in his voice was all too apparent.

"What for?" Atlas said.

"I'd just like to meet him, talk to him."

"I dunno. Charlie ain't big on company."

"Atlas," I said. "Why'd you come back here, right now I mean, at this time?"

The giant shuffled his boots, brushing wet leaves aside. "I got a call from Charlie's sister."

Professor Mantus gave me a conspiratorial glance. "She's still around?"

"Yeah, well she went to Detroit after the fire—"

"The fire?"

"Yeah. Listen, you can't tell nobody about this stuff, okay? Charlie trusts me and I owe him."

The professor and I both nodded, though we didn't know what we were agreeing to.

"Charlie's sister set their house on fire the day after she graduated from high school. Charlie'd been livin' in the swamp for quite awhile by then. There wasn't no one around to defend her. I guess the old man went after her once too often. She just kinda snapped. Set the place burnin' when the folks was sleepin'. The cops said the fire was accidental, but the girl told Charlie she done it. Their folks both burned to death."

I looked up at Atlas. "The sonofabitch deserved it," he said. "If there's any justice, that fucker's still burnin'. I don't know nuthin' about the old lady, but she couldna been much of a sweetheart, lettin' all that take place right under her nose."

"So you're telling us," Professor Mantus said calmly, "that Charlie's sister murdered their parents? What happened to her? She must still be alive."

"Oh, she's alive all right. I didn't know what happened to her for awhile. She just lit out, disappeared. I hadn't known Charlie very long then. I was still in school. Then, one day, I get a letter from her. It was meant for Charlie, care of me, with the Farwell Street address on the envelope. Charlie had told her about me, I guess. I didn't know, at the time anyway, that she'd been out to the swamp quite a bit to see him. The letter said she was okay and livin' in Detroit, but she was in some kinda trouble."

"How long ago was that?" the professor asked.

"Oh hell, I dunno. I was, maybe, fourteen—a good twenty years anyway."

"What kind of trouble was she in?"

"Drugs, mostly. She couldn't pay off some dealer, a guy called Coco. I guess she was hookin' then, mostly to pay for her habit, and she'd come up short. Anyway, she wrote that she could square it with this Coco guy if Charlie could do him a favor."

"What favor?"

Atlas frowned. He looked unnatural without his meaty smile. "Disposal," he said.

"Disposal? Disposal of what?"

Atlas's shoulders sagged. "You said you'd keep quiet, remember that. It was a body…a corpse."

"Jesus!" the professor said. "Whose?"

"I dunno. Probably some poor slob like Charlie's sister who couldn't pay for his juice, maybe a rival dealer or somethin'."

"Did he do it, Atlas? Did Charlie do it?" I was praying that he'd say no and let my conscience off the hook.

"Yeah, he did Jim. They brought it down from Detroit, wrapped in a tarp."

"You were there?"

"No, but Charlie told me about it. They left the body in that old, abandoned car, then Charlie took it way back into Purgatory, weighed it down with rocks, and sunk it."

"How could you let him do that, Atlas?!" I remember getting up and pacing nervously. "My God, we've got to tell the police about this."

I felt a powerful pull on my shoulder. I was whipped around like a little child and all six feet of me was lifted off the ground. I smelled Atlas's chocolate breath.

"Jim," he said, in the deep, calm voice of resolute menace, "we're friends and all. But I won't let you break your promise. Understand? It ain't happenin'."

The professor reached up and placed a chubby hand on Atlas' massive shoulder. "Put him down," he said softly. "Please."

I felt the ground again, but Atlas didn't let go of my jacket. I looked at Doctor Mantus. He rubbed his porcine nose and squinted at me in the dark. "Atlas was a kid when this happened, Jim. It was twenty years ago." He squinted more intently against the night. "Besides, do you know who The Boatman was, in Greek mythology? His name was Charon. He ferried the dead across the River Styx into Hades. Charon, Styx. Charlie Sticks. There's a connection here. We have to pursue this. If we go to the authorities, they'll just delay us. We're running out of time."

He turned his attention to Atlas, who gradually relinquished his hold on me.

"Jim won't say anything I'm sure."

"Will you?" Atlas said.

"No." It wasn't Atlas's threat, although that should have been enough reason for my acquiescence. I'd like to think it was for Meg, but I don't really think that was it either. I wanted to see the game played out. I wanted to know where all this was leading us.

"Good," Doctor Mantus whispered. "The, uh, 'favor' must have saved Charlie's sister, I'm assuming?"

"Yeah," Atlas agreed, releasing me with an apologetic smile. "She stayed in Detroit a couple more years, then when I left for college to play football, she came back here. She got clean, changed her life, kept tabs on Charlie."

"She called you recently, you said. Why?"

"She said she was in some kinda trouble again. She wanted me to look after Charlie. See how he was doin'. So I came. Besides, I thought it'd give me a chance to see Rusha and Yuri and Teena."

"Atlas?" I said.

"Yeah?"

"Charlie's last name. You're sure it's Sticks?"

"Yeah, well part of it anyway. He's got some kinda foreign-sounding name. I could never pronounce it, so I just called him Sticks. I think he likes it, really."

The professor looked at me, then at Atlas, his nose searching upward as if to check the giant's scent.

"And Charlie's sister," he said. "What was, what is, her name?"

We really didn't need him to tell us, but he did. "Rhea," he said indifferently, and began searching his pockets for another piece of chocolate gold.

Chapter twenty

Before he went back across Horizon Road that night, we
told Atlas about Rhea's torching of the new church building and
her attempt on my brother's life. He was flabbergasted. He'd talked
to Rhea on the phone many times and been to her house on a couple of occasions, but he'd never known her as anything but Rhea.
She'd not once used the name Lena Gossbach with him, nor said
anything about her relationship with Herk or her terrible fear of
God's retribution.

By the time he left, he'd agreed to meet us early the next
morning and take us out to Purgatory to meet The Boatman. Doctor Mantus thought it essential, and I admit that my curiosity was
piqued, although if he was supposed to be one of The Twelve, I
had no idea how we were going to convince him to leave that place.

As we watched Atlas's huge bulk fade into the night shadows, the professor and I resumed our seats on the back steps.

"We're crazy," I said, breaking a long and thoughtful silence.
"You know that, right?"

"I don't think so," Professor Mantus responded. "You don't
either, really. We're just doing what we're supposed to do."

"Which is?"

"In the story of the Twelve Labors, Hercules brought back
Cerberus, the three-headed dog that guarded the entrance to Hades."

"Funny," I said, (I'm sure the professor noted my sarcastic tone), "Atlas never mentioned that Full Count had three heads."

"None of this has been literal, Jim. Do you think I like being viewed as a pig? We're not meant to be literal about it. Atlas said the dog is cross-eyed, that he sees in threes. That's probably what we're supposed to know. Sybil isn't an antelope and your father isn't a dragon. It's a puzzle, a game. We're supposed to figure it out."

"With Meg as the stakes? It's a risky game."

"I don't think God threw her in the pot."

"What do you mean?"

"I'd guess somebody else bet her life…maybe her."

I don't think he could see my face crimson in the darkness. "So we're supposed to go get this dog? Then what? We listen to the advice of a canine councilor? It's ludicrous."

"I think it more likely that Charlie Sticks is meant to join the group."

"Oh, good. That's an improvement—a crazy old hermit who's an accessory to murder."

"Are you worried about the law or about God?"

"How about just plain morality?"

He turned to me, his nose jutting upward as if to catch the scent of hypocrisy. "Listen, Jim," he began, "if God is behind all this as you and your brother and the Council members seem to think, then you're saying the whole thing is divinely instigated. If you accept that premise, then is the behavior that leads us here; that leads the Body Disposer, the Stripper, the Drug Addict—is it immoral? Indeed, does conventional morality even apply? God sets the rules. Can't He break them?"

"Spoken like a true philosopher."

"No, Jim—like a theologian." He lit a cigarette and inhaled deeply. "Are you familiar with the story of the woman called Jael in the Old Testament book of Judges?"

"No."

"I'm sure your brother is. You can look it up. There was a character named Heber the Kenite, the husband of this woman

called Jael. The commander of the defeated Canaanite army, a guy
named Sisera, was running from the Israelite enemy when he happened upon the tent of Heber and Jael. Heber was away, running
down the remnants of Sisera's forces. Though she was his enemy's
wife, Sisera begged Jael for something to drink. She gave it to him
and pretended to befriend him but, while he slept, she took a tent
stake and drove it through Sisera's head with a hammer. God approved of this deceit and murder, according to the writer of Judges.
Deborah had prophesied earlier in the book that *the Lord will hand
Sisera over to a woman*. Was it immoral for Jael to kill a defenseless
man? What do you think, Jim?"

"I think that if literalists saw a sign in a hotel bathroom that
read 'Flush toilet paper only', they'd be picking their own turds out
of the toilet."

Professor Mantus chuckled. "Then don't be so literal here."

"How did you come to be a theologian?"

"I'm not. I've studied myths all my life, including the He-
braic ones."

"So you're saying the Bible is myth?"

"Some of it, perhaps. But some of it is probably true, as is
the case with Greek, Roman, Hindi, Muslim and Native American
myths."

"Then God is a myth?"

"I don't think so. We've surrounded Him with myth. We've
clouded Him, covered Him, *humanized* Him, if you will, with our
own fears and superstition. Noah and Moses, David and Elijah,
Mary and Peter—they weren't directed by their rabbi or priest or
church councils. They heard God in their hearts and minds and did
what He told them, guided them, to do. Man has corrupted his
own true vision of God with religion."

"I can't agree."

"No? Is what is happening here real? Do you think your
brother is being guided by God or is he just some fruitcake?"

"It's real."

"Has his *religion* embraced it?"

"No, but many people have."

"My point exactly. His religion has rejected him. If he lived in an earlier time he'd have been murdered for heresy. But the people around him, those close to him, even old heretics like myself, can see what's happening. It makes me wonder how many times *real* prophets have been locked away in padded rooms. But even when some prophet is accepted by people, it's never his own. The great religions and religious movements always grew out of something else—Buddha, Mohammed, Abraham, Christ, Luther, Calvin, Joseph Smith, et al."

"I'm a Christian," I said. "I have to follow it. Everything I know and feel tells me that Jesus Christ was God incarnate, that He died and rose again, to save me. *That* is my religion."

"Fine. I don't say you're wrong. I hope you're right. But I don't see everyone else going to hell because *you* believe it and *they* don't. If you think *that's* so, then you'd better put on some plastic gloves and start harvesting your own shit. You can also tell your people here to quit working on that new building." He pointed toward the stack of lumber piled next to the cement slab.

The Chrysler suddenly appeared out of the misty October darkness. Minnie looked tired as she got out of the car, but she was still very animated, like an engine that races just before it runs out of gas. She embraced me, beaming with insouciance. "Oh, Jim," she chirruped, "Dad is doing so well. He's going to live and we won't have to wait too long before he can come home—and your brother, his recovery is remarkable. Ginny and Larry brought the baby up to see him. He was well enough to hold little Ben and coo over him and ask about what's going on here. He asked for you. I told him you felt like you had to stick around here for a while. He nodded, as if he understood, and told me to tell you to 'follow what you feel'. It's really amazing, Jim, to look at him."

"And Meg?"

Her smile vanished. "Days," she said. The evaporation of her joy made me regret asking. "Maybe hours."

She tried to conceal her fear, but it was like attempting to hide an elephant behind a toothpick.

"I have to talk to you," I whispered as I held her, "alone." Sylvia was just getting out of the car.

"Now? Tonight?"

"Yes."

She leered seductively at me. "You're sure it's just to talk?" I think she must've felt my other need, pressing against the area of her stomach.

"I have to tell you about what's going on here. It has to do with your father." Her face suddenly grimaced in concern. "Nothing bad, really," I assured her. "Can you take Sylvia home and come back?"

"Yes."

"I'll wait."

As the Chrysler left me in shadowy darkness again, I returned to the porch steps, guided by the glow of Doctor Mantus's cigarette and the October moon. I resumed my place on the step next to him and we sat in silence for a few minutes, listening to the mild wind gossip playfully in the cornfield beyond.

"Why the Labors of Hercules?" I said, finally.

"I'm sorry, what?"

"Why use an old myth to bring this Council together?"

The Professor snickered and rubbed his snout with a chubby hand. "Every culture has had its religions, and every religion has had its hero—a kind of man/god."

"Like Hercules, or Heracles, or whatever he's called?"

"Yes. Half-man, half-god, a product of the celestial and the terrestrial, as with the Titans of Greek mythology. Their parents were Uranus and Gaia, heaven and earth. Zeus, their son, an immortal, impregnated Alcmene, a mortal woman. The event occurs, in most religions, either literally or metaphorically. Jesus, for example—"

"Is God's son," I said.

"And Mary's," the professor countered.

"But He was truly God."

"And truly Man—otherwise the Cross is superfluous. Listen," the professor said, "I'm not attacking your belief. I'm trying to illustrate that the *sense* of God is in every culture, every people. Really, I'm arguing *for* God. Religious belief is about man's search for God, his basic desire for Life and Good. Have you read Joseph Campbell at all, Jim?"

"No."

"He published a book in the late forties, before you were born, called *The Hero with a Thousand Faces*. In it, he takes the heroes from mythology, (or religion, whichever term you prefer), and fits them into a contiguous pattern, juxtaposing them for comparative evaluation. The similarities, on a general scale, are staggering."

"Such as?"

"Well, in the creation myths, for example: Man is formed from clay or dust. That's true of the Maori, Negritos, Winnebago, Yoruba, Hebrews, Christians, ad infinitum. In many of these myths, there's frequently dismemberment of the heroic figure, accomplished to create new life—Purusa among the Hindus, Tiamat in Babylonian stories, Tawi in Hopi culture, Adam in Hebrew and, in a more spiritual sense, Jesus for Christians. The Inca, Eskimo, Egyptian, Greek and Shoshone, to name a few, include incest in their accounts. It's also insinuated in the Judeo-Christian tradition. *And Cain went and dwelt in the land of Nod and Cain knew his wife.* Since Eve was the only other woman around, the inference is that this woman of Nod was Cain's sister."

I remember wishing that I hadn't brought it up, interesting though it was. I was so tired, and The Bore's monotonic voice was a lullaby to my sleepy mind. I concentrated on Minnie's return and the memory of that afternoon to drive away Morpheus with the Satyr. It worked for awhile. "But a few coincidences don't make all—or any—of these stories true," I said.

The professor seemed oblivious to my struggle. "Coincidences? Is that what you call them?" His scoffing amusement manifested itself in a kind of chuffling snort. "Even if you accept that explanation, the 'coincidences' are certainly more than a 'few'. The same pattern exists in almost every religious faith. Man offends the divine parent and loses his immortality. Eternity 'devolves', as Campbell put it, into time. Death enters the world. A single, androgynous creation—Adam for Jews and Christians—is broken into duality as in the dismemberment I referred to earlier. Adam's rib is torn from his body to create Eve. Then, the continuation of life must be accomplished through the reuniting of those entities—sex. A hero comes to set things right again. He is ordered by God, comes from God, *is* God in the Christian version. He is different, capable of closer proximity to the Celestial, a communicator with the Divine. He is initiated into his trials, his labors, with temptation. He is on a quest for the 'ultimate boon'—usually a return to immortal status. He is faced with obstruction and evasion, but is able to overcome these with the aid of the Creator."

"Like Jesus."

"Yes, *and* Hercules. He's guided through his difficulties. He triumphs. He becomes the master of two worlds. He comes to understand the phenomena of passing time—that every creature lives off the death of another. The cycle continues in him—his death for Life. He leaves the world as Redeemer, erasing the terror of death with the messianic promise of reconciliation with the Divine—burial in Mother Earth to be reborn with Father Sky, devolving to physical dust to gain spiritual immortality. The story is as old as man himself and found everywhere."

"Why are some religions so different then?"

"Such as?"

"Well, why do some believe in only one God and others in many?"

"Is there really such a difference, James? I mean in the strictest sense? The Muslims claim that Allah is the only God, but if that's true, then why are there different kinds of Muslims, like the Suni and Shiite? Same with the others. The Jews have their Orthodox and Reformed and Hasidic. Christians have Catholics and Lutherans and Baptists, each of which view the 'only' God from very different perspectives. I won't even get into the concept of the Trinity—"

"So you think we all believe in the same Deity?"

"Essentially, yes. But the single hero-figure of Jesus always has confused me."

"Why?"

Professor Mantus shivered, perhaps from the descending cold. "Well, if the Apostles are to be believed, and we assume Jesus wasn't crazy—which I think is a safe bet—then He's the only founder of a major religion to claim that He actually *was* God. Mohammed, Buddha, Abraham, et al, never so drastically confused the dividing line between the Divine and the human."

"Because Jesus was who He said He was?"

"Perhaps."

We sat in silence again for a few minutes, little death-destined creatures shivering beneath the dark canopy of a billion stars.

"Would you like to come inside?" I said. "I could use a little light and warmth."

He stood up and stretched. "No, I think I'll head home. We're in for an early morning. Six o'clock? Is that what Atlas said?"

"Yes."

"Okay. I'll see you then." He extended his chubby hand as I rose to see him off. His flesh felt cold, but strangely vibrant at the same time.

"How does my brother fit into all this?" I said as we walked toward the professor's car in the moonlight.

"I'm sorry," he responded. "I don't quite understand what you're asking."

"Is it God who's talking to him?"

"Most definitely."

"Is he one of Campbell's heroes?"

"He is to me. In that sense, it all fits."

"How?"

"The Divine is forcing us to associate your brother with the most popular of the Greek hero-myths. We're not meant to see him in any Judeo-Christian context, despite the fact that it's the central credendum of his own faith. His name isn't Paul or Elijah. His 'trials' or labors, whatever you wish to call them, are disguised parallels of the original Herculean myth. What this hero's 'ultimate boon' is here, I don't know, but God is communicating with him. Herkimer Gudsen knows the Celestial better than we do—is closer to It. If nothing else, we're privileged to see it happen. Now, if I talk about this much more, I'll never get to sleep, and I *am* exhausted." He placed his hand on my arm and squeezed it lightly. "Good night James, and think of this. Among most Prostestants, 'James' is not only an apostle, but another James is honored as the brother of Christ. Christ is the Good Son in whom God is pleased. Perhaps James Gudsen should not underestimate his own importance in this little adventure." He winked at me and was in his car and pulling out before I could respond.

I stood there for a few moments, I remember, looking up at the vast sky and wondering about what the professor had said. Death for life, the constant trade-off. Animals kill and maim each other every day for food, for status, for the right to mate, to defend their territory. It's what they are. What they're driven to do. How different are we?

I remembered clearly then, perhaps for the first time, wading through the murky water of the Mekong River, the others in the patrol stretched in single file before me except for J.C. who, invariably, brought up the rear.

His real name was Jeremiah Cabal. He was raised in the bayous of Louisiana. He was a devout Baptist, always reading the Bible and proselytizing among the troops. We called him J.C.—more for Jesus Christ than his actual name. He could make you feel uncomfortable with yourself, but I liked him. I was, I think, the only guy in our outfit he could even remotely define as a friend, although we never talked much and he always stayed behind when I went into Saigon with all the others, looking for whores. Captain Garcia, our patrol leader, whose second year of combat had almost completely desensitized him, referred to J.C. as 'God's Bitch'—a term that J.C. disliked intensely. (I might have said 'hated', but gentle J.C., I think, was incapable of hate.)

On that steamy-hot day in the jungle, when we were stretched out across the river like ducks on a carnival wheel, J.C. took the Cong bullets that, I was convinced, had been meant for me. When they opened fire, invisible behind us, the GIs ahead of us scrambled up the muddy bank and into the trees, losing three, maybe five of us to the single consequence of geography. After he went down, I tried to pull J.C. with me. I remember thinking that death surrounded the two of us like the blood in the river. I was certain that I would not be going home. The VC bullets popped in the water, raising little geysers. Slowly, some of our guys began to return fire.

I got J.C. to shore, but the mud sucked at my boots and pulled at his sinking torso, as if the earth could take sides. I didn't want to die because of a simple thing like mud. I let go, the murderous barrage driving me into the shelter of the trees. I could tell I was hit. The calf of my leg convulsed with the shock of intrusion, but I couldn't see the wound.

I lay down on the jungle floor. I looked out at the riverbank. Jeremiah, hit badly but still alive, was trying to crawl to us—to me. I watched him struggle, his face filled with the confusion of the hunted who don't understand the principles of nationalized virtue and vice or the inbred hunger for blood. I know he couldn't see me in the thick foliage, though he stared directly at the place where I was concealed. I heard the others yelling for him, but I was mute. He never moved toward their voices, but struggled ever steadily, the longest distance, toward my silence. Then, the indefinable occurred—that thing that causes your life to become different—the moment when you cross that line that becomes a wall between what you were and what you become. He stopped. He had a chance yet, but he quit trying. Jeremiah had decided to die. He smiled. He actually *smiled* at me, then he raised a bloodied hand and gestured. 'Leave', the hand said, 'go on, get away'. I got to my feet again, my leg throbbing from the bullet. I was determined to go back for him. Death didn't scare me at that moment. Death, like anything else, becomes devalued by volume and, other than death, what reason is there to be afraid?

At the exact moment when I moved back into the open, a Cong bullet shattered the back of J.C.'s head in a crimson spray. The smile went slack. The youthful face fell forward into the mud.

The body went still, the image of that moment forever imprisoned in the cold, gray chambers of my brain.

That night, we camped several miles away from the river. The bullet had been extracted from my leg. I was alive, but forever scarred. I remember gazing up at the star-filled sky through the canopy of the jungle, as I looked at it now in the cold clarity of a Michigan autumn. Jeremiah had once tried, as he did with everyone, to 'bring me to Christ', as he put it. I told him I wasn't big on religion. He said that religion is in the human heart. It can't be rejected, he said, because it is what we are.

Doctor Mantus had, in a different way, said the same thing. I felt the hot tears on my face. The stars melted together in liquid confusion. I remember saying 'thank you'. I don't know why or to whom, and the sound of my own voice scared me. Death for life. Who was next to be culled from the herd?

The headlights of the Chrysler caught me in my terrible introspection as Minnie pulled into the gravel driveway and parked beneath the ancient limbs of the undressing oak.

"You okay?" she said, as she walked toward me in the darkness through the dead leaves. "You looking for aliens up there?"

"No, God."

"You're looking in the wrong place."

I felt her comforting arm around my waist. "Let's go inside," she said. "It's cold out here. Buy me a cup of coffee?"

"Sure."

We kissed in the dark kitchen, then she flicked on the light switch and moved toward the sink. "If I let you touch me any longer," she said, "I'll be doing that slave-thing again and I'll never find out why you asked me to come back here tonight." She filled the coffeepot with water, then turned back to me.

"Maybe that wouldn't be all bad."

"Listen, if you hadn't told me it concerned my dad, I'd be spread out on that table right now wondering if I was ever going to be able to catch my breath again."

"I'm not that good," I said.

She laughed. "I don't believe in empty flattery. Besides, I don't give you all the credit. You've probably had some pretty good teachers. Even so, if they gave degrees for that sort of thing, you would have graduated *summa cum laude.*"

I think that's when she got a really close look at me. "Are you all right, Jim? You're as pale as a ghost."

"Yeah. I'm fine."

"Tell me about my father."

So I began to try and explain it all—the Council's formulation, Herk's dreams, our hope for Meg. When Doctor Mantus explained things, it all seemed reasonable. Coming from me, it seemed preposterous, even ludicrous. She listened politely, letting me ramble when I felt the need. I thought it would piss her off, but the connection between the Council of Twelve and her father seemed to fascinate her.

"No," she said, in response to my concerns. "The cretin thing doesn't upset me. My father is still Ben Tower. It even helps me to believe that his injuries weren't just *random.* I guess it's easier to accept tragedy if you can see some *purpose* in it. The only reason I could see for his injuries before was that he tried to save me. I feel less guilty now. You know what I mean?"

"Yes, I think so." I thought of Jeremiah.

She poured us both a cup of coffee and we sat down at the kitchen table. The house, normally so full of activity, seemed ominously deserted. It was like being one of only two people in a movie theatre. You knew no one else was there, but you whispered to your companion out of habit.

She sat in silence for a while, blowing on the hot steam rising from her coffee. I was content just to see her there. "God must've been planning this for a long time," she finally said as she winced from heat of the coffee on her lips. "Ouch!"

"What do you mean?"

"My given name, at birth, was Minerva—Minnie. You said the offspring of the Cretan Bull was the Minotaur. That's supposed to be me, right? Minnie Tower?"

"That's what we figured."

"Then all this was in place when I was born, or mom and dad would have named me something else, like…I don't know…."

"Eiffel? Sears?"

"Cute. I'm serious, Jim, don't you see what I'm saying? Even my divorce had to happen, and at the right time, so Doctor Mantus could make the connection."

"Sure, but it has to go back even farther than that. Larry Ladon, Aristotle Mantus—they were around long before you. Anyway, the last names are just as important as the first. You have to think that God knew about this from the time of the *first* Ladon, the *first* Springbok."

"He did. *Before I formed you in the womb I knew you, before you were born I set you apart.*"

"I remember Herk using that passage in one of his better sermons," I said.

"That's right. It was the first one I ever heard," she answered, pointing toward the living room. "Right in there. I memorized it. It's from the Old Testament. Jeremiah."

I saw his hand again, covered in Mekong mud and blood, directing me toward my destiny, away from the death that came from the trees across the river and whatever other source it springs from.

"Jim, Darling," Minnie said, her loving hands on my face. "Are you okay?"

It was then that I told her about J.C. She was the first to know of him in this other universe called home. The telling was the last link forged in an enduring connection—a complete, desired amanuensis. It was also the severing of a different chain. I remember that I cried. I remember that her tenderness led again to sex. I remember praying, sometime that night, that my existence in the world should never require another death.

Chapter twenty-one

Like us, like Minnie and me, the earth and sky coupled that night to produce a lusty sweat. But while ours dried on our tired bodies and was washed away in a brisk shower, theirs filled the world outside with a dense fog.

When Doctor Mantus arrived at around five-thirty in the morning and knocked at the back door, I was startled, since I'd been looking directly at the windowed door and he'd appeared before it, in the mist, like a phantom.

I pulled the door inward and the fog nosed its way across the floor with the professor, as if searching for an earthy teat on which to lock its misty lips and feed. The dry heat of the house, however, forced it to curl into billows and retreat outside.

Doctor Mantus looked very different in casual clothes. I was used to seeing him in tweeds, vest and tie. He had never succumbed to the tawdry, gaudy ugliness of seventies' fashion—never a leisure suit or bell bottoms. He was one of the few people I knew who, in spite of his ugliness, would not look back from the eighties or nineties at a picture of himself with regret. His appearance had always been consistently professorial, right down to the patches at his elbows, the tousled hair, the glasses perched on the end of the bizarre nose. This morning was the exception. He wore an old flannel shirt, rumpled corduroys and rubber boots.

"Morning James," he said cheerfully. "I'm famished. Would you have some bread for toast?"

I found the bread while he took a cup from the cupboard and poured himself some coffee. "Judas Priest this fog is thick. I couldn't see the house from the road," he said. "Any idea what you're going to say to this Charlie fellow if we can find him?"

"Nothing. I'm going to let you do the talking. I don't think we have any butter. Jam okay?"

"What kind?"

"Strawberry."

"Fine." He sat down at the Formica table. "I really think *you* should talk to him, though."

"Why?"

"No logical reason, really. It just seems like you should."

"I'm not even a member of the Council."

"You're Pastor Gudsen's brother—that's more significant."

Minnie appeared from the living room, drying her dark, wet curls with a thick towel. She was wearing jeans and a blouse that were somehow familiar to me, though they were too big for her in the hips and bosom. She resembled a playful teenager, modeling her big sister's wardrobe.

"Where'd you get those?" I said. "I don't remember you bringing a bag last night."

Her cheeks crimsoned a bit. "I borrowed them from Meg's closet. I didn't think your brother would mind."

"Just to drive home?"

"I'm going with you guys."

"No, you're not."

"Why?"

Professor Mantus seemed amused. He took his toast from me and grinned broadly as I looked down into his cavernous nostrils. I turned back to my primary adversary. "Because, Min, this guy is...I told you about him. *He dumps bodies,* for God's sake. He might carry a gun for all I know. Forget it. You're not going."

"And what do you intend to do if I ignore your orders, Mein Fuhrer?" she said.

"I'll be pissed."

I could read the professor's mind. *Good retort, James. You simply withered her with that bon mot.*

She crossed the kitchen and turned me around so that we were face-to-face. She put her arms around my waist and nuzzled her damp head against my chest. "No you won't," she said.

"I thought we agreed that I owned you." It was a poor argument, but the only one I had.

She put her mouth right next to my ear. Her breath made me shiver. My heart leapt. "Only a third, Sweetie. *God* has my soul. *I* keep my mind. *You* only get my body." She licked my earlobe, then stepped away. "Deal?"

I looked over at the professor. He was grinning and pretending not to listen. There is no figure more ludicrous or susceptible than a man caught in mid-erection. My authority wilted with it. Possession, I convinced myself, is relative.

A rapping at the back door startled me again as the huge frame of Atlas Johnson filled the window. Minnie opened the door and he stepped in, ducking his head down to avoid striking it against the frame. Behind him, Auggie Two-River slipped in, silent, with the fog.

"Jesus, Jim," Atlas boomed, "you ever seen this kind of pea-soup shit? I couldn't see the damn house 'til we got to the driveway. Never seen the like of it."

"I'm Minnie," Minnie said, extending her small hand. It was immediately enveloped in his paw.

Atlas laughed. "You were up at the hospital when I came in yesterday, right?"

"Right," she said. "I'm Jim's girlfriend."

"Well, I can see Jimmy ain't lost his taste in women. You'd best keep an eye on 'im girl." His voice lowered to a conspiratorial whisper. "He ain't known for his loyalty."

Minnie smiled. "I'm his *last* girlfriend."

"True?" Atlas looked at me. So did Minnie.

"True," I said. There was no hesitation.

"Well I'll be damned," Atlas bellowed. "One miracle right after another."

It was the first time I heard my love for Minnie spoken of in that way—as miraculous, I mean. It wasn't the last. I think I saw tears in her eyes, but maybe it was my own misty vision.

Doctor Mantus broke the silence. "Well, what do we need to take with us?" He stood up, strawberry jam ridged like dried blood along his lower lip.

"I brought the bag of chocolates for Charlie," Atlas said, "and some canned food, a new shirt and a jacket." He pointed to the canvas bag he was carrying.

"I don't know if that's a good idea," the professor said.

"Why? He don't have much."

"Because we may have to convince him to come back with us, to leave the swamp."

"What!" Atlas looked at me. "Jim, you never said nuthin' about that."

"We don't really know yet what we're supposed to do. I wouldn't worry about it just yet." My tone and expression told Doctor Mantus not to argue. "If we do have to talk to him about leaving Purgatory, we won't force him, I promise you. I'll keep my word. We won't say anything to the authorities. Okay?"

"I guess so." Atlas seemed somewhat placated, but I could tell he was still tense.

"I'm going to call the hospital, check on the patients," I said, "then we can go."

Robin Stym and Baxter Bird had been with Herk through the night. He'd slept well, was still sleeping. Ginny and Larry were scheduled to be there soon for the day shift. Rusha was going to watch her nephew at Ginny's house. No change in Meg. Ben was doing fine except for a tantrum the night before over being forced to turn the television off and go to sleep.

When I returned to the kitchen, Auggie, Minnie and Doctor Mantus were seated around the table. I told them what I'd learned. Atlas was peering into the open refrigerator. "Mind if I have some of these hot dogs?" he said, pulling an unopened package of eight from the fridge.

"We really don't have time to cook right now…"

"Oh I don't need to cook 'em," Atlas said. "I'll just eat 'em as is. Okay?"

I looked at Minnie. She shrugged. "Sure."

He tore the package open with his teeth, extracted a wiener, and gobbled it down in a couple of bites. He pulled one halfway out of the plastic and held it out to us as if he were proffering a cigarette. We all declined. He ate a second, then stuffed the damp package in his coat pocket. "Let's go then."

We decided that we should be together in one car in order to appear less obvious to anyone who might spot us out there and perhaps to be less threatening to Charlie Sticks, if he should happen to see us arrive. We took the Chrysler.

The fog was the worst I'd ever driven in, before or since. The radio was filled with school closings and delays. I turned it off. We rode in silence for a little while, moving along Horizon Road by memory rather than vision. Still, I ran through a stop sign that I never did see. Auggie pointed it out as it passed his back seat window.

"Please be careful, Jim," Minnie cautioned. She was sitting next to me in the front seat and I knew she'd not seen the sign either.

It was a nerve-wracking journey, slow and difficult. I stopped at least a dozen times where I didn't need to. The fog turned the well-known streets into dark, labyrinthine tunnels. It was a pilgrimage of faith. The invisible, or at least the barely discernible, guided us.

I remember turning onto what we thought was Washington Street. It felt like we were headed in the right direction and Atlas swore that we were, as vehemently as Auggie swore that we weren't. Occasionally, Atlas was able to spot some ghostly landmark through the mist and darkness—a half a billboard, a twisted tree that grew close to the road—enough to let us know we were on the right road.

We almost bypassed the junkyard. Fortunately, no one was behind us, so that when Atlas yelled, "There it is!" I was able to brake quickly and ease onto the gravel shoulder. I followed what seemed to be a narrow drive. Thirty feet or so from the road, we encountered a chain-link fence and locked gate. In the headlights we could see a sign arched over the top, the lettering painted free-hand by someone who wasn't a professional. It read: *Straight ahead: general refuse. Right: automobiles. Left: appliances. No returns. Deposited objects become property of Purgatory Landfill. The Management.*

Doctor Mantus said: "Abandon hope all ye who enter here."

Minnie offered a nervous laugh.

"We can't go in," Atlas said. "Turn right and follow the two-track along the fence. It'll get us around back." I did as I was told, barely able to follow the line of the fence that was only a few feet outside my window.

"Couldn't we have at least waited until the sun came up?" Auggie complained as he was crushed against the door by the combined weight of Atlas and the professor.

"Charlie don't like the daytime. He's up and about early in the mornin' and late into the evenin', usually huntin' for muskrat or possum," Atlas said. "He don't come out of the cover of the trees any other time. If you wanna talk to 'im, it's goin' havta be at one of those times."

"How will he know we're here?" Auggie asked.

"We got a special signal." Atlas tapped me on the shoulder. "The end of the junkyard property is comin' up here, Jim. Take a left and hold to the back fence. The ground gets really soggy here. You drift too far from the fence line and the car will get stuck."

We crawled along another hundred feet or so before Atlas ordered me to stop. "Kill the engine," he said.

He opened the door and got out. The rest of us followed. I could scarcely make out Minnie's head and shoulders on the opposite side of the Chrysler.

We were standing on a gravel rise that abutted the fence. As I watched Atlas, backpack in tow, move to the rear of the car, I was surprised at the silence. Except for our feet on the gravel echoing into the soupy fog, there was no sound.

"Stay close," Atlas whispered.

Somewhere, far beyond us, the dawn was breaking. I remembered thinking that for some people, somewhere, the rising sun this morning must be a comfort; but all we saw of it was a dim lightening of black into gray. A torch in a black tunnel would have offered better illumination—and warmth. I shivered as we huddled on the passenger side of the car and watched Atlas descend the gravel slope into the mist.

"Stay close," he repeated and the rest of us, in a line, followed. I could feel Minnie's hand clutching the back of my coat.

The ground sloped downward at a steep angle. Although I had the continual sensation of descent, I think it began to level out once we had gone a dozen feet. I suppressed a childish desire to ask Atlas to hold my hand and struggled against the mucky ground and dense fog to stay close and keep him in sight. There was something about the place that instinctively commanded silence. Except for our labored breathing and sloshing feet, we obeyed.

I could see, ahead of us, the bony arms and fingers of skeletal trees, gnarled together as if attempting to strangle one another—if dead things could harm dead things. At first, they were only a vague discoloration of the dominating gray—little black threads dropped on a dirty easel. Gradually, they became larger, more defined and numerous against the cadaverous fog. They were the ghastly wraiths that haunted this Necropolis where Charlie Sticks and Full Count lived and ruled alone.

Atlas abruptly veered to our left. I was glad to have the saturnine tree-monsters out of my direct vision. I could sense their spectral presence and I couldn't help but glance in their direction, occasionally, to see if they had moved.

Ahead, another form drew my attention. At first, I could hardly make it out. Gradually, as we neared it, the sketchy silhouette of an old car became more clearly defined. Atlas opened one door. It protested, groaning on rusted hinges as if it were an old man forced to put weight on his arthritic knees.

Atlas fumbled around inside for a moment or two, while we four huddled in the mist, our feet growing damp from the sodden ground.

"Ha. Here it is," Atlas proclaimed as he withdrew his bulk from the car's interior. "Thought maybe some thievin' little bugger had taken it, but it was right where I left it."

He held a baseball bat. It was a Louisville Slugger, professional size I think, but in Atlas' hands, in the foreground of his bulk, it looked Little League.

Without warning, he turned back toward the car and banged it hard on the rusty hood. The steely sound echoed through the hazy, gray vapor and returned to us in multiple, disquieting facsimiles.

"What the hell is he doing?" I heard Auggie whisper behind us.

"I think it's how he calls to The Boatman," I ventured. Although Atlas said nothing, a multitude of dents on the hood and bat seemed to confirm my supposition.

Atlas dealt the old wreck another precipitous blow. I felt Minnie jump beside me. It was amazing to me that the bat didn't splinter under such compelling brutality. I made a curious mental note that if I were ever to have a child who loved baseball, I would make sure he had that kind of bat. It was the first thought of its kind. Minnie looked at me and smiled, as if reading my mind.

"That should do it," Atlas said. He threw the bat back into the car and looked toward the swamp. The trees were gaining clarity with the increasing light, now resembling ragged beggars with patches of mossy fog clinging to their emaciated frames in tatters.

Ten, fifteen minutes went by. Professor Mantus was chain-smoking and pacing. Auggie leaned against the rear bumper of the abandoned car. He was praying. All I could think about was that the trunk at Auggie's back had once contained a corpse. Minnie and I whispered quietly to one another while Atlas consumed some more of the raw hot dogs. Our conversation was about nothing and everything—each seemingly insignificant sentence or word rich in the language of intimation and flexuous connotation. I realized that what I'd said back in the kitchen, a world away, was true. Minnie would be the last, the final, the only woman I would love, because she was supposed to be.

That's when we heard the dog bark and the sloshing of the Boatman's pole snaking across the fetid water.

"Here he comes," Atlas said. "C'mon. We've got to get closer."

We lined up behind him, again in single file, as he headed toward the trees. We still couldn't see anything. Atlas followed the dog's bark, but how, I don't know. It echoed twice each time and seemed to come from every direction—even behind us. I know Auggie sensed that too, because as I looked back, I saw his head also turned backward, over his shoulder.

We heard a scraping sound, like a boat bottom dragged on a pebbly beach.

"Charlie!" Atlas yelled. "It's me, Johnny."

We could still see nothing in the fog, but a low, ominous growl issued through the mist. It seemed very close.

"Shit," Atlas said. "Spread out and don't move."

We did as we were told, each of us eager to avoid any confrontation with the infamous Full Count.

Gradually, he became visible, crawling out of a gray cloud of fog, howling and snapping like a black banshee. He shadowed into focus three or four feet in front of me, then halted, growling savagely. He was bigger than I'd expected. The black hair on his muscular shoulders bristled. His jaws hung open. Drool clung to the corner of his mouth. His muzzle wrinkled back, exposing his sharp, yellow teeth. I could see the muscles in his legs and shoulders tense as he crouched low in a posture of aggression. I would have been overcome with fear if not for his eyes. They were a deep red color, which should have contributed to his sinister demeanor, except for the fact that they were turned inward, toward the furrowed muzzle, as if the poor thing was vainly trying to examine the end of his dripping snout. The effect was comedic, and I smiled.

Full Count's hackles stood erect. The snarl intensified. I know it sounds ridiculous, but to this day I believe he was offended by my amusement. I think that's what made him attack.

"Don't move!" Atlas shouted again, as the dog rushed at me. I was frozen. If Full Count had been an ordinary dog, I'm convinced he would have had my balls for lunch. Instead, he leapt at the image next to me, the phantasmal twin that only he saw. He landed on the ground behind me, a puzzled look of accustomed chagrin replacing the fierce lip-curl.

I turned around to face him. He rushed at me again, this time to the other side.

"Don't worry," Atlas said. "Like I told ya, he sees us all in threes and for some reason he never goes for the middle one, the one that's real. As long as you don't accidentally move into his path, he'll run by you all day."

"How do we get him to stop?" I asked, as Full Count rushed by me again.

Atlas took out the package of hot dogs and threw one on the ground right in front of Full Count's nose. The cur jabbed to the right, then to the left of the wiener, coming up twice with mouthfuls of weedy vegetation.

"How on earth does he ever eat?" Auggie said.

"I forgot." Atlas picked up the hot dog and held it right against the dog's muzzle. The mutt quickly got his teeth on it and wolfed it down. "Charlie always has to feed him by hand."

The professor laughed. Full Count growled as Atlas shoved another hot dog into his maw.

"A sop to Cerberus," the professor chuckled.

"Johnny?"

I turned around just in time to see Charlie Sticks emerging from the fog. At first, I thought one of the spectral trees had come to life. Charlie was as gaunt and bony as a person could be, I think, and still be classified as living. His ragged clothes hung on him and, I suspected, his flesh as well, although his arms and legs were covered by a filthy old coat and jeans that had been repeatedly patched. His skull-like upper face and haunted eyes gave the impression of a deep and continual abstinence, though whether from food or some other comfort, I couldn't tell. His jaw, chin, mouth and neck were hidden behind a greasy beard that hung in oily locks to his chest. His hair dripped in long, unruly snarls to his shoulders. He sported a goofy-looking hat, similar to one I'd been suffered to wear as a

child—square, with a short bill and long ear flaps that were designed to tie under the chin, though his were loose, the string having rotted away long ago. Just below the hat bill, a thick and lumpy
white scar traveled down his dirty forehead to the bridge of his
nose. It was so pronounced that it looked like some mole had been
burrowing beneath his yellow skin. I wondered if that was where
Charlie's father had struck him, a supposition that was later confirmed. His feet were covered with rubber boots, the kind that are
all one molded piece. In his bony fingers he held a thick and well-
worn pole, likely the same one he'd used to drive off Wendell Jackson and his cronies when Atlas was a kid. He carried it in front of
him, with both hands, like a weapon.

"These people try to hurt you Johnny?" he asked. His voice,
though threatening, was soft and raspy, as with one unaccustomed
to speech.

"Naw," Atlas drawled. "These here are my friends, Charlie.
Damn, it's good to see you, man. You ain't been puttin' on any
weight, that's for damn sure."

Charlie stared blankly at us for a moment, then lowered his
staff. "Count! Here!" The black cur, munching on his third name-
sake from Atlas' hand, immediately flew to Charlie's voice, standing
obediently to one side of his master, though I believe the animal
thought he was squarely planted in front of him. As it retreated
from me, I could see three large sacs dangling just below the stump
of its tail. It's multiple vision, as with the males of many species
including our own, mystically coordinated with its genitalia.

The dog took no notice as Atlas stepped forward and embraced Charlie's scarecrow form. He was, apparently, accustomed
to the giant's triple presence.

Charlie seemed uncomfortable with the amiable gesture,
perhaps because he had been touched with affection so infrequently
in his life. He merely patted Atlas' constricting arm and stepped
back.

"You bring me sumpin'?" he said.

"I did." Atlas pulled the chocolate coins and clothing from
his canvas pack.

The man's eyes lit up briefly, like a child's on Christmas morning, then faded back into insensate density. He took the gifts without thanks and clutched them to his chest. Slowly, he unwrapped two chocolate coins and slipped them into his mouth before holding out the bag in our direction. "Want?"

The men all declined, but Minnie, seeing The Boatman's disappointment, stepped forward and took one of the chocolates. Amazingly, Full Count allowed it.

"M-m-m, delicious," she said. Charlie smiled, then as quickly, lost it and turned to Atlas.

"Where's Rhea? She go back to Detroit? She an't come by long time now. Dinnin tell me nuthin'. Where she is?"

"I don't know how to tell ya this, Charlie," Atlas said. He looked like an overgrown child in the principal's office. "She called me to come look after—"

"She's in jail," I said. Better to get it out, be done with it. There are two ways to rip adhesive tape off a hairy arm—slow and fast. Fast was always best.

"Jail?" Charlie looked confused, muddled.

"She's been locked up, Charlie. She tried to kill somebody," Atlas said.

"Rhea? Kill?" He seemed to be lost in memory, the consciousness of another death.

"She had to," he said. "He hurt her. She had to."

"We ain't talkin' about your old man now, Charlie," Atlas said. "Somebody else."

"Somebuddy? Who buddy?"

"My brother," I said.

"Why?"

"She says the Boatman told her to."

"That's me. Boatman. I an't told her kill no buddy." I knew that Charlie's voice issued from somewhere inside the dense bush of his face, but the gray hair of his moustache hung so thickly over his mouth that it was impossible to detect any motion of his lips. He seemed to be completely frozen in place as he clung jealously to his 'gifts' and his pole. At his feet, Full Count continued to snarl at our multifarious images.

"I'm sure you didn't," Minnie said. Her loving heart revealed itself, as always, in the sympathetic expression on her sweet face.

"How she come to me now?"

"She won't be able to, Charlie," Atlas said. "At least for a while. We'll watch over her. Soon's they let us, we'll go see her, okay? You all right with that?"

"I dinnin tell her nuthin' to do."

"Charlie," I said. "Charlie?" He appeared to be lost in an interior fog—a comfort, perhaps, as assuaging as the surreptitious mist from which he'd come. "Charlie?"

"Yeah."

"You believe in God, Charlie?"

"God? Sure. God hates sinners."

"No."

"Sure. Bad peoples. God burns 'em." He cocked his head for a moment, like dogs will, as if listening to a sound the rest of us couldn't hear. "Rhea work for God. She say so."

"Rhea says the Boatman told her to kill. Are you God, Charlie?"

"Me? Ha, ha. No." He shook his long, wet locks so that they stuck to his cheeks. I could see the veins become visible on his temples and his sallow color crimson. "Rhea. God talks to Rhea. Boatman don't hear God. Rhea, she burn the old fucker-man. *Fucking fucker-man.* My fault. Oh, oh, oh. Beat my head old fucker-man. Can't stop the fucker-man. Can't stop. Prop me in a chair. Make me watch. Mama wrap my broken head." He touched the white scar above his bushy brows. "Fuck Rhea, fuck Rhea, daddy fucker-man. Mama, mama, blood and fucking. Burn fucker-man, burn."

"My God," Minnie whispered.

"Sorry," Atlas apologized. "Charlie just ain't right in the head."

"Charlie," I said, risking a couple of steps in his direction, despite Full Count's rising hackles. "God loves us. He doesn't hate anyone."

Silence.

I waited for someone to speak. I glanced at Professor Mantus, then at Auggie. They were looking at me expectantly. Minnie nudged my arm.

"Do you like it here, Charlie?" It was all I could think of to say.

"Home," he mumbled. "Safe." He looked back toward the dense fog bank that still drifted above the waters of Purgatory.

I decided to try a different approach. "You like baseball?"

His yellowish eyes became animated, widening with the interior vision that had, by necessity I suppose, become habitual. "Detroit Tigers. 1968 World CHAMPEENS! Denny McClain wins thirty-one. Mickey Lolich, fat man. Al Kaline. Mayo Smith bring Mickey Stanley in to play shortstop. Smart move."

"I know you listen to them, Charlie, but have you ever *seen* them play? Would you like to *see* them?"

"How see?" His wide eyes narrowed in cautious interest.

"If you come with us, we'll take you to see them."

He frowned heavily.

"Jim," Atlas said, "I don't think you should try—"

"Wouldn't you like that, Charlie? We can find you a nice, warm house to live in. We can get you new clothes. We can take you to see the Tigers play in Detroit. You could have chocolate every day."

"Season over," he said. "Tigers fucking third place." He started to turn away.

"Next summer then." He kept his back to me, but he didn't retreat. "You can see Rhea too. She won't come anymore, Charlie. She says you have to come to see her now. It's your turn. Wouldn't you like to see your sister?"

Charlie didn't move. He was still clinging to his meager possessions. "Rhea?"

"You have to help her now, Charlie. You left her before, remember? She had to fight alone."

"Jim," Atlas cautioned. "Don't do this."

"I'm sorry. I don't want to, but he has to come with us," I said. "The Council meets tonight. We need Charlie to be there. Meg doesn't have much time. We'll keep the authorities out of it, like I promised, but he has to come with us—now."

The professor nodded. "I think so, yes."

Charlie turned to face us again. Full Count snarled. "Couldn't help Rhea," he moaned. "Fucker-man wouldn't stop." Tears escaped his haunted eyes and made clean little snail-tracks along his dirty, sallow cheeks.

"No. You couldn't help her then Charlie, but you can help her now. You can help Rhea *now*."

"Johnny say?" He looked helplessly at Atlas.

"Yes," I said.

"Johnny say?"

We all looked at Atlas. He pursed his lips. "Yeah, Charlie," he said finally. "I think you should."

"Why?"

"Because God has need of you," Minnie said. Her voice was tender and soothing and sympathetic. She smiled at the pathetic scarecrow with genuine compassion.

"You God?" Charlie said, pointing a bony finger at me.

"No, no." I laughed "God is your Father—"

I knew my mistake as soon as I said it. Herk wouldn't have made such a stupid error—equating God with the most hated figure of this wretched man's life.

I expected a terrible rage, some kind of purging rant. Instead, all emotion drained from Charlie's few visible features. The eyes went blank. He dropped Atlas' gifts and his boat pole. He turned abruptly, sloshing off into the fog, Full Count close on his heels.

Auggie started to go after him, but found himself restrained by Atlas' iron grip.

"We can't just let him leave," Auggie protested.

"He ain't goin' anywhere without his pole. Stay put."

"What's he doing?" Minnie asked.

"I don't know."

"Listen," the professor said. "Shush."

Charlie wasn't far away, maybe ten yards or so, but sound carried so differently in this place that I couldn't be sure. The splashing boots stopped. There was a clicking sound—one I recognized, but couldn't place. Then, the spattering feet again.

"He's coming back," Atlas said.

Minnie sighed. "Thank God."

I remember seeing Full Count reappear, then Charlie's shadowy figure behind him.

"*Father fucking-man!*" he screamed, then his specter-image disappeared in a burst of light and explosive sound.

He might carry a gun for all I know.

I felt a terrible burning sensation in my legs, then cold numbness as they collapsed beneath me. It was a sensation I'd known before. As I went down, I saw Minnie falling too, her tan jacket pocked with spreading red stains.

Chapter twenty-two

I remember moving slowly and painfully to cover Minnie's body with my own. I remember asking God, in anxious and hurried prayer, to take my life instead of hers. I remember a flashing intuition of the phenomena of time passing into finality. I think I cried her name—or someone else did. I remember the sense of magic flight, the crossing of a threshold—something too deep and impenetrable to experience in the banal consciousness of everyday life. Then came a kind of soul-satisfying vision of fulfillment and imperishability. All this in seconds—surrounded by the noisy and irritating obscenities of reality.

We never lost consciousness. I saw the pain in her sweet face, heard her whispering endearments, rejoiced in her forced smile. Someone pulled me off and laid me again on my back. I saw the shafts of sunlight and rags of clearing fog. A leaf floated in the sky, clinging to the wind, dependent on the invisible to hold it in motion just a while longer. Disconnected, its seeding done, it would find its eventual way to the floors of Purgatory—more than carrion, a leafless tree, waiting out the cold. Silly thoughts for a silly creature—foolish and mortal, foolish and divine.

"Birdshot," I heard the professor say. "The goofy bastard used birdshot."

That's when I knew we would live.

"They're flesh wounds," Doctor Mantus said. He had Minnie's jacket and blouse open. I could see her pale skin, her black, teenager's bra, bright blood.

"Birdshot?" It was Minnie's voice.

"Small pellets," the professor said. "They broke the skin, but not much more. You've been hit three times, two in the chest, one near the navel. The bleeding's stopped already."

"Jim? What about Jim?"

"I'm fine," I assured her, though I didn't know if I was or not. I felt somebody's hands on my leg. "Four." Auggie's voice. "Three in the leg, one in the hand. Not deep. Can you sit up, Jim?"

I found that I could. "The Boatman?"

"Atlas has him."

"C'mon," Auggie said. "We've got to get you two to the hospital. Can you walk?"

In the background I heard the constant barking of Full Count. I could tell that he was running about on the watery ground, splashing back and forth, attacking the ephemeral clones of his master's enemies.

Auggie pulled me to my feet. I saw a blurred image of gold coins—uneaten treasure in a plastic bag. Then Minnie was next to me and we embraced. "My love," she whispered to me. "My dearest love." I touched her face with my wounded hand and left unorthodox rouge there.

The professor helped her move to the car and Auggie pulled my arm over his shoulder as we followed. Inside, I curled my arm around her. She laid her head on my chest. I looked at my hand. The pellet had penetrated the fleshy area of my palm. It was bruised and bloody, but I could see the ball shot. It was traumatizing, that's all. Minnie kissed it and held it between her own. The professor got in the back seat, next to Minnie, from the other side.

Through the window I saw Atlas emerge from the fog. He'd thrown Charlie's inert body over one massive shoulder and the Boatman's rubber boots dangled at his waist. Full Count was rushing back and forth in rabid fury at his feet. In his own limited vision, I'm sure the mutt believed that he had wounded dozens of us, but they were Pyrrhic victories.

Auggie opened the front door of the Chrysler and Atlas dumped the Boatman's limp form onto the seat. He moaned, but appeared to be unconscious. His hands, I think, were bound behind him. I heard the click of the seatbelt. "How you doin' Jim?" Atlas said.

"We're okay," Minnie answered, "just messy."

"Quite a woman you got there." Atlas winked at me.

"I know."

"What about him?" Minnie nodded toward the prone figure whose presence in the car had produced a gamey stench.

"After the shot, I had to take him down. He wouldn't quit struggling so I punched him. He's all right, poor crazy bastard. Ouch!"

Full Count had finally managed, by sheer coincidence, to lock on to real flesh, in the form of Atlas' calf muscle. The giant turned around and struck the cur a compelling blow on the top of its head. "Little sonofabitch," he mumbled. Auggie picked up the prostrate dog. It sagged, dumbly, in his arms. Full Count was quiet for the first time since we'd seen him. "Put 'em in the trunk," Atlas said.

Auggie did as he was told, then slid into the front seat next to the slumping Boatman, leaving as much room behind the wheel for Atlas as he could. It wasn't enough. He had to unclip Charlie's seatbelt so that he could push the limp body tighter against the door.

When Atlas, with some difficulty, was finally able to close his door, he started the car and turned back toward the landfill entrance and Washington Street.

"Which hospital?" he said as he turned onto the main thoroughfare. The rising sun had dissipated the remnants of fog. Traffic had picked up.

"No hospital," I said. "Take us back to Horizon Road."

"You crazy?" Atlas shouted. "I know it ain't but birdshot, but the pellets gotta come out. Those wounds gotta be treated. You both been bleedin'.'"

"Jim's right," the professor said. His voice, still monotonic and soft, was oddly authoritative. "If we went to the hospital, they'd call the police. By law, they'd have to. Your friend would go to jail. We can't have that."

"Look, I release you guys from your promise. As much as I owe Charlie, he needs to be locked up. He can't go around shootin' people for Christ's sake."

"It isn't the promise, Atlas," I said. "Charlie's supposed to be one of the Twelve."

"The Twelve? What the hell are ya talkin' about?"

"I can't explain it now. You probably wouldn't believe me if I did. I'm willing to forget about the shooting. Let's let it go at that, okay?"

Atlas looked in the rear view mirror. "Minnie?"

She smiled at me. "Whatever Jim says."

"Shee-it! The whole world's gone goofy." Atlas shook his massive head. "What about your wounds? I ain't taken' responsibility for that. I can't take them pellets out. You and Minnie need a doctor."

"There's a guy named Leo Herman—a general practitioner. I've known him since I was a kid. He's been the Gudsen family doctor for years. He's a member of the church too. I'm pretty sure he'll come to the house and I think his discretion can be relied upon. We'll call him."

"What about Charlie? If I'd known we were goin' to do this, I'd just a left 'im in Purgatory."

"No," Professor Mantus said. "He's got to be with us tonight for the Council meeting."

"You mean you intend to *keep* him?"

"He can stay at my place," Auggie said. "That way, Atlas can keep an eye on him. There's an old doghouse out back too. We can keep that crazy mutt chained up out there, if Atlas didn't kill it."

The Boatman moaned. "I think he's coming to," Auggie said.

"Aw shit!" Atlas exclaimed as he saw the manse up ahead. "Your yard is crawlin' with people, Jim. Don't these damn busybodies have homes of their own?"

"They're working on the new church building."

"Well, we pull in there and the whole damn world's goin' know what happened."

"Go to my place," Auggie suggested. "Pull 'round back. We'll go in through the kitchen, that way we won't be seen."

"Jim?"

"Sounds like the only sensible thing to do."

Atlas laughed. "The only sensible thing would be to get you two to the Emergency Room."

Yuri Theus and Athena were appalled when we came barging into Auggie's kitchen, looking for all the world like guerrilla fighters just back from an unsuccessful sortie. They'd been enjoying a leisurely brunch.

Professor Mantus quickly pulled them aside to explain it all, while Atlas gently placed Charlie's prone figure in a kitchen chair and tied him to it with clothesline that Auggie discovered in his basement. Minnie was laid on the sofa in the living room and Auggie helped me to a chair by the telephone.

I managed to get hold of Doctor Herman. He promised to come immediately, though he would have to cancel his appointments for the day, including patients already seated in his waiting room. My faith in him was not misplaced.

I limped into the living room, where Teena was already at work washing Minnie's wounds with warm water. Teena pulled a towel over Minnie's naked chest and seemed relieved when Auggie emerged from the bathroom with scissors, iodine and bandages. "Sit down, Jim," he ordered. I turned around and hobbled into a chair by the kitchen table. Auggie propped my bad leg on another chair, then began to cut away the leg of my jeans. "There's five!" Auggie said. "There's five pellets. Three in the area above your knee and two below."

"Six," I said, extending the palm of my hand for his perusal.

He shook his head. The high cheekbones lowered with his grimace. "Pastor Gudsen will never forgive me."

"What?"

"I promised I'd look out for you. He told me he was afraid something bad was coming. He had a dream or something—one of his visions maybe."

"When was this?" I winced as the iodine antiseptic burned into one of the wounds.

"Sorry. Yesterday. He told me that yesterday. Should I continue?"

"Go ahead."

I wondered what else I didn't know. I felt entirely unequal to the leadership that had, apparently, been thrust upon me.

Doctor Herman arrived just as Charlie Sticks began to emerge from Atlas' fist-induced fog. "Rhea," Charlie moaned.

"I'm takin' you upstairs," Atlas said to the Boatman. "No fuss now! We're goin' get you cleaned up. You stink like a damn pig sty."

"I'll help," Auggie offered, relieved, I think, to be replaced by someone who knew what he was doing. Atlas untied the groggy hermit and he and Auggie forced him up the stairs.

"What on earth has been going on here?" Doctor Herman said, as Doctor Mantus and Yuri Theus, who'd been exiled from the living room while Athena tended to Minnie, escorted him into the room.

Doctor Leo Herman was as kind and devoted a Christian man as I'd ever met. Though not obese, he tended to corpulence and a phlegmatic, reasonable, disposition. The sight of a bound lunatic and my bloody leg, however, clearly tested the boundaries of his moderate temperament. He set his black leather bag on the kitchen table.

"It was an accident, Doctor Herman. Could you see to Minnie first?"

"Minnie? Not Minnie Tower. Ben's daughter?"

"I'm afraid so. She's in there." I nodded toward the living room.

"She was shot too?"

"Yes."

"Who shot you? That wild-looking fellow?" The doctor had a flat nose, quite the opposite of Doctor Mantus', and not designed for holding spectacles. His were always sliding to the tip of his nose, which curved just enough at the end to keep them from slipping off altogether. He frowned at me through them, then pushed them up the flat ridge so that they might, again, slide down to their normally precarious perch.

"I promise you I'll fill you in later," I said. "Minnie needs your attention and we can't go to the hospital. Trust me. Will you help us?"

"I suppose the satisfaction of my curiosity will have to be subservient to Hippocrates, young man, but you're going to tell me all about it when I'm through."

Doctor Herman grabbed his black bag and turned abruptly toward the living room. I heard him greet Minnie tenderly. "Hello, Sweetie," he said. "It looks to me as if you've been hanging around with the wrong crowd." I heard her laugh, and that single sound went a long way toward easing my anxiety.

Doctor Mantus and Yuri took up seats across from me.

"Ya goin' ta be okay?" Yuri asked. There was genuine concern on his face.

"I'm fine," I assured him, though I was painfully uncomfortable. "It looks worse than it is."

We heard some shouting upstairs, then a door slammed, muffling the sound. I heard water draining through the pipes behind the kitchen wall and I guessed that Charlie Sticks was enduring his first shower in many years. I felt a wicked retribution in suspecting that his cleansing was probably as painful an experience for him as getting shot had been for me.

I looked at the professor, who seemed to be studying his cigarette with unwarranted interest.

"What are you thinking?" I asked.

"Huh? Oh, nothing. I'm just a bit disappointed, that's all."

"That I lived?"

"Don't be ridiculous—even joking."

"What then?"

"I thought it would turn out differently; that we'd learn more. We're no closer than we were."

"We have the Boatman. We have Charon."

"Yes, but where do we go from here? We're overlooking two—two people we've encountered already."

"What makes you think that? Besides, maybe Charlie will know who they are when we talk to him some more, or one of the other councilors will put us onto them when we meet tonight."

"Well, I'm quite sure one of us knows the other two already." He kept studying his cigarette, as more and more of it turned to ashes.

"Why?"

"Because in the original Hercules myth, the descent of the hero into Hades to capture Cerberus is the twelfth—and last—labor. I've missed something here." He took out a small notepad from his jacket and began writing. "Yuri here represents the Nemean Lion. That's one. Meg's cancer, symbolically personified by the nurse, Judy Crabbe, is two. I'm the Boar of Erymanthus. That's three. The woman we just met, Sibyl Springbok, is four, the Hind of Ceryneia. Five, the Birds of Stymphalus—Robin Stym and Baxter Bird. Auggie Two-River is six, the Augean Stables. Seven is Ben Tower, the Cretan Bull. Eight, we don't have."

"What was eight in the legend?"

"The Horses of Diomedes, I've told you." This was said with a degree of irritation, as if I was a dullard in his classroom who'd failed to remember a simple concept. I told him so and he quickly apologized. "It's not you, James, it's me. I feel like the answer is there and I'm overlooking it somehow. I think I was brought into this to explain it, and I'm not getting it done."

"You're really beginning to believe all this, aren't you?"

"Yes," he said, "I am." He returned to his notes. "Nine is Rusha, or 'Hippolyta', the Queen of the Amazons. Ten, we don't know."

"The Oxen."

"Yes, the Oxen of Geryon, the three-bodied monster."

"Then my father."

"Larry Ladon, yes. The dragon who guards the Apples of the Hesperides."

"And Charlie Sticks is twelve?"

"Or his dog, Cerberus in the myth."

"Damn," I said. "Full Count is still locked up in my trunk."

"Full Count?" Yuri echoed.

"Never mind that now," Professor Mantus said. "We'll tend to him in a few minutes." I heard cries of pain from both the adjoining room and upstairs. I must've looked anxiously in Minnie's direction, because Yuri said, "I'll check on her," and left the room.

"We're missing two," Doctor Mantus mumbled. "We're overlooking them."

"It *is* possible that we haven't come across them yet. You just gave them to me in the order that Hercules dealt with them in the myth, right?"

"Yes."

"If that's so, then none of them have come to *us* in the proper order. Why should we assume that Charlie Sticks is the final piece of the puzzle?"

"For one thing, are you sure that the order in which we *recognized* them is the order in which they *came* to us, or were *offered* to us? Those are two very different things."

"No, I'm not."

"Secondly, there's a great deal of Judeo-Christian imagery involved here, not solely Greek myth. You've told me about your brother's 'piercings' throughout his life. We know about his visions, the apostolic implications of the gathering of the Twelve, etc. How does all that fit in? What about Rhea Theomastix—her apparent recognition of what's happening? You told me last night that she was writing the word 'Labors' in Greek on the walls of her cell.

How does *she* connect? Just to guide us to Charlie? I don't know. I think I'm supposed to figure it out, but I can't seem to piece it all together."

At that moment, Doctor Herman and Yuri returned to the kitchen.

"How is she?" I said.

"Doing fine. I gave her something to help her sleep. I extracted the pellets and cleaned the wounds. She'll be fine, providing there's no infection. She'll be sore for a while, but fine. Now, while I do the same for you, I want to know what happened."

Doctor Mantus filled him in. Doctor Herman kept nodding, as if the incredible events of the last few months were simply the summary of an athletic contest or the acknowledgement of a grocery list. He cut away my pant leg with scissors and dropped the material on the floor. I tried not to watch as he calmly extracted each pellet from my leg and hand with a scalpel and tweezers, then disinfected and bandaged each wound.

"You can understand then," I said, when the professor had finished, "why we can't call the police about this?"

Doctor Herman pushed his glasses up the flat bridge of his nose with a gloved hand, unknowingly leaving a trace of my blood there. "Yes, I suppose so." He paused for a moment from his labors and looked directly at me. The blood smudge was unsettling, but I said nothing. "Where do you think all this is supposed to lead you? What purpose is there to it?"

"It has something to do with Meg," I answered, "with her survival. But we don't understand it all yet."

"Jim," the good man said, pushing his glasses back up his nose, "she has *terminal* cancer."

I looked at Doctor Mantus who was studying another cigarette. "I know."

Doctor Herman rose from his chair and went to the kitchen sink to wash up. "I'll continue to pray for her," he said as he scrubbed. "I'm sorry to rush away, but I have to get back to my office. I'm way behind. Too much pain in the world."

"I appreciate it, Leo."

"Yes, well, if I were you, I'd keep close tabs on the fellow who shot you. Next time he might use something more lethal, then I'd have some real difficulty explaining why I didn't report this incident." He dried his hands and put his coat back on. "See you in church." He grabbed his black bag and went to the door. "Pastor Gudsen is quite the topic around the medical water cooler. Did you know that?"

"I would assume it."

"His recovery from that stabbing is phenomenal, nothing short of it. No one can explain it. Being his family doctor, I've seen him through a lot of things, including that arrow in his head, but this…well…I'm sixty-one years old and he's the best evidence for God's existence that I've ever seen." He shook his balding head. "Have you seen him today?"

"Not today, no."

"When you do, please let him know I'm thinking of him."

"Sure."

"Frankly, I'll be glad when he's back. Pastor Bird does his best, I'm sure, but he's not the preacher your brother is. God bless." He closed the door quietly behind him.

Atlas and Auggie came down the stairs.

"Where's Charlie?" I said.

"He's watching television in Auggie's bedroom," Atlas said. "We got him cleaned up and Auggie gave him a new set of clothes. We clipped off a lot of his hair and shaved him. You'd never recognize him."

"He's like Samson," Auggie said. "As soon as we cropped his hair, he settled right down. Studied himself in the mirror for a while, then got interested in *The Price is Right*. He hasn't moved for ten minutes."

"Do you think you should leave him alone?"

"The only way out is down the stairs," Atlas said. "I made 'im promise to stay put if I bring him that damned dog and some chow. I'll go get the mutt. I still got your keys," he said, holding them up.

"I'll make him a sandwich," Auggie added.

"You look a hell of a lot better," Atlas observed as he headed for the door. "How's Minnie?"

"Not bad," I heard her say as she appeared in the archway that separated the kitchen from the living room. Teena stood next to her. "It wasn't the best date I've ever been on, but it wasn't the worst either. At least I wasn't bored."

"You need a new owner," I said.

"What? Your property gets damaged and you want a trade-in? Sorry, Buster."

"Someone who'll take better care of you."

"Already took care of that." She winked at me.

Teena looked confused, but the rest were laughing.

"Be right back," Atlas said and closed the door, shutting out the brilliant sunshine and the crisp, autumnal air. From the other side of Horizon Road, I could hear the buzz of power saws and the rattle of syncopated hammering.

"What time is the meeting tonight?" I asked the professor.

"Seven."

"All the Councilors will be there?"

"Except for Minnie's father—and your brother, of course. I've contacted the rest of them."

I looked at Minnie. She smiled sweetly. "You okay?"

"Fine. A little sore, that's all."

"We're going to have to keep this quiet, even among the Gospel Church members—the shooting I mean."

"As long as I don't walk around in a bikini, no one will know." She looked down at Meg's bloody blouse. "I'll need a change of clothes, of course."

"I think I've got something for you," Teena said.

"Good," I said, "then maybe you could take my car and drive Minnie home."

"Oh no you don't," Minnie said. "I'm staying for the meeting."

"I think you ought to—"

"Do exactly what I want to?"

I shrugged. "I'm beginning to feel married," I said. "You knew precisely what I was going to say."

Laughter erupted around the room. It was a great, warm sound.

"*You* could use a new wardrobe too," Minnie said, pointing at the bloody, discarded trouser leg on the kitchen floor. "Half-shorts are out this year."

"I'll send somebody across the street."

Atlas came back in through the door. He was cradling Full Count in his arms. The dog's eyes were open. He was busily munching on a hot dog and was, apparently, oblivious to his surroundings, though whether that was due to his preoccupation with his food or the blow to his head, I couldn't determine. Atlas took him upstairs and returned almost immediately.

"How's Charlie?" I said.

"Hungry."

"I'm on my way." Auggie was carrying a paper plate loaded with peanut butter and jelly sandwiches and potato chips.

"My stomach's sending out alarm signals too," Atlas said. "What say we have some lunch? A cheeseburger or three would be nice."

"I go," Yuri said. "Der's a MacDonnas coupla miles from here. I be back coupla minutes." He headed out the kitchen door.

"What're we goin' do with Charlie?" Atlas said. The question was directed at me.

"I don't know. He can stay here for now, I guess. He has to be a part of all this. We'll just have to keep a close eye on him."

"I think he'll be okay," Professor Mantus said. "The shooting thing was done in a panic."

"I agree," Atlas said, "but he ain't the most stable person I ever knew. No tellin' what he'll do. He's gotta lotta demons."

"He can't spend the rest of his life in that swamp," Minnie observed, as she sat down, gingerly, next to me.

"I think his sister is the key," Doctor Mantus mumbled.

"Key to what?" Atlas said.

"The place where those demons live."

Chapter twenty-three

Yuri brought back enough hamburgers and fries and milkshakes to feed an army. By the time we'd finished eating, got cleaned up and into some different clothes, the late autumn sun was low in the sky.

Minnie and I decided that we should get across the street to the manse and find out what was going on there. Naturally she was anxious about her parents and I, about my brother and Meg. Certainly there would be news. We agreed to keep silent about our own adventure that day—at least the part about getting shot.

Doctor Mantus opted to go home for awhile to 'freshen up' as he put it, promising to return at 7:00 P.M. Yuri and Auggie agreed to bring the Boatman over to the meeting of The Twelve at the appointed time. In the interim, Atlas was commissioned as turnkey.

"Try not to limp so much," Minnie said as we crossed Horizon Road. "You look like you've been shot in the leg."

"Very funny," I said. "Maybe next time you'll listen to me when I tell you a situation might be dangerous."

"God is good."

We were met in the yard by Rusha and Larry Ladon. Rusha hugged Minnie. and I saw her wince from it.

"Hey Son," Larry said. "You hurt yourself?"

"Just twisted my ankle a bit." I pointed at the new church site, primarily to deflect his attention away from the subject of my leg. "Looks like they made a lot of progress today."

He turned and looked admiringly at the new structure. "They got three walls framed in since morning. We got home from Holy Cross a while ago and there they were already."

"How's Herk?"

"I told him about the council meeting tonight and, of course, he insisted he should come. The doctors refused to let him, but they really are amazed at how quickly he's healing. They keep asking us about him and one guy's been poring over his medical records for days. They've been fighting off the media since word got out. Have you seen this?"

He held up a copy of the Saginaw newspaper. My eye went immediately to an old picture of Herk with his head bandaged. It had been taken after Auggie had accidentally shot him with that infamous crossbow. Meg was in the photo, standing between Herk and me, looking radiant and alive.

LOCAL CLERGYMAN CHEATS DEATH AGAIN, the headline read. PARISHIONER CHARGED IN STABBING.

"What about Meg?"

Knowing what they knew, there were no words. Larry's vanished smile spoke volumes. "Where's Mom?"

"She's inside with the baby. Sylvia was there for a while, but she's gone back to the hospital."

Rusha was studying Minnie's pale smile. "You all right, Sweetie?"

"Yeah, fine. Just tired, that's all. We've been through a lot of stress with dad and then Pastor Gudman. I'll be okay."

I heard a car pull in behind us and stop. We were blocking the gravel drive. Minnie turned around. "It's Sybil!" she yelled, and went off with Rusha to greet her friend, as Larry and I headed for the house, waving to and conversing with numerous parishioners who were leaving for the day after laboring on the new church building.

At seven o'clock, most of the councilors were crowded around the kitchen table: Yuri, Doctor Mantus, Larry and Rusha, Auggie, Judy Crabbe, Robin Stym and Baxter Bird. Caleb Bird and I were there by virtue of office. Ben Tower and Herk himself, of course, were absent. A quick explanation of Ben Tower as a new councilor resulted in the unanimous approval of Minnie, who was sitting next to me, as her father's stand-in. Atlas still had not arrived with Charlie.

"Atlas was on the phone with some friend of his just as we were leaving to come over here," Auggie explained.

"Friend?"

"Yeah, some woman, I think. She was calling long distance."

I looked at Yuri, hoping for a better explanation. He shrugged. "I came over before Auggie," he said. "I vasn't der."

"Atlas told me to go ahead," Auggie explained. "He said he'd be over with Charlie in a few minutes."

"Who's Charlie?" Judy Crabbe asked.

Frankly, I was relieved by the delay, since it gave me a little time to prepare the Council for Charlie's appearance—not only as a new member of the Twelve, but also as the brother of the person most of them knew as Lena Gossbach. Doctor Mantus helped me, fortunately, with the narrative about the day's events, both of us carefully omitting any reference to the shooting, Charlie's bizarre appearance, or his felonious history.

The primary topic, of course, was Pastor Gudsen and his welfare. Auggie was quick to relate that Herk, though he'd been at death's door less than forty-eight hours ago, had been practically healed when he'd seen him last night. Judy Crabbe testified that he'd shown up in Meg's room that morning in a wheelchair, accompanied by an orderly. Judy said, tears welling in her sleep-deprived eyes, that when he'd touched Meg's hand, the thin, cold fingers had slightly curled around his, though Meg was comatose and surviving each moment purely with the assistance of machines. Larry added that he and Ginny had seen Herk only hours before, and he looked well enough to come home. Larry passed the newspaper article around, commenting on the bewilderment of the medical staff regarding Herk's remarkable recuperation.

This created a general hubbub that died only when Doctor Mantus stood and harrumphed several times to draw the Council's attention.

"The, ah, existence of this group has nothing to do with Pastor Gudsen's condition, I'm afraid. It has, if I've been informed correctly, everything to do, rather, with the life of Megan Gudsen."

"Thank Christ," Judy Crabbe whispered. "Somebody's finally paying attention."

The professor continued, apparently unaware of the nurse's comment.

"Last winter, less than a year ago, Pastor Gudsen had a vision. Is that right James?"

All faces turned to me. "My brother told Meg and me that God had spoken to him, yes. He said it wasn't a vision or a dream, but the *voice of God.*"

"What did it sound like?" Auggie said.

"I don't know. *I* didn't hear it."

"Never mind that now," the professor said. Clearly, he was annoyed by Auggie's question. "What did the voice *say?*"

"That Meg would survive her newly-diagnosed cancer if—"

"If what?"

"If Herk did what God instructed him to do."

"Which was?"

"To gather The Twelve."

The earlier commotion was now replaced with a sanctuarial silence.

The professor continued. "At our last meeting, my first, it became apparent, as I explained then, that the myth of the Labors of Hercules was the allusionary model by which the Twelve would be brought together. Each of us here, (or even two of us, as in the case of Robin Stym and Baxter Bird), represent, in some fashion, one of these labors. Since our last meeting, Ben Tower, who obviously can't be here tonight, Miss Springbok," he nodded in her direction, "and Charlie Sticks, who should be here shortly, have been added. There's no doubt in my mind that the people gathered around this table represent certain characters in the Herculean myth and, therefore, belong here. Our problem is to find the last two, and I'm convinced that we probably have met them already. We're just overlooking them somehow. We need to put our heads together and figure out who they are—quickly. I think Megan Gudsen's life depends on it."

"Which of the mythical characters do the missing ones represent again?" Larry Ladon asked.

"The Horses of Diomedes and the Oxen of Geryon," I said. Doctor Mantus winked at me approvingly.

"So we're looking for horses?" Minnie said.

"As much as we were looking for a Minotaur and a bull from Crete when we found you and your father," Doctor Mantus replied. "We have to be metaphorical about this. I believe it's your names that are mostly significant. Ladon was the dragon that guarded the apples of the Hesperides. I'm the Boar of Erymanthus. Erymanthus sounds very much like Ari Mantus. The Birds of Stymphalus—Baxter *Bird* and Robin *Stym,* and so on."

"Vat 'bout me?" Yuri said. "Ma name an't like Nemean Lion at all."

"No, but you *were* a lion, a Detroit Lion football player, and the king who ordered Hercules to perform these labors was called Eurystheus—Yuri Theus. There's a nominative connection there too."

"So," Sybil Springbok said, "we need to find people whose names are similar to Diomedes or Geryon?" Everyone turned toward Sybil when she spoke and many when she didn't. She was so easy to look at. It wasn't really eroticism, just the mere pleasure of looking at something lovely.

"Yes, I think so," Doctor Mantus replied, "but there has to be some other connection to the myth as well—as with your dream Miss Springbok."

She smiled. "I'm sorry," she said, "please forgive my reticence, but this is all a bit difficult to swallow. Religion isn't my forte."

"This isn't about religion," I said.

She turned her doe-eyes on me and I remember wondering if Minnie could detect my discomfort.

"No? What then?"

"It's about God."

She smiled—a lovely, unnerving smile. "These things," she said. "They couldn't be mere happenstance? Coincidence?"

"No."

The answer came from a voice outside the circled conclave. Though it issued but a single word, I knew it. We all turned in its direction. I remember the moment vividly. It's often repeated itself in my dreams, to the point where that thin line, the distinction between what is real and what is desired, has clouded.

I knew then, that what I was witnessing was not possible. I know now, that it could be nothing else.

Standing in the framed opening between the kitchen and the living room were Ben Tower and the Reverend Herkimer Gudsen. Ginny stood behind Herk, tears flowing down her cheeks onto the thin-haired little head of her grandson. Sylvia was clutching her husband's arm in a similar attitude of wonder and gratitude. The bandages were gone from Ben Tower's head. There was no indication at all that he'd ever been hurt. Even the bald area where the surgeons had shaved his head was covered with hair.

"Daddy!" Minnie cried as she ran to him and embraced him. "Sweetheart," he said to her. I knew from that single response that Ben Tower would not be watching cartoons the rest of his life. Somehow, miraculously, he had returned in more than just a physical sense.

"What...what's happened to you?" Minnie said as she tenderly touched the side of his face that had been caved in by the crushing weight of nature. Ben Tower kissed his daughter's forehead and looked at her with such an expression of paternal devotion that she, too, was moved to tears.

"Pastor Gudsen came to Ben's room," Sylvia Tower said. She looked at Minnie. "I was sitting by the bed there, watching cartoons with your father, holding his hand. Pastor said that we had to go, that we were needed elsewhere." Sylvia was struggling to hold the image in her mind as if it were too large to be contained in such a meager vessel. "He...he walked up to your father and put his hands on him...and then..." Sylvia choked back the lump in her throat. "Then he began to unwrap the bandages. I came around the bed to try and stop him, but your father held tight to my hand. I think I told Pastor Gudsen to stop...I don't remember."

"I do," Ben Tower said. "I remember hearing that. It's the first thing I remember—after the bull's charge."

Sylvia broke into sobs and Ben put his free arm around her. "I...I'm sorry," she said after collecting herself. "It's not just that I have my husband back. It's something else too."

"What, Mama?" Minnie said, brushing her own tears aside.

"We're not alone," Sylvia finally said between sobs of joy. "We're really and truly not alone."

I looked at my brother. He bore that sad, martyr's smile that was so much a part of him. But there was also a change in him—something about him was new and indefinable. Even now, knowing all that has happened since, I find it difficult to explain. There is, perhaps, no real explanation. I know this: Herk had ceased to be, in my mind at least, primarily a brother. He would always *be* my brother of course, but that's not the way I thought of him anymore. His role in the world had gone way beyond such a paltry definition. The change involved the words confidence, faith, assurance, comfort, dependency—all of them at once—none of them adequate to real understanding. Herk had been transfigured somehow and perhaps Sylvia Tower had said it best—the change in him was the subtle transformation in all of us from the hope of religious faith to the certain knowledge of God's presence. The vagaries of myth, our pathetic attempts to ward off the confusion of random chaos, our puerile, impotent dependency on the icons of religious formula had been stripped away. Herkimer Gudsen was connected to God. We were not alone.

We all felt it. We all knew it.

Rusha embraced our brother then she stepped back, took his hand and stretched out his arm. He was wearing an old sweatshirt.

I don't think it belonged to him. He knew what Rusha was looking for. He pulled up his sleeve to allow her to examine him. Not only was the gash in his arm from Lena Gossbach's attack healed, but there was no evidence that he'd ever been stabbed—not even a scar. Rusha looked at her own bandaged arm. Her hand touched his collarbone, then the area at his side where the butcher knife had punctured a lung less than forty-eight hours ago.

"Yes," was all he said.

He took her arm, placed one of his large hands over her bandages. She told me later that her arm hurt, but not badly. It was like the annoying prickly sensation you experience when a limb has been deprived of blood—when it 'wakes up' after having 'fallen asleep'. Then he slowly unwrapped her bandages. There was dried blood on the inner gauze, but the arm itself bore no mark whatsoever.

Rusha, her eyes flowing with tears, kissed our brother's hand. "My Lord," she whispered. It was not an exclamation. It was a designation.

"No!" His voice was stern, emphatic, even reprimanding. "I'm only Herk Gudsen." His voice softened again and he smiled at our sister. "Just a man, Rusha. God has need of me, that's all, and we have need of Him."

We all stood in stunned silence for a few minutes. I remember hearing the bare branches of the forsythia bush, scratching the kitchen window, the sound of the October wind.

Auggie got up and reverently offered his chair to my brother. Herk sat down. The rest gathered around him.

"No, you're not God," Doctor Mantus said from across the Formica table, "but God works through you. Have you applied your healing ability to your wife?"

"Yes."

Judy Crabbe's eyes widened in expectation. "What happened?" Her voice was filled with anxiety.

"Nothing. No change."

"Then we have to see it through," Doctor Mantus said.

"Yes, we have to see it through. Meg's life requires the Twelve."

"But why this game, Brother?" I heard my thoughts spoken by my own voice.

"Game?"

"Yeah. Why the piercings—Ben Tower's accident—Lena Gossbach's attack? Why did they happen at all?" I felt Minnie's arms around my neck. I saw Ben Tower's smile of approval.

"It's not solitaire."

"What?"

"The game, Jim. There's more than one Player."

"I don't understand."

"Of course you do."

"Nothing bad ever comes from God," Caleb Bird said.

Herk nodded.

"Then someone is trying to stop us?" Baxter Bird said, addressing my brother rather than his own.

Herk said, simply: "There is always the Enemy."

We were all startled as the kitchen door opened suddenly behind us and Atlas Johnson, Charlie Sticks, the wind and a few dry leaves blew into the kitchen.

"Sorry I'm late," Atlas said, puffing from the exertion of pulling Charlie along and the normal strain of operating his own considerable bulk. He slammed the door behind him, while the other meaty hand was firmly locked on Charlie's collar. "I'll be goddammed if it wasn't Maddy on the phone, Yuri," he bellowed. "Jim, you remember Maddy—or you should anyway," he chuckled.

Ginny looked at the giant with sour-faced disapproval. I thought it was his intrusion upon the moment, but it might have been his allusion to my checkered past or, simply, his cursing. I felt Minnie's arms around my neck loosen. I didn't say anything.

"Rusha!" Atlas boomed. "Your slave-girl says Hi." It was one of the few times I would ever see my sister's face crimson in embarrassment.

"Why did she call?" Rusha managed, half-afraid, I think, to continue any reference to Maddy, but overcome with curiosity.

"She wants to come here! Teena's been writin' her, she said, tellin' her all about this place. She's tired of the club. Can ya believe it? Maddy wants to come *here*, give up the films and such." He guffawed. "She says she's found *God!*"

"Vy she doesn't yus come den?" Yuri said.

"Aw, you know Mad," Atlas said. "She ain't got the plane fare. I'm goin' wire it to her. Made her promise not to spend it on hooch. She says she'll be here in a coupla days."

I listened to Atlas, but my eyes were riveted on Charlie Sticks. His transfiguration was comparable to Herk's, but only physical. It was nothing short of miraculous the impact a simple shave, haircut, some soap and a new set of clothes could make on him. Except for the wary eyes, I wouldn't have believed him to be the same man. There was enough fear in those haunted eyes for an allied battalion on a Normandy beach.

"I want go back, Johnny," Charlie said.

"Take it easy old pal," Atlas whispered, reassuringly. "These people won't hurt you."

"Now! Got to go now!" Charlie said. He began struggling to free himself from Atlas's iron grip. It was as useless a motion as that of a single shaft of wind-blown wheat before the steel blades of the harvester.

"No, no, no, no!" Charlie screamed. He gave himself up to his terror and collapsed on the linoleum. It was the only way Atlas would have let go. His skinny body writhed frenetically on the floor. He screamed gibberish. His body convulsed in uncontrollable spasms.

Everyone rushed to him, encircling the terrified man in an attempt to aid him, but no one knew what to do. When anyone reached for him, his screams multiplied in both number and volume.

"Is he epileptic?" Rusha shouted above the din.

"No!" Atlas said. "He's really scared—of what though, I don't know."

"I am here," Herk said softly, and stepped through the crowd. He calmly watched Charlie as the Boatman's gray eyes rolled up into his head and bits of spittle and blood appeared at the corners of his mouth. The awful screaming had stopped, but Charlie was convulsing in death throes. Herk knelt down and placed his hand on the heaving chest. "In the name of our blessed Lord, Jesus Christ," he said softly. "Go away!"

Charlie's face twisted into a terrible grimace. He laughed—the low, wicked, guffawing of the unrepentant murderer in the electric chair. "Fuck you," he growled.

"*Go away!*" Herk repeated. *Go home.*" The words sounded almost comical in the presence of such malevolence—like a child who's irritated with a playmate. "Go home," he said again.

Then Charlie's body went limp and he lay still.

"He's dead," someone said.

"No," Herk whispered as he gently rubbed Charlie's damp forehead. "He's beginning to live."

Charlie's eyes opened. He smiled. "I gonna be okay?" he said.

Atlas lifted him to his feet as if he were nothing more than a small child, his eyes never leaving Herk.

"Yes," Herk said.

Charlie embraced him, laying his head on my brother's shoulder. The clean-shaven face was turned to me. Charlie was smiling through his tears.

"He's one of the Twelve," Herk said.

"We believe so," the professor answered, "yes." Everyone else was too astonished by what they had witnessed to speak. "He's Lena Gossbach's brother."

"Yes," Herk said, "of course." He placed his large hand on Charlie's head as he held him. I saw the scars from earlier piercings still there and it hadn't escaped my notice, when my brother had walked to the table, that he still limped.

Herk held Charlie for a few minutes in the stunned silence, patting his back and whispering comfort, before he gently guided him to a chair. The wild man sat there placidly, a docile grin on his face.

"What did you just do?" Atlas said.

I remember thinking what silly creatures we are, we humans. Animals accept what we give them, whether we use guns to kill them or medicine to cure them. They don't wonder at what superior intelligence can do. They accept it and live or die, because they have no other choice. It happens to us, and we wonder where it came from or, sadly, if it ever happened at all.

"I did nothing," Herk said. "God has placed a claim on him."

"Charlie? Hey man," Atlas said, stepping forward and shaking the Boatman's shoulder. "You all right, Buddy?"

Charlie Sticks looked at him with distant eyes. "Yes," he said quietly. "I'm home."

Atlas looked back at Herk. "What's he mean—he's home?"

"God lives in him now." Herk sat down.

The others, initially too stunned to speak, now became animated, and a general clamor ensued.

"He performed an *exorcism!*"

"No, he just calmed the guy down."

"He's been cured himself. Didn't you see? No wounds."

"He called on the Lord. It's a miracle!"

"He is Christ!"

I saw my mother, calmly silent in the midst of the din. She was watching her son; the son she'd always favored; the son who'd been the focus of her life; the pivotal, all absorbing polestar in her universe; and I began to know why, as she, somehow, had always known.

This day was a vindication for her—the intendment of her directed life, the summative experience that justified her partiality and erased my own, petty grudges. She was the earth-woman who had accepted the sky as her lover and had produced in the encompassing act a contemporary, mythic hero.

She smiled at the wonderment around her. She was serene and fully confident in the eye of the whirlwind of chaos and confusion that swarmed around her. I felt my jealousy melt away.

"Please," Herk said. "Please! Would everyone be seated?"

The whirlwind dwindled to a murmuring breeze. When all eyes were turned to him, he said: "We need something to eat. Mother, Minnie, Sylvia, would you be so kind...?"

The request had a normalizing effect. The supernatural, as is often the case, became subservient to the natural—the epiphany of the spirit drowned in the grumblings of the body.

Ginny moved to her calling. Minnie and Sylvia hurried to assist, both of them having become familiar with Herk and Meg's kitchen in the process of helping to feed all the workers. Atlas leaned against the wall, mouth still agape, slowly becoming aware that the world had shifted and would never again be such a burden. At that moment, Professor Mantus seemed to be the only person, other than my brother, who could find his voice.

"Why do you think," he asked Herk, "that God would heal *you* so quickly—that he would give you the power to erase Ben Tower and Rusha's wounds or drive away Charlie's demons and yet not allow you to cure your own wife?"

Herk shrugged. "I don't know for sure, except that we've been set on a course and we have to follow it. Rusha, Ben and this man"—he put a hand on Charlie's emaciated shoulder— "are meant to be part of the Twelve. It's my task to bring them together, keep them together. Beyond that, I have no power. Meg's life is outside my care, but not God's. It will take *all* of us for God to save her."

"A deal's a deal," I said.

"Yes."

There was a long silence, as the stunned disciples looked at each other—looked to each other, perhaps wondering, like me, what would happen next.

"The Oxen of Geryon," Doctor Mantus said, quietly. "They're next, and I keep having this nagging sensation that one of us knows who they—or it—is."

"Can you describe the myth again?" Rusha said, emerging from her stunned silence. She was rubbing the smooth skin on her forearm where the wicked gash had once been. She didn't look up when she spoke.

The professor obliged. "Geryon was a three-headed, three-bodied monster, the offspring of Chrysaor and Callirrhoe, a daughter of the Titan, Oceanus. He was a king, the king of Tartessus, and owned the finest stock of cattle in the ancient world. Heracles was sent to steal them. Hera, Queen of the gods, tried to help Geryon protect his herds, but Hercules wounded her, killed Geryon, and brought the oxen to King Eurystheus in a golden bowl."

"What are we supposed to learn from that?" Baxter Bird said. "How can that story help Mrs. Gudsen?"

"We're supposed to find some three-headed monster?" Robin echoed.

"None of this is literal," Doctor Mantus said. I could see that his joy rested in subtler miracles. "Perhaps we're looking for three separate people who have some connection to one another."

I turned to Minnie behind me. She had turned away from the sink, where she was working, toward me. She'd heard it and thought the same thing. She nodded.

"Yesterday," I said, facing the others around the table, "three policemen were out here investigating the attack on Her...on Pastor Gudsen."

My brother smiled benignly at me.

"Yes, go on," Professor Mantus said, his ugly nose lifted in the air as if to catch a scent.

"They're brothers. They all have the same name."

"Which is?"

"Young, I think it was. Wait a minute." I started searching my wallet for the card the Adonis had given us.

"It was Yonger," Minnie said.

"Yep, she's right." I'd found the card.

Doctor Mantus thought for a moment, then excitedly pulled his little notepad from a pocket and began scribbling.

"Then that's it!" he declared.

"How could you possibly know?" Sybil Springbok said.

"The name, Yonger," Doctor Mantus chuckled in his snorting, piggish way. "Don't you see?"

I confessed that I didn't. Sybil wasn't alone in her confusion.

"Juxtapose the two syllables of their name."

"Regnoy?"

"No, no," Doctor Mantus cried impatiently. "Just take the last syllable, the G-E-R, and put it in front of the first. Don't invert the *letters*."

"Geryon," Sybil said.

"There," Doctor Mantus said. "Geryon, the three-bodied, triple-headed monster. Then there's the connection with Hera, too. Remember, Jim? Hera, Rhea?"

"You're right, Professor," I said. "We *did* have it all along."

"What's the other one? The last one?" Herk said.

"Diomedes," Doctor Mantus said. "He was a wicked king who fed human flesh to his horses."

The phone rang in the background.

"I'll get it," Ginny said, leaving the sink where she'd been preparing salad.

"There's a doctor at the hospital," Judy Crabbe offered, "who raises horses—pure-blooded Arabians. It's his passion. He breeds them for racing. One of his stock ran in the Kentucky Derby last year. He's from Pakistan, I think. He's a strange combination. His father's a devout Muslim and his mother's Jewish...Israeli."

"What's his name?" Professor Mantus said.

"Doctor Mudeez," Judy answered.

"He's dad's doctor," Minnie said. "I've talked with him."

"What's his first name?"

"That's easy to remember. His mother's great hero was Moshe Dayan, the Israeli soldier. Not too many Muslims named after Jewish generals."

"Moshe Mudeez?" Auggie said.

"No," Sylvia said. "He was the doctor who operated on Ben. It's Dayan, Dayan Mudeez."

"Diomedes," the professor said. "Number twelve."

"Jesus!" Atlas exclaimed.

Ginny reappeared in the kitchen. She was pale. She looked as if she'd been punched in the stomach. Her arm rested on the stove. She was holding herself up, barely. Larry Ladon rushed to her. "Ginny, Darling," he said, "what is it? What's happened?"

For some reason, I was watching my brother. He closed his eyes. His hands, folded on the table in front of him, white-knuckled in his grip.

Ginny was fighting back tears as Larry placed an arm around his waist.

"My dear son," she said to Herk.

He didn't turn around. His eyes stayed closed. "Darling!" She struggled to go on. "That was the hospital," she said, her soft, tremulous voice more frightening than any scream a damned soul could produce. "It's Meg, Darling. She…she passed away a few minutes ago." Ginny broke into agonized sobbing.

Everyone turned to look at my brother. We were all thinking the same thing. At this grand moment of epiphany, nothing mattered anymore.

He opened his blue eyes.

The facial expressions around the table were identical. They were the synchronic manifestations of cold despair, as if spring and summer had forever gone out of the world.

Judy Crabbe fainted.

Herkimer Gudsen wept.

Chapter twenty-four

Herk rose from his chair after what seemed an interminable time, though I'm sure it was only minutes. "I need to be alone," he said. As he turned to leave the room, I went to him, anxiously searching his gentle face. His blue eyes were fierce with grief.

"You didn't start all this to save Meg," I told him.

He knew what I was thinking. "No." Unconsciously, he took my hand and felt the thick bandages. "What's this?"

"Nothing," I lied.

He smiled, as a knowing parent smiles at a child's simple deceptions. He gently engulfed my wounded hand in both of his. I felt a prickly sensation. "Keep them all here," he whispered, "I won't be long." He pushed past me and went into the living room.

"Where Good Son goes?" Charlie Sticks said. "He comin' back?"

Ben Tower was sitting next to the Boatman. He put his hand on one wasted arm. "It's all right," I heard him say. "Faith."

Ginny looked at me. As always, I had no answers. She wiped her face with her apron. "Perhaps we should concentrate on supper," she said.

It was a good suggestion. When the spirit is drained, fill every cavity of the material. It is *some* comfort.

"You go ahead with that," I said, "you go ahead with that."

Minnie grabbed my arm. "I think you should let him be alone if he needs to," she said.

"I'm going to the bathroom."

"Oh, sorry." She kissed me as I left.

As soon as I shut the door, I began to unwrap the bandages around my hand. The last of it was sticky with blood. I peeled it off. The area around the puncture was swollen. The purplish mound looked worse, if anything. I had expected it to be gone. I thought my brother might have healed me too. I was wrong to think that he could.

I knelt there, on the hard floor, and prayed. I asked God to care for Meg's soul. Like a petulant child, I wanted to tell him that I would no longer believe in Him. *I won't love you anymore and you'll be sorry.* But I was the one who'd broken a promise. He'd kept His end of the bargain—a deal's a deal.

I could beg exception—that's all. Every guilty man does that. Jeremiah Cabal knew. How many times, I thought, must someone die because I haven't the courage to suffer? God must be angry—or at least sadly amused. "Help me," I whispered. "Help me." There was nothing else to say.

The words of one of Herk's sermons came to me. 'God made a perfect world,' he'd said, 'and we have made it go wrong. Now, He insists that we clean up our own mess.'

I rose from my knees. I found fresh gauze in the bathroom closet and rewrapped my hand. I returned to the kitchen where the others were quietly eating or talking. Minnie left her parents to stand by me. "Jim," she whispered, "I'm so sorry about Meg. I know you loved her."

"Not enough," was all I managed.

The others watched me as I sat down. There was no staring, really, just furtive glances away from the study of food. They all wanted to ask me when my brother would rejoin us, but they knew I didn't know.

Atlas had taken the chair my brother had vacated, next to Charlie Sticks. They were conversing in hushed undertones—a significant feat for them both. The formerly wild man seemed tame and calm, though that constant look of childish confusion remained. Ben and Sylvia Tower were also quietly whispering. Rusha and Sybil stood in a corner, surrounding the devastated Judy Crabbe, who was sobbing uncontrollably and would not, despite their efforts, be comforted. Doctor Mantus peered at his notes on the table as he noisily slurped down his soup. The three Birds— Caleb, Baxter and Robin, were sequestered in another trio. Alone, Auggie Two-River appeared to be praying. My mother and father stood by the stove, dishing the soup into bowls, Yuri Theus acting as waiter.

Minnie and I sat down next to her parents. Yuri brought us some soup. It emitted the finest aroma and I think I would have felt better had I eaten, but I wanted to feel empty.

As I watched him eat, I was astounded by Ben Tower. I'd seen, close-up, how badly his head had been mangled. There was no evidence at all of the terrible injury—none. It seemed to me that he ought to be doing something else—talking to reporters, preaching of his healing from a pulpit, following my brother into the living room to comfort him—anything besides eating soup. I looked down at my bandaged hand. Minnie touched my arm and smiled at me. For a moment the pain went away. It was miracle enough.

Professor Mantus abandoned his soup and stared at me, his head cocked to one side like a curious animal.

"It's over," I said to him. "There's no purpose to this anymore."

"You think so?" He wiped the oil off his chin with a paper napkin.

"Yes."

"I don't agree."

"Why?"

"The Twelve are still important."

"How?"

"Do you seriously believe, James, that our only relevance is to save a single life? Are you suggesting that something that God has planned, as you pointed out, for generations, has no worth or purpose? You think we should disband and go home?"

"Yes."

"If the Apostles had done that after Christ left them, there would be no Church."

"Yes, well, we're not apostles and Herk is not the Son of God." Minnie's hand was on my arm again. It said: 'Listen, listen.'

"He may not be Christ, but he bears as great a resemblance to that Life as I do to the mythic boar."

"Really." I hated the caustic insinuation of my own voice.

"Yes, really. Didn't I just see him heal the Boatman? Were you here for that?"

"He makes me feel good," Charlie said.

"He calmed the poor man, that's all. Charlie was afraid. He's been living in—"

"Purgatory? Hell?"

"Isolation. He's not used to people. He panicked. Herk got him to settle down, that's all."

"And the disappearance of your brother's wounds? Ben Tower's?"

"Fast healers."

"From a crushed skull, a punctured lung? C'mon, James."

I looked at my bandaged hand. "He couldn't heal me."

"Couldn't or wouldn't? You're not one of the Twelve. Perhaps you're not meant to receive the same…treatment. Did Christ heal everyone? Did He step down from the cross? I noticed that your brother still limps."

"It means nothing."

"No?" Doctor Mantus lit a cigarette. "*You* told me what an unusual child your brother was. He was always talking about God. He always wanted to be a Pastor. What about all the piercings? He heals people, drives out demons, if we're to believe our own eyes. Before that, you told me about how he faced off against the pharisees, (your word), of his own church, including your father." Larry turned away from the eyes that examined him. "The name, Gudsen, even poor Charlie recognized its significance." Charlie smiled, amused to be, for a brief moment, the subject of conversation. "Jesus rescued the fallen woman. Forgive me, Rusha, but I see you as Magdela.

"Coincidence, vague approximations that could be applied to hundreds of people."

"Even the miracles?"

"They're performed by televangelists every Sunday afternoon. Before them, it was done in tent revivals. Cheap magician's tricks."

"You're wrong, Jim," Minnie said. "I love you desperately, but you're wrong. What happened to my father was a real miracle—nothing less."

"Then God did it, not Herk. He said so himself. As for the rest of it, there are more voids than substance."

"For example?"

"All right. Our mother and father. Why aren't they named Joseph and Mary? Herk's the Good Son, I'm his brother, James. What about Larry and Ginny?"

Professor Mantus fumbled with his lighter. He clicked it a couple of times, studying the flame. "Your mother's name is Jenny or Ginny?"

She was standing at the end of the table. She'd been listening like everyone else. "Ginny," she said. "It's short for Virginia."

Doctor Mantus smiled, his triumphant grin lifting his ponderous nose to reveal his refutative teeth which, metaphorically at least, were capable of inflicting serious wounds.

Larry, as always, stood at my mother's side. "Mr. Ladon," the professor said. "May I ask what your full, baptismal name might be?"

"Lawrence Joseph Ladon."

There was a tittering whisper around the table. Doctor Mantus looked at me and raised his eyebrows. "What do you think?" he asked.

"Bullshit!"

I don't yet know what made me so angry, so unwilling to accept what appeared to be Truth. I think it was a desire to be sensible, to put the supernatural aside. It's easier to make sense of the natural and I wanted very much for the world to make sense. But then what does 'sensible' mean, to feel or to be felt? The ability to act or be the object of an action? The sense of touch, or being Touched? As is always the case with Truth, I was confused.

"You know better," Doctor Mantus said, calmly responding to my outburst by lighting another cigarette. "You know better, James."

"Despite her name," I argued, "my mother was no virgin when Herk was conceived."

"I suppose not. And Mr. Ladon was not a carpenter."

"No."

"Tell them about your dream, Ginny," Larry said suddenly.

I could see that his suggestion took my mother by surprise. She blushed and averted her eyes in maidenly disconcertion. When she turned back to look at our father, her expression was unpleasant. It was apparent that she didn't want to do what he was suggesting. To his credit, Larry was not intimidated by her withering glance. "Tell them," he repeated.

"I don't know," she began, "why or if this is necessary. It was a very private experience. I've only told one person." She glared sharply at Larry. "And apparently that was one person too many."

"Tell us," Charlie Sticks said. "I like to hear. Won't tell nobody."

My mother's hands were on my shoulders. I took one and squeezed it.

"It happened just after I learned I was pregnant with Herkimer," she said. "You have to understand that I was raised in a strict Lutheran home. Pregnancy outside marriage was, well, unthinkable. I loved Larry so much, but he was married to Theda. I knew that if I had the baby, I would have to raise it alone. My father, your Grandpa Watkins, Jimmy, would have been so ashamed. I felt like a...a...prostitute." She started to cry at the memory of it. I began to realize then, as children often do when they mature, that pain and love travel in the same heart and *that* conveyance is drawn by a lame horse down a well-traveled and muddy road.

"I couldn't go to my regular doctor," she continued, "because he was a member of our church. So I went to see this other man. A girlfriend of mine told me about him. He had a small clinic on the East Side, on Farwell Street."

"My ole stompin' grounds," Atlas said. "Not a good place for a white girl, especially then."

"This doctor, he told me he could well, you know, get rid of the baby, for a hundred dollars."

"He'd do an abortion," Sybil said.

"Yes." Ginny's grip on my hand tightened. "He told me it would be best. No one would ever have to know. *It takes about twenty minutes, he says, and then you can go back to your life.* I wasn't sure that was where I wanted to go. I almost agreed right then, but something...conscience? fear? God?...held me back. I told Doctor Harrad I'd think about it."

"How do you spell that?" Ari Mantus interrupted.

"The doctor's name?"

"Yes."

"H-A-R-R-A-D. Like the big department store, in London, only with an 'a' instead of the 'o'. He died a few years ago. I saw his name in the obituaries."

The professor looked at me and smiled.

"I went home that night. I was considering the...option, very carefully. I remember praying. I remember feeling terribly empty. I cried myself to sleep."

"And you had this dream then?" Rusha asked.

"Yes. It doesn't seem real anymore. You'll laugh, I'm sure."

"We won't," Doctor Mantus assured her. "Please continue."

"I woke in the middle of the night. I remember looking at the clock. It was around three or so. I closed my eyes again, but I *sensed* a presence. It was the same feeling I'd had when I was a girl and I was vacuuming and didn't hear my mother come into the room behind me, but I *knew* someone was there. Have you ever felt that?"

It was a rhetorical question, but Sylvia Tower and Auggie Two-River answered her simultaneously. "Yes."

"I was frightened. I was living alone in the house that Larry had just bought for me. It was a strange place—unfamiliar. I thought that there might be an intruder."

"It must've been very difficult," Rusha said.

"I...I forced myself to open my eyes. I saw light on the floor. Someone had turned on a lamp, I thought. I remember saying something like *Don't hurt me, please.* Then I turned toward the light."

She was quiet for a moment, perhaps daring a single smirk to appear so that she'd have an excuse not to continue. There were none. She had a captive audience.

"There was a man standing at the foot of my bed. He was enveloped in intense light. The light didn't shine *on* him though, so much as it seemed to come *from* him. There was nothing threatening about him. He smiled at me. It was a kind smile, loving almost. His skin was smooth and youthful, but his eyes were...old. It's hard to describe, though I remember it exactly, like it happened only minutes ago. I've replayed it in my mind a thousand times. I guess it was just that age was indefinable in him, like it didn't apply. He had long, white locks of hair that fell to his shoulders. It wasn't the whiteness of age, though, but rather the color of purity. He was clean-shaven, or his face was just hairless. It was youthful too. He wore some kind of robe, but most of him was covered in intense light. You won't believe me, but he had...he had wings...feathered wings, like a bird—three of them." Ginny looked around at the astounded faces. "What I'm describing," she continued, "are the things I saw as the light dimmed in one area and grew more intense in another—sort of *snatches* of appearance, in a wavy glow. It was difficult to see, but very clear at the same time."

She stopped again. She let go of my hand. I turned in my chair to look at her. Her eyes were distant, dreamy. Her chest rose and fell rapidly. She had a strange, euphoric smile on her reddened face, primary contributor to a general aspect of rapture that seemed to possess her. I was afraid for her, yet she looked, to me at least, positively beautiful.

"Did he say anything?" Professor Mantus said. There was a sharp edge of impatience in his voice. "Did he tell you who he was?"

"Seraph. He said he was Seraph."

"An angel of God," Caleb Bird whispered.

"He said I was...a...a vessel. Yes, *vessel* was the word he used. I remember his exact words. His voice was beautiful, like the caroling of bells. *You will bring forth God's will,* he said. *Your child will open many paths to Him who loves you, to Him who died for you. Faith, woman, faith. You are the vessel from which God pours out his new word upon the world.* Then he was gone. The room was dark again. I lay back in my bed. I felt Herkimer move in my womb. I fell asleep."

There was no sound when she finished. Even the autumn wind outside seemed to hush and lay silent.

Doctor Mantus stared at my mother for a long time before he finally spoke. When he did, his voice sounded thunderous against the quiet. "You said, Mrs. Gudsen, that you'd had a dream, yet you say your eyes were open, that you had woken up. Are you telling us that this experience of yours was real or not?"

Ginny smiled at him—wisely, I thought. "You mean was the image of the Seraph real or was it a real dream? All I can tell you is that what I saw was real. Does it matter that I slept or not while it happened?"

"I think so, yes."

"Not to me. I did what I was told to do. I had my baby. If you have seen my son—what he is, what he can do—then you must know, yourself, if it was real or not."

"Yes." He glanced in my direction. "Yes, I suppose that must be true." I knew then that he hadn't asked the question for *his* benefit.

"Then why all this mythological bullshit," I said. "Why use myth, like the Hercules legend, to bring us together. Why would the One True God use myth?"

"Which God? Allah? Vishnu? Jehovah?"

"The Christian God, the Triune God, Jesus Christ."

"Only the Christian perception of God is real?"

"It's the only correct one."

"And before Christ? Before Jesus came into the world? Was it only the Jewish God?"

"Christ has always been the True God, incarnate or not."

"Which Christ? The Roman Catholic Christ? The Gnostic Christ? The Lutheran Christ? The Mormon Christ? You are reducing God to petty parochialism, Jim."

"And you're making Him too ecumenical—too large to see."

"Since when is it easier to see what is small than what is large? I look at your lovely Minnie, for example, and I think that I wish I'd had a daughter like that. I think that Ben and Sylvia Tower are fortunate. I think that she's pretty and intelligent and if you're not a fool, she'll grow old with you. I think I know what she sees in you. I have no desire to make love to her, though she *is* beautiful. I know she would die for you and, I'm sure, you would do the same for her. These are all perceptions I have of Minnie Tower. You have many of the same perceptions, but not all of them. Are mine false, then, and yours true? Minnie is who she is. Our perceptions of her don't change her. So it is, I believe, with God. Every man lives his life allegorically. We, each of us, have a personal 'mythology' and we tend to gather together with those who think similarly. Your brother's perception of God would not allow him to condemn Baxter Bird and Robin for their homosexuality. Was he right? I don't know. But God has spoken to Herkimer Gudsen several times and, unless I'm misinformed, He's never addressed the topic. We've gathered around your brother because what he's doing 'fits' who we are and how we see God. God speaks to each of us mythopoeically and our response is to develop our own mythos of who He is. Our fault lies in the Inquisitions, the Jihads, the witch hunts and condemnations that parochialism serves. I believe we are being shown, by God, a larger vision of Himself, connecting all cultures and all times to Him. I think that's why Ginny Gudsen had her 'dream' and had her baby. I also think it's why God chose a Greek myth to bring us together."

During his discourse, he had risen from his chair and leaned across the table toward me. It was the first time I'd ever heard passion in his voice. Now, apparently somewhat abashed by his outburst, he resumed his seat and calmly lit another cigarette.

Attention quickly shifted away from him as all eyes looked at the area behind me, and I knew my brother had reentered the room. "Understand," Herk said with quiet resolution, "that when our Lord said 'No one comes to the Father but by Me', he meant it. You are witnesses to what He does and can do. Myth is, as Doctor Mantus has said, perception. The *idea* of God must be grasped first, then there can be the perfect marriage of Myth and Fact, of Heaven and Earth, of Perception and Truth. The way to that Truth is Jesus Christ."

"Amen," Auggie whispered.

"Jim," my brother said as I stood and faced him. "I want you to contact the Yonger brothers. Invite them here."

"Why?"

"Because I ask it. Because the Twelve must still be brought together."

"Judy." His blue eyes found Nurse Crabbe in a corner, still finding comfort in Sybil Springbok's embrace. "You know this Doctor Mudeez. You must convince him to join us as well."

Judy's wet eyes widened. "You can't be serious, Pastor Gudsen. He's a *Muslim*. What possible interest would he have in coming here?"

"I don't know. Perhaps to find a larger perception of God." Herk glanced at Professor Mantus and smiled. It angered me that, under the circumstances, he was capable of it. "At any rate, he must be brought into the fold, and *you* must do it," he said, returning his fierce blue eyes to Judy.

"What about Meg's funeral?" I said. It was a cruel interjection. Sadly, as I think of it now, it was meant to be.

"Meg will be taken to Sarow's," he said. "I've already arranged it with Frank. I called him a few minutes ago."

Frank Sarow was a mortician, one of the best. He was also a member of the Gospel Church. He was the happiest man I'd ever met. He and his wife Polly and their five children lived in a large apartment over his funeral home. They were all overweight and jovial, even though they lived in the constant company of death.

"So," I said, "a deal's a deal."

"We didn't make it in time, Jim."

I laughed. It was a bitter, grim laugh. "God put a timetable on it, did He? He gave you a deadline line, Brother? Or was the line just dead?"

"*James!*" Ginny said.

"He told me to gather the Twelve and Meg would live. That's all I know. There is life beyond this world, Jim. I intend to finish what I promised to do."

"*Screw this!*" I shouted. I pushed past him, past the whole crowd of lunatics and into the welcome space of the living room. My leg was on fire.

Herk followed me. "Jim. You have to stay with us." The others gathered behind him.

Minnie squeezed through and rushed to me. She hugged me.

"We killed her, Min, you and me. You didn't know though. You didn't know. It was me."

"No," Herk said. "A disease killed Meg. Don't let one kill you too. I need you."

"Why?" I said, my vision grown bleary through my tears. "I'm not one of your precious Twelve."

He put his hands on my face, forcing me to look up at him. "God has need of you."

It was then that Atlas discovered that Charlie Sticks had disappeared.

Chapter twenty-five

I t was after ten when most of us ventured out into the October darkness to search for Charlie Sticks. Ginny and Larry stayed at the manse to attend to their grandson, who continued to sleep through the ruckus in an upstairs bedroom, probably because he rarely slept at night. Everyone else was involved in the search.

We decided that a fanning operation in every direction from the manse would probably be the best strategy. Charlie had no car and probably no sense of where he was or, for that matter, where he was going.

Auggie and Atlas checked Auggie's house first, the supposition being that Charlie wouldn't run off without Full Count. They were right. The mutt was gone too. There was no sign of Charlie.

Minnie and I took the area directly behind the manse. The conjecture was that Charlie, after rescuing his dog, may have backtracked across Horizon Road to throw off his pursuers or, simply, to head for the forest which stretched out in a long line beyond the dried fields, where he might feel safer. He was used to the shelter of trees.

The moon was exceptionally bright in the cloudless night, enabling us to find our way without the necessity of any artificial light. Minnie discovered a path of broken stalks through the dried-out corn, so we followed it, though a foraging deer could have made it. Still, the stalks seemed to be bent or broken in a direction *away* from the house, so we stayed with it until we came out of it against the line of trees, where we stopped to rest for a minute.

Our breathing, visible in the cold autumn air, gradually slowed, and in the ensuing quiet we could hear others of our party calling for Charlie in the distance.

"I don't know why they're doing that," I said, "if he was going to come to us simply in reaction to a vocal summons, I don't think he would have left in the first place."

"Why did he leave?" Minnie said.

"I don't know. Maybe it was a reaction to all that hocus-pocus. I know it scared me."

"Jim," Minnie whispered. She touched my face. "What's wrong?"

"My leg is killing me. Aren't you sore?"

"Yes. I didn't mean physically. Something else is gnawing at you. I know Meg's death...well, I know how much you cared for her."

"Do you?"

"I think so."

"Do you know she asked me to make love to her, almost in the exact spot where we're standing now?"

Minnie's shocked expression made me hate myself even more. I don't know why I told her. No one ever needed to know. I could have taken it to my grave and everyone would have been better off. It wasn't enough that I killed Meg, now it was necessary to tarnish her memory and hurt the girl I wanted to marry. What the hell was wrong with me?

"Why...why would she do that? Minnie said. Tears glistened in her wide eyes. The October moon reflected in the little pools gave her an otherworldly appearance.

"Because her messianic husband couldn't get it up." I lit a cigarette. I saw the desperate pain I'd created. "It was before I met you, Min. Nothing happened. She ran back to the house."

"But the baby..."

"It's Herk's. He was cured or 'healed' or whatever you want to call it—not only of impotency, but sterility as well. Another miracle. From impotence to omnipotence in a single day."

"You loved her."

"I guess so."

"What did you mean, at the house, when you said we killed her?"

"I struck a deal with God. He'd save Meg, and I'd give up my greatest pleasure."

"Sex."

"Yes. I *could* have too, except…"

"What?"

"I didn't think I'd fall in love with someone else. I didn't know there could be greater pleasure, greater meaning."

"Jim," she said, placing her soft hand on my cheek. "You didn't kill Meg. This is all much larger than that." She kissed me. "*God* is much larger than that. If it was that easy to manipulate God I would have found you much earlier. Besides," she said, "I couldn't regret what we did if it cost me everything."

She made it right, or showed me how it could be. I felt a sudden lightness and my heart leapt again. I put my hand to my chest and quickly pulled it away. I always despised Hawthorne's Dimmesdale.

We heard a barking in the distance. It was echoing out of the woods.

"Full Count?" she said.

"Could be. Let's go see."

I started to move into the trees. She grabbed my arm. "Who's Maddy?"

"You don't need to care about that anymore—ever."

She studied my face for a long time. "Okay," she said, and followed me into the forest.

Twenty minutes later, we emerged into a moonlit clearing and stopped to listen. Above our own labored breathing, we heard the approach of someone—or something—to our right. Branches and dry leaves snapped and chattered at its approach.

"Jim," Minnie whispered.

"S-h-h. Just stand still and wait."

My eyes strained against the shadows to see what...who, it might be. After what seemed like an eternity, a huge, dark shape moved stealthily into the clearing about twenty yards away and stopped.

"Atlas?" No one else was that big.

"Jim?" He turned toward us then and traversed the mist-covered ground between us in a few colossal strides. "Any sign of Charlie?" he said. His perfect white teeth shone in the shadows. Despite his smile, he looked as though he labored, like his name-sake, under the weight of the world.

"We followed a trail through the cornfield," I told him, "and then came through the trees. We thought we heard the dog."

"Me too, but I ain't heard anything else for a while. You guys okay?"

"I don't think I can go much farther," Minnie said. "It's not every day you get shot, see your father miraculously cured, and then go hiking through thick woods. I think my mind and body need a little rest."

"Was it just this morning we were in Purgatory Swamp?" Atlas said. "Seems like a coupla weeks at least."

"You think that's where Charlie's headed?"

"Probly, though he's headin' in the wrong direction. I gotta find the little bastard. I feel responsible."

"Jim," Minnie said. I felt her hand clutch my arm. "I'm so dizzy. I..."

She collapsed. Her body just seemed to fold up and reextend itself onto the fallen leaves.

"Min!" I knelt next to her, my own heart rattling against my chest like a frustrated ram doing battle with a brick wall.

Atlas knelt across from me. He listened to her heart, checked her pulse. "She's okay, Jim. She's fainted, that's all."

"I've got to get her back to the house." I tunneled my arms under her and lifted. I felt something give. A sharp pain burned through my leg. "Oh, shit!"

Atlas took her from me with gentle ease. Standing there, her prostrate form across his arms in the moonlight, he looked like Shelley's monster with the little child.

"You lead the way, Jim," he said. "I'll carry her out."

"What about Charlie?"

"He'll have to wait."

It was a slow trip. Atlas moved, despite his burden, much faster than I, as I struggled to keep up on my damaged leg. By the time we emerged from the cornfield and crossed the yard to the manse, I was utterly spent.

Inside, Ginny and Larry were sitting together on the sofa in the living room. They quickly moved out of the way so that Atlas could gently lay Minnie down on it.

"What happened?" Ginny said, hovering like hope in the background. "Is she all right?"

"She'll be right as rain with a little sleep," Atlas said. "Anybody come back with news of Charlie?"

"No," Larry said. "You're the first ones to return. We just put the baby in his crib for the night. He's a bit fussy." Larry, it was plain to see, was tired. He and Ginny had spent their days at Holy Cross and their nights tending to little Ben.

Atlas, like most bachelors, failed to catch the hint to keep his voice subdued. "Jim," he boomed, "can I borrow your car?"

"Take mine," Larry said, hurriedly offering his keys.

I was covering Minnie with an afghan. "Where're you going?"

"Well, Purgatory is east of here and I'm fairly sure that Charlie is movin' south, toward town. I don't know if he's lost or he knows where he's goin', but I thought I'd try drivin' south and criss-cross the east-west roads that he might run into. Maybe I could spot him. I can't just sit around here knowin' he's flounderin' around out there somewhere."

"Of course you can't," Larry said. "The ignition key is the round one."

"Be careful," I said. "Remember, Charlie *is* capable of violence."

When Atlas was gone, I gently lifted Minnie's head and shoulders and slid under them so that my lap became her pillow. The position, like my life, gave me intense pleasure and pain simultaneously. She groaned, just for a moment, then quickly returned to the regular, soft breathing of insensate slumber.

Ginny stood over me, smiling, as Larry took a chair. "Poor thing," she said, bending over to move a strand of hair from Minnie's face. "She's so tired." Then she did a remarkable thing. She kissed my cheek. She whispered, "I love you, Son." I could never remember such intimacy from her. Not that she'd never addressed endearments to me before, but I only remembered them as afterthoughts, as secondary remarks, coming on the heels of expressions of devotion to my brother. They had always been catch phrases, equalizers. *Oops, James might feel unloved. I better say something to him too.*

This time, Herk wasn't around. I think that he may not have even been in her thoughts.

"I love you too, Mom," I said.

She smiled, warmly, fully, at me—perhaps even with a measure of pride. "Can I get you some coffee or something?" she said.

"An ashtray, maybe."

"Okay." She did, then she sat down in the chair next to Larry. He'd been watching with contented interest and a ready ear. It was, I think, my first moment alone with both my parents.

"She's a lovely girl, Jim," Larry said, pointing to Minnie's slumbering frame.

My hands played unconsciously with her black curls. "Yes, she is. I want to marry her when all this is over."

The incongruity of Ginny's smile and her tears told me she approved though she said nothing.

We sat in silence for a few minutes, then Ginny said: "It's all true, you know, Jimmy."

"What is?"

"My dream, your brother's communications from God, the miracles we saw tonight. I've known something like this would happen from the moment Herkimer was born. He was different from everyone else. He *is* different. You know it too, don't you?"

I sighed. Back to Big Brother again.

"You have to stop believing though, that I love him more than you. I don't—and you believing it hurts me. You have *that* kind of power, Jimmy. Only those you love can really hurt you."

"It's impossible *not* to love Herk more than me, Mom. *I* love him more than me."

She laughed. The sheer joy of it made me smile. "Pish-posh," she said. She really said that. "I never even considered ending my pregnancy with you. You were always easier to love. I love Herkimer devotedly, don't get me wrong. But I've always loved you just because of *who* you are and *what* you're supposed to be. Your brother is God's gift to the world. You are God's gift to *me*."

My jaw must have been hanging open.

"There, I've said it." She wiped away a track of moisture from her cheek. "Let's put it to rest. Besides," she said, "you were always your *father's* favorite."

"True?" I said to Larry Ladon.

He looked uncomfortable. He squirmed a little in his chair. "Guilty," he said.

"Why?" It wasn't a question as much as it was the declaration of a mystery.

"Because you make mistakes," he said. "I see *me* in you. When I look at your brother, I see God."

I laughed. I couldn't help it. Larry didn't seem offended. "You mean I was the imp."

"No," he said patiently. "You were, are, just *real*. Besides we, you and I, have never been at odds."

"Does it irk you to follow him now?"

"No. It's what I'm supposed to do."

We heard the kitchen door open then and a draught of cool air slithered into the living room. My brother appeared, framed by the entryway, closely followed by Sybil Springbok and Rusha.

"Any luck?" I said.

"No," he answered. "Charlie seems to have disappeared."

"Do you have any idea—or insight, as to where he might have gone?"

"No."

"The hospital called while you were out looking for him." Larry said. "They've been looking for you. They're very upset that you left without signing the proper release forms. They want you to come in tomorrow morning and either continue to stay there under observation for a while or sign a waiver absolving them of any responsibility for your 'injuries'. Ben Tower too. They didn't know Ben was with you. The woman who called said they spent several hours combing the hospital looking for you two."

"Why just now?" Herk said. "They called earlier...." His voice trailed off for a moment. "They must've known *I* wasn't there if they called here, about...Meg."

"I said that too, two different units, different doctors, different floors. Apparently, they got their wires crossed. They didn't know Ben was even gone until about an hour ago when the nurse on duty went into his room to give him his medication. You guys have caused quite a ruckus."

"I'll take care of it," Herk said. He looked pained to have been the source of such confusion. "My son, how's he doing?"

"He's asleep," Ginny said.

Herk's blue eyes found Minnie. "Is she okay?"

"She fainted, but she'll be all right. Just too much for one day."

"Too much for one life," he muttered. I knew he wasn't talking about Minnie. "I'm going to check on Ben." He turned and limped from the room.

"He'll wake him up," Larry said.

Ginny shrugged. "Don't worry, I'll watch him."

Rusha and Sybil sat down, heaving simultaneously unrehearsed sighs. "We've been all over the area," Sybil said, "and not a sign of him. I don't understand how he could have disappeared so quickly."

"My dogs are killing me," Rusha added as she pulled off her shoes and massaged her feet.

Gradually they all began to return. First the Bird brothers and Robin, then Ben and Sylvia Tower, Auggie Two-River and Doctor Mantus, Yuri and Teena Theus. None of them had seen any trace of Charlie Theomastix.

Naturally, Sylvia and Ben were concerned about Minnie, especially when Herk returned to the room and Doctor Mantus and I related the story of that morning's events in Purgatory Swamp. Minnie gradually awakened during our narration. She was a bit disoriented at first, remembering only the forest where she'd fainted, but gradually she became acclimated to her surroundings. After telling me how foolish she felt for fainting and 'having to be a burden', she sat up and followed Doctor Mantus's account with interest.

"We didn't know Charlie had the gun," he said. "He must've been hiding it in his boat. He was able to get off only one shot before Atlas wrestled him down."

"You should never have taken Minnie with you, Jim," Ben Tower said. It was the first coherent sentence I'd heard from him since he was injured.

"I know."

"He didn't 'take me', Daddy," Minnie said. "I went of my own volition, *against* his wishes. We argued about it. Don't blame him." She squeezed my good hand. "He couldn't have stopped me."

Ben was easily convinced, perhaps remembering his own attempts to control his determined daughter. "No, I suppose not," he said.

"Your hand," Herk said to me, "that's what happened. You were shot."

I nodded. "It's not that serious. They were small pellets, shot in a wide spray. They barely broke the skin. We're okay."

Minnie nodded in affirmation and patted my leg as she tried to get comfortable—without much success.

"Where's the nurse?" Doctor Mantus observed. "Where's Miss Crabbe?"

"She went back to the hospital to talk to that surgeon," Herk said. "The one who's supposed to join us—what's his name?"

"Mudeez," the professor answered. "Dayan Mudeez."

"Yes. She left right after Charlie disappeared. She said she wanted to talk to him now, knowing that he would be at the hospital tonight. Wednesday, tomorrow, she said, is his usual day off. She wanted to talk to him right away—about the Twelve."

"What's the hurry?" I said. It sounded cruel, but it wasn't meant to be. Cruelty and stupidity are born bedfellows. "I didn't mean it that way, Brother," I said.

"I know." There was a terrible sadness in his eyes and in the tone of his voice. "In the morning, I'm going over to the funeral home to…make arrangements. I also have to go to the hospital and square things with them. Jim, I think you need to talk to the Yonger brothers while I'm gone and convince them to join us here, Thursday afternoon. That's when the Council will reassemble. Perhaps Doctor Mantus could go with you."

"Me too," Minnie said. "I think I could help. One of them likes me. It might bolster our chances of drawing them here. That is, if it's all right with Jim."

She looked at me. I nodded.

"Good," Herk said. "One o'clock Thursday afternoon then. Everyone all right with that?"

"Why not tomorrow?" I suggested. "If Judy says that it's this doctor's day off, wouldn't it make more sense to reconvene then?"

"Tomorrow would be easier for me too," Sybil Springbok said. "My sitter's not available on Thursday and…"

"It's *supposed* to be on Thursday," Herk said firmly. There was no further argument.

"What about Charlie Sticks?" Rusha reminded us.

"I don't know yet," Herk answered. "I only know that he's doing what he's meant to do, whatever that is."

"Perhaps that's counter to what we're trying to do," Doctor Mantus suggested.

"*The good man brings good things out of the good stored up in him,*" Herk said.

"What happened to Charlie tonight, Brother?" I asked.

Herk hesitated for a moment. "He was touched by the finger of God. He'll come back to us. I know it."

"Why were we out looking for him then?"

"Because I don't know *how* he will return."

"You whispered something to Charlie," Professor Mantus said to my brother, "just before he disappeared. I'm sure of it."

"Yes."

"May I ask what it was?"

Everyone turned to Herk, waiting.

"I told him: *Blessed are the eyes that see what you see,*" he said.

Doctor Mantus nodded, searching the vast reservoir of his mind for a connection. It didn't take him long. "That's something Jesus said."

"Yes."

"Why did you say it?"

"Because he needed to hear it."

"Pastor Gudsen," Doctor Mantus began, squinting through his coke-bottle glasses, his great nose testing the scent of things as if his brain could smell. "Did we waste our time looking for Charlie?"

"I sense it, yes. He has something to do, though what it is, I don't know."

"Is that how you know we're supposed to meet on Thursday instead of tomorrow? You 'sensed' it?"

"Doctor Mantus," Herk said, casting his sad, pearly smile in the direction of the professor's porcine face, "isn't that how we all ultimately operate? Your intellect brought you to the logical conclusion that you should die. Yet here you are, among us. It wasn't thought that brought you to us, was it?"

"Perhaps not," the professor retorted, "but it *was* that very ability that was the reason for my being here."

"How so?"

"It was my knowledge of myth—the classics—that was needed to unravel this code of yours. It was I who made many of the connections that have brought the Twelve together—including myself."

"And the 'connections', as you call them—they were the product of your mind? Or were they there for you to discover, to sense, to feel? It wasn't your conscious which brought you here, Doctor Mantus, but your conscience—not what you *thought* that made the connections, but what you *felt*."

"Aquinas says that *conscienta* is our knowledge applied to our own actions. That's all I've done."

"If that's true, then conscience loses universality."

"I don't follow."

"If you're raised a Catholic, Doctor Mantus, your knowledge of what confession means will prompt you to visit a priest. If you're raised a Lutheran, you'll confess *en masse* in liturgy, or in the privacy of your own bed. The Roman or the German would be predisposed to guilt by Aquinas's perception of conscience if their roles were reversed. Simply put, a good Jew would feel guilty about eating a pork chop, a Christian would have no qualms about it at all. It's *knowledge*, what we've been taught, that directs what Aquinas calls conscience. It doesn't apply to everyone. That's why he's wrong."

"*Thus conscience doth make cowards of us all.*"

"No. Hamlet didn't have the solution either. *Their best conscience is not to leave't undone, but keep't unknown.* Shakespeare contends against Shakespeare. Words are instruments of thought, Doctor Mantus, and thought is merely the servant of inspiration—the sense of the Spirit—God."

"So God directs you?"

"God directs us all. Religion can't define or guide."

"If God directs us all, then why are some men evil?"

"*All* men are evil. Some are just better actors. By that I mean that they have a better 'sense' of how to play their roles—and they accept direction. *That*, to me, is conscience."

The kitchen door slammed and Atlas Johnson entered the house—alone. The debate had run its course anyway. We'd all known who would win—even Doctor Mantus.

"I been to hell n' gone," Atlas said as he entered the living room. The baby started to cry upstairs. Larry sighed and gratefully accepted Ginny's gesture to stay where he was as she hurried from the room.

"Did I do that?" Atlas said.

"It's all right," Sybil Springbok said. "Babies cry." She smiled warmly at the giant. *That* insinuation did not escape him.

I asked him if he'd seen any sign of Charlie. It took him a minute or so to tear his eyes away from Sybil's tawny beauty. "No, not a trace, man. I dunno where the hell he's goin'."

My brother opened his mouth to speak, but Doctor Mantus anticipated him. "He's going where he has to go, where he's supposed to go."

What miracles couldn't work had been accomplished in a few minutes of disputation. Aristotle Mantus was an apostle and that, in itself, was a small miracle.

Chapter twenty-six

That night, Minnie went home with her parents. They insisted. I hated to see her go, but it was as much for her good as theirs, so she acquiesced. She needed to rest. So did I.

Sybil left to pick up her son, while Doctor Mantus returned to his lonely book-lined hermitage to prepare for his morning classes. The Birds flew to their unprocreant nests. Auggie Two-River, Yuri Theus and Atlas went back across Horizon Road to join Teena and settle in for the night. Larry and Ginny took my nephew back to their house, leaving Rusha and I to tend to our brother.

The three of us stood in the yard as the last of the cars pulled away. The October moon had brightened even more and cast shadows across us from the skeletal framework of the new church building. For some odd reason, the shadow pattern made me feel uncomfortable and I suggested that we go inside, but Herk wanted to 'take in the cool air', so we sat for a few minutes on the porch where he'd nearly lost his life.

"How did you do what you did tonight?" Rusha asked our brother when we were settled.

"What do you mean?"

She rubbed her smooth, scarless arm where the bandages had hidden her wound. "To me…to Charlie."

"I didn't do anything Rusha," he said without taking his eyes off the moon. "You know that."

"Yes, I know. But why *you*, Herk? Why not someone else?"

"I don't know. Does it matter?"

"Somehow it does, yes."

We sat in silence for a few minutes. November was coming, and even in her heavy coat, Rusha was shivering. Herk seemed oblivious, though he was just in shirtsleeves. Finally, he said: "What do the others think?"

"Auggie says you're the Christ," I said.

"Then you need to straighten him out. I'm not Jesus. He *was* God incarnate. I'm just a man. This isn't about me."

"Isn't it?"

"No. You've known me all my life, Jim—or most of it. Don't you know me?"

"You're a man who loves God, I know that. I think you're supposed to teach me about Him."

He looked at me and smiled. "All of us are like the trees around here." He pointed at the bare trunks and gnarled branches that stood like skeletons in the yard. "We soak up the blessings of sun and water as if it were our right. We grow slowly. Most often we're green. Occasionally, rarely, we show flashes of brilliance, of color, of insight—then we're barren and dormant—until life is renewed in us. We grow a little more. We spread our seed. If we can avoid the axe or disease long enough, we get large enough to be venerated—but we all die. The winter comes when we can't recover anymore, when it's too much for even the toughest among us. If we're lucky, it comes slowly, by degrees, by aging. But we're always dreading it, wondering why—as if God should love one tree more than another or favor a particular forest. Don't you think He's made it abundantly clear that all the trees are the same? The fact that that one still stands in the middle of that cornfield," he said, pointing to a solitary maple, "was not God's will. It was probably because some farmer wanted shade while he worked his crops. We're subject to God, you see, but we're also subject to one another. That tree still stands by a man's will, not God's."

"*You're* not still here by man's will. No doctor cured *you*."

"Oh there are times when God steps in. Once, in Jesus, he even walked among us. He offers us life beyond death. But he of-

fers it to all of us. We would like to be able to believe that because
we are in the Lutheran forest, we are favored—we will be spared.
But there is a Catholic funeral liturgy just as there is a Lutheran
one, a Buddhist one, a Hindu one. Our *knowledge* has brought us
religion. Religion is the product of man's thought, as variant as the
trees—subject to our cultures, our languages, our environments,
our histories. But men of God *know* God, regardless of what forest
they were born into."

"Jesus is the way to know God, though. We can't deny that."

"That's true, Jim, but you say that as if there were no salvation *before* the Nativity. There was no time *before* Him. Jesus was,
is, God. If that's true and I believe it is, then redemption has always
been there. 'I am the Alpha and the Omega,' Christ said, the beginning and the end. God is God. There's redemption for Adam,
for the pagan Greek, for the pious Hebrew, for the law-bound
Muslim. The problem is that we have stuffed God into a church or
a synagogue or a mosque; a Bible, a Koran, a Torah, a myth—and
forgotten that He lives in our hearts, our souls. God is God. Our
vision of Him is too small. I think that's what I'm supposed to
teach. It *feels* right."

"It sounds right," Rusha said.

"Then Christ—" I began.

"Is God. Yet our immediate assumption is that He is only
our God, addressed by *our* name, properly understood in *our* book,
celebrated in *our* church. If you'll excuse a tired cliché, we can't see
the forest for the trees. God forgive us, we have made of Jesus a
myth, a kind of superhero, a Hercules, and we have forgotten that
He is not only the Son, but the Father and the Spirit. If Moses re-
vered the Father, he also adored the Son."

"What you're suggesting is ecumenicalism."

"What I'm *insisting* is that God will not be diminished by
words like ecumenicalism."

"C'mon, brother, somebody has to be right, don't they?"

"We shouldn't care who's 'right'. We should only seek God
out—pray to Him, love Him. He created us. *How* He did it

shouldn't matter. It stands to reason that He will save us too. *How* he does that shouldn't matter either."

"Then Christ is superfluous."

He stared at me sharply. His blue eyes flashed in the moonlight. I think I was afraid.

"I'll preach all my days of Christ. He is God and Redeemer. He is *my* Saviour, but I won't judge others. Peter didn't find Jesus in the liturgy of his church or in the pages of a Bible—nor did Matthew or Mark or the gentile population of the ancient world. Handel got the words to his *Messiah* from the Bible, but not the music. Did God inspire Darwin? Shakespeare? Jefferson? We're too small. We're so very, very small."

He turned his sad face to the starry canopy of heaven, and sighed. "I miss Meg," he said—so softly that the words were barely discernible. He didn't break down. He didn't come apart. He just said it. At that moment, I was glad I wasn't him—perhaps for the first time. I would later read how Theseus told Hercules: *Men of great soul can bear the blows of heaven and not flinch.* But Herk flinched that dark October night. He flinched.

"Will you two go with me to the funeral home in the morning?"

"Yes," Rusha answered immediately. She put her arm around our brother's shoulders and kissed his cheek. I could see her wet eyes glisten in the moonlight. There was no dragon in them now, only the tender sympathy of the saint.

"What about the Yonger brothers?" I said. "You wanted me to contact them. It may take some time for me to convince them to come to the council meeting." I knew then, as I do now, that my recalcitrance had nothing to do with the Yongers. I just couldn't tolerate the thought of seeing Meg in a coffin.

"I've changed my mind about that," Herk said. "I sense now that they'll come to us of their own accord. Go with me, Jim, please."

"Could we pick up Minnie on the way?" I thought I might be able to stand it better if she was there. I still found it difficult to

accept the possibility that Herk might have loved Megan more than
I did.

"Sure."

"What are we going to do about Charlie Sticks?" I said. "If
he comes back, if he can even find his way back, and Judy manages
to talk this Mudeez guy into coming, then what? We'll have the
Twelve together, then what to we do?"

"I think Charlie is on God's business," Herk said. "I don't
know what he's doing, but he's being guided—inspired. Whatever
he's up to, it's God who leads him now."

"That's what you meant when you told him that he was
blessed for what he'd seen?" Rusha said.

"Yes."

"But you don't know what he's seen?"

"No."

"Do you know," Rusha said, "what day Thursday is?"

Herk considered her question for a moment, as did I. I
wasn't sure who she was asking. I'd lost track of the days. I was sure
Herk had too.

"It's October 31st," she said.

"Halloween," I said, finally connecting.

"All Saints Day," she added. "Is that why we have to meet on
that day instead of tomorrow? Is it supposed to be on a day to
honor the saints, a 'hallowed eve' in Christian tradition?"

"It's also Reformation Day," Herk said, "when Luther was
forced to the conviction that faith alone was needed for salvation. I
don't need to tell you two, raised in the Lutheran church as you
were, that Luther changed our view of God. Veneration of the
saints, good works, fasts, pilgrimages—even the sacraments, became
unnecessary. People should not be dependent on pope or priest or
any other man for salvation. We've all been taught our catechism
about Luther. I think he guided us to a larger vision of God. Sadly,
we've changed it again. Always there are the religionists, who insist
on form instead of function, law instead of Gospel, tradition instead of revelation. The *church* always seems to become the object
of worship, rather than *God*." Herk lowered his head and looked at

the traces of his own blood on the steps between his knees. "I don't know why Thursday has to be our meeting day. I just *know*, that's all."

"Perhaps it's symbolic of that larger view," I said. "Halloween is a day for magic and animism too—the glorifying of life and nature and myth. The day was commemorated by pagans long before the Catholic Church and Luther."

Herk smiled at me, but he said nothing. Rusha stood up and stretched. "You got a cigarette, Jim?"

I lit one for her and handed it over. "What a crazy thing life is," she said, taking a long drag and expelling the smoke into the cold, autumn air with her own warm breath. "A few weeks ago I was the Queen of the Amazons, now I'm sitting here freezing my tush and talking about theology with two brothers I didn't know I had."

"Do you miss it?" Herk asked.

I expected her to say 'no', even if it wasn't true. Instead, she took several drags on the cigarette. "In some ways, yeah," she finally answered.

"What ways?" I asked.

"I think it was the eyes—the look in their eyes and on their faces. When Maddy and I did our thing, it was exciting, you know? They watched us with…hunger, desire, maybe even adoration. It was a power trip. I really felt like a Queen."

I remembered watching her. The image came clearly to mind and I felt an awakening in my groin. She was right. At that moment, at the Amazon Club, before I knew who she was, I would have handed her my soul for a few more moments of that voyeurism.

"Why did you leave?" Herk said.

"Because there's something greater here," she whispered, "something more wonderful than Self. I didn't know that's why I left at the time, but it's why I stay. It's a lovelier thing to adore than be adored; to love than to be loved."

We sat in silence for a while, my erection reducing in direct correlation to the vanishing incestuous image in my mind. I knew how my sister felt. I, too, was beginning to love what I'd become, but I missed the freedom of what I'd been. What we've learned to know as evil, I was convinced, is pure self-indulgence. The rest of the bad stuff is just error—the difference, perhaps, between demons and sinners.

"Well," Herk said, "I want to be at Sarrow's early tomorrow. Can we leave around eight? That all right with you guys?"

"I'll need a ride," Rusha said.

"We'll pick you up."

"I'm afraid I'll need one right now too. Dad took the car."

"I can take you," I said. "You get some rest, Herk."

"You sure?"

"No problem."

But it was. I could barely bend my leg to get behind the wheel. I don't quite understand yet how I got through that difficult, miraculous day.

When I pulled into the driveway of the house where I'd grown up, all the lights were out.

"They must've gotten little Ben to finally go to sleep," I said to Rusha. "You have a key?"

"Yeah. Dad had one made for me." She fumbled in her purse until she found it. She put her hand on the door handle, then hesitated. "What do you think is going to happen?" she said.

"What do you mean?"

"Where do you think this is all going?"

"I don't know."

"What was he like? As a child, I mean."

"Herk?"

"Yeah."

I laughed. "I don't think he ever was one. He was…stoic, you know, like an adult. Quiet desperation and all that. He was always more of a father to me—to Ginny too."

"He is special."

"Yes."

"Why would this woman try to kill him? From what I can tell, he was always very kind to her. Her face was…savage, Jim, wild. She scared the hell out of me. Why would she do such a thing?"

"I don't know. I guess life forced her to concentrate on herself a little too much."

Rusha smiled. "And now this brother of hers."

"Charlie."

"Yeah. I worry about what he might be up to. You think Herk's in any danger?"

"He's always been in danger. We all are."

"I'd like to believe that isn't true."

"So would every beast that ever walked the earth. But predators are here. The predators are *always* here. They have to be. No good story was ever written without conflict. Neither was any good life ever lived."

"When did *you* become so philosophical?"

"You don't think it's true do you? I'm telling you, Rusha, safety is only a façade. Governments, churches, prisons, schools, hospitals—they're institutions created to keep us from panic. They declare that they will protect us from foreign invasion, from evil, from criminals, from ignorance, from predatory microbes. But they fail. Again and again they fail—and they'll continue to fail. They are assurances, that's all, like the wildebeest that feels secure in the bosom of the herd. We're supposed to live in jeopardy. It's the way of things."

"But we're safer with those institutions aren't we?"

"As a species, maybe, not as individuals. They didn't save Lena Gossbach. They didn't save Meg. Given enough time, they don't save any of us—not in this life."

"Well," she quipped, "now that I'm completely at ease, I think I'll go inside and try to get some sleep." She opened the door.

"I'm sorry," I said.

She turned and looked at me. "We came close, didn't we, you and me?"

"That's how we'll always be."

"What?"

"Close."

"I think so." I'm almost sure she winked at me through the shadows.

I watched her walk up the driveway where Randy O'Connor and I had once bombed my brother with water balloons and I wondered how much she'd had to suffer in her life at the hands of her terrible mother, and how much more suffering was ahead for her because of her proximity to me.

When I arrived back at the manse, only the kitchen light was still on in the house. As I painfully extracted myself from the car, I glanced toward the cornfield and thought I saw, in the moonlight, the shadowy outline of a human figure.

I was thinking, of course, that it might be Charlie Sticks. Maybe he had circled back, perhaps he'd found a weapon. This could be the man who had shot me earlier that day. Even if it wasn't Charlie, whoever it was could not be up to anything good, hunkering among the cornstalks. I became aware, gradually, that I was trembling.

I wanted to ignore it, to go on into the house, to that illusion of safety. Instead, I went into the field. I decided to face the predator. Better to fight than be brought down in panicky retreat. Something scurried before me in the dry husks. My heart throbbed frantically against my chest, like a condemned man pounding futilely on his prison door. I was only mildly relieved when I saw the white, downy tail of a rabbit bounce away from my intrusion, through the stalks. Something larger was still there, standing inhumanly still, just ahead in the moonlight. "Who's there?" I said, and the strength of my own voice startled me.

No answer.

I wanted very much to turn around. Warmth and safety. Names for things that felt good. Not real.

Whoever was standing there, he hadn't moved, though I was certain he could see my approach. He was waiting quietly, even calmly. I saw the outline of his head, just beyond, looking toward me, just above the husks. Waiting.

He was smaller than I was. If he wasn't armed, I might be able to take him.

"Last chance to talk to me," I said, "then I'm coming."

Nothing.

I pushed aside the last leafy barriers, my body coiled tensely for the assault. Then I saw it, clearly. I laughed, giggled really, like a little child. It was the silly, joyful titter of relief and release, the realization of misjudgement and the delaying of death and danger to another place and time.

Before me stood the dilapidated remnants of a scarecrow, whose presence had long since gone unnoticed in the enveloping greenery of the rising corn. Meg had put it there last spring, when the dead stalks had been green youth. I remembered how she'd borrowed one of my old shirts to clothe it, the tattered remanants of which now flapped in the autumn wind as it tunneled through the rows.

The cancer had been in remission then, a mocking façade, like the scarecrow itself—enough to keep the Black Predator away for a few weeks, hiding, lurking patiently in the middle of animation, in the growing advancement of life. Now it was just an image of death, hidden by dead things.

Meg, our dear, dear, Meg. How could she be gone? How could God let this happen to his children—to his special child—to Herkimer?

I looked at it for a few minutes. I remember Meg stuffing a burlap bag with straw to form its head, the noise of church builders in the background. I remember telling her that it wouldn't keep the crows at bay. She'd told me then, that if the image of man didn't frighten them away, nothing would. Nothing else in this world, she'd said, was truly frightening enough.

I tore the thing down. It felt good to destroy something. I left its parts scattered in the field and returned to the house.

Upstairs, I passed Herk's bedroom, which was immediately adjacent to mine. I paused at his open door to listen. The light from the hallway revealed that he was in his bed. I could hear the gentle respiration of untroubled sleep. *Your wife died tonight, Brother,* I wanted to say. *Aren't you ashamed to rest so comfortably?*

As if to answer me, he turned over and reached for Meg's absent form. He pulled her pillow close and sighed deeply, then became aware of the light. He sat up.

"Jim?"

"Yeah, it's me. Just on my way to bed."

"You all right?"

"Sure. Right as rain." I knew that he understood what I was thinking.

"What are you so afraid of?" he said

"You, Herk. Who *are* you?" It was a question I'd been asking myself my whole life.

"Still?" he said. "Do you still have no faith? I'm your brother. Go to bed."

He lay down again.

I turned off the hall light, and did as I was told. It seemed a virtuous thing.

Chapter twenty-seven

Herk had to shake me into consciousness the following morning. As he left the room, I struggled out of bed and into the bathroom. My leg was pretty stiff, and for a few minutes it was misery to put any weight on it. But once the blood began to circulate, the leg loosened up. I removed the bandages. There were purplish mounds wherever the pellets had burrowed in, but the seepage had stopped. My hand, too, was beginning to heal.

The hot water and steam felt fantastic. I stayed in the shower a long time, allowing the caressing water to massage me, like the caring hands of a mother on a child. When I emerged, I felt clean, invigorated, fresh, purged.

I didn't have to rewrap the wounds. The water had reduced the welts to nothingness, like a stream wears a rough edge round. I almost bounced down the stairs.

Herk was at the kitchen table, a cup of coffee in front of him. When he raised his head to acknowledge my approach, I could tell he'd been praying. His face bore that otherworldly look—the flushed and fevered visage of the martyr.

"Do you want to call Rusha?" he said. "Let her know we're on our way?"

"Sure. I'll call Minnie too."

"Yes."

"Are we going to Sarrow's right away or are we stopping at the hospital first? It's on the way."

"Ah yes," he sighed, "the hospital. I suppose we ought to straighten that out first."

He was clothed in his black suit and clerical collar—an outfit I hadn't seen him wear for quite some time. Unlike our Catholic brethren, the donning of priestly accouterments had become somewhat passé among the Lutheran clergy. I had to remind myself that we weren't Lutherans anymore.

The morning air was crisp. The sun shone brilliantly—unusual for late October in Michigan. Minnie was ready when we pulled into the Tower Ranch by the corral. She too seemed reenergized as she bounced out the door and closed the short distance to my car in long strides. Herk got out of the passenger seat to allow her to sit next to me, despite her protests.

"How's your dad this morning?" he asked.

"They're still sleeping," she answered. "He's going to be okay though, I know it."

"Yes," Herk agreed, as he settled in the back seat. "He is."

As we drove up the dirt road, Minnie studied the buffalo herd, grazing serenely in the pasture. "It's hard to believe," she said.

"What?"

"That just on the other side of that fence is death."

"They just want to keep living," I said, and leaned over to kiss her on the cheek.

Rusha, too, was waiting when we arrived.

"Any word about Charlie?" she asked as she climbed into the back seat with our brother. Ginny was at the door, waving. I waved back and she went inside. "No," Herk said. "Nothing. Did my son sleep at all?"

"Didn't hear a peep. Ginny just gave him his breakfast bottle."

From our childhood home to the hospital, the conversation was mostly small talk between the women. We passed the old Temple Theatre, I remember. That grand old building had been constructed on lumber money almost a hundred years ago. Ginny had told us when we were kids that she'd seen Gregory Peck perform there live on stage, sometime in the early thirties when he was a struggling unknown. Later, it had been converted to a movie house, the only one in Saginaw that still had a stage and all the ornate decorations of a bygone era. The marquee outside announced the new film, *The Godfather,* as its latest offering.

"I've seen it," Rusha said, recalling the night of the fire. "It's great."

"I want to see it too," Minnie said. "Everyone's been talking about it."

"Some sort of religious film?" Herk asked.

The girls laughed and I tried to fight back my own amusement. The remark was so typical of my brother. He was one of a rare minority of Americans, (perhaps the Amish and a few death row inmates), who paid no attention to Hollywood.

"It's about the mafia," Rusha said, "based on Mario Puzo's book. Marlon Brando plays the title role."

"Oh," Herk said, feigning knowledge. I was pretty certain he didn't know who Marlon Brando was. It was the closest I think he'd ever come to lying. Derisive laughter can do that.

The hospital entrance was a scene of bedlam. We learned that some reporter had been assigned to follow up on the story of Herk's stabbing by interviewing the victim. When he discovered that Herk had disappeared and was physically able to leave, he began hounding the staff for details. One of the volunteer workers, a high school kid, had told him about Herk's miraculous recovery. That same reporter had covered the story of a year or more ago when Herk had survived the crossbow bolt. The journalist had put two and two together and called his editor. That was at about 7:00 that morning. Since then, Holy Cross had been inundated by the media. There were television camera trucks all over the parking lot and hospital security guards were having a difficult time keeping them from blocking the main entrance. We knew that they would soon invade the manse if they hadn't already. The church members coming to work on the reconstruction of the new building would find no sanctuary at Horizon Road *this* morning.

I told Herk to forget it, as we sat in my car and watched the meleé from a safe distance across the street. We weren't sure, at that time, that all the hubbub concerned us, but when Minnie turned on the radio, our doubt was removed.

"...*is once again in the news. This former Lutheran pastor survived a terrible accident just before Christmas of last year when he was accidentally shot through the head by a neighbor, who was using a crossbow to shoot at a target. The six-inch steel projectile (referred to as a bolt) that was shot from the weapon penetrated Gudsen's skull and became embedded in his brain. Miraculously, he survived, apparently without any damage to his thought processes. The object was never removed. A few weeks after this incident, Gudsen was removed from his position as an ordained minister at St. Luke's Lutheran Church over philosophical disagreements with his superiors concerning doctrinal issues. As a consequence, he began his own congregation. This group grew large enough over the next few months to finance the construction of their own building on Gudsen's farm on Horizon Road in Bennet Township. Earlier this month, this new church building was burnt to the ground. Arson was suspected. Only days ago, Pastor Gudsen was attacked and stabbed several times by a troubled woman, a former prostitute and member of the cult, on the steps of his own home. Cindy Belostra, a high school senior who volunteers at Holy Cross Hospital, declared in a special WKNX interview that Pastor Gudsen was near death when he was brought in and none of the doctors believed he would survive. Late yesterday afternoon, this same source tells us, Herkimer Gudsen left the hospital with another critically injured patient, both men apparently completely restored to health. Is it yet another miraculous recovery for the 'Saginaw Survivor'? Stay tuned for more details of these startling developments after Neal Petrie with the weather and Joe Lascomb gives us the latest WKNX update on Henry Kissinger's progress at the Paris peace talks.*"

I turned the radio off. "Think it's not about you now?" I said.

Herk shook his head. "They called us a *cult*," he said. "A *cult!* Do they think I'm some kind of Charlie Manson?"

"I don't think they meant that, Pastor Gudsen," Minnie said, gingerly twisting toward him. "We're just not affiliated with any established church."

"What do you want me to do, Herk?" I said. "Why don't we just forget it for now and you can come back later and straighten out the paperwork after all this has died down a little."

"I told them I'd come in this morning," he answered. "Maybe the media people won't notice me."

"Yeah, I'm sure a six-foot-five guy dressed in clerical clothes would be extremely inconspicuous."

As always, he ignored my acerbity. "How about around back? Is there a way to get in there?"

"I don't think so," I said. "Well, wait a minute. There's an employee entrance. I used to use it all the time when I worked here, but you have to have a key."

"You don't have yours anymore?"

"I had to turn it in when I quit."

"Drive over to the Emergency Entrance on the west side of the building."

"I think I ought to know where *that's* located," I said. Minnie nudged me. When I looked at her, she frowned disapprovingly.

"Rusha, if you wouldn't mind," he said, as I put the Chrysler in gear. "I'd like you to go inside through emergency and find Judy Crabbe. She should be at the fourth floor nurse's station or somewhere in that area. Ask her if it would be possible for her to get the paperwork together and meet us at the employee entrance in back. We'll wait for you there. Could you do that?"

"Sure," she answered, "but will she be able to get the papers we need? I mean you have to go through accounting and everything, don't you? How can she do that?"

"Our insurance will take care of the money end of it. They have all my papers. I just want the release forms. Judy knows everyone in the place. I don't think it should be too difficult for her."

"Won't she be risking her job, Herk?" I said. "Her bosses are going to be pretty angry when they find out she's helped you to circumvent hospital protocol. Can you really ask her to do that?"

"The only thing I'm trying to avoid here is notoriety. Besides, I don't think she's going to be a nurse much longer anyway."

"What? Why?"

"God has something else for her to do."

I kept thinking that we ought to be tending to the funeral arrangements for Meg, rather than playing James Bond for the sake of my brother's sense of responsibility, but I kept my mouth shut because I didn't know what he knew. I drove to the Emergency Entrance. Rusha got out, then I drove back to the main street to find the little access road that led to the rear of the hospital. We were there in a few minutes, parking illegally in some doctor's space. Its owner was probably taking a break from the exhausting work of losing to Death, by playing golf somewhere in Cancun.

We sat there for perhaps a half an hour before Rusha emerged from the employee's door and hurried over to the car.

"What's up?" Minnie said as Rusha climbed in.

"She's going to get everything together," Rusha said, "but she said it's going to take her a while—from one hour to two or three. She'll meet us where I came out," she pointed to the door where two nurses were just emerging.

"We should go to Sarrow's then and come back," I said.

"We can't," Minnie countered. "What if she comes down while we're gone? We can't do that to her. We'll just have to wait."

I twisted around in my seat to face my brother. "Look, why don't we just come back tomorrow, or the day after. I know you gave them your word, but you can't help it if they've caused this circus. Besides, you're asking Judy to steal so you don't have to lie."

"Jim!" Rusha said.

"There's more to it than that, Brother," Herk said. His voice was calm, devoid of any anger. "I don't know if I'll be able to come back. This needs to be taken care of now."

He was so placid, so absolutely sure of himself. I think that's what infuriated me.

"What...what does that mean?" Rusha said. "That you might not be able to come back. Do you know something that you're not telling us?"

"I don't really *know* anything, no, but I think it's going to get worse."

David Turrill

"What is?" Minnie said.

"This whole thing," he answered, with complete equanimity, as if 'getting worse' was nothing to fear.

"Have you had some kind of vision, Herk?" I said. "Another dream? What's going on?"

"No, nothing like that...nothing certain. I just *feel* like something is going to happen."

"What you said about Judy Crabbe—not being a nurse anymore. Did you just 'feel' that too?"

"No. Judy told me that. She wants to devote her time—all of her time—to the church. I just told her to follow her heart."

"And you, Herk?" Rusha said. "What about you?"

"I think I'm going to have to leave."

"No!" Rusha shouted. Tears rippled down her face. She took our brother's large, scarred hand in hers and kissed it. "No," she said, "we need you here."

He smiled sadly at her and pulled his hand away. He put an arm around her shoulders and kissed her forehead. "Sh-h-h," he whispered.

"Where...where will you go?" Minnie said. There was genuine terror in her voice. My own heart was beating the terrible, adrenal rhythm of dread. Herk was our connection to Goodness—all of us. I think we didn't fear what would become of Herk or us, but a return to what had once been. I began to realize that he'd changed us all that much.

Rusha turned her tear-stained face to me, but I had no answers. How does one respond to possibility?

"Let's wait," he said.

I turned off the engine and looked at the bare trees in the little arbor beyond the lot. I'd looked at it many times when I'd parked here to go in to work. I thought it was quite amazing how far I could see through the trees when the leaves were gone. There was a clearing beyond and a new subdivision under construction. I'd never noticed it before. Autumn has a tendency to expand a person's vision.

377

We sat in silence for about twenty minutes, all of us eyeing the door where Judy was supposed to appear. Rusha finally broke the silence by asking me for a cigarette, and that single request was enough to prime the conversational pump.

"When you say you'll have to leave," Rusha ventured, "what do you mean? Can't you tell us anything more? You can't expect us to just forget about that. Right now, at this moment, dozens of people are working to rebuild the church—your church. They're doing it for you, Herk. You can't just walk away from them. Who'll take care of things? People have given up their property, their jobs, their *lives* for you."

"No," Herk said, firmly. "They've given themselves to God. It's God who moves them. He's led us all this far and He'll lead us on. He'll lead *you* on, Rusha, although your path isn't mine."

After that, there was silence. I think we were all stunned by possibility.

It was noon before Judy Crabbe finally appeared at the glass door and pushed it open. She was carrying a bundle of papers that, after a frantic search for a pen in the glove compartment of my car, Herk signed. He kissed the homely woman on her rough cheek and blessed her. I think it was the first time I ever saw her smile.

We escaped unnoticed and began the drive across town to Sarrow's Funeral Home.

"Do you think the media has discovered that Meg is...gone?" Minnie said. "I mean, wouldn't they inquire about her if they're so interested in finding out about you?" Again, she twisted around to address Herk. Again, she winced. "Wouldn't they find out that she's at Sarrow's?"

"Eventually, I think, yes," Herk responded. "But perhaps they haven't figured that out yet. I hope not. I don't want this to be a circus." The evenness and surety of his voice once more appalled me. If there was grief there, it was well hidden. At the time, I took it for apathy. Now, I know it was just iron *trust*.

There was no one there when we pulled into the parking lot behind Sarrow's, except for the family cars and a business limousine. Frank Sarrow didn't hire any outsiders. Every member of his large family was involved in the business in one way or another. His two grown sons were both licensed undertakers. A married daughter did all the accounting. Another drove the hearse. A third acted as a Greeter. Even the little ones set up chairs and cleaned. Mrs. Sarrow played the organ at services held at the Funeral Home. Most of the family still lived in the spacious rooms above the funeral home, and I remember being awed by the quiet and dignified way in which the children, by years of habit, moved about. They'd been taught from infancy that their footsteps must not be heard downstairs. They lived, like Anne Frank's family, consistently in the presence of death.

As we entered the building, Frank Sarrow greeted us at the door. He smiled broadly, as he always did, and shook hands all around while Herk introduced the women. "I'm so sorry about Meg," he said to Herk, as if he'd known her all his life.

He was wearing old clothes, instead of his customary black suit. "I was just on my way downstairs," he said, "to get Meg ready for the showing. I picked her up late last night, so I haven't yet had a chance to...prepare her." He said this as if he was talking about psychological counseling rather than draining what was left of her bodily fluids and replacing them with some embalming liquid. "Let's go to my office and fill out the paperwork." He turned toward the other end of the wide vestibule and we followed. "Please forgive my appearance," he continued. "I expected you earlier. I just changed. Both my boys were called away on another pick-up out of town, so I'm tending shop by myself. I had to choose between waiting any longer for you or tending to the...to Meg. I hope you're not offended."

"Not at all," Herk said. "I apologize for our lateness."

"Tut, tut," Sarrow said with a wave of his chubby hand. A diamond ring, set in a gold band, sparkled on his finger. "Don't think twice."

I saw, in a room to our left, an open casket surrounded by flowers. An old woman lay there, alone, her aged hands folded on her breast in the artificial semblance of sleep. I never saw, in my life, anyone sleep that way. I wondered if anyone ever had—before it became the posture of death, I mean.

Mr. Sarrow led us into his office, where Herk signed the necessary papers, answered the necessary questions, wrote the necessary check to expedite this last, and most unnecessary of life's obligations.

"May I see her now?" Herk asked after we'd finished.

"Oh dear!" Mr. Sarrow exclaimed. "I didn't think you'd want to do *that* until I've had an opportunity to make her...more presentable. You see, as I said, it was very late when we picked her up and I really haven't—"

"I want to see her now, Frank," Herk said.

"If you could just give me until this afternoon, Pastor Gudsen. I've already called our hairdresser. You need to choose something from her wardrobe to wear and bring it in, or I can send someone out to your place for it. We'll have her looking beautiful for the showing tomorrow. Why don't we wait until then? Now," he said, rising from his leather chair, "the casket models are just down the hall. I'd like to recommend, if I may, the natural wood over metal. There's so much more *warmth* to wood, don't you think?"

Herk placed his large hand on Frank Sarrow's chest as the latter attempted to pass us. "Frank," he said calmly, "she's my wife. I want to see her now."

Sarrow had to look up at Herk as most people did. "She died of cancer," he said. "I know that you know that, but she's very emaciated—very thin. She's lying on a marble slab in the mortuary downstairs. She's still in the body bag. You'll wish you hadn't seen her that way. Believe me, what you're asking is very unconventional."

"My brother is a very unconventional kind of guy, Mr. Sarrow," I said. "Let him do as he wishes, then we'll leave you to tend to your work."

The poor man sighed deeply. I think he somehow felt that death was his shared responsibility unless he could deceive us. We were not to look at the ugly face of the Reaper, but the lovely deception of sleep. It was his art, and what is art if not deception?

That was what I thought then. I've learned some things since.

"Very well," he said, "but remember that I tried to stop you. The image will stay with you for a long time." It was his charge for viewing an unfinished canvas.

We entered a dark, closet-like corridor just beyond the casket display room. Mr. Sarrow pulled a string attached to a small chain. A bare lightbulb flicked on directly above us. We could see a heavy wooden door at the far end. The mortician jangled some keys, and the door opened. There was a strong draft coming through it. It was cold and fresh and unscented—like winter.

Sarrow flipped a switch, revealing concrete stairs. "That's strange," he said.

"What is?" Herk said. "The cold?"

"No, no. We always keep it cold down here. No, I'm talking about the draft. Oh, watch your step, please. These stairs are a little steep."

When we descended the last few steps, the mystery of where the air was coming from was solved. There were dried leaves on the painted concrete floor and shards of glass lay next to a wall on our right. The broken window was above our heads, the kind commonly found in basements, protected by an outside aluminum well. The cold autumn air was whispering through it, whisking the dry leaves across the open floor. I remember thinking that the window had been purposefully broken. All of the glass was knocked out of the frame, as if someone had wanted to avoid being cut while attempting to crawl through it.

"Oh dear," the undertaker said. "Now how could that have happened? The kids next door I'll bet. They like to play baseball in my parking lot when there's no cars. I've scolded them dozens of times. Well, now their parents will have to pay. They need to learn that this is a *business!*" He said it very defensively, as if most of the world did not believe it.

He turned away from the window and went to an intercom box on the wall. He pressed a button. "Purse?"

"Yes Frank?" The voice on the other end was sweet and fruity—like Aunt Bea on *Mayberry RFD*. Mrs. Sarrow had the rather appropriate name of Persimmon, but everyone called her Purse.

"I want you to send Molly down here immediately with a broom and dustpan. Someone broke a window, probably those little devils next door, and there's leaves and glass on the floor."

"Oh dear! Molly's at school, Frank," the box answered in lilting static. "I'll come down myself."

"Very well." Mr. Sarrow turned to Herk. "Your wife is in this room," he said, and opened a door labeled MORTUARY A – KEEP OUT.

He turned on a light as we all followed. The room smelled of unclean cleanliness, like the scrubbing designed to eradicate disease rather than the light washing that catered only to the eye.

"There must be some mistake," Frank Sarrow said. We were looking at a marble table surrounded by stainless steel sinks and shelves of bottled chemicals. The single glaring light above the marble slab reflected off its empty surface.

"I was almost certain I put her in 'A', but I must've placed her in 'B'. I'm so sorry for the mix up. We'll have to go to the room next door. Please forgive me, I must be going senile."

I looked at Herk as we shuffled across the concrete floor to Mortuary B. He looked calm, serene, unafraid—but I was certain he was thinking what I was. Perhaps he even knew.

"My God!" I heard Frank Sarrow exclaim as he switched on the light in the second room. I didn't have to look to know that it, too, was empty. He rushed from that room and through a door further down the hall that was labeled CREMATORIA. He emerged from there in seconds, mild panic in his narrowed eyes. He practically ran to the steel double doors against the only remaining wall. He pressed a button and the doors opened to reveal an empty freight elevator. "My God," he said again. "She's gone! How can she be gone?" His shirt was soaked in the icy perspiration of fear.

"Gone?" Rusha said. "You can't be serious. Are you sure they didn't take her to a different funeral home?"

"I picked her up myself," he said. "I brought her down here in that elevator. I put her in the main lab, Mortuary A. I *know* I did!"

He looked up at the broken window.

"He did it," Herk said softly.

Frank Sarrow was dialing 911 as Purse appeared at the base of the stairs with a broom and dustpan. "Oh dear," she said. "What a mess."

"What?" Minnie said. "What did you say, Pastor?"

"He did it," Herk repeated. There was a bizarre grin on his thin face. "Charlie. He did it."

Chapter twenty-eight

As always, Herk was right. The Yonger brothers *did* come to us. The three of them arrived at Sarrow's Funeral Home just minutes after the stupefied mortician called 911. Several other squad cars responded as well, and within half an hour, the parking lot at Sarrow's looked, with all its flashing red lights, like a giant pinball machine.

We sat quietly with two of the brothers, the detectives, in the smoking lounge of the funeral home, as they grilled the miserable Mr. Sarrow. The third brother, Donny, (for Donatello), the huge one who still wore a uniform, was outside somewhere.

I noticed that the Adonis, Rafe, kept looking first to Minnie, then Rusha, then Herk. I think he was amazed to find my brother so well and hardy. Apparently, he'd been listening to the news. The reason for his fascination with the other two was, well, obvious. He seemed almost unaware that I was in the room. It gave me great satisfaction to notice that Minnie was purposefully ignoring him. The same could not be said of my sister.

"So," Detective Raphael Yonger said, "you picked up the body around ten thirty last night from Holy Cross Hospital at Mr. Gudsen's request? Is that right?" He was talking to Frank Sarrow, but looking at Rusha. She was smiling at him.

"Yes," the mortician answered, too distraught to notice that Yonger's eyes weren't on him.

"Did you do any kind of examination at the hospital?"

"Of course," Mr. Sarrow said, obviously appalled that the officer would even ask him. "I followed the procedures outlined by state law."

"Which are?"

"To speak to the attending physician; sign the paperwork attesting to time and cause of death; and conduct my own tests to corroborate the doctor's findings and verify that the patient was deceased."

"And?"

"She was."

"No, I mean after that. What did you do then?"

"I brought Mrs. Gudsen here, in my hearse."

"You brought the body inside?"

"Of course. I rolled the guerney onto the elevator which opens to the outside, as I showed you, and took her down to the mortuary."

"And what time was it then?"

"Close to midnight, I think. Eleven-thirty, maybe."

"You took the body off the guerney?"

"Yes. I placed Mrs. Gudsen on the marble table in Mortuary A, where I showed you."

"Was the window broken then?"

"No, of course not. I would've noticed."

Detective Yonger took his eyes off Rusha for a moment to make certain that his sibling was writing down every detail, then returned them to their pleasure. The homely brother seemed oblivious of everyone.

"Then you went upstairs? I mean to your residence on the second floor?"

"Yes."

"Did you go to bed right away?"

"I watched a bit of TV, then I retired."

"What time was that?"

"About one, just after *The Tonight Show* ended."

The image of Frank Sarrow munching potato chips and laughing at Johnny Carson's monologue while Meg's corpse lay on a cold slab in the basement below him was somehow intensely disturbing. I glanced at Herk. He was studying the detective's face, perhaps sizing up his new recruit, who had no idea what was in store for him.

"Did anything disturb your rest? I mean did you hear glass breaking, or any other unusual sounds?"

"No, nothing. I'm a very sound sleeper."

"And the next time you went to check on the…on Mrs. Gudsen, was when you had these people with you?"

"Yes. I was supposed to meet with them earlier this morning, so I was waiting until after that to start work downstairs. They were late. I waited for a while, then went back to our apartments to change into my work clothes. That's what I'm wearing now. I was on my way down to the mortuary when they arrived. I don't understand any of this. It's never happened to me in thirty years in this business. Why would anyone want to steal, to abduct, a…person…from…I just don't understand it." He shook his head, miserably envisioning, no doubt, the bad publicity that would naturally result from this. Winged dollars flew before his dazed eyes.

"Do *you* have any idea, Pastor Gudsen, why anyone would want to steal your wife's body?" Rafe Yonger said. "Forgive me, but I have to ask."

Rusha, Minnie and I turned our heads simultaneously in my brother's direction. None of us had said anything about Charlie yet. We didn't know if we should.

"I'm not sure why, no." I believe he was telling the truth.

I think Rafe Yonger was willing to let it go at that. I didn't know why I should have felt relieved at that moment, but I did. Then the satyr, his brother, spoke for the first time since they'd arrived. "Do you have a suspicion concerning *who* might have done this?" he said.

Again, all eyes settled on Herk.

"Who?"

"Yes, who," Mike Yonger said.

"I have a…suspicion, yes."

Rafe Yonger looked surprised, as did Frank Sarrow. The latter had not heard my brother's remark about Charlie, since he'd been occupied with his call to the police.

"Can you give us the name, please?" Mike Yonger's pencil was poised over his notepad.

"I can't really do that. I *won't* do that. I'm sorry." Herk's voice was as implacable as a woman's breast—soft, firm, and untouchable—outside the bounds of trust.

I wasn't really surprised. Herk believed that Charlie had a role to play out and he would follow that. In spite of the horrible image, ever present in my mind—the depiction of our beautiful Meg being dumped into the stagnant waters of Purgatory Swamp—we would follow him and, like him, say nothing about Charlie.

"You can't do that!" Rafe Yonger said. "What are you talking about? You *have* to tell us if you have any idea who the perpetrator might be."

Herk just shook his head.

"Mr., uh, Pastor Gudsen, I don't think you quite understand. A crime's been committed here, several of them actually, amounting to felonious charges. If you withhold vital information, you could be arrested for obstructing justice or worse, abetting the felon. I'm sure you really don't want *that.*"

"Detective Yonger," Rusha said, smiling sweetly. "My brother is an ordained minister. Even though he's been removed from the Lutheran pulpit he is still, constitutionally, a pastor. What you're asking goes against his conscience and clerical privilege. It won't be long before the reporters at the hospital find their way over here. I'm sure you wouldn't want me to explain to them why the Police Department arrested this gentle man who's the focus of so much media attention right now. He's trying to recover from a vicious murder attempt. His wife has died of cancer and her body stolen. Now, you arrest him? I think it would seem rather heartless to the general public, don't you?"

Her voice had taken on that sultry, Amazonian tone. For an instant, I thought I saw the dragon eyes. It was clear that Minnie was no longer an object of the detective's attention. His eyes were attached to Rusha.

"Miss Gudsen—"

"It's Ladon."

His quizzical frown required explanation.

"We're half-siblings," she said.

"Oh, forgive me, I didn't know. Miss Ladon," he began again, "your husband or boyfriend must find it difficult to say no to you."

"I'm unattached right now," she answered.

"Really. How unfortunate."

"Do you think so?" she said, coyly.

"Actually, no."

Mike Yonger rolled his eyes. "The fact remains," he insisted, "that to withhold information from an investigating officer is—"

"I think Miss Ladon has a valid point, Mike," Rafe Yonger interposed. "I'm sure Reverend Gudsen wouldn't keep anything from us if he felt that, in good conscience, it wasn't privileged information." The satyr frowned dramatically. "But perhaps, by that same conscience, he would understand that we have to pursue this investigation or be guilty of neglect of duty. Given that, I think that he might be amenable to assisting us in some way that would allow *all* consciences to remain clear. What do you think, Pastor?"

Herk's head was down. His fingers pressed against the sides of his head while his elbows rested on his long legs. Whether he was praying or merely thinking, I couldn't tell. With my brother, thought and prayer were intimate associates.

When he finally looked up to respond, his blue eyes were full on pain. "We're going to look for him. I think I know where he is. You're welcome to come along, you and your brothers."

"You said 'brothers'," Rafe observed. "Plural. How did you know I have another brother?"

"*My* brother told me," Herk said. "Is he here?"

"Yeah," Rafe Yonger admitted. "Donny's outside."

"The three of you are welcome to go with us—no one else, *and* we keep this away from the press as much as possible. Agreed?"

Rafe Yonger looked at his frowning brother, then at Rusha. She pressed her back against the sofa, preening like a lioness. "Yeah," he said, "okay."

"Good. We'll leave tomorrow morning." Herk stood up.

"Whoa, wait a minute. Tomorrow? How far is this place?"

"It's here, in Saginaw. Not far."

"Then why not go now?"

"Tomorrow is the day," Herk said, "that we're supposed to go. You're meant to go with us. That's the only explanation I have."

"Impossible," Mike Yonger said.

"Detective," I said, drawing Rafe's attention briefly away from Rusha, "I know this is a bit unconventional, but my brother knows what he's doing. He's not being deceitful. He believes that this is supposed to happen. Not just the theft of his wife's body, but your part in it as well. I think he even *knew* it. I don't know if you're religious men or not, but you need to understand that Pastor Gudsen is being directed by God. He believes that. We believe that. I know how it must sound. I've had my problems with accepting it myself, but you know that he's survived a bad accident and, just a few days ago, as my sister mentioned, an attempted murder. You can see that he's very much alive and healthy. You know that he was stabbed several times by Rhea Theomastix, including once in his arm. Look at it. There's no scar, no evidence of the wound at all."

Herk pulled up the sleeve of his jacket to allow them to inspect. I knew he was opposed to such theatrics, but I also knew that the physical was often the greatest witness to the metaphysical— sadly, for most of us, the only reliable one.

Mike was skeptical, but I could see that Raphael was deeply impressed.

Rusha too, related her story—how Herk had healed her the previous evening. She displayed her smooth, unblemished arm with pride, and Rafe Yonger was particularly attentive, inspecting her appendage with even greater interest than he had with my brother's, lingering in front of her while he held her hand, and her eyes held him.

At that moment, Donatello Yonger entered the lounge. His colossal physique filled the doorway.

Rafe Yonger reluctantly released Rusha's hand. "Anything?" he said.

"The guy wasn't careful, that's for sure," the giant answered. "There's footprints all over, in the dirt beyond the window well. There's material on the window frame where something snagged on a piece of glass. I'd be willing to bet that if we compare it to the body bags the hospital uses, we'll have a match."

"Good."

"The guy had a vehicle. The tire tracks indicate that it was heavy, a pick-up maybe."

"Anything else?"

"Yeah. I think he had a dog with him."

"A dog? Why the hell would he bring a dog along for something like this?"

"I don't know, but there's dog pawprints all over."

"How do you know it wasn't just a stray that came sniffing around later?"

"Well, for one thing, some of the thief's prints are on top of the dog's, which means the dog would have been here at the same time, or earlier. The dog scratched some paint off the side of the building, peed on it too, right by the broken window. It wouldn't do that, I think, if the glass wasn't broken while he was there. It's like he was *waiting* for his master to get the job done and come back out. There's no evidence that he was anywhere else around the place. Mrs. Sarrow tells me they don't own a dog. Neither do the nearest neighbors. We checked."

"Full Count," Herk said.

I nodded.

"Beg your pardon?" Rafe Yonger said.

"That's the dog's name. Full Count."

"You *do* know who this guy is."

"Yes."

"You'll tell us then?"

"I'll take you to him—tomorrow."

Mike Yonger shook his head. "No way. If you don't tell us now, we'll have to take you into custody until you do."

"Whatever you feel is necessary," Herk said.

An awkward silence ensued during which the satyr and the giant studied their recalcitrant sibling.

"I have a compromise for you," Rusha said finally.

"What would that be?" Rafe Yonger said, smiling.

"You let us return to the manse on Horizon Road. We'll all promise to stay there until you arrive tomorrow morning, then we'll take you to the person responsible for this."

"That's ridiculous," Mike Yonger scoffed. "How do we know you won't leave? You could break the agreement, go off without us, maybe try to get revenge on this fella—or maybe even protect him for some reason."

"One of you could stay with us—keep an eye on us, so to speak. Perhaps, Detective," Rusha said, addressing Rafe Yonger in her most seductive voice, "*you* wouldn't mind watching me for an evening?" I almost laughed. "I make a mean lasagna. You could get to know me, I mean us, better. You could stay up all night to make sure we behave. I'd even keep you company."

Rafe Yonger smiled. It was the kind of admiring grin the heroic knight gives the dragon—just before he's eaten.

"What a crock of shit!" Mike Yonger exclaimed.

Mrs. Sarrow squeezed past the bulk of Donatello Yonger with no small difficulty, and entered the room.

"Frank?" she said, in her Aunt Bea voice. "There's a reporter outside. He wants to know if he can talk to you for a few minutes."

"Oh God," the mortician said, "I'm going to be ruined."

"No," the eldest Yonger said, "not yet."

"Well?" Rusha smiled. "Are you going to take us out of here in handcuffs, Detective, or shall I go home and put the lasagna in the oven?"

"You used the word 'home'," Mike Yonger said. "Do you live at the Pastor's house?"

"The manse is home to many people," she answered, "even though they don't reside there. Me included." She looked at Rafe. "What do you say?"

"Okay," he said. "It makes sense. Okay."

"Well, great," Mike Yonger said, but he said it as if the idea was anything but.

The lone reporter was ushered into Mr. Sarrow's office, where Mike Yonger and the mortician met with him. Donatello took his samples and left with the other patrolmen. Herk and Minnie and I fled to the Chrysler, while Rusha, a voluntary hostage, rode behind in Detective Yonger's unmarked squadcar.

We passed a television van with its logos emblazoned on the sides. It was pulling into Sarrow's driveway as we were pulling out.

"Looks like we made it just in time," Minnie said.

"They're still going to be all over us at the manse," I said. I looked at Herk in the rearview mirror. He was pressing his fingers against his head again, and frowning conspicuously. "It had to be Charlie, huh?"

"Yes," he answered, straightening up and folding his arms across his chest. The pained expression, however, remained.

"Why would he do that, Herk?" I knew he wouldn't have the answer I wanted, but I felt compelled to ask anyway. Sort of like a kid asking if there's a heaven for hamsters.

"I'm not sure. He was supposed to do *something* that's all I know. I guess this is it."

"But what's he going to do with the…with Meg. Why would he take her? To bury her in that swamp? What does that accomplish?"

"He's trying to save her, I think."

"Save her? Save her for what, Herk? She's dead!"

I felt Minnie's restraining hand on my arm. I didn't need for him to say anything because I knew what his answer would be. *I don't know. It's supposed to happen. God wills it.* Ignorance and fatalism, I thought, the shaman's tools. Then I felt ashamed.

Minnie broke the disturbing silence, as she looked at the squadcar close behind us. "You think Rusha really likes this guy or is she just a great diplomat?"

Herk was clearly relieved by the change of subject. "I think our sister is a bit smitten."

Smitten? Who uses a word like that anymore? Only my brother and people born before 1900. It was an innocuous way to say that Rusha was itching to get laid—to be struck, smote, smitten, pierced. Why was every thought of mine a criticism?

"I think so too," Minnie said. For a terrifying moment I thought she was reading my mind, but she was only responding to Herk. That was how we all operated now—in response to Herk. "She really seems to like him, and vice-versa. I don't think he would have consented to this without her."

"No," Herk answered solemnly, "probably not."

"We're going to Purgatory tomorrow morning then?" I said, primarily to return us to unpleasantness.

"Yes."

"We bring Charlie out with us?"

"Yes."

"What about Meg?"

"I don't know."

"You don't know."

"No, Jim, *I don't know.*" There was an edge of irritation to his voice.

"And what if he decides to shoot at us again?"

"He won't."

"He won't?"

"No."

"Jim," Minnie said, "what's the matter?"

"The matter is that you and I were filled with buckshot a couple of days ago, remember? Charlie's sister tried to kill Herk and Rusha. I'm a little nervous about the Theomastix family, that's all. You think that's unreasonable?"

"Charlie's only doing what he's supposed to do," Herk said.

"Yeah? Well so was Judas, and we all know how that little scenario turned out."

"I don't think Charlie is dangerous to anyone now except, perhaps, himself."

"No?" I said. "Where do you think he got the truck for this little escapade? You think he borrowed it from one of his many friends?"

Herk didn't bother to respond. I looked in the rearview mirror. He was clutching his head. His hands, and the thinning hair on his pate were all I could see. That should have been enough for me to know that I should leave him alone, but something urged me on. "And what about the Twelve? Is that all done now? Did anyone bother to ask Judy if she'd had any success in getting this Jewish/Muslim doctor to join us?"

Herk raised his face and looked at me. I could feel his blue eyes drilling into the back of my head. "That's enough, Jim," he said, his gentle voice barely discernible. He touched my shoulder. I felt my anxiety slip away. It was like the acceptance of death—a letting go, a willing capitulation. It came by his hand. Minnie touched me too. We turned onto Horizon Road.

The media *had* found us. The wide yard of the manse resembled a military bivouac. There were vans and cars and strangers everywhere. I pulled onto the gravel shoulder about a hundred yards from the driveway. Rafe Yonger pulled in front of me, and also parked. He sat there for a moment, then got out of the squadcar and approached the driver's side window of the Chrysler.

"Looks like our peaceful evening isn't going to be so peaceful, Detective," I said.

"I'll put a call in and have some patrolmen over here to clear them out. It may take a while, though."

"Where's Rusha going?" Minnie said, as she pointed toward the squadcar.

"Damn it!" Rafe Yonger exclaimed.

Rusha had left the police vehicle and was quickly approaching the yard of the manse.

"What's she up to?"

I saw someone stop her as she turned up the driveway. From that distance, it looked like Caleb Bird, but I couldn't be sure. She talked to him for a minute then she abruptly turned around and came back to us.

I got out and went with the detective to meet her. "What the hell were you doing?" he said. He was angry, but she took no notice and smiled pleasantly.

"Getting rid of unwanted company," she answered softly. A television van sped past us, then another. As we stood there, gawking, a caravan of newshounds sped by us, moving in the direction from which we'd just come. I looked back at the Chrysler. Herk was hunched down in the back seat, covering the window side of his face with his large hand. Not a single member of the exodus even glanced in his direction, so intent were they on whatever rabbit they were now chasing.

"What the hell did you say to them?" Rafe asked Rusha.

"I told Caleb to tell them that Herk had stolen Meg's body and probably left Michigan. The real story, I told him to say, was at Sarrow's Funeral Home."

"You told them *Herk* took her body?"

"Why not? If they believe he's gone somewhere, they'll leave us alone for a while."

I laughed. "Oh Frank Sarrow is just going to *love* you."

Rafe Yonger tried not to smile, but he wasn't succeeding. "What about all those other people?" he said, pointing in the direction of the manse, as the last of the media whizzed by us.

"They're just working on the new church building. It'll be dark in an hour," she said, studying the late October sky through the bare branches above us, "then they'll go home."

"And what happens when the mortician tells the media that Pastor Gudsen didn't take the body—that he was just there a few minutes ago?"

"Then they'll come back here, I suppose. But, by *that* time, you will have established a perimeter around the manse to keep them out."

Rafe Yonger shook his head. "And why in hell would I do that?"

Rusha's vixen smile widened. "To preserve any evidence; to maintain the integrity of a crime scene; to get a hot plate of lasagna. You choose." She sauntered back to his squadcar, well aware, I was sure, of his eyes on the accentuated wiggle of her derriere. She opened the door and got in. The detective looked at me.

I shrugged. "She's a very determined person."

"No shit."

Atlas Johnson, Yuri and Teena Theus, Auggie Two-River and Ginny and Larry Ladon together with Baby Ben, joined us for dinner that night.

We should have felt as though we were under siege, but Rafe Yonger had so effectively cordoned off the place, that a wide perimeter beyond which the returned media camped gave us a sense of privacy that we'd not experienced in a long time.

Our guests, in fact, had had a difficult time getting through, even though they'd been cleared by phone ahead of time.

After Herk said the blessing, we all sat around the table in the kitchen, stuffing ourselves with Rusha's promised lasagna. Uncharacteristically, Atlas took a small portion and then moved it from one side of his plate to the other with his spoon, until it grew cold.

He, along with the other 'visitors' had been secretly instructed not to discuss Charlie—or even mention his name. It wasn't difficult to see that this deception bothered the big man. Atlas wasn't good at deceit. I think that's why God gave him such broad shoulders.

"Maddy's on her way," he said, breaking into the conversation as though he was only voicing his thoughts, which, in fact, was probably the case.

Rafe Yonger had just been expounding on his mother's penchant for Renaissance art and its subsequent manifestation in the names of her three sons—Raphael, Donatello, and Michelangelo. What Mrs. Yonger hadn't anticipated was that, because of her, her sons would continually be identified with cartoonish turtles in the minds of a later generation.

"Who's Maddy?" Rafe asked, as he spooned a second helping of steaming lasagna onto his plate.

"A friend," Rusha answered. "We used to work together."

"Oh yeah?" Rafe said, his mouth stuffed with pasta. "Where do you work?"

"I'm unemployed right now."

Ginny frowned. All of us feared the next, inevitable question, but Rusha was cool as ice.

"Where *did* you work then, with your girlfriend, I mean?"

She just said it. "The Amazon Club."

"Rusha..." Minnie whispered.

My sister held up a silencing hand. "You can't begin a relationship with a lie."

It wasn't the first time I would be awed by my sister's integrity.

Rafe Yonger put down his fork and stared at my sister. When he spoke, it was very softly, and the cavalier tone of his voice had evaporated. "That's the old strip club, the one that Vice closed down a little while ago."

"Yes."

"You were a waitress there or something?"

"Or something, yes."

"What?"

"The feature act—Maddy and me; the Queen of the Amazons and the Slave Girl. I'm out of it now though—for good."

"Because the place is out of business?"

"No, because I don't want to do it anymore. Jim, my brother here, reunited me with my father. My other brother," she looked into the gentle smiling face of Herk, "has helped me to find God. I'm done with that life."

"That's good."

"Yes, it is."

Rafe Yonger studied his lasagna for a moment, then looked at Rusha again. The entire company, I could see, was waiting for his reaction—most especially my sister. She was braced stiff with the intractibility of reality, though I knew he could hurt her with the slightest trace of judgment.

He smiled. "I'll bet you were the Queen."

Rusha cocked her head, a defiant expression on her face. "That's right."

"Thought so. Great lasagna," he said simply, toasting a forkful in her direction before it disappeared into his mouth. He munched contentedly while he stared at her. The message had been received. Tears formed in my sister's wide eyes.

The detective was shot to death twenty-odd years later, when he went to a suspect's apartment to question him about a homicide. The guy just opened the door and fired. At the funeral, her four grown sons surrounding her, Rusha told me that Rafe Yonger, in their two decades of married life, had never asked her another question about the Amazon Club or any other part of her disreputable past. He loved her that much.

"So," I said to Atlas, "when is Maddy due in?"

Chapter twenty-nine

Ginny and Larry Ladon had fought their way through the lines of police and media shortly after the lasagna feast to return home with little Ben, to begin another combative night with my insomniac nephew. They'd been instructed to contact each member of the Twelve and have them all meet at the manse at six the next evening.

Atlas, Yuri, Teena and Auggie had stayed until eleven o'clock or after. We told everyone about the disappearance of Meg's body and Herk tried to answer questions as well as he could, but I knew he didn't have the answers. Atlas had pulled me aside as soon as he'd had the chance, to grill me about Charlie. I'd told him what I knew. His faithless anxiety matched mine and it was frustrating to respond to his continual interrogations with my brother's irritating and habitual response of 'I don't know'. It made me feel as though I was hiding something from him. Maybe I was. I think now, perhaps, that I knew more than I was telling.

By the time Auggie departed for the night with his house-guests, (soon to expand to four), the media had dissipated sufficiently to allow them to walk across Horizon Road relatively uninhibited.

Rafe Yonger was as vigilant as he'd promised—particularly in regard to Rusha. The two of them were still talking quietly on the steps of the back porch when Minnie and I went up to my room around midnight.

Herk appeared to have no problem with Minnie staying the night. In his own way, he knew that marriage was more than a piece of paper or a public avowal, though he'd never have condoned it for himself. He was the most egotistically humble man I knew.

Minnie and I lay on my bed together for a while, examining each other's wounds in a very unclinical fashion. I was practicing 'kiss it and make it better' medicine on her flat stomach when she pulled my hair, forcing me to look up at her.

"Why did you act that way today?" she said.

I raised myself up on one elbow, amazed again at the intense ability of women to focus. "What way? What are you talking about?"

"You *know* what I'm talking about—the way you kept goading your brother in the car."

"Sibling rivalry."

"Oh no you don't," she said, sitting up against the bedstead and pulling the sheet across her waist. It whipped rudely against my face in the process. "You don't get away with a flippant cliché. What was going on there? That's the closest I've ever seen Pastor Gudsen to being angry. What were you trying to accomplish?"

"You can call him Herk, you know. He's not God."

She was silent for a moment. "*That's* what this is, then."

"What?"

"You. You're envious of him, aren't you?"

"No." I think I was telling the truth. I think I'd gotten past that. I told her as much.

"Then why were you so obnoxious this afternoon?"

"I think it's God I'm mad at."

"God? Why? For not choosing you?"

"No, the exact opposite. I *have* been chosen. What pisses me off is that I don't know the why, the how, or anything else about it. It's like being put into the game at quarterback, late in the fourth quarter of the championship game, with your team down by two touchdowns and you've never played any position except nose guard. God doesn't condescend to speak to me. I never know what's coming. I'm not even sure about what's been."

"Neither does anyone else, not even your brother."

"But why? Why shouldn't we know? If we're chosen to do this, why shouldn't we be given some kind of reason?"

"I don't know. It's the way God works, that's all." She got up from the bed with the sheet wrapped around her. She went to the window and looked out into the deserted yard with its barren trees. She shivered and hugged herself. She was still thin enough that her hands clutched her back. "Why does it have to get cold?" she said. "Because the earth is tilted and it turns? No point in lamenting the fact. Some things just *are*, that's all." She turned and looked at me.

"I was jealous of Herk all my life," I said, "but I don't think I envy him anymore. It isn't that. I just keep thinking that he spent so little time with Meg when she was dying. He wasn't even there when she drew her last breath. He doesn't seem concerned now that what remains of her is rotting in a plastic bag in some lunatic's shack. It just pisses me off that he's so damned *calm* about it!"

"You think it's apathy."

"What else could it be?"

She came back to me. "Faith," she said.

"And what is that?"

She stood in front of me. "I think it's an unconquerable sense of certainty that God's in control—and only what's ultimately good for us will happen to us."

"Like your ex-husband breaking your jaw?"

I could see that even the recollection was painful and I wanted to take it back.

"Yeah, even that," she whispered. "If he hadn't done it, I would've stayed. Even though I'm sure now, I didn't love him. I would've stayed. His brutality brought me to you. Should I regret that?"

"So God directed you to get a divorce?"

"Maybe."

"But why put you through all of that? Why didn't we just find each other first, before all that?"

"I don't know. Maybe he had to learn something too. Maybe it's because pain is how we learn best."

"It's a wicked tool."

"No more wicked than a suturing needle. It's what we need." She looked at the antiquated clock on the wall as she crawled back into bed. My eyes followed hers. It was almost two o'clock. "I need to sleep. Happy Halloween," she said, and she kissed me.

"The end of autumn," I mumbled.

Rusha woke us around nine. She and Rafe Yonger were at work in the kitchen when we stumbled downstairs. The earthy aroma of greasy bacon permeated the house. My stomach growled like a predatory beast, alert long before my mind or spirit.

Herk was already dressed and reading the newspaper at the table. "Morning," he said, glancing up at us. The gooey remains of some hen's offspring was smeared across the plate in front of him. Now he even had the detective waiting on him.

"Eggs?" Rafe Yonger asked cheerfully.

"Sounds great," Minnie answered. "I'm famished."

"How do you like 'em?"

"Sunnyside up and sloppy."

"Done."

"I'll just have toast," I said.

Herk laid the newspaper on the table and turned it toward me as I sat down opposite him. The headline, emblazoned in large letters across the front page read: BODY STOLEN FROM FUNERAL HOME, GRIEVING HUSBAND SUSPECT. "It appears that I've become a criminal," he observed.

The phone rang. "Not again!" Rusha started toward the wall phone hanging next to the kitchen door. "I'm taking it off the hook."

"Who's calling?"

"Everyone. Members of the congregation, mostly—media, crackpots, you name it."

"What're you telling them?"

"That Herk's not here—except for our people, of course."

She lifted the receiver. The anger on her face dissipated into recognition. She exchanged a few pleasantries, then extended the phone toward me. "It's the Professor."

He had no pleasantries for me. "Jim, what the hell is going on?" He sounded anxious, excited. His voice, perhaps for the first time since I'd known him, was animated. "Meg's body has been stolen? Is that true?"

"Yes."

"But it wasn't Pastor Gudsen's doing."

"No. Rusha fed the reporters that lie to misdirect them."

"I thought as much, good for her. It was Charlie Sticks, wasn't it?"

"Think so, yeah. We're going over there shortly."

"Wait for me. What about the Geryon Monster?"

"What?"

"The Yonger brothers."

I turned around as the kitchen door opened and Rafe's two brothers entered the house. "They're here too."

"Good. I'll be there in ten minutes. Don't leave without me."

"I don't know if—" He didn't allow me to finish. I heard the dead, monotonic buzz of disconnection.

By the time I ate some breakfast and showered, he'd arrived.

The temperature had dropped considerably overnight, and dark clouds drifted in the great canopy. They made the sky seem close and weighty, as if God's hand was pressing down from above. Dry leaves rustled across the yard and collected in swirling mounds against the foundation of the old house. The sun appeared, then vanished, then came back again. When it was there, my jacket made me sweat. When it was gone, I shivered. In autumn, you never knew what protection to use.

A considerable delay was occasioned by the continuous arrival of congregation members to work on the new church building. They'd all read the morning headlines and out of 'deep concern' (a euphemism for busybodying), needed to be placated by Herk, and reassured that their Shepherd had not led his flock astray.

Caleb was instrumental in this endeavor. My admiration for him continued to grow. In my eyes, he was a better disciple than I was. He kept things going—no miracles, no mysticism—just fortitudinal faith and the ability to lead by example. I imagined that the Big Fisherman must have been very much like him. None of Christ's brothers were ever Apostles. The Catholics would even deny they ever existed. Such faith required distance.

We didn't leave until after noon. Rusha and the Yonger brothers went in Rafe's unmarked Ford. At first, the detective refused to let Atlas and Doctor Mantus accompany us. I think it was probably because the former's size made him look like the muscle for some mob boss and the latter resembled a porcine Peter Lorre. But, as she would many times over the years, Rusha convinced Rafe to change his mind. The giant and the professor rode in the Chrysler with me and Minnie and Herk. The media had lost patience during the night and the last of them had evaporated with the morning fog.

It was a ten-minute drive to the Purgatory Landfill. As we circumvented it on the two track and pulled around to the back of the chain link fence, I saw a pick up truck, fairly new, parked haphazardly near the old abandoned car that was a perpetual landmark.

We parked and got out. Atlas fetched the baseball bat from inside the old wreck and struck the hood with Pavlovian certainty, summoning Charlie to come to us. The Yonger brothers inspected the truck.

"I'm sure of it," Donny Yonger said. Atlas was standing near him and I think it was the first—and last—time I ever saw anyone who came remotely close to matching the former bouncer's size.

"Sure of what?" I said.

"A pick up was reported stolen last night in a tavern parking lot, not far from Sarrow's Funeral Home," Rafe explained. "I don't have the plate numbers with me, but it's the same make, model, year and color. Apparently, your brother's brought us to the right place."

"Yeah."

"What's with the baseball bat?"

We decided then to tell the Yonger brothers almost everything about Charlie—his ties to Rhea, their personal history—only omitting Rhea's murder of their parents and Charlie's body-dumping activities. (Even Rusha's charm had its limits). When we began to talk about the events leading to the formation of the Twelve and Charlie's part in it, I was surprised to discover that Rusha had already told Rafe Yonger much of the story, probably while the rest of us had slept last night.

Rafe and Donny were particularly interested in the description of Charlie's 'exorcism', if that's what it was. Clearly, those two were beginning to accept it all, while Mike hung back, assiduously writing in his notebook, an expression of scornful contempt on his face.

After fifteen minutes had passed, Atlas rang the unorthodox bell a second time, the metallic sound echoing unnaturally through the watery bog beyond.

"What do we do if he won't come out?" Mike said.

"I'll have to call for a boat," Rafe replied. "We'll have to go in and find him."

Another ten minutes went by. Atlas was about to play Quasimodo again when the muffled barking of a dog emanated from the sodden forest.

"Full Count," Minnie said, unconsciously rubbing the wounds on her stomach. "He's coming."

Mike Yonger reached for his gun, cradled in a holster under his suitcoat.

"No," Rafe warned. "Leave it. No weapons."

We all fell silent, like the expectant observers of an execution. Only the momentary beeping of a forklift on the other side of the chainlink fence in back of us disturbed the stillness. Then we heard the Boatman's pole, eerily splashing in the stagnant water as it moved somewhere behind the protective thicket.

Then it stopped. The air was as silent as midnight in winter. The sun broke through for a brief instant, and on its heels, Charlie's disembodied voice floated over the surface of the swamp. "I got her." It came like a lover's whisper, low and husky with excitement, through the trees. We didn't see him, but I felt the unsettling sensation of being watched. I felt exposed. We waited. Somewhere, deep in the swamp, a crow cried out its raucous warning.

Mike Yonger stepped forward, his leather shoes making popping suction sounds in the mud, as if the earth was trying to pull him in. "Charlie Theomastix!" he shouted. His voice startled us all. "I'm Detective Yonger of the Saginaw Police Department. Please show yourself. You're under arrest for auto theft, unlawful entry, destruction of private property and—"

"Shut up, Mike!" Rafe Yonger glared at his sibling.

Full Count began barking in his deafening staccato. His snarls seemed to resonate from behind every tree. He was an entire kennel erupting at an unwelcome and threatening intruder.

I was certain Charlie's voice was mixed in there too, but the dog's maniacal din drowned him out.

"You stupid son of a bitch," Atlas said. "Charlie!" he shouted. "It's me, Johnny. No one's goin' arrest you, Buddy. Don't go. It's all right."

Mike Yonger turned toward Atlas. "This is a police matter, and I don't like the way—"

"Shut up," Rafe Yonger reiterated. Michelangelo fell silent obediently, but sullenly. Full Count ceased his caterwaling simultaneously, and the unearthly quiet returned, like a sinner to his imperfection.

We waited, breathlessly. Minutes passed. There were no sounds from the swamp, either of retreat or advancement. No sounds, only the tacit air of anticipation.

Then Herk, almost at a whisper, said, "Come."

I swear there was no way that Charlie could have heard him. I barely heard him and I was standing right next to him.

"There he is," Professor Mantus said. Ironically, the man with the most limited vision was the first to see him. But then, vision doesn't have to be physical.

Charlie slowly emerged from his cover of mist and foliage. The Boatman was steadily poking his raft forward. Full Count sat on his haunches, tensely awaiting the opportunity to do battle. Next to him, at Charlie's feet, was the large plastic bag containing the body of my sister-in-law.

"I have her," Charlie said. "I bring her." As he drew nearer, I could see his shaved features. The terrible scar on his forehead was much more noticeable with his cropped hair. But that wicked mark was diminished by his ecstatic aspect—the face of the prophet in the presence of God.

Full Count again began growling and snapping, but he was silenced by a sharp word from his master.

Herk waded into the shallow water to meet the raft as it grounded. He stood there for a moment, ankle deep in the muck, staring at Charlie Sticks. The Boatman leaned against his pole and smiled.

"Thank you," Herk said softly, then lifted the remains of his wife into his arms and headed back toward us.

When he was close to our future brother-in-law, he said, "Charlie comes with us back to the manse. No cuffs, no arrest, at least not now. He won't resist you. I'm not pressing any charges. The stolen truck and other problems we can deal with later. I guarantee his cooperation. Okay?"

Rafe looked at his brothers. Mike was still holding handcuffs. "Rafe," he said, "you'd be breaking every rule in the book. You'd be jeopardizing our careers."

"Who's going to know?" Rafe said. "There's just *us*, Mike."

"Yeah, and sooner or later that looney," (he pointed at Charlie), "is goin' go in front of a judge. We're goin' be called to testify. They're goin' ask us where and when the arrest was made, then what? We add perjury to all this? Do we say 'sorry judge, but the holy man here decided it was best to wait.'? C'mon man, we gotta do this properly."

Donatello Yonger stepped forward. Though he physically matched his brothers' combined sizes, he rarely offered his opinion. Apparently, he now felt compelled to speak. "He's right, Rafe."

"Damned straight I'm right. You gotta think about your future—*our* future."

Rusha watched our brother as he carried the body bag to the pickup and laid it reverently on the bed of the truck. Then she planted herself in front of the wavering detective.

"You know," she said, "that there's a higher authority than the law. You've become a part of something here that's extraordinary—you know that. I told you about the Twelve. You and your brothers are destined to be a part of that, as well as Charlie Sticks. It can't happen if you're going to bind yourself to law. You can't worship a code. You can't love a statute."

I could see what a prisoner he was to her. I knew what his response would be, having been incarcerated there myself.

"All right," he said, "we'll see how it develops. We've stretched things this far, I guess we can be flexible a little longer."

Rusha smiled at him. He was trying very hard to appear as though he'd made a decision.

"I never thought I'd see the day when your professional judgement would be clouded by a piece of ass," Mike said.

Rafe Yonger immediately lunged toward his brother, the 'clouded judgement' erupting into a violent storm that manifested itself in the lightning ferocity of his eyes and his thunderous voice. "You son of a bitch!" he shouted.

He'd apparently forgotten that he'd come from the same litter. I think he would have hurt Mike if Rusha hadn't grabbed his arm and restrained him. "Tell her you're sorry," Rafe said. "Tell her you're sorry or I swear I'll never talk to you again."

Mike looked sheepishly at Rusha. "I apologize," he said. "I didn't mean anything against you. I'm just trying to do things by the book."

"If 'the book' prompts you to attack people," she said, "you should try some different reading material."

Rafe smiled. So did Donatello.

Charlie left the raft and, with Full Count in his arms, he stood by, the obedient disciple, waiting for instruction. He looked, and acted, completely differently than he had when I first saw him.

Though he was, again, covered in grime, and the stubble of a new beard was beginning to appear, the light in his eyes was disturbing—like the irritation one experiences when a bright light is suddenly turned on in a dark room. For a few minutes, at least, you knew it was easier to negotiate in accustomed shadow.

"What I do now?" Charlie said.

"You're coming with us," Herk responded. "You're never coming back here again, okay?"

Charlie shrugged. "Okay." Full Count growled a little, then settled his small head comfortably into the crook of his master's arm, seemingly content to await further developments.

"Let's go then," Herk said.

"Wait a minute," Rafe said. "What about the truck?"

Herk turned to Charlie. "Where are the keys?"

"Inside."

"Why did you take it? Why did you steal the truck, Charlie?"

"Couldn't carry the lady all this way. Some folks left it sitting with keys. I got in. God gave to Charlie."

Atlas smiled. "Didn't think you knew how to drive old pal."

"Charlie go very slow. People yell at me. They say bad things. I was happy to stop."

"Charlie and I and the dog will go in the truck," Herk said. "Follow us back to the manse."

"Then what?" Mike said.

"We'll see."

As we headed home, Minnie sat next to me as before, with Atlas and the Professor in the back—now much more comfortable in my brother's absence. I felt that way too.

"What in hell are we doing?" I said after lighting a cigarette.

"What do you mean?" Minnie said.

"How did I ever get here? I'm following a stolen pickup truck with my sister-in-law's corpse in the back through the business district of Saginaw as if I was just out for a Sunday drive in the country. The people I regard as most intimate in my life, I didn't even know a few months ago. I've discovered who my father is and learned that I have a sister who's an ex porn star, along with two others I've never met. My brother is some kind of strange prophet who performs miracles. And, in the middle of all that, I've found God, or rather He's found me."

Minnie laughed, then her face turned serious. "Would you go back if you could?"

I knew what she was asking. She wanted to know if this new world I'd stumbled into, this strange new world of which she was the central figure, was a place I really wanted to inhabit.

"No," I said. "That other place, where I used to be, was too…real. It had it's own kind of value. It was a miserable place, but I knew what to expect. It was free of magic or romance or faith. I could count on a straight road. It was as boring as a Kansas landscape, but it was predictable. Sometimes, too much can depend upon a red wheelbarrow."

"I never liked Williams either," Minnie whispered. "Give me Keats or Shelley anytime."

"I guess I've come to love the world," I said to her, "mostly because you're in it."

She smiled and took my free hand. "What did you mean when you said things can be *too* real?"

"They get away from Truth."

"Aren't they the same things?"

"No. Reality just *is*. Truth is how we know it."

"The eye of the beholder?"

"I don't think so. It's like the sexual act. Porn is real. A close-up of copulation is, by definition, sex. It's what we do, but it's not the way we know it. How we apply it to ourselves, within the parameters of our magical vision, *that* is truth. It's not our view of things, it's what we are. It doesn't change what the thing is. It enhances it. We don't see it differently, we only see it *Truthfully*."

"Am I beautiful then?"

"Yes."

"And what would you say to someone who disagrees?"

"Your vision is limited."

She squeezed my hand. I looked in the rearview mirror. Atlas was beaming his broad smile while Professor Mantus' magnified eyes studied the back of my head. There was a kind of grin spreading there too, beneath the extensive nose.

Privacy was a part of the older world that I *did* miss.

When our caravan pulled into the yard of the manse, we were all grateful to find that the media had, out of boredom perhaps, continued to stay away. Herk spoke with Caleb Bird for a few minutes, instructing him to send the volunteer workers home for the day, except any of the Twelve who might be there. Since it was a weekday, a Thursday I think, their numbers were quite small anyway.

When they had dispersed, Meg's body was removed from the truck, carried into the house and up the stairs, where it was laid out, still in the body bag, on Herk's bed. No one had the courage to open it.

By then it was mid-afternoon. We all migrated to the kitchen, where we had some lunch and nervously awaited what we hoped would be the first gathering of the complete Twelve. I confess I didn't know then why we were so filled with expectation. I know now.

Chapter thirty

I remember everything about that night, everything I saw anyway. I remember that darkness closed quickly around us and out of its compressing shadows little monsters haunted the yard and the porch, their cries for beneficence disturbing the still air like the wailing of the damned.

The children came in droves, mostly the offspring of our own congregation, brought here because cautious parents trusted that we would not poison candy or slip razor blades into apples. It was another generation of man hiding behind masks of wickedness, still searching for the sweetness of life.

We'd forgotten that it was Halloween. Rusha was about to make a run to the party store down the road for treats, when Robin Stym and Baxter Bird arrived, toting bags of candy. Apparently, they were more conscious than the rest of us of the necessity to propitiate the generational handiwork of our own perverted fascination with madness and devilry.

Skeletons and mummies, ghosts and vampires, zombies and hags appeared at the door—death and decay brought forward this one night, to mask the mortality we all wear underneath. Upstairs, real death held sway.

Larry Ladon and Ginny arrived at dusk, my insomniac nephew in tow. They looked exhausted, and I felt a stab of sympathy. Herk seemed oblivious to their suffering and, at that moment, to his son. He gave little Ben a cursory kiss, then handed him back to our mother as he greeted Auggie Two-River and the Theuses. Ben Tower and Sylvia showed up just before the appointed time of six. Minnie was again reduced to tears at the sight of her vigorous father. Sometimes it's necessary to see a miracle several times before it can be believed.

Eighteen of us crowded into the large kitchen, pretending that we knew our purpose. At six, we were still not complete. Rusha and the Birds tended to the trick-or-treaters, occasionally visiting for a few minutes with the parents they recognized. Full Count, chained to the giant oak in the yard, alerted us to every intruder, while Charlie kept a parental eye on his pet from the window. Mike and Donny Yonger were constantly at his elbows, watching him with similar dubiosity. Their careers depended on his continued presence and they had no intention of allowing him an opportunity to bolt.

Sybil Springbok appeared at around six thirty, full of apologies for her lateness. She'd been out with her son Jamal, who, she declared proudly, had been a Zulu warrior, non-pareil. She'd lost track of time, watching her 'Shaka' plunder the neighborhood. She'd dropped him off with a sitter then hurried over to the manse as quickly as possible.

I hadn't noticed that Atlas was absent until she'd breathlessly discarded her coat and asked after him.

Auggie told us that some woman had called for him just before they left to come across the road. "I gave him the message. He asked to borrow my car. I gave him the keys and he took off. Said he'd meet us over here in an hour or so."

Sybil was obviously disappointed. Her luxurious smile faded. "A woman, you said?"

"Yeah," Auggie responded, munching one of the dozens of caramel apples that Ginny had brought along. He seemed oblivious to Sybil's fervid acuity.

"Did she say what she wanted?"

"He was supposed to pick her up."

"Oh. So he'll be bringing her here?"

Auggie shrugged. "Guess so."

Sybil poured herself a glass of cider and I lost track of her in the crowd as Herk approached me.

"What now?" I said.

"Judy's still not here with Doctor Mudeez." He seemed very agitated. "It's almost seven."

"Are you sure she knows about it?"

"I checked. Dad called her this afternoon. She said she'd be here and she'd bring the doctor."

Full Count began howling in the yard again. Herk limped to a window, looked anxiously out, and returned to me. "More kids," he said.

"What are you planning to do?" I said. "I mean, when they get here."

He put one large hand on my shoulder and studied me with his pale eyes. It almost felt as though he was leaning on me, though he stood upright. "Hold God to His promise. I'm going upstairs. When Judy and Dr. Mudeez arrive, send the Twelve to me." He turned away.

I grabbed his arm. "Robin and Baxter count as one," I said, "so do the three Yonger brothers. The Twelve are actually fifteen. You want all fifteen?"

"Yes."

"What about me?"

"Only the Twelve, Jim."

"Why?"

He smiled.

"Okay," I said. "Never mind." I didn't want to be there to see his defeat anyway.

We milled around for the next hour, pretending we had some purpose. The trick-or-treaters became more sporadic, then faded into the darkness completely. We sat in the living room, like patients in a doctor's office, engaged in uninspired prattle, too afraid of an answer to ask what was wrong. Even Doctor Mantus said nothing. The only sounds were the occasional whispers of small talk or the grunting of my nephew as he sucked down another placating bottle of formula.

At nine thirty, Judy Crabbe finally walked through the door-way, sputtering apologies to anyone who would listen. Behind her, a dark man in a dated sharkskin suit stood silently by. This, I assumed, was Dayan Mudeez, the last member of the Twelve, the son of a Muslim and a Jew, the respected surgeon we'd heard so much about.

Judy anxiously explained that Doctor Mudeez had been called into emergency surgery around five thirty, just as they were preparing to leave the hospital to come to us. It'd been a difficult case. A young man and his girlfriend, high school kids, had been drinking. They'd run head-on into a Semi. The girl had died instantly, her neck snapped like a dry twig. Doctor Mudeez had saved what was left of the boy by amputating his legs, repairing his ruptured spleen, and suturing his lacerated face. It had taken over three hours in the operating room. Judy had assisted. There was no one available to let us know.

"Where's the Pastor?" Judy said, glancing anxiously around.

"Waiting, upstairs," I answered. "He went up quite a while ago. We haven't seen or heard from him since."

"The newspapers said—"

"I know. It's a lie. He's here."

"And Meg?"

"Here too."

"My God!" She put her hand over her open mouth.

"The Twelve are to go up and join him."

"Right now?"

"Yes. As soon as you got here."

Judy took the doctor's hand and led him through the crowd. I think he must have been wondering why he'd agreed to come. Any sensible man would. There was a dubious frown on his face, mixed with a hint of incredulity. It was the expression Father Damien might have had when he first saw the denizens of Molokai. But Judy Crabbe was not a person whose wishes were easily set aside, and he followed her up the stairs.

Doctor Mantus, then Rusha and Rafe and the other Yongers joined the entourage. Auggie escorted Charlie. Robin and Baxter held hands. Ben Tower, Yuri Theus, Sybil and, finally, Larry Ladon all began the ascent to the upper room where Herkimer Gudsen and his dead wife waited.

Caleb Bird tried to follow. I stepped in front of him.

"Only the Twelve," I said. I think he'd known, but the disappointment was there anyway.

"Not even you, Jim?"

"Not even me."

He turned slowly away and sat in a chair in the corner. Sylvia Tower, Minnie, and my mother silently congregated on the shabby, threadbare sofa. Yuri's daughter, Teena, had seen too great a miracle in her father's reclamation to launch any protest. She offered to make a pot of coffee and disappeared into the kitchen without waiting for a response.

I sat down and lit a cigarette. We waited in silence, each of us occasionally glancing at the shadowy stairwell. Teena brought the coffee. We didn't know what was supposed to happen, but we knew, somehow, that what was transpiring upstairs would send us forward into a difficult future, or drive us back into an even more difficult past.

The baby cried. Ginny went to him, covered him with a blanket. He went back to sleep. "It's a day for miracles," she said as she sat down again.

I think she was referring to little Ben's napping. I didn't ask.

From the second floor, a kind of chanting issued. The Twelve were speaking in unison, like a psalmic choir—or a coven.

The chanting stopped. A door opened. Hurried footsteps clattered on the stairs. I heard Judy's pleading voice. "Wait! Please wait!"

The surgeon, Doctor Mudeez, appeared. He looked at us. "They're crazy," he said. "I've encountered saner people in asylums." He was red-faced, even against his dark skin. The arteries in his neck were visibly expanded in stress. He unconsciously loosened his tie and took a deep breath as Judy rushed into the room behind him.

"Please don't go," she said. "You *have* to be here."

"Judy," he said. "You've always been a top-notch nurse—one of the best I've ever worked with. That's why I agreed to come with you. But what you've gotten yourself involved in here is dangerous. It's *criminal.* In my faith, it's *apostasy!* You told me you needed me here to try to heal someone, not perform some kind of half-assed ritual on a corpse!"

Tears were flowing down Judy's rough cheeks. She looked desperate. I wanted to intervene, to help her, but something told me I shouldn't. I could feel Minnie's eyes on me.

"I never said 'heal'," Judy shouted. Her fear was turning to anger.

"What?"

"I never used that word. I told you you were needed to help *restore* someone."

"Restore? Judy, you restore furniture, not people. You're arguing semantics. You *know* you misled me. You didn't tell me you were involved in some crackpot cult."

"Please," Judy said, returning to her plaintive tone. "It can't happen without you."

"What you expect to happen *can't* happen. That woman's dead. She's been wasting away with cancer for a year. *You* are encouraging her grieving husband in his sick fantasy. I thought you were smarter than that, Judy. You could lose your license. I could lose mine. I never would have believed that you'd get me involved in something like this!"

"Please stay," Judy pleaded. "*Please!*"

Herk was suddenly standing behind her. No one had heard him approach over Judy's mendicancy. Even *he* looked anxious. I could see fear in his eyes, behind the calm façade. Things were falling apart.

"We're not crazy, Doctor," he said. "We're trusting in God's promise."

Mudeez seemed to calm a bit, but he remained adamant. "If you believe that God will resurrect your wife, Pastor Gudsen, then let Him do it. Bury her, like any good Christian, and leave her to Heaven."

Herk hesitated. He seemed to be listening to someone or something else. "She's not supposed to go to Heaven—not yet. She's supposed to stay here, with me. I've gathered the Twelve. He will restore her, as He did Lazarus. You've seen what He did for Ben Tower. Did *you* heal Ben Tower?"

"No, I didn't. I know about *your* recovery too, Pastor. They weren't miracles. The body has an amazing capacity to heal itself. I've seen many supposedly 'miraculous' cures in my career, but I've never seen anyone come back from death. It doesn't happen. I find it particularly interesting that you and Mr. Tower left us before anyone could properly examine you and then you dupe my gullible nurse into falsifying your discharge papers. Miracles don't happen. Resurrection doesn't happen. I think you know that."

There was a terrible silence. Then Herk said: "It has happened."

"Only in myth."

"Jesus is not myth."

"Yes, I know," Mudeez said. "Mythology is *other* people's religions. I hope you'll let those policemen upstairs do their duty, as they seem to want to, and remove your wife's body for a proper interment. I'm sure you loved her. Let her go." He turned and was gone before my brother could respond. Judy began to follow him, but Herk seized her arm and held her back.

"I can't let him leave," she said, struggling to release herself. "Meg...for Meg."

"No. He's not the one," Herk said. "Let him go."

Doctor Mantus entered the room, which was slowly reoccupied by the others. "It *has* to be him," the professor said. Full Count barked outside as we heard Doctor Mudeez pull out of the yard and up the gravel drive. Judy collapsed in the only available chair.

"I think it's time we do what we should have done in the first place," Mike Yonger said.

"I agree," Donny said.

They both looked at Rafe who, in turn, looked at my brother. "Maybe they're right, Pastor Gudsen. You said yourself that whatever you were hoping for here required all of the...your, uh, people. Isn't that right?"

Herk looked defeated. Worse, he seemed *disillusioned.* It was something I'd never seen before and never wanted to again. Followers can always doubt. In some way, I think it's their duty. Such a luxury is never afforded a leader. That's how, perhaps, fanaticism is born. Doubt thins the flock and makes the Shepherd obsolete. Faith makes Him an icon.

"Man, that sonofabitch was sure in a hurry!" The booming bass voice came from the kitchen as the screen door slammed behind it. "He damned near ran us over in the dark." The huge frame of Atlas Johnson filled the archway leading to the living room. Sybil Springbok's face, I noted, abandoned its disconsolation and broke into a warm, receptive smile.

Rusha was the first to notice the small figure that was partially obscured by Atlas' huge bulk. "Maddy!" She cried as she rushed forward.

"Hippie!" Maddy shouted, extending her arms as she stepped into general view from behind her gigantic escort.

The two women embraced and kissed each other lightly on the cheeks, European fashion. I tried, unsuccessfully, to erase the erotic image of the Amazon Queen and the Slave Girl from my mind.

"How did you get here?" Rusha said, taking Maddy by the arm and pulling her into the center of the room.

"Atlas was kind enough to pick me up at the airport," Maddy said. "Didn't he tell you? I wanted to come. I heard so much from Teena about this place I had to see for myself. Besides, the club...well, it just wasn't working out. Oh, I'm so happy to see you, Hippie. You look great, postively *radiant!*"

Rafe Yonger stepped forward, his hand extended.

"And this must be the reason," Maddy giggled.

"I'm Rafe," he said, simply. He looked at Rusha as Maddy shook his hand vigorously. "Hippie?"

"An old nickname," Rusha answered. She was blushing. That was something I'd not seen before.

"Pleased to meetcha," Maddy gushed. I was afraid, for a moment, that she might drool. Then she spotted me.

"Jimmy!" I'd just stood up. She almost knocked me back into the chair again as she embraced me and planted a rough, wet kiss on my gaping mouth.

I hurriedly escaped, but not soon enough to avoid a scathing frown of disapproval from Minnie.

"Maddy," I said, holding her at arm's length. "This is my girlfriend, Minnie Tower."

"Nice to have you here," Minnie said, obviously lying through her teeth. "I've heard you're an old friend of Jim's."

Oblivious of the trouble she'd created, Maddy innocently compounded it. "We go way back," she said, shaking Minnie's hand. "A course Jimmy goes way back with a lot of girls, don't cha, Sweetie."

"Is that so?" Minnie said. Although I'd always been honest with her, told her about my past exploits, she acted as if she was hearing about them for the first time. "What else can you tell me about 'Jimmy'?"

Rusha rescued me by pulling Maddy away to introduce her to the others in the room. Our father was the nearest. "Dad," she said, "this is Maddy Foxe. Mad, this is my father." Larry obviously was not pleased by this living reminder of his daughter's disreputable past, but he forced a pleasant smile and shook Maddy's hand. Rusha pulled her quickly away.

"And this," she said, "is Professor Mantus. He teaches at the university here in town."

"How very nice to make your acquaintance," the Doctor said, emitting a piggish squeal and squinting through the thick spectacles. "Miss Foxe is it?"

Maddy laughed. "That's my stage name," she said, staring at the professor's porcine features.

"It is?" Rusha said.

I was equally surprised. I'd never known her by any other name.

"Yeah. Well don't look so shocked, Hippie. Atlas told me you weren't going by Rita anymore either. What did he say? Rusha?" My sister nodded. "Anyway, I took the name 'Maddy' sorta from my last name, Mead. My real first name is Dian. I'm gonna use my real name from now on. I'm through with the business."

"Dian Mead?" Professor Mantus said. "That's your name?"

"Yup."

"May I ask you a question, Miss Mead?" The normally withdrawn and levelheaded academic was very animated and nervous. He was trying to light a cigarette and his chubby hands were shaking badly. It was apparent that Maddy was influencing this uncharacteristic behavior, but I had no clue as to why. I glanced at my brother. He was smiling. *He* knew.

"Sure," Maddy said, "ask away."

"Do you own a horse?"

"Well now, that's a silly question. Naw. Always wanted one though, ever since I was little. My old man was a carny and—"

"A carny?"

"Yeah, ya know, a carnival worker. He worked all the state fairs and stuff. He ran a carousel and I used to love to watch him feed little kids into the thing. They'd go 'round and 'round on these beautiful white and gold horses. They went up and down on the poles. When business was slow, he'd let me ride as much as I wanted. I can still hear the music." Her eyes were distant. Behind them, her mind was experiencing greater vision, seeing farther, through dimensions of time and space that, internally at least, were not barriers.

"You said the carousel operator, your father, would 'feed' the machine with the children," Doctor Mantus said. "That's an odd way to put it."

She laughed. There was something utterly charming about Maddy, her naiveté perhaps—the porn actress who didn't know guilt. "That was my daddy's word for it," she answered. "He'd wake me up every morning in our little trailer and say 'C'mon, Cupcake, eat yer cereal. We gotta go feed the horses.'" She paused for a moment. Nostalgic tears filled her eyes. "He was a good daddy. Two years! I was only with 'em for two years. He died in June of 1960, cancer. I had to go back to livin' with my ma." She wiped the moisture away. Her smile returned. I'm not sure it had ever left. "Sorry," she said. "Why do ya wanna know this stuff anyway, perfesser? You need some kinda background check to join this group?"

Rusha laughed, as did several others.

"Indeed you do, Miss Mead," Doctor Mantus said, "and you just passed with honors."

"I don't think I get ya," she said, her blue eyes wide in standard Maddy confusion.

"Me either," I added.

Doctor Mantus grinned in my direction, though I was too far away for him to see me.

"The Horses of Diomedes," he said. "Diomedes. Dayan Mudeez. *Dian Mead.* We had the wrong person. Miss Mead is the final link in the chain. *She* is supposed to be the Twelfth."

I hadn't been alone in my slowness. Doctor Mantus's statement created a rupture in the tumor of doubt and silence that had grown around us. Everyone began talking at once. Judy Crabbe seemed wonderfully mollified, as if the flight of Doctor Mudeez had been her personal failure. She began, in fact, to cry. I heard her mumble "Praise God!" Hope had been restored. A stone had been rolled away. The weight of the world had been lifted from our backs by a demure demimonde in the company of a colossus named Atlas Johnson.

The group gathered around Maddy like adoring pilgrims around a common vision. Auggie touched her arm, then withdrew. I think he was trying to determine if she was real or not. I wanted to tell everyone there that this person was just Maddy Foxe—a girl who'd kissed and fondled my half-naked sister. I'd known her—in the most Biblical sense of the word—yet I hadn't known her at all, hadn't recognized her. Her father was a half-Gypsy carny who'd 'fed' children to his constantly circling horses. *Maddy's the real star of the act,* Rusha had told me once at the Amazon Club—a prophecy fulfilled.

Herk moved through the crowd around her and took Maddy's hand. "I want you to come with me," he said. She followed, without question or protest. Maybe it was a miracle of faith, maybe it was just that Maddy was accustomed to doing what authoritative males told her to do, I don't know. But she followed, even when he released her. They went up the stairs.

The others did too, the remaining Eleven. Atlas knew, instinctively, where I had not, that he couldn't follow. He stayed with our small group in the living room. We returned to our mute vigil and watched the clock on the wall that had lost its meaning.

The praying chorus upstairs began again. The hands of the clock didn't seem to move, but each time I looked up, they had secretly shifted. One of them hid behind the other. It was midnight.

In the yard, Full Count barked. Minnie went to the window. "It's snowing," she said.

I joined her, put my arm around her waist.

"Do you feel it?" she said.

"Yes."

"What is it?"

I lit a cigarette and looked at the moon beaming its secondary light through the obscuring snow. "Peace, maybe. I don't know. Meaning?"

"I love you," she said "but I've never stopped feeling like a single entity until this moment."

"Yes," I agreed. "Something with us. Atonement?"

"No. At-one-ment."

It was a minor epiphany, but Minnie was right. Humanity had been mispronouncing that word for centuries.

From behind us, Caleb Bird whispered. "They're done. They're coming down."

Then I, too, heard the footsteps on the stairs.

Epilogue

T here is the Invisible and the Visible. There is Heaven and Earth. There is Mind and Matter. There is Eternity and Time. The Tree of the Fall was the teleological impetus, whether myth or not, by which Humanity was driven into the scope of time and mortality. The Tree of Calvary was the flame that drew us back to the Light, to Eternity. Every creature lives on the death of another. Herk's journey was the realization of the kinship of the anomaly of time and imperishability. "I and the Father are one," Jesus said. So he was. So Herk is. So we will be.

The invention of Time counts thirty years since that Hallowed Eve when God kept his promise to Herkimer Gudsen.

Now, our church is called 'New Age' by those outside it. They're wrong. It's a misnomer of the basest kind. What we know is very old—man's sense of the Infinite through myth and metaphor made incarnate, then reversed again. We have learned that the Kingdom of God is within us. Nothing can remove it. We are at peace.

Since 1975, I've been the Administrative Pastor of the church on Horizon Road. There are no judgments here. Denominations, gender, race, sexual preference, even dogma mean nothing to us in the presence of Greater Truth. Religion has too long mistaken denotation for connotation. We're working to change that.

We did complete the church building. Six years later, we had to build an addition, a cathedral-like sanctuary that dwarfs the original structure. The cornfield has become a parking lot large enough to accommodate three thousand cars. For the moment, at least, it's adequate, but the Council has determined that we'll have to expand again if we're going to accommodate our burgeoning congregation.

We have several other churches of course—seven in Michigan and another five outside the state. The problem is that people want to be a part of *this* place, where it all began. For those who live too far away to be regular members, it has become a pilgrim's shrine.

Caleb Bird was the first to follow a Macedonian Call. He's now in Milford, Connecticut. Baxter and Robin followed him there. They remain together, proselytising among the gay community, and heterosexuals as well—with some success, I'm told.

Atlas Johnson and Sybil Springbok were the second couple to be married in the reconstructed church, only two months after Minnie and I took our vows. They have four kids, including Sybil's son, Jamal. That young man is an assistant pastor with me now. Atlas and Sybil's youngest daughter, Celia, is in pastoral training. She won't be the first woman to hold a position in our clergy. That honor went to Teena Theus years ago. None of our ministers are 'ordained'. Only churches that have given up on the possibility of God's continuing dialogue would require such a rite. Teena's father, Yuri, still holds a position on the Council and runs the Ladon Orchard.

Charlie was never charged with anything. The pick-up truck was wiped clean of fingerprints and found by deerhunters. It had been abandoned in the wetlands known as Shiawassee Flats, not far outside the city limits. The owner was happy just to have it back. Further investigation was dropped. Charlie came to work as the custodian at the church. Occasionally, he accompanies us to Tiger baseball games in Detroit. He lives across the street in Auggie Two-River's expanded Boarding House. Charlie's sister, Rhea, was released from psychiatric care in 1983. She lives with her brother now. She rejoined the church and has become a calm and fearless lover of God.

Auggie himself is the sexton for our cemetery that is immediately adjacent to the Boarding House property. My mother is buried there, not far from where I first saw Auggie's father herding cows. Since mother's death three years ago, Larry lives with Minnie and me. Since the kids moved out, there's plenty of room. Larry's had a hard time coping, but he knows about resurrection. At almost eighty, he does what he can for the church, and he knows how to wait.

Donatello Yonger married Maddy. Two years ago, they moved with their kids to Racine, Wisconsin, where my oldest son, Jeremiah, is the pastor of a Faith and Revelation Church. They went there at Jeremiah's request. Simply put, more colonizers were needed.

Rusha, my widowed sister, tries to hide her pain. Next spring, her youngest, John, will be graduating from high school and heading to Ann Arbor to study law. I think that then she'll come to live with us. Minnie is like a sister to her and I think she would feel too lonely in the big house where she raised her family. She could help us with dad, too. He's becoming more and more feeble.

Mike Yonger never married. He has enough time in with the police force to retire next year, but I don't think he will. He loves his work too much. All of his spare time is spent here. Given the chance, I think he would have married Judy Crabbe. Their irascible temperaments were suited and they were dating when Judy was killed in an automobile accident. Sometimes, usually at dusk after Vespers, I see Mike across the road. He stands near her headstone. He waits too.

Minnie's parents are growing old, but they've been blessed with relative good health. Ben Tower still serves on the Council. He's a patriarch of the church and is regarded with deep veneration. He's frequently called upon to witness to the miracle that God performed on him. When she can, Sylvia helps Minnie with the Sunday school program and the ever-continuing feeding of the hungry.

Doctor Mantus is now completely blind, but he refuses to give up his house or his pride to come live with us—an option that has been repeatedly offered. With characteristic determination he's overcome this handicap too. He's learned braille, and the church recently purchased a talking computer for him.

He, too, still serves on the Council as one of the Ruling Elders. He's become a man of great faith and often leads special prayer gatherings. Empowerment came to Doctor Mantus in the upper room. His monotonic mumblings are now the dynamic, grandiose orations of the saint. Our members flock to his services, most never having been aware of his 'thorn of inarticulation', as he likes to call it. Teaching people to talk to God has so much become his vocation that I jokingly refer to him now as 'Praying Mantus'. His love of word games has helped him to accept it in good humor. In addition, he has a nose for the future. It was at his urging that I've written this narrative. Each of us, he says, (that is the Twelve), must do so. He is assiduously working on what he calls The Good Son Testament. From what I've seen of it, it's Truth.

Dayan Mudeez died that Halloween night in 1972. He left the manse irritated and angry. He must have driven directly to his palatial home across from the eighteenth green of the Saginaw Country Club. There, according to the article in the newspaper the following day, he surprised two intruders who were ransacking his house. They were inexperienced thugs, kids really, looking for drug money. They hanged him from the railing of a balcony at the summit of the main stairway. The idea, apparently, was to make the murder look like a suicide. They left their fingerprints and muddy boot markings everywhere. The cord they used to hang him came from the drapery in the doctor's bedroom. Valuable *objets d'art* were left behind while the doctor's change drawer was cleaned out, along with a small amount of cash in his wallet. They got thirty dollars, mostly in change. Then too, there was the broken window above the kitchen sink. Glass particles in the drain meant that it was shattered from the outside in. Mike Yonger was put in charge of the case. He had the culprits in custody twenty-four hours after the housekeeper found her employer. The killers were sentenced to life in prison. I don't remember their names.

Doctor Mudeez was interred in the B'nai Brith Cemetery behind Temple Israel Synogogue on Potter Street, where he rests still. I remember Judy weeping and tearfully lamenting that Mudeez had died for nothing. We all knew better. Judy, I think, did too.

My brother, with his infant son, disappeared on November first. There were too many questions to address. He could have stayed, I suppose, and fought the accusations and insinuations. After all, he had the proof. This option I proposed to him, but he didn't want to sensationalize or commercialize what God had done. "A profiteer," he quipped, "is never honored in his own country."

We didn't hear from him for almost a year. As the winter of 1973 approached, I received a letter from an H. Ladon. It was postmarked ten days earlier from Lucerne, Switzerland.

Jim –
We are well. Moving again soon. Good-bye. Keep the faith.
H.

There was no return address—no way to write back. None of us has heard from him since. I've said, too often perhaps, that he's dead. Ginny would have none of it. Strange, that Herk doesn't know she's gone.

Today, a quiet Sunday afternoon in October, one of those perfect autumn days of cool light and clean air, Doctor Mantus accepted our invitation to dinner after another of his riveting prayer services.

My six-year-old grandson Joel, already an expert with a remote, had just placed a disc in the DVD player, as the professor and I settled into the comfortable chairs that had long ago replaced the curbside furnishings of my brother and Meg's occupancy.

"What *is* that?" the professor said.

"I'm sorry?"

"On the TV."

"Oh. Some animated movie that Joel's put in."

"What is it?"

"I don't know." I turned to my grandson, who was stretched out on his stomach, elbows on the floor, his little hands holding his head at what would have been, for me, an excruciating angle. "What're you watching, Jo-Jo?"

"Aw, can't I finish?" he whined, assuming, as children must, that some adult was about to ruin their happiness. "I didn't finish yestiddy," he said. "Can't I finish?"

"Sure you can, Buddy," I laughed. "I just wanted to know what it is."

"Herkaleez," he said.

"What?"

"*Herkaleez!*" he snapped impatiently. "Herkaleez is gonna rescue Meg from Hades. It's cool, Grandpa. Watch!"

I looked over at Doctor Mantus. Though he couldn't see the movie, he was smiling. "So it goes on," he said.

The professor and I retired to the porch steps after dinner. I'd quit smoking years ago, but Aristotle Mantus was determined to retain this one vice. He lit a cigarette and coughed in pleasure.

I waved to Charlie Sticks as he moved through the shadows of the oak and evening to clean the church, Full Count's great-grandpup bouncing around his heels. Three balls had never been an impediment to the original sire or his offspring. Charlie smiled and waved back.

"When will we be able to tell it all?" I said.

"When the time comes."

Charlie opened the door of the sanctuary and entered. Nearby, under the cornerstone of the building, is an empty body bag. Someday, someone will find it and wonder why Holy Cross Hospital buried it there.

"When do you think that time will be?"

"Every religion has those who saw. Subsequent generations have to content themselves with what those witnesses wrote. Then, it's a matter of faith."

"Do you think they're still alive?"

"Yes."

"Still on the road to Golgotha," I whispered.

"What?"

"Nothing."

Minnie and Joel joined us. "Grandpa," he cried. "Grandma says I can burn this sparkler I found in the basement. Wanna watch?"

Minnie followed him into the yard, carrying the butane lighter I use to light the grill.

"You can't hold it though, Jo-Jo," she said. "Grandma will stick the sparkler in the grass and you can help me light it. I don't want you to get too close."

After slow ignition, the firework streamed sparks as my delighted grandson danced around it. A large moth fluttered out of the darkness and joined him, swooping and circling. The heat and sparks wounded it. It faltered, flailed, regained its strength, and swooped again, a powdery Icarus. It circled close, closer. It blazed in deathly harmony with its *inamorata*, then the conjoined flames faded into wisps of gray smoke, evaporating in the returning gloom.

That, I thought, is our relationship to God. We are drawn to Him out of the darkness. We can't help ourselves. If we get too close, we can get hurt, but the alternative is endless night, endless winter. If we're willing, on the other hand, to trust, to go all the way, we can *be* the flame too. We can, like the moth in my autumnal night, join the Light in dispelling the darkness—if only for a moment.

"For this is the marriage of heaven and earth: Perfect Myth and Perfect Fact: claiming not only our love and our obedience, but also our wonder and delight, addressed to the savage, the child, and the poet in each one of us no less than to the moralist, the scholar, and the philosopher."
—C.S. Lewis, *God in the Dock, Essays on Theology and Ethics*

"Eternity is neither future, nor past, but now. It is not of the nature of time at all, in fact, but a dimension of the consciousness of being that is to be found and experienced within, upon which, when found, one may ride through time and through the whole of one's days. What leads to the knowledge of this transpersonal, transhistorical dimension of one's being and life experiences are the mythological archetypes, those eternal symbols that are known to all mythologies and have been forever the support and models of human life."
—Joseph Campbell, *Thou Art That, Transforming Religious Metaphor*

Acknowledgements

I would like to thank my editor, Deborah Meghnagi, for her insight and suggestions. I would also like to thank my friend, John and my daughter Amy for their multiple readings, ideas, and criticisms. A special thanks to the poet, John Keats, who died so young and knew so much.

About the Author

David Turrill is a teacher, theater director and writer who lives on a farm in Rockford, MI, near Grand Rapids. He is the author of two other books - *Michilimackinac, A Tale of the Straits* and *A Bridge to Eden*. He is the father of two children and grandfather of three. His wife passed away in 1996. He is a Vietnam veteran.

The fonts used in the book are from the Garamond family

An Apology for Autumn

The Toby Press publishes fine writing,
available at bookstores everywhere. For more information, please
contact *The* Toby Press at www.tobypress.com